"My firm has  disappearance." He turn find myself looking at with strawberry-blonde woman?" I shake my head. "Her name is Danielle Hurst. She's been missing for five days. The police are focusing on the theory that she left town with a boyfriend, but Danielle's parents believe the police are overlooking connections to other disappearances."

The longer he speaks, the harder it becomes for me to breathe. It's like history repeating itself. My parents claimed I'd run away with a boyfriend. It's why no one came for me. No one ever came. I try to remember the grounding exercises my therapist taught me. *Name five things you can see.* I glance around frantically. Files. I see files. Files and a stain on the carpet near my right foot and—sympathy. I see sympathy and pity exuding from those brilliant blue eyes. Pity for me. I can't breathe!

He continues softly as though trying to blunt the blow. "We believe the disappearances, including Danielle's, have ties to another incident which occurred three years ago."

Spots float in the air between us, circling round and around.

"Eva? Eva!" I hear his voice as if from a distance, but I can't answer, still can't breathe. I grope blindly for the desk at my side and jolt from my chair, ready to run before the familiar darkness comes to reclaim my soul.

Praise for Elisabeth Scott

"Elisabeth Scott delivers strong character development and an exceptional plot with just the right amount of relationship and romance. You'll be kept guessing—along with her characters–until the very end!"

~Erin Tunnell

~*~

"Block off plenty of time because once you start Thirteen Scars, you won't want to put it down. Elisabeth Scott is a gifted storyteller who weaves suspense and intrigue among a cast of captivating characters. Thirteen Scars will keep you in its grip until the very last page. My favorite novel this year!"

~Susan Allred

~*~

"Debut author Elisabeth Scott knocked it out of the park with Thirteen Scars! This riveting romantic suspense gripped me from page one and never let up."

~Katherine Hawthorne
Sinful Surrender *series*

Thirteen Scars

by

Elisabeth Scott

Thirteen Scars

Cover Art by *Diana Carlile*

The Wild Rose Press, Inc.
PO Box 708
Adams Basin, NY 14410-0708
Visit us at www.thewildrosepress.com

Publishing History
First Edition, 2021
Trade Paperback ISBN 978-1-5092-3639-8
Digital ISBN 978-1-5092-3640-4

Published in the United States of America

Dedication

To God for the vision and ability. To my kids for their unwavering belief in me. To author Katherine Hawthorne for friendship, inspiration, support, and painful honesty. I never would have started without you. To my friends and family for reading as I wrote with so much excitement, encouragement, and anticipation. I never would have finished without you. To Erin, the grammar queen who questioned everything. You rule the world! To editor Dianne Rich for believing in my book and taking a risk on me. To my mom who loves me no matter what, and finally, to my dad who seemed to believe he could do anything if he just kept trying. I did it, Dad. I actually wrote a book! This is for you.

PROLOGUE

Darkness. It's all I've known for days, maybe weeks. I catch glimpses of light when Demon comes, but his visits are irregular, leaving me with no real sense of time as I lie here alone in the sweltering black. At first, I feared his visits, anticipating the pain and humiliation he inflicted. Now, the longing for human contact, for any break in the dark isolation outweighs my fear. Demon has become my hope, my only hope.

It's been a long time since his last appearance. I can tell because the cut is healing, and my hunger has all but disappeared. The dripping faucet in the corner keeps me alive, but only barely. Sometimes I try not to drink, try to will myself to just fall asleep and never wake up. It's an out the fighter in me just won't let me take. Time after time I crawl toward the incessant dripping until I feel the mud beneath my palms and know the faucet is within reach. The more I use the water, the more the mosquitoes come, seeking the moisture eroding the dirt floor but finding my sweaty body instead. What blood Demon doesn't claim belongs to them. I have no protection against their assault, no clothing to cover the wounds Demon inflicts.

Demon is an angel of pain. He is beautiful, my Demon. I wish he was hideous. In my heart it would make things easier. In the brief flashes of light that precede his entrance, I can see the backlit glow of his

1

clean bright hair, the cut of his immaculate suit. I smell the scent of his evil, and it's deceptively alluring. He never appears to be someone who could hurt me, but each time Demon comes, his soft, sweet words whispered in my ear are accompanied by his invasion of my body as he convinces it to betray me, to feel pleasure with his pain. Each time he comes, the pleasure rushes, but the cut follows. One cut on my inner thigh. One cut for each time he has possessed me. Like some fucked-up notch on a bedpost.

Each time he leaves me, I have another notch along with a single Cliff Bar. Just enough to keep me alive until the next time, if I ration it. I wish I could say I didn't eat them, that I resist, but like with the water, my body has a mind of its own, and my fighter craves the fuel, falsely believing it will one day make a difference. Logically, I know it's not enough, but my foolish heart wants to hope anyway. Stupid fucking heart. Maybe Demon will cut it out and save me from myself. Maybe I want him to. Maybe this night, as the wind outside howls and sleep sucks me under, the darkness will swallow me whole and carry me where Demon can never find me again.

CHAPTER 1

Eva (Three Years Later)

"Clemmie. Clemmie baby, give Mommy a kiss," I cajole, trying to get my two-year-old, Clementine, to decide I'm more interesting than the crackers she is currently crumbling into a soggy mess on her highchair tray. "Mommy has to go bye-bye." Those magic words bring her eyes to mine, and the swell of tears in her baby blues heaps on the guilt. I should have left while she was happy and content with her crackers, but after last night's dreams, I needed a dose of her baby sunshine to refocus my thoughts, anchor me in the here and now.

I lean in and nuzzle her messy cheeks, sucking in the scent of the baby shampoo I still use on her unruly red curls as I tickle her pudgy belly.

"No, Momma!" she squeals between giggles, her toothy grin giving me just what I need to push myself out the door and start my day.

After one last check to make sure my outfit is camouflaging all my problem areas, I grab my purse and keys from the dated kitchen counter and turn to my aunt while opening the back door. "Call me if you need me. I should be home on time today. Oh, and no chocolate milk. I didn't think she would ever go to sleep last night."

Aunt Polly smiles and winks at me. "Don't you worry, baby. Me and this little munchkin will be just fine, won't we, Clemmie?"

Clemmie giggles and swats her gummy cracker-covered hands at the finger Aunt Polly uses to tap her nose.

Waving, I slip out into the cloyingly humid Alabama heat before Clemmie notices I've left. I unlock my old Toyota 4Runner, happy it's finally out of the shop and I don't have to drive Aunt Polly's giant sedan. The scent of oil from the mechanic shop still lingers as I slide into the seat, but the comfort of the familiar leather is not diminished.

The SUV wasn't new when I scrimped and saved to buy it over ten years ago. It survived my college years and carried me off to my first official counseling job before more recently carrying me to the hospital to have Clemmie. Now it carts around her car seat as well as myriad toys and random discarded fries that litter the floor. It might not be perfect, but it's mine. Few things are these days, so I don't take it for granted.

My growling stomach reminds me to hurry or I won't have time for my usual breakfast stop. The Daily Grind is the relatively new business venture of my high school best friend, Tessa Taliaferro. I consider it my duty to support her by stopping in on my way to work each morning since she has always been by my side and even made the move to Magnolia Ridge with me. The "bestie discount"—as she calls it—also helps stretch my tight budget.

The old-fashioned bells jingle as I push through the door after parking in one of the sparse downtown spaces. Tessa waves from behind the counter where she works the line of people at the register. The scent of pastries and freshly brewed coffee elicits an audible grumble from my stomach, causing the man who came in behind me to chuckle.

My face heats as I realize he heard. I don't want this man's attention, not his or anyone else's. I quickly duck my head and turn to slip out of the shop knowing Tessa, who is used to my neurosis, will understand. With my hair covering my face and my eyes on the floor, I whip around then suddenly trip and go flying. Just as I'm about to face-plant, strong arms catch me and settle me back on my feet. Before I can catch my breath, I'm looking up, way up, into eyes so blue I could drown in their depths.

"Whoa, pretty girl. You okay?" His voice is deep and rumbling, like water rushing over rocks. Dark hair falls over his gorgeous eyes, and full lips that look like they've worn a lot of smiles tip up at the corners.

I open my mouth to answer, but nothing comes out. My embarrassed blush deepens. His hands slowly drift down my arms before letting go and falling to his sides. The unfamiliar and unwanted heat suffusing my body pulls me back into last night's dreams and pushes me toward the panic attack I was barely able to stave off this morning. I struggle to breathe, feeling the weight of stares that I know must be picking apart all my flaws. Thankfully, Tessa unknowingly creates a distraction by calling my name in greeting, and I manage to make my escape when the man turns.

CHAPTER 2

Ashe

Damn. She ran from me. I didn't mean to embarrass her. I couldn't help the quiet laugh when I heard her stomach rumble. I'd been staring at her since I followed her into The Daily Grind for my morning caffeine boost. Her outfit was bland, and though feminine, it was a bit shapeless. What caught my attention was the mess of tousled dark curls framing her softly beautiful face. I couldn't look away. When I chuckled, I'd expected her to laugh too, but it was like she just folded in on herself and then tripped over my shoe in her haste to get away.

As soon as I caught her, the heat of her felt like it all but singed my hands. Then she looked up at me with eyes that were such a vibrant mix I couldn't even claim their color. I was lost. The feel of her beneath my hands was soft and so very warm, but then she ran away without a word, like my very own little White Rabbit. She may have taken off down a rabbit hole, but I am damn good at chasing rabbits. My first clue, her name…Eva.

I make my way up to the counter, because rabbit to chase or not, caffeine is a necessity. My newest case is a bit out of the norm, and even a boatload of coffee won't make what I have to do today any easier. Without coffee, it will be impossible.

"Good morning. What can I get for you?" The perky strawberry-blonde barista eyes me suspiciously as she waits to ring up my total. After ordering the largest coffee possible and a cheese danish to go— Because everyone needs a little fuel with their caffeine, right?—I flash my most charming smile and decide to do a little fishing.

"So, you know Eva?"

The barista's eyes narrow, but she bags my danish and motions for me to move farther to the side of the counter where more privacy is available.

"How do *you* know Eva? I've never seen you with her before. What did you do to make her run out like that?" She fires questions at me without bothering to answer mine as she slides the danish across the counter and places the steaming coffee in front of me.

I hold up my hands in surrender. "I promise; I didn't mean to scare her. She tripped and then ran away without saying a word."

"She looked upset, and she never misses her morning latte. Who are you anyway?" She plants her hands on her hips and gives me a glare.

Fearing I'm about to be wearing my coffee, I swipe it from the little spitfire's reach and take a cautious sip. I'm glad my little rabbit has a friend as fierce as Blondie, so I decide to just be honest.

"Look, I don't know Eva, but I think I'd like to. I want to at least apologize for accidentally tripping her and maybe buy her that latte. Here's my card," I say, setting the coffee back down and slipping a business card from my wallet.

She tentatively takes it from my hand and slips it in

her apron pocket without reading it.

"Would you just give her the card and tell her I'm sorry and want to make it up to her?"

Blondie nods before rushing away to help another customer.

I grab my caffeine and sugar fix then smile to myself as I walk out. I didn't learn much, but now I know where my little rabbit is every morning. I don't intend to miss her tomorrow.

CHAPTER 3

Eva

Could this day get any worse? With my luck, probably. I was already dragging after missing the two extra shots of espresso Tessa always adds to my daily skinny latte, then my first client of the day was a no-show, which means I have to call his court referral officer, and now I'm suddenly stuck with a two-hour group session to lead because my coworker, Jake, had to leave to handle an emergency with his mom, who's in the early stages of Alzheimer's. I don't usually mind covering for him, but why did it have to be today? My face flushes again just thinking of how stupidly I acted this morning.

I know as soon as I get off work, Tessa will be calling to find out what happened. What the heck am I going to tell her? She's been my best friend since we were pulling each other's hair on the playground in kindergarten. She'll know if I lie, so I guess I'll just tell her the truth, because saying, "I got embarrassed because the completely gorgeous man behind me laughed when my big fat stomach growled, so I decided to trip over his feet and go mute before running away," won't make her think I'm crazy at all. Ugghhh! Why am I so neurotic? Shouldn't I be able to counsel myself out of all my issues? Apparently, I can help people work through their addiction problems, but I can't get myself back to normal.

I used to be normal...before. Now, after an abrupt and unsuccessful end to years of therapy, I'm just really good at faking. Don't get me wrong, I'm still a very competent substance abuse counselor, but now I choose to ignore my own issues. Most days the avoidance works well for me, but apparently not today. Maybe I just won't answer my phone when Tessa calls. I'll pretend to be busy, and when I go to The Daily Grind in the morning, everything will reset and be fine again. Yep, I think that's the best plan. Avoidance for the win. I grab the file for my no-show, but the phone buzzes before I can make the call.

"Eva? You have a visitor. I've already had him sign a confidentiality agreement." Our receptionist, Jolie, is nothing if not efficient. With so many outpatient clients to manage, she has to be.

"I'm not expecting a client until after the group session. Who is it?"

"Mr. Lincoln with LCR Investigations and Security."

"LCR?" I've never heard of LCR, though being contacted by someone investigating one of my clients is not completely out of the norm.

"That's what the business card reads. Should I buzz him back, or would you prefer to come to the lobby?"

"Just send him back, but please warn him I have to be in group in twenty minutes."

"No problem. I'll let him know."

I hear her calling Mr. Lincoln to the desk as she's hanging up. The buzz of the security door echoes down the hallway, and I stand and straighten my long flowy shirt to make sure it sufficiently covers the slight baby pooch I still can't seem to get rid of before walking toward the open door of my tiny office. I step into the hallway, already extending a hand, but my greeting dies in my throat as I look up into the cerulean gaze of the man from this morning. No way! My heart races, and my mind immediately goes straight to the worst-case scenario.

"Are you following me? How did you get my name?" My fear and the safety of being on my own turf makes me bold. "What do you want?" He simply stares at me, looking as shocked as I feel.

"Whoa. Calm down, little rabbit," he says, smiling at me while holding his hands up in surrender. "I'm not here for you. I'm looking for Julie Jones."

Julie. I haven't been called Julie in years. Three years, to be exact, and little rabbit? What the heck? I work hard to keep the anxiety off my face. I need to play it off, find out what he wants.

"What do you want with Julie?"

"Well, pretty girl, that's between me and Ms. Jones, but nothing nefarious, I promise." He quirks a disarming grin and crosses his heart with his finger. "We have a mutual acquaintance to discuss. It's just business."

Mutual acquaintance. Well, that certainly sounds like it's something related to a client. Perhaps this is a coincidence after all. I glance around.

Jolie is up front in the lobby, and Malcolm, another counselor, is just down the hall in his office.

No one can take me out of here or hurt me without them knowing. I, of all people, know safety is an illusion, but this building is safer than most.

"If you'll just direct me her way, I'll be happy to leave you alone…for now, anyway."

I don't have time to keep standing in the hall, and if I'm honest, now that I know this has nothing to do with the incident this morning, I'm curious which client is currently in trouble.

"I'm Julie, um, Julie Evangeline Jones. I go by Eva." I stammer, almost choking on my first name. I clear my throat and indicate my office with a wave. "This is my office. Come in. Feel free to have a seat." My windowless and minimalistic office feels crowded with Mr. Lincoln's large frame situated on the small love seat intended for clients, and by the time I settle in my chair and swivel it to the right toward him, his relaxed demeanor has disappeared. The grim look on his face has me feeling unsettled, so I fall back on my professional persona and pull on the confident mask I wear for clients.

"Mr. Lincoln, I'm not sure which client you would like to discuss today, but I need you to understand I can't even confirm or deny someone is a client unless he or she has signed a consent form authorizing me to talk to you."

He shifts uncomfortably and refuses to meet my gaze, instead pulling up something on his phone.

"Please, call me Ashe. I'm actually not here to talk about a client. My firm has been hired to investigate a disappearance." He turns his phone toward me, and I find myself looking at a picture of a beautiful woman with strawberry-blonde hair. "Do you recognize this woman?"

I shake my head. "Her name is Danielle Hurst. She's been missing for five days. The police are focusing on the theory that she left town with a boyfriend, but Danielle's parents believe the police are overlooking connections to other disappearances."

The longer he speaks, the harder it becomes for me to breathe. It's like history repeating itself. My parents claimed I'd run away with a boyfriend. It's why no one came for me. No one ever came. I try to remember the grounding exercises my therapist taught me. *Name five things you can see.* I glance around frantically. Files. I see files. Files and a stain on the carpet near my right foot and—sympathy. I see sympathy and pity exuding from those brilliant blue eyes. Pity for me. I can't breathe!

He continues softly as though trying to blunt the blow. "We believe the disappearances, including Danielle's, have ties to another incident which occurred three years ago."

Spots float in the air between us, circling round and around. "Eva? Eva!"

I hear his voice as if from a distance, but I can't answer, still can't breathe. I grope blindly for the desk at my side and jolt from my chair, ready to run before the familiar darkness comes to reclaim my soul.

CHAPTER 4

Ashe

Damn! I knew this interview was going to be difficult, but I never would have dreamed the kidnapping survivor I need to speak to would be *her*— Eva. She looks nothing like the edgy defiant blonde I expected from the picture in her file. Her knuckles are white from her death grip on the arm of the chair, and I'm not even sure if she heard what I just said. "Eva?" Her face loses color, and one hand goes to her throat as if she's struggling to catch her breath.

"Eva!" I reach for her just as she staggers from her chair. *Shit!* Everything seems to happen in slow motion.

She makes a grab for her desk as if to keep herself standing but misses in her panic, the momentum carrying her toward an impact with the floor. Her head clips the corner of the desk with a sickening thud before I manage to catch her.

"Fuck!" I sink to the floor and scoop her head into my lap. "Eva?" Her dark curls cover her face. When I carefully sweep her hair to the side, I suck in a sharp breath. Blood is matted at her scalp and seeping down toward her left eye. I don't think the wound is serious, but it definitely looks gruesome.

"What the hell did you do? Get away from her!" My arms tighten around Eva as the hulking stranger yells at me from the doorway. He's big, but I think we're evenly matched. He drops to the floor and reaches for Eva, but I won't give her up without a fight.

"Stay back," I growl.

"Mal?" Her voice is weak. "Why are you yelling?" Her hand reaches toward her head, but I gently restrain her.

"You hit your head. Just lie still a minute, babe. Okay?" I say, looking around the office for something to cover the wound and stop the bleeding.

"Babe? What the hell, man? She's not your babe! I already told you to get away from her." The guy shoves his way closer and tries to wrench Eva from my grasp. My curse is cut short by her pained whimper. We both instantly still. "Eva, are you okay? Do you want me to call an ambulance?" he says softly, his concern evident on his face. I relax my grip, but only slightly. I still don't know this guy. Eva blinks slowly then turns her head toward the door with a wince.

"I'm okay, Mal. I don't need an ambulance." She tries to sit up, but I don't release my hold. "Mr. Lincoln, I'm fine. Please let go."

"Ashe. My name's Ashe," I say as I comply with her request and gently assist her to a seated position.

Her eyes close, and she sways for a moment before steadying herself with a palm on the floor.

"Mal, can you help me up?" she asks.

"Let me call Jolie for the first aid kit first." He uses her desk phone to make the request then stoops as though he is going to try to carry Eva.

She puts up a hand to stop him.

"I can do it myself. I just need a little help."

We both move quickly to take a side, slowly

helping her stand and move to the love seat. I settle myself beside her in the limited space before the other guy can. Who knew I could be so territorial? I just met this girl today, but for some reason she already feels like mine, and no way is *Mal* getting his grimy hands on her. What kind of name is *Mal* anyway? I think he looks more like a Jackass.

The redheaded receptionist zips into the room carrying a first aid kit. "Eva! What happened?" She sinks to her knees in front of the love seat and starts pulling supplies out of her case. "Mal, can you grab some damp paper towels?"

He straightens from his stance leaning against the desk, and the death glare he was directing at me softens when he looks at her.

"Sure thing, Jolie." He heads down the hall but not before checking in with Eva to make sure she doesn't mind being left with me.

Really? Do I look like I'm trying to hurt her? I was worried she'd still be frantic once she came to, but her response is calm as she sends Jackass on his way. The redhead, Jolie apparently, starts dabbing at Eva's forehead with alcohol wipes causing her to flinch and grab my hand. I'm pretty sure she doesn't realize it, but I'm not above being glad that at least subconsciously she seems to know I won't hurt her.

"I'm so sorry, Eva. I'm trying to be gentle. Are you sure you don't want to call an ambulance or go to the doctor? It seems like the wound stopped bleeding, but you could have a concussion." She swaps from the alcohol wipes to the damp paper towels when Jackass returns so she can wipe the blood close to Eva's eye before applying antibiotic ointment and a bandage. My biggest fan resumes his post at the desk—and his glare.

"I just tripped. It's no big deal. I promise I'm fine. I think I'll just call Aunt Polly to come pick me up."

Tripped? I don't know much about panic attacks, but I'd swear that's what I saw. She shoots me a look that dares me to contradict her before looking around as though searching for her cell phone. Loud knocking sounds from the front of the building, startling us both.

"Oh no. I forgot about leading the group session. I'm late." She starts to stand as Jolie grabs the now closed first aid kit and excuses herself to let the new arrivals sign in. I keep my hold on her hand gentle but use it to ensure she stays seated.

"No way. You're in no shape to do anything right now. Let me give you a ride home." I need the information Eva can provide, and I can't take the risk that she might run or refuse to talk with me again. Plus, if I'm honest with myself, I feel guilty for being the cause of the panic that resulted in her pain.

"Not happening," Jackass says, and "I don't think so," Eva says at the same time.

"Who are you anyway, and why are you here?" he demands.

"Asher Lincoln," I say, reluctantly dropping Eva's hand and reaching in my wallet for business cards before handing one to Eva first then to Jackass. "I'm one of the owners of LCR Investigations and Security. My reasons for being here are between Eva and me."

I can literally see Eva's discomfort returning at the mention of my firm. She clasps her hands in her lap trying to hide the tremble. I also don't miss how her breathing has quickened. The look in Jackass's eyes and the clench of his fists tells me he's also noticed and is gearing up for another protest.

Damn it! I need a way to get the information without sending her running again. I can't give up on finding Danielle while there is hope she's still alive, but I also can't deny that hurting Eva, even just by asking questions, is going to be nearly impossible. Asking her to relive what had to be the worst experience of her life will kill what peace she's managed to find in the last few years, not to mention that it will likely cost me any chance of knowing her beyond today. I have never been so conflicted about a job. I've never been so conflicted about a woman either.

CHAPTER 5

Eva

My eyes dart back and forth between the two men. Testosterone hangs like a heavy fog over the room, and if I don't get out of here, I feel like I might choke. Of course, that's probably more from anxiety than testosterone. It's been over six months since I've had a panic attack. I thought I was finally free, finally moving forward. I thought no one here would ever know, that I'd never have to talk about my past again. I just want to be normal. Spots begin floating in front of me again, and I realize I haven't taken a breath. Closing my eyes, I inhale slowly through my nose and exhale from my mouth. When I open my eyes, the room is silent and two male gazes are fully focused on me.

"That's it. I'm taking you home," Mal demands.

"Mal, you can't. I have a whole group of people here waiting for a group session."

"And you're going to lead a two-hour session with a bloody knot on your head and hands that won't stop shaking?" Mal protests. "Yeah, right. You've lost your mind!"

I flinch because it hasn't been that long ago since I basically did, though Mal doesn't need to know that. "Jake had to leave, so who's going to cover group if you carry me home? It won't work. If I'm not leading group, then you have to." Mal curses and runs his hand down his face in frustration. "I'm okay now anyway. I can drive myself."

"Like hell!" Ashe interjects. "Look, I get that you don't know me, but I promise I just want to make sure you get home okay." He directs his attention toward Mal and says, "I'll take her straight home, and she can call you the minute she arrives. You have my card, so it's not like you can't track me down if need be. Hell, call and verify my identity if it makes you feel better."

Ashe turns back to me and places his hand over mine. "I promise you'll be safe. No more questions, just a ride." His blue eyes peer into my hazel ones, and I see nothing but sincerity reflected back. I know I shouldn't trust him, but for some reason his touch is warm and calming.

I glance at Mal. He must read the decision in my expression because he nods and hands me my cell phone from my desk and grabs my purse from the drawer. He gently tugs me to my feet and places the purse on my shoulder. "Text me the minute you get home. I mean it. The very minute. Don't make me come after you."

"I promise." I step toward the door and feel Ashe's steadying hand at my back.

"Give Clemmie a kiss for me and get some rest. Don't stress about group. I've got it covered." Mal ushers me out into the hallway, but before Ashe can follow, Mal grabs his arm and mutters something in his ear. Ashe glares but nods before escorting me to his truck and opening the passenger door. If my head wasn't pounding, I'd probably pay more attention to the vehicle, but as it stands, I simply endure the thick overheated interior. I rest my head against the too-warm leather seat and close my eyes. I hear Ashe open his door and slide in. The feel of his hand near my right cheek causes me to flinch away and pop my eyes open.

"Easy, little rabbit. You forgot to fasten your seat belt. I just want to make sure you're safe." Though he is very circumspect while fastening my seat belt, just his proximity is causing that uncomfortable heat again, and I don't mean anything related to the hundred-degree temps outside. I have never been more thankful to live close to work. I need some distance from this man. Turning my head, I look out the window, hoping maybe he'll get the hint and not talk to me. He told me no more questions, but I'm not sure I trust him. Mr. Asher Lincoln and his firm don't need to know anything about me.

I moved to Magnolia Ridge for a fresh start. So far, it's worked. I've made a new life for myself and Clemmie. We've been happy living with Aunt Polly and being a part of this community. I don't intend to let this man ruin it all for me. My past is in the past. I was a random victim of a random crime. I'm nobody's victim anymore, and I won't be made to feel like one. I can feel my fear and anxiety morphing quickly into anger. It's not that I don't feel sympathy for this other woman—I do. I know what it's like to be taken, but rehashing my past is not going to bring her even one second closer to being found. My past has nothing to do with this investigation. I moved five hours away and changed everything about myself just to make sure no one would know me or ask questions. The chances of being in the same place as my captor at the same time again are almost statistically impossible, especially since he's probably dead.

Ashe cranks the truck and turns the air on high, but I'm so caught up in my thoughts I miss that we never move. I shoot him a questioning glance. He's looking at me expectantly.

"I need your address, Eva," he says softly. I rattle it off and turn back to my window. Ashe drives carefully for the few miles to Aunt Polly's. I'm grateful he doesn't talk, so I have time to think up the quickest way to get out of this car when we arrive.

"Listen, I said no more questions right now, and I meant it. You're in no shape for it mentally or physically, but that doesn't mean we can avoid the conversation. It's important. You may be the only person standing between life and death for Danielle."

I don't respond. I can't. As soon as we pull into the driveway, I'm opening the door, and only his hand on my arm keeps me from being halfway up the brick walk. "Rabbit, don't even think about it. I'm coming around to help you out." He gives me a stern look. "Don't move."

I feel his eyes on me as he circles around the front, almost daring me to challenge him. For some reason, I don't. I wait until he has the door fully open and reaches for my hand. I hesitate, a little afraid of his intensity. His expression gentles.

"I promise, I don't bite. I just want to help." He winks just as I place my hand in his grip. A laugh wants to escape, but I hold it in. I fear a small grin may have eluded my self-control, though I quickly corral it before Ashe can notice and take it as encouragement.

As he carefully extracts me from his vehicle, I notice Aunt Polly smiling widely at the top of the front steps. Her long, wavy ash-blonde hair is loose, and her peasant skirt is swirling around her legs in the tepid breeze. I'm not sure what Ashe will make of her throwback style, but there is no one on earth I love more, except my daughter.

"Who do we have here?" Aunt Polly asks as we make our way up the walk with Ashe's hand now burning at my back. "He has manners. I like him already."

A full-on laugh shakes Ashe's frame. "Thank you, ma'am. I'm Asher Lincoln. I—"

"He's a friend from work," I interrupt. He eyes me suspiciously but doesn't contradict my statement. The last thing I want is to worry Aunt Polly. I've caused her enough stress the last few years.

"Um, yeah, Eva had an accident at work, so I wanted to make sure she arrived home safely." Aunt Polly's gaze swings to me and sharpens. She looks me over before brushing the curls away from my face to examine the bandage.

"Girl, what did you do?" she asks, fretting over the injury.

"It's nothing, Aunt Polly. You know how clumsy I can be. I just tripped." She narrows her eyes and looks toward Ashe as if waiting for him to verify my accounting of events. Thankfully, he has his game face on and doesn't confirm or deny what I said. Just as I think Aunt Polly is about to launch into a full-scale interrogation, she notices Ashe's hand, which is still at my back, and breaks into another beaming smile.

"Well, Mr. Lincoln, I'm glad you were there to help." Aunt Polly starts to reach to shake his hand but is interrupted by the sound of crying coming from the baby monitor. "Excuse me just a minute. I'll be right back." She hurries into the house, leaving me alone on the porch with this handsome man I barely know.

"Eva." Ashe turns me to face him. "I don't want to upset you, but I do still need your help. I keep my word, so you don't have to answer anything right now, but please, just look up Danielle Hurst. Several articles have been written this week. Read about her. I promise she's worth saving. You're my only lead right now, and if my theory is right, you're not safe either until this kidnapper is caught."

Not safe. Not safe. The words echo around in my aching head, stirring me back into a near panic. I jerk my arm from his grasp and hurry toward the front door just as it re-opens. Clemmie toddles out full tilt with Aunt Polly close behind.

"Momma! Momma! Momma!" she squeals happily before clamping her arms around my leg for a hug. I hoist her up onto my hip and bury my face in the baby smell of her messy ringlets before Polly can see the fear on my face or delay Ashe's departure. Clemmie giggles, and we make our way quickly into the house without a backward glance.

CHAPTER 6

Eva

The heat inside my prison has become unbearable. Moisture clings to the air and suffocates me with every breath. The usual scent of human waste is long gone, and I can't remember the last time I needed to make use of the makeshift latrine in the corner. My thigh burns with the latest cut. For a while, I would try to clean myself and the cuts with the water from the faucet. I wasn't going to let Demon win. I would survive. I would never be his victim.

Now, time has ceased to have any meaning, and the blackness before me stretches endlessly. No one is coming. I've never been close to my parents, and not hearing from me for a long period of time would be more a relief than a red flag, but I was sure someone from work would have reported my disappearance. I was still new, but I'd made friends...at least I thought I had. Chanda and Karrie had invited me to join them for drinks, along with some of the other staff. I'd been so excited to be included and to meet new people. I'd worn my favorite little black dress and drank with my friends, dancing until my body was sweaty and my head was throbbing. When the drinks ran out, I volunteered to buy the next round. I made my way to the bar and then—nothing. Just nothing. My mind is a blur of perceived sensations...attraction, fear, pain, light, darkness, movement. It makes no sense. I remember nothing between walking to the bar and waking up here.

Still, I believed someone would come, someone would care, but I don't believe anymore, and I don't care. I suck in another thick breath that only adds to the heat brought on by my already fevered state. I slide my hand down my grimy body to trace the marks on my inner thighs. My right thigh has six parallel scars in various states of healing. The left now has seven, and it's the seventh that is going to be my salvation. I feel the raised puffiness of the wound and the sticky fluid oozing out as I press it. I imagine the mark is red to match the heat emanating from it. I'm hoping the dirt from my hands will speed up the process of the infection. I find it ironic that after all I've suffered and survived, an infection will be my final release. I've been too weak to crawl to the faucet, and the sweat on my body has all but dried up. It can't be long now. Please don't let it be long.

I jerk awake, struggling for enough air to scream. My head throbs, my body is wracked with phantom pain, and the soaking-wet sheets are tangled around my sweaty legs. The scars on my thighs burn, and my hand unconsciously rubs them as I count over and over, assuring myself there is no new mark. The details of my room slowly sink in as my eyes adjust to the dim glow of my ever-present nightlight. I'm not there anymore. I'm home. I'm safe.

Dreams sometimes haunt my sleep as well as my waking hours, but I haven't had this particular one in almost a year. My life has settled into a contented routine now that Clemmie is no longer an infant and sleeps through the night. I work, I come home and play with my sweet girl, and then after I put her to bed, I watch movies with Aunt Polly or read a book in my room. Some nights are restless, but maybe that's true for everyone.

My life is simple and uncomplicated. I don't date. I don't go out with friends other than Tessa. Dating and friends are a risk. I don't take risks. Tessa, Polly, and Clemmie are the only ones who have ever loved me or needed me, and all I need is them. I can't let Asher Lincoln and his questions destroy the peace I've built for myself. I can't let my past touch Clemmie. She is pure unfiltered sunshine and the only thing that keeps the memories at bay. She can never know she was born of the deepest darkness.

CHAPTER 7

Ashe

Damn it! I run my fingers through my hair for what must be the fiftieth time today. Paperwork is scattered all over my desk awaiting my attention, and all I can focus on is the one file on top—Julie Jones, or rather, Eva. Never could I have imagined they were one and the same.

Danielle Hurst's parents had come to LCR two days ago with an outrageous theory. What they were asking for was far out of my purview, but John Hurst was a friend. Before he retired from the Magnolia Ridge police department six months ago, he'd been an important source of information for our business. He'd helped LCR more times than I could count, so when he came in begging for a few minutes of my time, there was no way I could turn him down. We've had service agreements with the Magnolia Ridge PD and several other local law enforcement agencies for years, so it was relatively easy to begin collaborating on this case.

According to John, Danielle is the fourth young woman to disappear in Alabama under similar circumstances in the past three years. Normally three disappearances spread out over such a span of time and in different areas of the state wouldn't have caught anyone's attention, but John used to live and work near the coast in Mobile. Julie Jones's case was big news in that area.

She had been missing from the Mobile area for almost two months when she was found on a farm naked, tortured, and unconscious in a tangle of debris from the aftermath of an EF-3 tornado in Tuscaloosa. John and his partner had made the three-and-a-half hour drive up to Druid City Hospital to interview her. Julie was barely in any shape to talk, but told a harrowing tale of captivity, assault, and torture though she had no idea how she'd been taken or by whom, other than the vague impression of having met a stranger at the bar. The only name she had for her abductor was Demon, a title her mind had concocted because it sounded similar to the name of the unknown stranger. She had no concept of even how long she'd been gone.

John had kept his own personal notes on the case, claiming he just couldn't let it go even after moving north to Magnolia Ridge shortly after. The picture in the Jones file is of a boldly smiling young woman in her twenties with sparkling eyes and straight reddish-blonde hair, nothing like Eva's midnight curls. Eva...shit, I needed to get my mind off her and back on the case.

Over the past few years, at least two young Alabama women—three, including Julie—had been listed as missing for extended periods of time. Unfortunately, the first two were murdered. Celia Wayne had been found in Selma six months after disappearing from a dance club an hour and forty-five minutes away in Birmingham. Other than some nicks discovered on the femur, her body was too badly decomposed to determine whether she had borne similar treatment to Julie, but the coroner's estimated time of death showed she had likely been alive for at least two months after her disappearance.

The second case was Amy Lacklan, who disappeared from a dance club in Huntsville. Her mutilated body was found over an hour away near the small town of Fort Payne nine weeks later. Though the dance club connection was tenuous at best, the physical characteristics of the victims were similar enough to be disconcerting. Both women were close to Julie's age and build with similar reddish-blonde hair, however, the most convincing evidence to tie these disappearances and murders back to Julie Jones were the cuts found on Amy Lacklan's body.

If John's theory is correct, LCR is hunting a man who travels the entire state and is intelligent enough to keep his prey for months on end without getting caught. Danielle could be his fourth victim. Like the others, she disappeared from a crowded nightclub, the most popular in Magnolia Ridge. With her strawberry-blonde hair, she fits the killer's type.

The local police have promised to look into John's theory out of respect for his former position, but LCR will also help because we owe John several favors. Danielle is his only child, and knowing she could be in the hands of Julie's Demon is eating him up from the inside. He knows he can't save her on his own, but he obviously believes he has a chance with our help.

A sharp knock at my door precedes the entrance of my partner, Jackson Rose. Rosey and I served in the Army together as MPs. Our military police background gave us the inspiration for LCR, though it was quite a few years after our separation from the Army before we had the necessary education, training, and credentials to make it a reality. Rosey drops his large frame into one of my brown leather chairs and kicks his feet up on the front of my desk. "Linc, you ready to cut out of here yet? Con and I are about to check out the new pub downtown for drinks. You in?" Liam Connery is the third member of the LCR triplets, so nicknamed by our staff because all our birthdays are in June. Each year we host a giant joint birthday party that never ceases to get out of hand. Con is the primary reason things usually go off the rails. His background as a member of the Security Force, the fancy Air Force name for MPs, makes him the perfect third for our company. His often-outrageous behavior is what makes him the life of every party.

"I don't know. I'm still reviewing some of the files from the Hurst case," I reply, shoving Rosey's feet off my desk and off the aforementioned files. He chuckles and rights himself in the chair.

"All work and no play make Linc a dull boy," he quips with a rare grin.

"How very original." I roll my eyes and reach again for Julie's file. Somehow, I can't think of her as Eva when I'm working. It's like I need Julie and Eva to be two separate people in my mind. I can't read the facts of this case, the specifics of her injuries, and the details of her experiences if I see Eva's face in the victim photos. Julie is the victim. Eva is my little runaway rabbit. My rabbit who has a baby bunny. Damn.

I can't get the image of the chubby-cheeked toddler out of my head. Her red curls bounced all around her smiling face before Eva scooped her up and disappeared inside. Nowhere in my file is a child listed. What if Eva is married? Have I been flirting with a married woman? No husband was mentioned yesterday when we were debating calling for a ride home. My brain starts tossing around scenarios. Perhaps the little one isn't hers. No. She called Eva "Momma". Wait, a daughter wouldn't have been mentioned in the file because the file is three years old, and the little girl couldn't be much more than two.

My mind suddenly takes me to a dark place, and I begin frantically flipping through the file until I reach the medical records. They are nowhere near complete since this isn't the official police report, but John kept good documentation. I skim past the list of injuries to the information I'm looking for. A rape kit was performed due to evidence of repeated assault.

Fuck! Every muscle in my body contracts with rage before I wrestle them back under control and continue reading. No DNA was found. I keep skimming but find no mention of a pregnancy test anywhere. Could I be jumping to conclusions?

The loud smack of Rosey's hands on my desk causes both me and my files to jump. "What the hell, Rosey?" I yell while trying to get my heart to beat normally again.

"Just trying to get your attention, bro. What just happened?"

"Nothing. I just had an idea I needed to confirm." I close the file and try to act nonchalant while pushing it to the side.

"Right, nothing," he says, eyeing me suspiciously before rising and walking to the door. "Whatever. You in for drinks or not?"

"Not tonight. I'm ready to go home and crash," I say while stacking my files as though getting ready to leave. Rosey nods and closes my door on his way out.

As soon as I'm alone, I lean my head back against my chair and try to figure out how to help Danielle without hurting Eva.

CHAPTER 8

Eva

"Momma, watch!" Clemmie squeals as she toddles around as fast as her little legs will carry her, chasing the other kids in the toddler section of the city splash pad. Her fiery hair is plastered to her head and dripping into her eyes, but the giant smile on her face shows she couldn't be happier. She and a little girl with floppy braids interspersed with multicolored beads discover a puddle at the same time and begin stomping and splashing each other amid countless giggles.

My heart lightens for the first time in the last couple days. I've allowed my fears to overwhelm me and have been upsetting everyone around me. I decided this morning that two days of hiding out at home, avoiding the coffee shop, and aimlessly drifting through work while vacillating between a need to know more about Danielle Hurst and a fear of getting involved was too much. I was falling back into old habits, old harmful patterns, and I refused to drag Clemmie down with me. It was time to face my fears and go on the offensive.

I woke up on the couch this morning after yet another restless night filled with memories disguised as nightmares. Clemmie was gently patting my cheek. Her lips were pulled into a concerned pout.

"Momma sad?" she'd asked in her sweet baby voice. I'd looked into her innocent eyes and known I needed to pull myself together for her. I had never let the darkness touch her, and I wouldn't start now. I'd cleared all the remnants of my emotional eating binges from the house, took a shower to clear my head, and packed a bag for Clemmie before heading to the park, knowing a Saturday of sun and fun would be just what we both needed. I'd invited Aunt Polly, but she seemed excited about a quiet day to herself at home.

"I wet, Momma." Clemmie giggles before wrapping herself around me in a squishy hug. She brings me back to the present. I smile and tickle her pudgy belly.

"Now Momma wet!" Her sweet laughter is exactly what I need as she claps her hands before hugging me again even tighter. After a few more minutes of tickles and loves, Clemmie runs back into the water to rejoin her new friend. By the time I notice her rubbing sleepy eyes, my clothes are dry, we've both gotten our share of sun and laughter, and we're ready to head home for a nap.

I fasten my sleepy girl into her car seat and head home. Clemmie is asleep before we even make it a block, and I sing along quietly to the music streaming through the radio, enjoying the breeze from the open sunroof as we cruise past the recently harvested cotton fields along the backroads.

I don't notice the large truck speeding up behind me until it's too late. I've just rounded a bend in the road when it appears in my rearview mirror right before ramming into the back corner of my car, causing my head to hit the steering wheel and sending us spinning. I scream for Clemmie as the 4Runner tilts and rocks, threatening to tip over. I can hear her shrill, frightened whimpers before the car finally comes to a jarring stop nose first against a culvert in a deep ditch.

My head makes another sharp impact, on what I don't know. Colors whirl in a kaleidoscope, and nausea pushes into my throat, choking me. "Clemmie, baby, Momma's coming. It's okay."

Frantically, I try to twist my body to unhook the seat belt, but it sticks. Clemmie's wails increase, and my efforts to calm her are useless. I have to get to my baby!

I can't think. My head pounds, and fireworks explode behind my eyes while I yank repeatedly at the seatbelt. Tears stream down my face unchecked, and panic steals my breath as I drown in the shadows with the sound of Clemmie's cries echoing in my ears.

CHAPTER 9

Ashe

Trailing someone on rural Alabama roads is not an easy task to complete undetected. Eva seems to be taking every backroad in the county, and I'm struggling to keep enough distance between us while keeping her in sight.

I've been surveilling Eva for the last couple days, and this is the first time she's deviated from her routine of work then home. Something melted in my heart watching her laugh and play with her daughter. Their love for each other was evident, and I knew I was a jerk for spying on them. I just couldn't help myself. I feel responsible for scaring her at work, but I also can't discount my belief that she's the key to finding Danielle Hurst alive.

Caught up in my thoughts, I round a curve, realizing I've lost sight of Eva. The road ahead splits, and though either direction could take her back home, I suspect she planned to continue her lengthy route and chose to take Willow Road on the left. After meandering over several hills and around quite a few curves with no sign of Eva, I find a cut-through road on the right and decide to try to find her on the other route.

The road is a pretty straight shot through a residential neighborhood that delivers me right where I want to be. Hanging a left on Route 14, I increase my speed a bit on the rarely traveled farming road, hoping to catch up, knowing Eva won't recognize my truck since it's just one of many we keep for surveillance work. The ringing of my phone startles me as I slow for the sharp curve ahead. Tapping the screen on the dash, I answer Con's call. "Hey. What's up?"

"Linc, I just want to let you know I have a lead on the Logan case, so I'm headed to Cullman. I'll be back later tonight."

"Okay. No worries, man. Let me know what you— Shit!" Just around the curve, a white 4Runner just like Eva's is off the embankment, smoking and crumpled against a cement culvert in the deep ditch. Jerking my truck to the shoulder, I ignore Con's voice calling my name from the disrupted call. I don't have time to answer but give my location and yell for him to call 911 before jumping from the vehicle.

Fuck! I never should have let her get away from me, I think as I scramble down the gravel into the ditch. I hear the hoarse panicked cries before I ever see Eva's daughter still strapped into her car seat in the back. Her eyes are filled with tears, and her tiny face is scrunched up and red from sobbing, but at a quick glance she appears otherwise unharmed.

On the other hand, Eva is slumped sideways toward the passenger seat, the gravity of the vehicle's tilted position pulling her downhill. She isn't moving. I'm stuck for a moment, unsure whether to try to calm the child or check on Eva, afraid to move either and risk further injuries.

I finally make my way to the passenger side and wrench open the front door as wide as possible. Shoving my head and shoulders through, I get my first good look at Eva. Her tangled hair covers the clear beginnings of a black eye and a purpling knot on her forehead. They join the cut from the accident in her office, which has broken open to slowly seep blood.

"Eva!" I'm afraid to touch her. I can see her chest rising and falling, but she shows no indication of waking. "Eva, please wake up," I beg.

Sirens sound in the distance while the toddler continues to wail in the back. "Hey, sweetie. Shhhh. It's okay." I try to soothe her. "I'm going to take care of you and your mom. I promise."

Reaching back from my awkward position, I let the little girl hang on to my fingers. I alternate between trying to calm her wails and checking to make sure Eva is still breathing.

The fire medics are the first to arrive. They move me out of the way and begin working to get the girls out of the mangled vehicle. "Sir," I hear as one of the police officers who just arrived approaches where I stand uselessly watching. "Sir. Can you tell me what happened? Did you see the accident?" he asks. "Do you know the victims?"

Considering my answer carefully, I decide to be vague and let them make their own assumptions. If I tell the absolute truth that I've only met Eva once, they will just send me home.

"Yes. Her name is Eva Jones, and that's her daughter in the back. I didn't see what happened. I was too far behind." I glance back toward the car and see a stretcher has been brought to the driver's side. One of the fire medics has the little girl on her hip, trying in vain to soothe her as she walks in our direction.

"Sir, I'll need your contact information," the officer states. Pulling a business card from my wallet, I hand it over, having the odd thought that I may need to order more.

"LCR. I've heard of y'all. You guys have a contract to work with the department."

"We try to keep a good working relationship with local law enforcement." The inconsolable wailing gets louder as the fire medic joins us. She's gently swaying back and forth, shushing the toddler to no avail. As soon as they're in range, the little girl inexplicably leans forward and reaches for me. Assuming I'm a friend, the medic releases her to my arms. I struggle for a minute to situate her correctly on my side, but her cries immediately calm to whimpers, and she lays her head on my chest. The medic gives me an incredulous look before patting my new companion on the head and turning back toward the rest of her crew.

"Clemmie ont Momma." Big, sad emerald eyes look up at me before she tucks her head back under my chin. Her thumb goes into her mouth, and she quietly sniffles. *Ont?* Oh...wants. She wants her mom.

"I know, sweetie," I croon as I look her over for any injuries. "Do you hurt anywhere, baby girl?" She shakes her head.

"Clemmie ont Momma," she mumbles around her thumb. Clemmie. Odd name, but whatever.

"Can you carry her to the ambulance?" the officer asks. "She seems fine, but she needs to be checked out."

Nodding at the officer, I carefully make my way

back up the embankment where an ambulance has joined the fire medics and the two patrol cars. A paramedic approaches and reaches toward Clemmie. An earsplitting wail escapes her tiny mouth, and her fists grab onto my shirt with a death grip.

"Shhhh, Clemmie. I've got you. It's okay." The paramedic indicates for me to sit on the back bumper of the ambulance. I hold Clemmie through the whole exam, shifting her as needed so the paramedic can be thorough. Clemmie cries loudly throughout the whole process, never once letting go of her grip on my shirt. Patting her wild curls, I whisper calming words in her ear. Her cries have almost stopped when she spots her mom being carried up on a stretcher.

"Momma, Momma, Momma," she pleads over and over, reaching toward Eva's unconscious form. Moisture pools behind my eyes at the little girl's pain and my inability to make anything better. I can't help Eva right now, but I vow to do everything in my power to protect this child who has put her trust in me.

CHAPTER 10

Eva

"Julie, my beauty, why do you make me hurt you so?" Demon whispers in my ear. "I only want to make you feel good. You remember how much pleasure I can give you, how much you wanted me."

I can't see him in the darkness, but I feel the caress of his warm hand on my cheek attempting to lull me into a false sense of comfort. I try to turn my head away, but I can't move. Oh God, why can't I move?

"I know you've missed me since you ran away, beautiful Julie, but don't worry, as soon as you've learned your lesson, we'll be together again."

Demon's hand slowly drifts from my cheek down to my neck before making its way to my breast for a loving caress and a gentle squeeze. My arms can't push him away. My mouth won't voice a sound, though in my head fear bounces around searching for an outlet. "Soon, Julie, very soon."

I open my mouth, and finally my silence is replaced with screams.

"Eva. Eva, it's okay. You're okay," a deep voice says, but I don't trust it. Demon could still be here. I fight the strong arms trying to restrain me, thrashing, trying to run. "Eva, open your eyes. It's Ashe. You've got to be still. You'll hurt yourself."

In the background something beeps furiously. I thought I was safe, but no one knows Demon like I do. I'll never be safe again. Other urgent voices filter through before a warmth floods my veins and carries me back under.

CHAPTER 11

Ashe

"Man, this could just be a coincidence, but I don't think so," Con says as he sips the lukewarm hospital coffee.

"I agree," Rosey adds.

The two of them had converged to meet me once they realized I was planning to stay overnight. We now stood huddled in the corner of the dated and uncomfortable hospital waiting room. Eva was lucky to finally be in a private room instead of the ER, where I'd had to wait outside the locked department door. Thankfully, I felt comfortable leaving her now that she was sleeping peacefully under the influence of the sedative. "It could be random, but the odds of her having a wreck only days after you start asking her questions about her abduction are slim."

"It wasn't just a wreck, guys. The back bumper of her 4Runner was crumpled. MRPD pointed out black paint transfer from another vehicle."

"Damn!" Con curses. "Some idiot ran her off the road with her toddler in the backseat? They could have been killed."

"Is the baby okay?" Rosey asks. I nod and run my hand through my hair in a nervous gesture I've repeated about a million times today.

"She's fine, just upset and wanting her mother, but Eva's sedated." I glance at the closed door to Eva's room down the hall. "Eva's aunt took Clemmie home. She was torn between needing to take care of Clemmie and not wanting Eva to be alone. It's why I offered to stay. I met Polly when I dropped Eva at home Wednesday, and she seems to be under the assumption we're dating."

Con sputters, nearly spitting out his coffee. "Dating? You? Mr. One Night Stand? You've got to be kidding." Rosey tries to hide a smirk. I flip Con off, but he just laughs. "Seriously, man, you don't even know this chick. She's just another job."

"She's the key to finding Danielle Hurst," I argue, not ready to admit anything more than that. Eva has already begun to get under my skin, but I can't explain why, and I don't intend to justify myself to my friends. "Danielle is somewhere out there right now suffering, and Eva is our only lead."

"Chill, Linc. He didn't mean anything by it. This just isn't typical behavior for you." Ever the peacemaker, Rosey eases the tension.

"If you could have seen her earlier, you wouldn't have been able to leave either. I walked in from grabbing food at the vending machine downstairs, and she was screaming. She was terrified. Nothing could calm her. She kept saying she needed to run, and the nurse had no choice but to inject a sedative to keep her from hurting herself." I run my hand down my face, feeling the scratch of stubble. "Look, you guys have seen her file. Her abductor was never caught. He's still out there and may be doing the same things to Danielle while we stand here and argue about whether or not I should be here."

"No worries." Rosey lays a conciliatory hand on my shoulder. "I'll get in touch with our PD contacts and see if I can get any information off the paint transfer from the wreck. Con still needs to make the trip to Cullman that got diverted today, but after that, he can start working on re-interviewing Danielle's roommate and the families of the other two victims." Con nods his agreement. "It's late. We'll head out and check in with you tomorrow afternoon."

Rosey pats me on the shoulder, and Con punches my bicep on his way to the elevator. I pass a nurse coming out of Eva's room as I head back in. He nods at me before continuing down the hall. The room is dark, but through the sliver of light from the closing door I see her shifting restlessly.

"Eva," I call out softly while moving to turn on the pale fluorescent light behind the bed. I guess the nurse must have turned it out to help Eva sleep better. "Eva," I say again. I don't want to wake her, but she seems agitated. Suddenly she bolts upright in the bed.

"Demon!" she gasps while struggling to free herself from the covers wrapped around her legs. "Light! Where's the light?"

"Eva, it's okay. I'll get the light." I hurry to the main switch, flooding the room with brightness. Eva's breathing slowly evens out, but her eyes remain blank. Moving cautiously toward the chair in the corner of the small room, I sit quietly and wait, trying not to spook her. Within a few minutes, her body relaxes, and she closes her eyes before slumping back in a sprawl, immediately asleep. I wait to make sure she's truly settled before I switch the harsh overhead fixtures off.

Carefully untangling the sheet and blanket from her feet, I pull it up to her chin, assuming being fully covered is important to her. I make my way back to the uncomfortable chair and spend the rest of the night contemplating how I'm going to explain my presence when Eva truly wakes up.

CHAPTER 12

Eva

Soft fingers brush the hair from my forehead before gently holding my hand. My eyelids feel as though Mobile Bay sand has burrowed underneath while also burying me with its weight from above, but Mobile is no longer my home. I shift slightly to see if my body is as heavy as my eyes and groan as all the aches and pains make themselves known.

"Eva? Eva, baby, it's time to wake up." The voice from my childhood makes me increase my efforts to open my eyes and clear the cobwebs from my head. "Come on, Eva, Clemmie wants her momma. Wake up, sweetie."

The soft fingers return to stroke my forehead, and their gentle upward motion gives my eyes the motivation they need to creep open. Bright daylight suffuses the room, making me squint as I try to locate the source of those fingers. Aunt Polly sits to my right, dressed in one of her typical bohemian skirts and flowing tops, her fashion sense having never outgrown her childhood in the late sixties. "There you are, Eva girl. I was beginning to think you were going to sleep all day. How are you feeling?"

Since I'm not really sure how to answer that question, I ask the one that is burning in my brain.

"Clemmie? Where's Clemmie?" I try to sit up, but Aunt Polly lays a restraining hand on my shoulder.

"Don't worry. She's perfectly fine. Tessa is at the house. They were having a fine time playing with dolls when I left. I'm more concerned about you," she says with a worried frown. "The doctor said your head injury looks worse than it is, and you probably only lost consciousness because the tilt of the car had blood running to your head."

I try to sit up while my foggy brain processes the overload of information. "Hold on." Aunt Polly reaches over me and presses a button on the rail to raise the bed to a more seated position. "Better?"

I nod. "Clemmie's really okay?" Noting the pale sunlight filtering through the hospital blinds, I realize it must be morning. Tears well up, flooding my eyes. "I was away from her all night?"

"Eva, I promise, she was just fine. She was so exhausted she fell asleep in my arms, and I just carried her to my room and let her sleep with me. I even made sure a night light was on."

Gratitude for this woman who is more of a mother to me than my own ever was overwhelms me. Before I can voice my thanks, a brisk knock on the door interrupts. A dour-faced woman in a white doctor's coat scurries in.

"Good morning, Ms. Jones," she greets me while flipping through the chart in her hands. "I'm Dr. Fillmore. I hear you had an eventful evening. How are you feeling today?"

Eventful evening? I guess that's one way to describe being run off the road. "My head and pretty much everything else aches, but nothing feels major."

"Good. Your CT scan from last night came back normal, so it looks like there's no concussion." She proceeds to shine a light into my eyes and run a few other checks before continuing, "Everything looks fine, so now let's talk about why you're still here. Can you tell me what caused your episode last night?"

Episode? I look to Aunt Polly in confusion and see deep concern in her expression. "I don't understand. What do you mean?"

"What's the last thing you remember?" Dr. Fillmore asks as she flips through the chart yet again.

"I remember the crash and trying to get to my daughter then waking up here." I glance back to Aunt Polly only to find she's avoiding eye contact and fidgeting with the garish material of her skirt, a sure sign that something is wrong. "Aunt Polly? What don't I know? You said Clemmie was fine. What happened?" I feel my chest start to tighten. Polly reaches for my hand and holds it tightly in hers.

"Ms. Jones, you woke up screaming last night. Not only were you physically fighting the friend who stayed with you but the nursing staff as well. We were forced to use sedation. You seem fine now, but is that something that happens often? I'd be happy to give you a referral to our staff psychologist."

"No. No thank you. I…um…I'm sure it was just a bad dream or something." I can feel Aunt Polly's censure, though I refuse to look her direction. I don't need therapy, and I don't plan to rehash my history for someone I'll never see again. Whatever happened, I'll figure it out on my own. The doctor looks displeased.

"Hmm, well it's not often we have to sedate people for a 'bad dream.' I can't force you to accept the referral, but I highly recommend you see someone who can help." She closes the chart, signaling the end of her visit. "I'll have the staff get your discharge papers ready, and I'll have them include contact information for our staff psychologist in case you change your mind. Someone will be in shortly to disconnect the IV." She nods to Aunt Polly and exits as abruptly as she entered.

Soon enough I'm discharged and seated in the passenger seat of Aunt Polly's ancient sedan with a plastic bag of my belongings in my lap. Staring out the window as we pass the cotton fields, I pretend I don't feel the weight of her questions hanging in the air. I don't want to talk right now. I just want to see Clemmie and know for myself that she wasn't hurt. I'll worry about the rest later. I've had bad dreams before; it's nothing new, though I don't typically lash out physically. At least I don't think I do. It's not like I've been sharing my bed with anyone to know. Friends with benefits only works if you actually let men get close enough to be friends. Friends, wait…

"Aunt Polly?"

"Hmm?"

"The doctor said I was fighting my friend in my sleep. How was Tessa there last night? I thought she was having a beach weekend? She couldn't have gotten home that quickly."

"It wasn't Tessa, honey. She hurried back when she heard about your accident and came straight to the house this morning to watch Clemmie." She glances hesitantly over at me while we're stopped at an intersection as though she knows I'm not going to like what she's about to say. "That nice Mr. Lincoln who brought you home from work is the one who called in your accident. Clemmie took a liking to him and just wouldn't let go. When he found out I was worried about leaving you at the hospital alone but had no one to keep Clemmie, he offered to stay."

No. That can't be right. Surely, I heard wrong.

"What?" I ask while Aunt Polly pretends to be very concerned with her driving. "Aunt Polly? Can you repeat that?" I stare pointedly at her profile.

"He's such a nice man, honey, and he seemed so worried about you. One of the police officers vouched for him too." She pauses and looks back at me once she parks behind the house. "Don't be upset." She smiles, pats my knee, and climbs out of the car while I sit there in shock.

CHAPTER 13

Eva

Settling my aching body on the bright-red sofa, I brace for my daughter's exuberant greeting. Clemmie breaks free from her teddy bear tea party and throws herself full tilt into my lap. I withhold my wince and hug her tightly while breathing in her sunshine scent and allowing it to fill my lungs. It feels like the first full breath I've taken since I woke up. Clemmie squirms in my grip.

"Momma, owie!" I relax my hold enough to allow for her wiggles, but I'm not ready to release her quite yet. "Boo-boo?" she asks while poking at my bruised forehead. I gently grab her finger and kiss it.

"Yes, baby. Mommy has a boo-boo."

"Mommy has a big boo-boo," Tessa teases from the floor beside the forgotten tea party. She smirks as she makes her way from the worn hardwood to join me on the couch.

"What? You don't like my new look? I heard black eyes were all the rage this year." I attempt a grin but fear a grimace is closer to what I manage when Tessa's expression turns pained. "Don't worry, I'm sure it looks worse than it feels."

"Clemmie," Aunt Polly calls from the kitchen, "want to help make Mommy a snack?"

"Nak! Nak! Nak!" Clemmie chants over and over as she scrambles from my lap and toddles as fast as she can to "help". I can't take my eyes off her, so relieved she escaped the accident unscathed.

"Ahem." Tessa pulls my attention back in her direction. "Now that it's just the grownups, what the heck happened? I hit Panama City for the first time in years, and you end up in the hospital? Seriously?"

I recount the prior day's events as calmly and succinctly as possible while Tessa covers her mouth in shock. "It was on purpose? Someone ran you off the road and just took off?" she asks incredulously. I nod. "Who would do that? Things like that don't happen in Magnolia Ridge."

"I really don't know. Maybe it was a drunk driver who didn't stop because he was afraid of going to jail. He was certainly driving way too fast."

"It was a man?"

"Um…I don't really know. It all happened too fast to tell. Aunt Polly says the police are investigating and will be sending someone by to get my statement." Clemmie chooses that moment to wiggle her way back between us, precariously balancing a paper plate with an assortment of fruit, cheese, and crackers.

"Nak!" Clemmie proclaims proudly while presenting her offering with a happy grin. A cracker tumbles into my lap before I can fully stabilize the plate. My little imp snatches it and scrambles down to feed the crumbling treat to Jo-Bee, her favorite purple bear, while Polly arrives with three glasses of iced tea. Tessa snatches a grape, and the next half hour is filled with food and laughter as we all enjoy Clemmie's antics.

Soon the eye rubbing commences and the whining follows, sure signs that nap time has arrived. Tessa stands and swoops my sleepy daughter off the floor mid-meltdown. She blows a raspberry on Clemmie's tummy and earns herself a sweet giggle. I slowly lever myself off the couch, and Tessa pretends to fly Clemmie into my arms. With a final hug and the detangling of Clemmie's fingers from her long rosy-blonde strands, Tessa heads out with a promise to check in after she's unpacked.

"You should probably try to take a nap when you put her down," Aunt Polly says as she picks up the remnants of our snacks. "You look exhausted."

"I feel exhausted," I confirm. "A nap sounds perfect, just don't let me sleep more than a couple hours or I'll be awake all night."

"No problem, honey," she throws over her shoulder as she heads into the kitchen. Clemmie wiggles to get down, and I hold her hand as we head down the hall. After a trip to the potty and a quick song, she snuggles in to rest.

My bed is calling my name, and my steps drag as I make my way to the room next to Clemmie's. I had dropped my shoes at the door when I entered the house, so it's quick work to shed the outfit Polly had brought to the hospital and replace it with my favorite sleep shorts and tee. I move yesterday's rejected clothing choices off the heirloom quilt covering my bed and vow to myself that I will hang them back up tomorrow.

The white plastic bag labeled *Personal Belongings* rests near my pillows where Polly must have placed it. Its only contents are my bloodied clothes, my purse, and hopefully the cell phone I haven't even missed.

None of those things are of greater interest to me right now than sleep, so I toss the bag to the wingback chair in the corner.

Unfortunately, my aim has never been very accurate, and the bag lands sideways on the edge of the chair, spilling out its contents. Not wanting to risk Clemmie barging in and seeing bloody clothes, I move to grab them. My heart stops when I get close. My belongings aren't the only things that spilled. A chill washes over me, and my breath comes in sharp pants. I back away, stopping only when my body hits the closed door. I slide down to the floor as dark clouds obscure the image of the pristine Cliff Bar lying innocuously on my carpet.

"Julie, my beauty, why do you make me hurt you so? I know you've missed me since you ran away, beautiful Julie, but don't worry. As soon as you've learned your lesson, we'll be together again." Demon's hand at my cheek slowly drifts down my neck before making its way to my breast for a loving caress and a gentle squeeze. *"Soon, very soon."*

My hand reflexively covers my breast as the room comes back into focus. Oh God! I remember. It was a dream, I tell myself over and over as I rock back and forth on the floor seeking my own comfort, but the evidence of the lie I tell myself is lying just a few feet away. I can't deny it any longer. Demon has returned to possess me.

CHAPTER 14

Ashe

"You know, we'd probably get more done if your head was actually in the game," Con nags from across the conference table. I startle and realize I've been staring at the same document for probably fifteen minutes without seeing it. "I can finish this up. If you're that worried, just go check on her."

Her...Eva. She's part of a case, and I shouldn't be thinking about her at all except for how she can help us find Danielle, but I had to drag myself away from the hospital this morning when her aunt arrived, knowing Eva would find more anxiety than comfort in my presence.

"I'm good. We need to get through the rest of this." I glance up at the whiteboard. Pictures, notes, and drawn lines mark all the connections. A theory is starting to take shape in my head, and Danielle's life matters more than my worries over a woman who is practically scared to death to be around me.

"You are far from good, brother, but I'm okay with denial if you are." Con spins his chair around and makes his way to tape another link to the whiteboard. He's been sequestered here in the conference room with me since his return from Cullman two hours ago. We don't typically work Sundays, though some of our investigators and security consultants do. This case is different, and with a woman's life in the balance every second counts.

Shifting in my seat, I try to alleviate some of the stiffness resulting from sleeping in a hospital chair and stretch my neck from side to side. We are missing so many pieces of the puzzle. We know the locations of the clubs the women disappeared from and the locations where their bodies were ultimately recovered, but other than Eva—no, Julie. I need her to be Julie here. Other than *Julie*, we have no idea where the women were held. Julie holds the key to how this predator thinks. Like most victims, she probably knows more than she thinks she does. I need to push her, but I'm afraid I can't.

"Oww! What the hell?" I yell as a rubber band smacks me in the head. Con laughs so hard he almost tips his chair over backward.

"Man, I wish you could've seen your face. That shit was funny." He grabs another rubber band and shoots. I dodge, and it bounces harmlessly off the window behind me. "You were doing it again."

"Doing what?"

"Mooning over the girl."

"Mooning? Seriously? You been reading your mama's romance novels again? Dude, go watch some ESPN," I grumble.

"Hey, don't diss the romance novels, man. They're like a how-to guide for the female gender. That's why I wake up happy and you wake up lonely and *mooning*."

"I don't *moon*." Growling, I javelin my heavy pen right toward Con's smart mouth. Reflexes honed from years of military service allow him to catch the pen and fire it right back at me, but I anticipated that reaction and am already on the move.

"I'm grabbing more coffee," I announce as I head toward the break room. Something grabs my attention though as I'm passing the whiteboard. Something looks off, but my phone rings before I can place what it is. I answer without looking at the screen, my eyes still glued to the board.

"Mr. Lincoln...um...Ashe?" The older female voice is anxious though familiar, but the child crying in the background makes it hard to distinguish. "Shhhh, Clemmie, it's okay." Clemmie? There can't be more than one child with that name.

"Polly? Is something wrong?"

"It's Eva. I don't know what's wrong, but she asked me to call you. She's been like this for an hour and she won't talk to me and—"

"Whoa, slow down. What do you need me to do?" I'm already grabbing my keys and notice Con doing the same. I'm already walking out the door before she answers. Clemmie's wails increase in volume as Polly's attempts to calm her fail.

"Can you come?" That's all I needed.

"I'm on my way. I'll be there soon." I end the call and increase my pace.

"What's going on? Do I need to call Rosey?" Con asks as he follows right on my heels.

"No. I'm not sure what's happened, but it must be bad for Polly to call me after only meeting me once. Just follow me."

Con and I make it to Eva's in record time. Polly greets me at the door with a sniffling Clemmie on her hip. "I'm so glad you came. I didn't know what to do.

She hasn't been like this since before Clemmie was born. She—"

Polly breaks off as she notices Con behind me. Giant teddy bear though he is, his appearance tends to give off a more dangerous vibe. The long blond hair he vowed not to cut after the military is tied in a loose knot at the back of his head. When combined with his permanent scruff and the ink visible on his forearms, he can seem formidable.

"Ma'am, this is my associate and friend, Liam Connery. He was with me when I got your call. Can we come in?"

"Oh, I'm sorry, where are my manners? Yes, please, come in." Even in an emergency, Southern manners always win out with the older generation. She leads us into a homey but brightly eclectic living room. "I just didn't know what to do. Wait, I think I already said that. I'm so worried, and Eva isn't talking. All she said was to call you, and Clemmie doesn't understand what's happening with her momma, and..." Her eyes well up as she finally pauses for a breath. I lay a comforting hand on her shoulder.

"Where is Eva?" I ask. Polly directs me down a hallway toward a bedroom. Catching Con's eyes over her head, I make sure we're on the same page. He nods and speaks sweetly to Clemmie, trying to make her laugh as I head down the hall. I knock softly on the door and call Eva's name. There's no answer, but I hear her moving around inside. After a couple more tries, I decide it's now or never. My nerves are shot, and I need to know what's going on.

"Eva, It's Ashe. I'm coming in, okay?" Again, I don't get a response, but the doorknob turns easily in my grasp. As I edge the door open, it sticks at halfway. "Eva?" Leaning through the tight space, I realize the door is pressing against Eva's hip as she rocks back and forth on the floor. I swallow the curse that wants to escape and work to gentle my expression. Wedging my large frame through the tight opening, I adopt a casual tone and try to keep my distance until I understand what's happening.

"Hey there, little rabbit." I fold myself down to the floor, so I can be eye level with Eva. "I heard you were missing me, so I thought I'd come pay you a visit."

She glances up at me for a moment but then resumes rocking. I sit quietly for a minute trying to figure out what to say so I don't mess this up. Eva's complexion is so white it's almost transparent, making the bruises on her face starker. The midnight tendrils of her hair are gripped tightly in her fists as she buries her face in her knees and rocks faster. I'm so distracted watching her that I almost miss her softly spoken words.

"He was there." Her voice is barely a whisper, but she finally looks up at me. Tears trail silently down her cheeks, and my heart stutters. She looks so lost, and for the life of me, I can't think of anything to say.

CHAPTER 15

Eva

I don't even really know this man, but still he came. His was the only name I could think of when Aunt Polly asked who to call. His big body looks strange sitting on my bedroom floor in his casual jeans and T-shirt. He keeps his distance, and I'm glad because I think if anyone touched me right now, I would crawl out of my skin. My thoughts are flying through my head, unable to land, except the one I want to block out. He was there.

"I don't understand. Who was where? Was someone in your room?" He jumps up and starts checking the window latches as though looking for evidence of an intruder.

"Hospital," I blurt. He turns and moves cautiously closer before kneeling in front of me and leaning down to make eye contact.

"Rabbit, tell me who was at the hospital. Let me help." Rabbit. I don't know why he calls me rabbit, but the sound of the word from his mouth is the sound of security and safety to my ears. The constriction in my throat loosens, and I'm finally able to take a full breath.

"Demon. He was at the hospital. I remember."

Ashe looks concerned but not alarmed. "Baby,

that's not possible. I was there all night. Maybe it was just a dream or maybe it was—"

"No!" I yell, pulling at my hair in frustration. I feel my body rocking again, but I can't stop the motion. Without it, I might become brittle and shatter. "He. Was. There!" A knock on the door has me skittering closer to the bed.

"Linc, everything okay in there?" a man's voice asks.

"Shhhh, Rabbit, it's okay. It's just my partner," Ashe soothes with a placating hand outstretched. "We're all good in here," he calls out to the man behind the door before rearranging himself in front of me once again. "I'm sorry. I promise I'm listening, okay? Please tell me what happened."

I take a deep breath and force the words to come out of my mouth. "I had a nightmare at the hospital." Ashe's eyes are intent on mine, but I shift mine to the hem of the nightshirt I'm currently wrapping around my fingers. I don't want to see the disbelief filter into his gaze. "I didn't remember it at first, maybe because of the sedative, but the doctor told me a friend was there. I'm guessing that was you."

Glancing up through the curtain of my hair, I see his nod before returning my attention to my shirt. "I think Demon wanted me to know he was really there. He left proof." I point toward the spilled hospital bag, seeing his tennis-shoe-clad feet as he stands and moves toward the chair.

"Eva, I don't know what I'm looking for. All I see is your clothes."

"The bar," I whisper as my fidgeting with the T-shirt increases along with my heart rate.

"Okay, I see the Cliff Bar, but honey, what does that mean?" I see his shoes move back in my direction, and he stops a bit closer this time before crouching and laying his hand over mine. I startle but am surprised to find his touch feels more like comfort than an invasion of my space. He gently unravels the twisted ends of the shirt from my fingers, and I realize they were turning a mottled shade of purple. Pinpricks of electricity shoot through them as the circulation returns. "Now, please tell me about the bar." He removes his hand and sits back to listen.

"When Demon had me, he needed to keep me alive, so every time he came, he left a Cliff Bar like some sick form of payment for my suffering. He got what he wanted, so I could live for a few more days. Every time, it was the same exact bar. Every time." I peek hesitantly through my lashes to gauge whether or not he thinks I'm crazy. "That bar. It fell out of the bag from the hospital. It's not mine. I would starve before I ever touch one again." Ashe's shock is palpable. I rush on before I lose my nerve. "He said we'd be together again soon. He...he touched me." My arms cross, shielding my chest as tears flow unchecked down my cheeks to drop to my fingers.

CHAPTER 16

Ashe

Exiting Eva's room, I stalk straight out the front door in an effort to contain the rage coursing through my system. My muscles are straining, and my knuckles are white as my hands grip the railing of the small porch. A hand on my shoulder has me spinning. Thankfully, Con dodges my swing seconds before my fist would have connected with his jaw.

"Damn it, Linc! What the hell?"

"Call Michael Ayers at MRPD and see if he can head this way. No sirens. Call Rosey and get him here too."

I can see the questions in his eyes, but we've been partners long enough that he makes the calls before he asks them. Lacking patience, I take the steps two at a time and pace the front yard. The image of Eva huddled on the floor, fear all but leaching from her pores, is burned in my mind. Contacting a detective I know personally was the only way she could be convinced to let me call the police.

Her story is outrageous, but her conviction is clear. I find myself believing her. Like Eva though, I know the police may find her story unlikely and coincidental, but just the possibility of the protein bar having fingerprints makes their involvement a necessity.

"Rosey and Ayers are both on the way, now tell me what the hell's going on," Con demands.

"I messed up." I run my hand through my hair in frustration. "He got to her."

"He? Man, what are you talking about? Spell it out."

"Demon. He got to her in the hospital. He put his fucking hands on her and then decided to leave her a sick little gift." By the time I finish explaining what happened with Eva, Rosey has arrived, and Con is just as concerned as I am. I leave him to brief Rosey while I check on Eva. When I left her, she was calmer and had begun to shift her focus more toward worrying about how her reaction had affected Clemmie.

Sweet smells drift from the seventies-throwback kitchen, seeming at odds with the heaviness of the situation. I follow my nose to where Polly is pulling what appears to be a second batch of cookies out of the oven. Clemmie stands on a chair at the small table pretending to mix with her own plastic bowl and a long wooden spoon. She gives me a crumb-covered grin and flings her arms in the air, letting the spoon clatter to the floor.

"Up!" I glance over at Polly who nods her assent before I pick up the little girl and accept her cookie-scented hug. Polly hands Clemmie what appears to be the second half of her cookie, and while she munches happily, I ask the question that has been burning in my mind since I arrived.

"Why me?" Polly doesn't even pretend to misunderstand.

"I don't know really." She taps the toddler on the nose, eliciting a giggle. "I had just laid Clemmie down for a nap, and as I passed Eva's room, I could hear her crying. She wouldn't let me in. She just pushed your card under the door, so I called."

Eva picks that moment to enter the room, her slightly damp hair and freshly scrubbed face evidence of a recent shower. Her thin sleep clothing has been replaced with yoga pants and an oversize sweatshirt despite the oppressive heat outside. Her eyes are still slightly puffy, but overall, she recovered quickly.

Clemmie immediately defects to her mom and tries to feed her the final bites of the now-mangled cookie. Eva adeptly turns the tiny hand back to Clemmie's mouth where the cookie remnants disappear along with the sticky fingers. She avoids my gaze by turning to rummage in the fridge. "Your card fell out of my hospital bag with everything else."

"Oh, I put it in there," Polly interrupts. Eva turns from the fridge with a small container of orange juice and looks at her aunt quizzically before shaking the juice. "Well, I had to have some way to contact him, and it's not like you were forthcoming with truthful information when I first met him. Mr. Lincoln—"

"Ashe," I correct.

"Ashe gave me the card at the hospital, so I could check on you. I programmed the information in my phone and stuck the card in your bag, so it wouldn't get lost."

Eva looks chagrined but nods her understanding and continues her explanation while sharing the orange juice, which now sports a bendy straw, with her daughter. "The card was lying on the floor beside…well, it was just there, and somehow I knew you would help." She averts her eyes before adding,

"I'm sorry I dragged you into all this. It's okay if you need to go. I'm fine now."

Go? Not likely. Has the woman lost her mind? "Not happening, Rabbit." The tension in her frame relaxes incrementally before ramping up again at the knock on the front door. "It's okay. It's just my partners and the detective I told you about. Can I let them in?"

She nods before turning to hand Clemmie to Polly and squaring her shoulders. With a deep breath, she follows me to the door.

CHAPTER 17

Eva

The only positive about this situation is that summer in Alabama ensures plenty of daylight is left for Aunt Polly to keep Clemmie busy catching lightning bugs in the backyard as they make their evening appearance. I wish I could be outside with them because inside the house our living room is crammed with people. Large groups of people make me nervous, but this group of the giant male variety cranks my anxiety even higher.

Ashe sits on one end of the sofa, taking up more than his half, while I occupy the other. I wish I could remember his partners' names, but I can't since I was barely breathing through the introductions. The bulkier one with the dark, military-short hair is seated in the overstuffed purple chair across from me. The blond, shaggy one with the mischievous look has flung himself into the matching chair across from Ashe and propped his ankle on the opposite knee after reconsidering propping it on Aunt Polly's well-loved hand-painted coffee table.

Detective Ayers has opted to stand and is hovering in a way that shoots my nerves into overdrive. I've already given a statement about both the wreck as well as the Cliff Bar and watched as Ayers collected the "evidence" from my bedroom. I can tell the detective is skeptical, but Ashe is doggedly determined to argue his points.

"Look, Ashe, I came out as a personal favor to LCR. Stuart and Clark were on tap to get the statement about the wreck, and they could have easily handled this too," Ayers says. "There's not really anything I can do other than run the bag and the bar for prints, and you know as well as I do that isn't an instant answer. Even on the miniscule chance that we get something, it just proves someone touched the item, not that the person left it for her or had harmful intentions."

"What about the hospital?" the dark-haired partner interjects. "If someone was there, they should be on the hallway security footage, right?"

"I was in her room most of the night. There are only a couple of small windows where he could have gotten in. Reviewing that footage shouldn't take long," Ashe agrees.

"That footage won't be available without a warrant, and we are nowhere close to having grounds for that," Ayers interjects. "Look guys, I'll do all I can, but without a bit more to go on, my hands are tied. This may just all be a coincidence. The bar could be something the hospital provided. There's no way to know."

Ashe shifts forward and starts to argue, but the dark one shoots him a quelling look before standing to shake the detective's hand and escort him to the door. I need some air. Bolting from the sofa, I dart toward the kitchen. My hands are shaking, and nausea is creeping up my throat. There's nothing anyone can do. They don't even believe me.

What if I'm wrong? What if it was just a dream? What if it *is* real and Demon takes me again? I plant my hands against the sink and retch into the basin. My stomach is empty, but my body doesn't stop heaving. When my reflexes exhaust themselves, I turn and sink to the floor, closing my eyes and dropping my head back against the cabinets. I sense his presence before I hear the fridge open and close, but I don't open my eyes. Something cool touches my forehead and feels like heaven.

"Drink some. It'll help." Ashe's voice is low and comes from right beside me. Opening my eyes, I find the source of the coolness is a bottle of orange juice. Ashe has situated himself on the floor beside me though not close enough to touch. I shake the juice before opening it to take a sip. I keep my eyes averted, fearing what I will see in his.

"Better?" he asks. I nod and look toward the backdoor, hoping Clemmie is still happily occupied outside and won't see me like this. Ashe reads my mind. "I checked on her before I grabbed the juice. She's perfectly content." I nod again, my words not yet ready to make themselves heard.

"We've gotta quit meeting like this, little rabbit," he quips. My lips involuntarily tip up into a small grin. "You know, I don't think I've sat on the floor this much since I was a child."

The humor does what he intended and opens a small fissure in the cocoon of fear that had wrapped itself around me. When he stands and offers me a hand up, I don't hesitate to take it. I drop it as soon as I'm steady though, the warmth transferring from his body to mine making me uncomfortable.

"Thank you," I murmur, straightening my cozy sweatshirt to cover my hips and glancing toward the living room.

"Don't be nervous. Rosey and Con left. What can I do to help?" I look up into his blue eyes, and instead of the pity or disbelief I expect to see, I find nothing but sincere concern.

"Um...I don't know. I just want to wake up and find this was all a dream."

I place the orange juice on the counter and walk to the window overlooking the backyard. Clemmie is toddling around, wildly swinging a purple butterfly net Polly picked up for her at the dollar store a couple weeks ago. She looks so happy, so innocent. I can't let this touch her. My back straightens, and my resolve tightens. I'm not Julie anymore. I'm Eva, and Eva is stronger than this. Eva protects those she loves. Turning back toward Ashe, I feel some of my fire return.

"What's that look, little rabbit? Whatever it is, I think I like it," he says, staring intently into my eyes.

"Tell me what to do, what you need. I'm ready to fight."

CHAPTER 18

Ashe

I pace the conference room like a caged animal. Eva will be here any minute, and while the information she holds may be the key to finding Danielle Hurst, I know how hard this will be for her. I wish I could spare her. When she was just a name on a file, it was so much easier, but now she's Eva. She's the rabbit I'm getting closer to catching every day, at least I think I'm getting closer. I don't usually doubt myself, but Eva is different. For once, I want to do things right.

I spent most of last night tossing and turning, worried about her and her little family. I had one of our security specialists, Sebastian Villani, watching the house all night just to make sure they were safe. Villain, as he's known at LCR, hung up on me about the tenth time I called for an update.

"Dude, sit! The floors can't take much more," Con throws out as he enters and takes a seat.

"Neither can I," Rosey adds as he finds his own place at the long table. "You've been a nervous ball of energy all day."

"She's fine, and she's on her way. Moss is on her. He just checked in," Con adds.

"What the hell? Why is he calling you?" I growl.

"Oh, I don't know, maybe because you've turned

into a psycho helicopter mom overnight? Our guys know what they're doing. If they weren't capable, they wouldn't be working for us." I know Con is right. I'm not even sure why I'm acting this way.

"Look, man, we made a plan when we met first thing this morning," says Rosey the Reasonable. "We're not going to scare her. We need her help. If it turns out her captor is harassing her again, we have enough people to protect her and find Danielle too."

"If? What do you mean if? We know he's a killer, and we have proof he's harassing her," I yell.

"We don't have proof. We have a protein bar, and a very common one at that. It could have come from anywhere. It doesn't mean anything without more evidence to support it."

A distressed sound comes from the doorway just as Rosey finishes speaking. Eva and Jillian, our administrative assistant, are at the door. Eva turns and flees back down the hallway toward the elevator. Rosey and I both head after her. He turns to me at the conference room door with a staying hand at my chest. "I've got this. Trust me."

I look him dead in the eye and see the truth of his words. He takes off after Eva and catches up to her at the notoriously slow elevator. He doesn't touch her, and I can't hear what he says, but she glances up at me before nodding to Rosey and following him back to the conference room.

I inhale a relieved breath and move aside to let them pass. The scent of vanilla and orange blossoms tickles my nose as Eva walks by. It only makes sense that my little rabbit would smell like flowers. The scent calms me and centers my thinking.

Eva takes a seat opposite Con and Rosey and crosses her arms defiantly over her chest. Where I expected to see fear, I see anger. Eva can't be more than five foot, six inches, but her eyes are shooting sparks at my badass six-foot, three-inch partner. I didn't think I could like this woman more, but now I do. After Jillian checks to see that we have all we need, I close the door. Eva jumps right in.

"Look, you, I don't remember your name, but don't ask me to come rip open my soul to help you if you're not going to believe me anyway. I had enough of that from my parents when they accused me of running away with a boyfriend and making up a story for attention when he ditched me. You're not the police, and I don't have to tell you anything." Damn, my rabbit is a tiger! I can't help but grin.

"Whoa. Please. Let me explain," Rosey starts. "First of all, I'm Jackson, and that's Liam," he says pointing.

"And that's mom," Con interrupts, pointing at me. Rosey coughs out a laugh, and I glare, but I can see Eva doesn't understand.

"Inside joke," I clarify. "Just ignore him."

Eva turns her attention back to Rosey, who continues, "I know what I said sounded bad, but that's not the way I meant it. I was just trying to get us to focus and think in terms of evidence. I believe you, Julie. I really do. I just have to be able to prove it, or what I believe doesn't matter."

"I understand," Eva concedes, but I can tell she is still on guard. "Please don't call me Julie. I go by Eva now."

"Right. I'm sorry. I knew that," Rosey apologizes.

He looks to me for help.

"Eva, we don't want this to be uncomfortable for you, though we know it will be. I wanted Rosey, um, Jackson and Liam in here because Jackson has a unique talent for profiling and tracking, and Liam is our tech expert. They'll both be listening for different things, but if you'd prefer we talk alone, I'll make that happen."

"No. I'm willing to try it, but can I change my mind later if I want to?"

"Of course. Is it okay if we record this?" I ask. "It will let us go back and listen when we have questions rather than have to bring you in again."

"Umm, sure, I guess." Hesitant Eva is back. I hate that we caused that, but Danielle Hurst's life is on the line, and we've run out of leads. We agreed earlier that Con would be the one asking the questions since his laid-back vibe tends to help others relax, and because my partners feared I would be too cautious. They were probably right, since all I want to do right now is grab Eva and run away from what she's about to face. Unfortunately, I can't, so I push the button to start the recording.

CHAPTER 19

Eva

My hands have been clasped so tightly under the table that they have begun to lose circulation. I release them and try to flex away some of the cramping. I'm trying my best to keep up a brave image, but inside I'm shaking apart. It's been years since I've told my story, but I haven't forgotten a single detail. I close my eyes and take a deep breath.

"Eva, are you ready?" the scruffy blond one, Liam, asks. I open my eyes and see sympathy in his.

No. Not at all. "Sure," I reply. I glance around the table. Liam seems to have a list of questions ready in front of him, and his body language is relaxed. Jackson has a notepad and pen poised to take notes, and Ashe, well Ashe looks almost as nervous as me. He has neither pen nor paper, and his hands are steepled on the table as he leans forward intently.

"Okay," Liam begins. "Let's start with a little background. We've read reports, but we're looking for insights into what may not be in the reports. We've compiled a list of questions we think will help fill in the gaps of what we don't know." He pauses to shuffle his papers then begins. "Tell us a little bit about what your life was like before the abduction."

Well, that was certainly not what I expected, but it

was easier to talk about than anything else, so why not? "I had just graduated from University of South Alabama with my master's in Clinical Mental Health Counseling. My parents and I have never been close, so I lived in dorms or with other college students off campus while I was in school. Once I finished, I moved back home for a few months, planning to take the time to save up the money to get my own apartment. I was offered a great job at one of the facilities where I'd interned, and everything except my home life was going good."

"What was happening at home?" Liam asks.

"My parents are very conservative, and after years of buckling down to get through school, I just wanted to let loose a bit. I started making new friends at work and going out on the weekends. I was twenty-three, so I didn't really feel like my parents should have a say, but they expressed their displeasure in everything from my choice to work in the field of substance abuse with people they felt were undeserving, to the way I dressed and the people I dated. Everything they said just amped up the tension and made me more determined to earn their poor opinion of me."

I pause. The only sound is the scratch of Jackson's pen on paper. Ashe nods at me in encouragement, and Liam just asks more questions.

"You mentioned dating. Who were you dating at the time?" A better question might have been who wasn't I dating at the time, but I attempt to answer.

"I wasn't ready for anything serious. I just wanted to have fun and meet people. I went out with a couple guys from work and a few people I met at clubs around town."

"Can you give us a list after we're done talking?" Liam slides a spare piece of paper across the table along with a pen he grabbed from the container centered on the table.

"Okay."

"Were you promiscuous?"

"What the hell, Con?" Ashe yells as he surges out of his chair toward his partner. Jackson jumps in between them, both hands on Ashe's chest as he struggles to hold him in place.

"Linc, calm down. You know it needed to be asked. Con could have been a bit more tactful, but it's part of the profile. We need to know this guy's type." Judging from the look on Ashe's face, his partner should be running right now, but Liam simply stares unflinchingly at me as though waiting for an answer.

"Yes." All eyes turn to me and the room quiets. The tension continues to hang heavy, but silence prevails. "Yes. I slept around. My parents made sure I understood that everything that happened to me was my own fault, that I deserved it, so if that's where this is going, I already know. Move on."

I refuse to hang my head in shame. I'm not proud of the person I was back then, but I've worked hard to be something better. I've done everything in my power to be worthy of the second chance I was given.

Liam sits silent, looking chagrined. Jackson speaks as Ashe falls heavily back into his chair. "Eva, that's not at all where we were going." As if realizing his posture looming over the table could be intimidating, he abruptly sits. "We believe this killer has a specific type of woman he targets. If we can figure out why he took you and why he took Danielle, it might help us figure out his end goal or even give us clues to where he might be holding Danielle. No one deserves what happened to you. Believe me when I say that your parents were wrong. Serial killers aren't placed on this earth to punish those who step out of line. Natural consequences are real, but that's not what happened to you. It wasn't your fault."

His expression holds nothing but sincerity. Liam and Ashe nod their agreement. Other than Aunt Polly, no one has ever defended me, yet these three men who barely know me view me in a better light than my own parents. My lips tremble, but I refuse to let the welling tears fall. If I start crying, I might not be able to stop, and these men actually deserve my help. Out of all the times I've had to tell my story, this might be the most important.

CHAPTER 20

Ashe

The questions were brutal, and her answers were heartbreaking. I'd read her file, several times in fact, but it was nothing like hearing the account from her lips. The shadows under her eyes were beginning to match the bruised shades of her forehead. I could tell she was exhausted after working all day then coming straight to this interview, but she refused every break we offered, accepting only a bottle of water she rarely drank but seemed to need in order to occupy her shaking hands.

So far, we've learned that she spent a lot of time in dance clubs and wasn't very discriminating in her dating. The man she suspects was her captor approached her in a club while she was buying drinks, and he seemed attractive and friendly. He was not someone she had ever met before. She had no memories beyond that until she woke up trapped and alone. She couldn't remember his name, only that in her head she called him Demon, perhaps because it sounded similar to his name. We were getting to the harder questions now, and I knew Con was about to start asking about her impressions while in captivity. I was afraid of not only her reactions but mine as well. Having known her less than a week, I really shouldn't care as much as I do.

Con clears his throat and jerks my attention back to the present. "Okay, now that we've got the easy stuff out of the way, I need to ask a few more difficult questions. Are you okay to keep going?" Eva fidgets with the water bottle for a minute before nodding her consent. "Can you give us your impressions of where you were held? We need every detail you can think of."

"It was dark, always dark. No windows and only one door that locked from the outside. The walls felt like wood, and the floor was packed dirt." Eva's eyes seem to haze over and lose focus the more she talks. "There was an old mattress in one corner, a makeshift latrine in another, and a leaky faucet I could use for drinking."

Silent tears begin trailing down her cheeks, but she doesn't acknowledge them. She doesn't even seem to realize she's crying. I can sense Rosey's discomfort, but when he looks at me for guidance, I subtly motion for him to let her continue.

"I hated that faucet. I wished so many times that it wasn't there. If it just wasn't there, then I wouldn't have to choose. I didn't want to choose. Why did he make me choose?"

She completely breaks down and can barely breathe for the sobs. I can't help myself. She looks so alone. Jumping from my seat, I quickly move beside her. She has bent herself double and seems to be trying to make herself as small as possible. I fear she will be on the floor in minutes. I don't want to scare her by touching her, but neither am I going to let this courageous woman spend any more time on the ground. Gently lifting her up, I carry her to one of the sofas at the back of the room. She doesn't seem to notice she has even moved. I sit with her in my lap and shift her, so her head is against my chest. To my surprise, her arms latch tightly around my neck, and she burrows in closer. Looking around, I notice that Rosey and Con have left us alone in the room.

I brush Eva's hair back off her face, but she turns it to hide in my shirt. I don't want to push her, so I leave her alone and just brush my hand softly up and down her back until she starts to calm. A knock at the door precedes Rosey's entrance with a soft drink. "I thought she might need the sugar," he says softly before handing me the bottle.

"Call her aunt and let her know Eva will be later than we planned," I request. Rosey nods and exits as quietly as he entered. "Eva?" She shifts in my arms but doesn't look up. I place my finger under her chin and tip her tearstained face up to mine. She refuses to make eye contact and moves to dislodge herself from my hold. Though I don't want to let her go, I know she won't appreciate feeling trapped. She settles beside me and takes the soft drink once she finishes fidgeting with her clothes. I almost ask her if she's okay, but the answer to that question is obvious. The silence hangs for a few minutes while she takes a few sips and seems to pull herself back together.

"Rabbit?" She finally looks up at me through a thin curtain of dark curls. "I want to understand. Why did the faucet matter so much?" She stills for a moment before turning her body away from me and hanging her head. I can't see her face behind the hair.

"Every time he would come, he would remind me that he was not a monster, that he was fair because he was giving me a choice. He provided the water, but I had to choose to drink it. He said I wanted him, craved what he did to me, that my body's reaction and my choice to drink rather than die proved it. I tried so hard not to drink, but in the end, I gave in every time. So, you see, it really was my fault."

CHAPTER 21

Eva

Clemmie is already asleep before I make it home, and the absence of that little daily dose of brightness adds to the heaviness in my chest. After a small sip of orange juice, the only thing my unsettled stomach can handle, I fall into bed exhausted. My earlier tears have drained my energy and left me feeling exposed and raw. I let down my guard, and the resulting turmoil invades my dreams.

A small sliver of light pierces the darkness for the first time since I woke up in this place. My eyes burn and refuse to focus. I squint into the brilliance and see the most beautiful sight I've ever witnessed. A man is outlined in the glow. His hair is gleaming and bright, and a breath of fresh air laced with sandalwood follows his entrance. I want to see his face. I know it will be beautiful. I'd prayed for the first time in years, prayed for someone to save me, and now he is here. I reach for him, too weak to move toward him on my own.

"Julie, my beautiful Julie." My savior's voice is a sensual whisper...and familiar. Wasn't there a guy at the bar? Daniel, Damon, Devan?

"Please, please get me out of here," I beg.

"Out? Oh, Julie. You chose to be here. You wanted to come with me. Don't you remember?" he soothes. I

wrack my brain but all I find is a void.

"No. No. No." I shake my head, my agitation building. "Please, just let me out!"

"Sweet Julie, you can leave here any time you want." My tension leaves on an exhale. I try to stand, but my legs won't hold me. I fall back to the sweaty mattress. My last meal was days ago, and it was mostly alcohol. Shit! I just need to get out of here. I crawl toward the path of sunlight leading me to the door. An expensive leather shoe suddenly blocks my way.

"Oh no. That's not the way." The path of light slowly reduces back to a sliver before disappearing completely, along with every semblance of hope.

My eyes have lost their adjustment to the darkness, and I feel around blindly trying to get back to the safety of my mattress, the only security I have. The steady drip, drip, drip of the faucet helps reorient my direction. I sense him, his sandalwood scent stronger than before, closer. Just as I touch safety, I feel his hands encircle my waist before I'm lifted and tossed, falling to my back with a thump that takes my breath and leaves me gasping. I feel his body lay down beside me in the grime, and then his hand finds my face and begins to stroke.

"Breathe," he whispers into my hair. His hands begin to gently roam my body. I flail my weakened limbs trying to cover myself. "No, no, sweet Julie," he sing-songs as though I'm a misbehaving child. "You are so beautiful, so perfect," he croons as he easily overwhelms my defense. "We're going to create such a sweet future together."

Tears leak unbidden from my eyes and trail into my tangled hair. His weight shifts over me as his hands become bolder. I push against his suit-covered chest, but he captures my hands, holding them above my head in one of his own. "No. Please! I don't want this."

"Oh, but you do. You agreed to come home with me at the bar. You said you wanted me." I whimper and shake my head in denial. "Don't worry, love. I'm not a monster. I don't want to hurt you. I'm going to make you feel so good. I'll give you exactly what you need."

In the quiet moments after, I lie still, shattered. "I knew you were the one, Julie, the one I've been searching for." He caresses my face, and I turn it away. "This time will be different." I sense his movement and hear a rustling sound as he says, "I have a present for you. I want you to always choose me just like I chose you." He grasps my hand and presses something that crinkles into my palm, forcing my fist closed. "My gift is a choice. I said you could leave this place any time you want. I don't lie." His hand caresses me as he speaks. "I've provided you with food and water, but you have a choice. Any time you want to escape from this place, you can refuse them. The choice is yours, Julie." His fingers tighten to dig into my leg, and a burning flash of pain sears across my inner thigh. My scream is swallowed by his mouth on mine. "Shhhh," he whispers against my lips. "It's necessary for the purification."

He takes his time composing himself, even washing his hands in the dripping faucet. I stay completely quiet and still, not wanting to draw any more of his attention. My body aches, and I can feel the slow trickle of blood from the burning wound. It's not until after the door closes behind him and the lock clicks into place that I curl into a ball and vent my pain into the black.

CHAPTER 22

Ashe

After yet another restless evening of late-night TV and being hung up on by Villain, who is now officially assigned to Eva's nightly protection, I drag myself into the office and straight to the break room for coffee, waving distractedly at Jillian on my way to Con's office. His door is closed, but I barge in without knocking.

"What've you got?" I ask as I collapse in a chair in front of his desk. He was working on gaining access to the hospital security cameras when I left to follow Eva home last night. The police may have to wait for warrants, but we're not the police.

"Damn, man, ever heard of knocking?" Con's long hair has escaped its tie and is down around his shoulders. Some strands are sticking up, evidence he has been running his hands through it, something he does when he's working out a difficult tech issue.

"Nope. Don't believe I have. Now seriously, what have you found?"

"You could have at least brought more coffee. You really suck as a partner."

"Con, my patience is thin," I growl.

"Whatever. Get Rosey in here so I only have to do this once." He sighs. I immediately text Rosey and glare at Con while we wait.

"What's so urgent? I was on the phone with Larken, the detective in charge of Danielle's case," Rosey comments before grabbing the only empty seat.

"Con has something new," I say before all eyes turn to Con.

"Okay, so while none of this will be admissible in court or helpful from a law enforcement standpoint, I was able to get into the security cameras for the hallway outside Eva's hospital room. The footage is grainy and black and white, but check this out."

Rosey and I make our way around the desk to the largest of Con's computer monitors. An image of the hallway is paused. "So, I started at about the time we were with you in the waiting room and worked my way back. What you're going to want to see starts before our arrival, at around 6:00 p.m."

The footage documents the activity in the busy area, but Con suddenly pauses it as a nurse enters Eva's room. "This nurse enters Eva's room just five minutes after another nurse left. He stays for about five minutes and slips out just before you run in."

"I was running because I heard her scream, but I didn't see anyone coming out of her room."

"Well, that's not all." He forwards the video a few hours and pauses again. "This is you leaving the room to come meet with us." He points to the screen. "Now look what happens shortly after."

The video begins again. Shortly after I leave, the same male nurse goes back in. We keep watching until I pass him coming out on my way back in.

"Shit! He walked right past you," Rosey exclaims.

"Now look, we can't prove he's Demon, but the

timing is awfully coincidental as is the fact that he seems to know where the cameras are and keeps his face averted. I can guesstimate he's about an inch shorter than you based on pausing the image where you two pass. Other than that, the only thing I can tell is that his hair is light," Con explains.

"It seems like enough to assume if you ask me," Rosey says. "You said Eva was upset and having nightmares both times you left the room. I think we're looking at the only known images of Demon."

"You know what that means, right?" I ask. "If Demon is here harassing Eva, then he may have left Danielle somewhere unguarded."

"Two birds, one stone? We find Demon, we can save Danielle and protect Eva," Con says.

"I don't understand the change in his habits." Rosey sounds concerned as he makes his way back to his seat. "According to Eva's account, she was never moved once she woke from the drugs she was given at the club. That means Demon probably transported the women directly from the club to the kill location while they were incapacitated and killed them in the same area where they were held."

"Okay, so what are you getting at?" Con looks as confused as I feel.

"Why didn't Demon leave when he took Danielle? According to his pattern, he shouldn't still be here. It doesn't make sense."

"What do you think that means?" I ask, returning to my own seat while Con leans back and props his feet on his desk.

Rosey's expression mirrors the concern I know must be apparent in mine. "We've conducted so many interviews and made comparison after comparison trying to triangulate based on his past actions where he might have taken Danielle, but what if we've been wrong all along and the one place we assumed she would never be is exactly where she is? Here."

My heart stops. "If you're right, then—"

"Then Eva is in much more danger than we thought," Con finishes.

CHAPTER 23

Eva

My dreams have been overtaken with what most would call nightmares, but I can only describe as memories. For a long time, the dreams were infrequent. Now, they are nightly.

It's been just over a week since I found Demon's gift. Nothing further has happened, and the week has been boring by usual standards. Boring should be good, but it's not. I can barely eat, and the loss of weight has been dramatic. I'd be thrilled any other time, but the cloud of apprehension, the heaviness of waiting for what comes next, has me on edge and ready to crumble.

Work has been typical. I cover my individual sessions and lead the groups I'm responsible for. I stop by and see Tessa every morning for my skinny latte, and we chat about mundane things since she worries about upsetting me. Even Aunt Polly is keeping things light and focused around Clemmie. Thankfully, my beautiful sunshine girl is oblivious to the tension surrounding her. For me, it feels like a powder keg ready to explode.

To make matters worse, Ashe has been virtually absent. It shouldn't matter, and I shouldn't care, but for some reason I do. Those private moments in the LCR conference room forged a connection of some sort. We aren't even dating, have never even kissed, but he feels safer to me than anyone ever has. I think he feels it too, but he respects the distance I've enforced since…well, just since.

He does call each night to make sure we're okay and to let me know what he can about the progress LCR is making in the Hurst case. The search has taken a turn with the verification that Demon is likely here in Magnolia Ridge. LCR and law enforcement have been working tirelessly to locate Danielle, but she remains lost. Ashe says he thinks they're close. For her sake, I hope they are. I hope someone comes for her like no one ever did for me.

Ashe introduced me to two of his employees, Villain and Moss, who trade off following me around like shadows. Villain is around six feet tall with a runner's build and light-brown shaggy hair while Moss is a few inches taller and built like he spends every day in a CrossFit gym. His skin is a smooth dark chocolate, and his head is shaved completely bald. The pair of them look as though they could handle anything the world could throw at them.

Though I should feel safe, I simply feel alone. I don't know these men who always lurk in my peripherals, and I don't trust easily. They are not like Ashe who, defying all logic, makes me feel safe despite the short time I've known him. For now though, I sleep with all my lights on and wish for things that can never be. I ignore Mal's observation that I'm distracted at work and avoid the ever-watchful eyes of Jake, my other coworker.

"Eva?" The intercom from the phone on my desk

jerks me out of my thoughts. "You have a delivery up front."

Jolie has a mischievous lilt to her voice that makes me suspicious. Thankfully, I'm between client sessions, so I make my way to the lobby. As soon as I open the security door, I see a teenager in the uniform of a local restaurant delivery service.

"Miss Jones?" he asks, then at my confirmation has me sign an electronic device accepting my delivery. The bag he hands me smells heavenly, and my stomach rumbles for the first time in days. "Have a good day," the boy says as he heads back out toward an older car with a lighted magnetic sign on top.

"Wait, let me grab a tip!" I call after him.

"No need. It has already been taken care of," he replies.

As soon as I get the bag back to my office, I look for the receipt or something to clue me in. I find the little slip of paper that thanks me for choosing The Golden Dragon, and on the back is just a short note that says, *I was listening.* I warily open the container to find my favorite, Mongolian chicken with veggies instead of rice. Ashe. Our very last conversation was about favorite foods.

The smell wafting from the open container is more than I can resist, and pretty soon I've eaten my limit of half the container and dropped the rest in the break room fridge for later. Feeling better than I have in days, I tackle some of the clinical notes I need to finish and consider calling Ashe to thank him. Not wanting to distract him from anything important, I decide to wait and call after work.

The rest of the day moves pretty quickly since it's

my turn to cover afternoon group. Once finished, I collect my leftovers and lock my office. With a grumbled goodbye from Jake and a distracted wave from Mal, I head for the back parking lot. Aunt Polly's sedan has returned to service as my primary mode of transportation since my 4Runner is still in the shop. I should probably feel bad since my having her car leaves Polly stranded at home, but I don't. I feel relieved. Making it through a day at work right now while having to worry about Aunt Polly and Clemmie driving around unprotected would be impossible.

I could say the house is quiet when I arrive, but I'd be lying. Clemmie's squeals are nearing glass-shattering decibels as she streaks through the house dragging Jo-Bee behind her by one arm. Aunt Polly sighs from her seat overlooking the chaos. I'm not sure what to say, so I just eye her questioningly. "Don't even think about giving me that look, young lady. You're the one who left her those cookies even though you know how hyper sugar makes her."

"What?" I'm confused. "I didn't leave any cookies."

"Yes, you did. They were on the table this morning. Clemmie loved the cute little bunny shapes. She made them hop all over the table before she ate them."

Bunnies? Villain and Moss have never come inside the house before, but could Ashe have enlisted their help to surprise Clemmie too? Unfamiliar warmth at his thoughtfulness makes me smile.

"Momma!" Clemmie snags my leg on her next pass and hangs on like a monkey as I pretend to shake her off. When she finally collapses to the floor in a giggling heap, I swoop her up.

"I love you, baby girl." I smile as we drop our foreheads together and rub noses.

"Lub ew too, Momma!" Clemmie drops a smacking kiss right on my lips then squirms to get down. I leave her playing with Jo-bee and take advantage of her distraction to quickly change into more comfortable clothes. The whirlwind of preparing and eating dinner, bath time, and bedtime follows. It's close to 9:00 p.m. by the time I remember to call and thank Ashe for the gifts.

"Lincoln," he answers on the second ring.

"Hey."

"Rabbit? Is everything okay? What's wrong?" he asks anxiously. I quickly reassure him that we're fine and thank him for the gifts. "What gifts, Eva?"

"I'm impressed you remembered my favorite takeout, and Clemmie loved the bunny cookies, though sugar makes her really hyper, so maybe only one next time," I ramble, my nerves getting the best of me.

"Eva, listen to me. I didn't send anything. I'm coming over." His voice holds a hard dark edge of urgency. He's still talking, but the phone falls from my trembling fingers as I rush to the bathroom and lose everything left in my stomach.

CHAPTER 24

Ashe

I arrive at Eva's faster than should be possible. I slam to a stop and run to the front door. I knock, well maybe pound is a better description, on the door. Polly answers almost immediately, wrapped in a worn terry cloth robe. Her relief is evident. Reading the urgent expression on my face, she steps aside and allows me entry without a word.

Eva is seated on the couch with an irritable and squirming Clemmie caged in her arms. She looks up as I enter. With the exception of the fading bruises, her face is devoid of color. I haven't seen her in a week, and a magnetic pull I don't understand draws me to her side. I sit on the sofa, close, but not too close, careful to give her space. Clemmie wiggles and fights to get free, but Eva's hold only tightens.

"Eva, baby, let me take her," Polly requests softly, walking toward Clemmie with her hands outstretched. "She's fine, honey, just mad because we woke her up."

Eva's hold gets even tighter, and Clemmie squeals, "Owie, Momma! No!" Eva immediately adjusts her grip and reluctantly surrenders her daughter to Polly, who turns a children's show on the television and lowers herself into a glider rocker with the now-distracted little girl. Eva's gaze never leaves Clemmie.

"Rabbit? I need you to explain what you meant on the phone. You scared me when you mentioned gifts." She slowly redirects her focus in my direction.

"I thought you sent me lunch."

Lunch? That was hours ago. "Okay...I don't understand. Can you be more specific?"

"Around lunchtime, I was called to the front for a delivery. It was takeout from The Golden Dragon. I wasn't expecting anything, but it had a note that just said 'I was listening.' "

"So, what made you think it was from me?" Her face flushes as though embarrassed, and she turns to hide behind her hair, a gesture I'm finding is a self-defense move for her. Instinctively, I reach and gently place a finger under her chin to turn her face back toward me. "Rabbit, don't be embarrassed. I would have sent it if I'd thought of it. Hell, I should have sent it. I've just been too damn distracted. Okay?"

She nods. "Um, well, the last time we talked, I mentioned The Golden Dragon was my favorite, and the order was exactly what I told you I liked best. The note made me think it was a sweet way for you to let me know you paid attention to what I said."

My heart starts pounding, and a suspicion begins to form in my head. "Okay, what happened next?" I ask, almost fearful to hear.

"Nothing. I ate half the food, finished work, and brought the leftovers home. When I got here, Clemmie was wild on a sugar rush, and Aunt Polly blamed me for leaving her cookies, but I didn't. I assumed you had one of your guys drop them by."

"Eva, I would never leave something for Clemmie without checking with you first, especially not food since I don't know whether she has allergies or not." I glance over at Clemmie, who has been rocked back to sleep by Polly.

"I should have called and checked with you I guess, but it was just food, you know? The cookies were shaped like bunnies, and I was…well…never mind. I just should have checked."

"You were what?" She shakes her head. I want to push, but other issues take precedence. "Okay, well back to Clemmie. What exactly was left and where are they?"

Eva stands and starts pacing back and forth. A single tear escapes before she slashes it away with the back of her hand. She starts to talk but is too emotional.

"Clemmie ate them," Polly interjects. "That's why my Eva's so upset." She looks down at the sleeping toddler while continuing to rock in the glider. "I've told her to quit worrying, there's nothing wrong with our baby. She's been nothing but normal all day."

"I just can't help worrying." Eva turns to me wringing her hands. "I just keep wondering if I should take her to the ER to be checked out?" She bites her lip and wanders over to run her palm over the disheveled red ringlets.

"Honey, she's fine. Other than being a little wild from the sugar earlier and a bit irritable from being awakened less than an hour after going to bed, she's felt fine," Polly reasons. Eva glances at me, but my knowledge of childcare is nonexistent.

"How are *you* feeling?" We've talked about Clemmie, but Eva hasn't mentioned if she's had any ill effects.

"Physically I've felt fine all day. I mean I threw up

earlier, but that was fear."

"What if we make a quick trip for blood work, then I'll stay the night here on the couch in case you need anything," I propose as a compromise. Eva seems to be considering the option.

"Well I think that's a wonderful idea," Polly says, taking action before Eva can protest. "I'll grab a pillow and some blankets," she announces before slowly standing and transferring Clemmie into Eva's arms.

I'm pretty sure she must have used some kind of magic because Clemmie never wakes or so much as moves. She disappears, leaving me with my rabbit, who looks like she's ready to bolt again. She sways a little in that unique mom sort of way that seduces children to slumber. Clemmie is already asleep, but I can practically guarantee she won't be waking up while Eva's doing that. She adds pacing to her sway as though it's necessary, but I know she's suddenly avoiding me for some reason. She's had a rough night though, so I leave her be and wait awkwardly for Polly's return.

The older woman bustles in with an armful of quilts almost as colorful as her personality while Eva quickly excuses herself to grab her daughter's bag.

"Can I trust you with my niece, Asher Lincoln?" The question is accompanied by a piercing stare.

"Yes, ma'am. I just want to keep her safe."

"See to it that you do, and I don't just mean physically. For some reason, she lets you closer than anyone else. It's been a long time since I've seen her as happy as she was when she came home today. She was smiling from ear to ear because she thought someone took the time to take care of her."

The thought of Demon playing with her emotions like that enrages me because not only was she scared, she was hurt. I understand now what she was about to say earlier and why she stopped herself. She wanted it to be me.

"She better not just be a means to an end," Polly warns.

"No ma'am, she's not."

Polly drops her voice to a whisper as movement sounds from the direction of Clemmie's room. "No one has ever truly cared about that girl. She's had to take care of herself her whole life, even before everything happened. She deserves to be more than a passing thought on your mind or a tool used and discarded after you get what you want."

CHAPTER 25

Ashe

The visit to the ER was short and anything but sweet. Eva was anxious and reserved, and Clemmie was terrified of having her blood drawn. All the crying must have depleted her energy because she slept soundly all the way home in the car seat Eva transferred to my vehicle. Since neither of them were showing any signs of having been harmed, the doctor sent them home with instructions to call after four tomorrow afternoon to get the results of the blood work.

The house is still brightly lit when we return, and Polly is waiting up for a report from Eva. Clemmie never stirs as Eva transfers her from the car to her bed before heading to her room, claiming fatigue. Polly soon follows, after ensuring I have everything I need.

Once the family has settled into bed, I step quietly out to the front porch and call Con. "Dude," he groans. "Damn, what time is it?" I hear the rustling of sheets in the background.

"We have a problem."

"I'm up. What do you need?" Con is instantly alert.

"I have a suspicion, and I need you to prove it or prove me wrong. I really hope I'm wrong."

"I'm listening."

"Someone sent gifts to Eva and Clemmie today.

Gifts made to seem like they came from me."

"What the hell?" Con growls.

"Yeah, but the problem is that Eva's gift was lunch from her favorite restaurant. Not only that, but it was her favorite dish, which is an uncommon order. She thought it was me because we had discussed that very thing on the phone."

"Ahhhh. I see where you're going with this and why you called me instead of Rosey."

"Yeah, well, it gets worse. Cookies were left inside Eva's house on her kitchen table for Clemmie."

"How the hell did anyone get past Villain and Moss?" he yells.

"That's one of the questions I plan to find an answer to myself. What I need from you is to find out how this guy knows so much. Get this, Clemmie's cookies were shaped like rabbits." Having heard me call Eva rabbit on more than one occasion, his mind instantly goes where I need it to.

"You're thinking he got to her phone."

"Bingo." I pace the small porch. "I haven't told you the worst though."

"Seriously?"

"Eva thought her lunch was from me, and Polly thought the cookies were from Eva, so both of my—" I fake a cough to cover my mistake and my own shock. "Um, both of the girls ate the food."

"Are they okay?" Con asks quickly.

"Both seem fine, but I'm staying the night on the couch. We went to the doctor for some blood work just to be sure. In the morning, I'm bringing Eva to LCR, and I want you to run an eval on her phone. It makes me sick to think that bastard has been spying on her right under our noses."

"Look, if anything's there, you know I'll find it. Just keep those girls safe."

"Will do." Hanging up the phone, I secure the locks before grabbing a seat beside the pile of blankets on the sofa. I text Villain to advise him that the threat level has escalated, and I'll be staying the night. Thankfully, the charging plate on the end table works with my phone. My shoes come off next before I shut off the lights and try to make myself comfortable on the sofa that probably barely fits Eva's frame.

I turn the TV to one of my favorite late-night rerun sitcoms with the volume on low, but sleep is elusive as Polly's words sit heavy on my mind. A rustle behind the couch snaps me to instant alertness before I bolt to my feet. Eva jumps back with a squeak, her hand on her chest and breath heaving.

"Sorry," she whispers once she calms. "I didn't mean to sneak up on you."

"What's the matter, little rabbit? Can't sleep?" I rotate my shoulders and relax my posture.

"No. I thought I'd grab a snack." She hesitates. "You can join me if you want?"

"Sure." She makes her way to the kitchen, and I follow her, smirking at the cookie monster sleep pants covering her cute ass. *Yes, I'm a guy. We look.* She turns as though she feels my gaze, and I quickly avert my eyes.

"Um…do you like yogurt?"

"Yogurt? Rabbit, I eat real people food. How 'bout cookies? I'm pretty sure cookies and milk are the standard for late-night snacking."

"Are you sure cookies are a safe choice?" Eva

teases.

"I could be persuaded to take the risk if you will," I counter.

She smiles shyly. Her skin is without makeup, and her dark curls are swirling all around her face. It strikes me how beautiful she is without her normal shields.

"Ashe?"

"Huh?" I try to refocus on the conversation.

"I asked if you liked chocolate chip. Aunt Polly made some yesterday."

"Uh yeah, chocolate chip," I stammer. Good grief, what is wrong with me?

"Here you go."

She hands me a small plate with several cookies and turns to fix the requisite milk. I feel like pouring it over my head to cool down because for some reason I feel sweat trickling down my back. After handing me the milk, she grabs a small container of fat-free yogurt from the fridge and heads toward the table.

"Uh, we could maybe sit, um, in the living room, you know, like if you wanted to." Damn! That was so bad I want to kick my own ass. I take a deep breath ready to try to ask in a less fumbling way, but Eva just nods and walks that direction after grabbing a spoon from the drawer and dropping the top from her yogurt in the garbage.

She plops down on the far end of the couch and curls her feet up beside her as though out of habit. Fuzzy pink-and-orange socks peek out from the hem of the cookie monster pants, making me smile. The woman is actually fuzzy like a rabbit. I chuckle to myself, and she narrows her eyes at me in suspicion. That expression changes to surprise when I carefully take my seat at the other end of the small sofa, balancing my cookies and milk carefully.

We eat in silence for a few minutes before she blurts, "That's one of my favorite shows."

"Mine too. I used to watch it with my dad." A discussion ensues about favorite characters and the merits of certain popular plotlines. Soon we're relaxed and laughing together at the rerun antics. I can't remember a time I felt so comfortable with a woman.

I offer her one of my cookies since she has been eyeing them for a while. "No thanks. I like them, but they don't like me back."

I'm sensing a theme here—Asian dishes with veggies instead of rice and yogurt instead of cookies. My little rabbit really does eat like one, but why? I mean sure, she's curvy, but only in the best ways. Tonight's going well, so I don't want to talk about anything that might upset her, including her diet and the possible violation of her phone. It can all wait until tomorrow.

Somehow, in the course of our fun, we've migrated closer on the couch. I only notice because I smell her subtle vanilla citrus scent. It smells like cookies and woman and home. Before long, Eva's head begins to nod. Eventually, it finds my shoulder, and I settle her against my chest. Her breathing is slow and even.

I find my own eyes closing despite my desire to stay awake, so I can keep tangling my fingers in her wild curls. Up close, I can see the strawberry-blonde roots just starting to show and wonder if she'll ever return to that color. Finally, my eyes revolt and close against my will. Settling into a light sleep that is only interrupted when Eva becomes restless and moans, I run my hand down her back over and over until she settles and we both fall into benign dreams.

CHAPTER 26

Eva

"Ahem." The sound intrudes on the blissful absence of thought and the warmth that surrounds me. I squeeze my eyes more tightly shut and hope the sound goes away. "Ahem!"

The sound only gets louder, and I wrestle my eyes open to find myself in the living room with Aunt Polly hovering over me with a curious expression. "You two sure are looking mighty cozy," she says with a grin.

Jerking upright in shock, I turn to see that my nice warm pillow was actually a quietly snoring Ashe. He must have covered us up since one of the patchwork quilts is draped around me. Though I can't remember when I've slept so deeply or peacefully, the vulnerability scares me in the light of day. I try to inch myself off the couch only to stop short when Ashe moves his arm and my head jerks back. The curse of curls, my hair has somehow wrapped itself around the button on Ashe's cuff. Aunt Polly laughs so hard she has to sit down, and that laughter awakens Ashe.

"Good morning, Rabbit," he rumbles in a sleep-laden voice. Clearing my throat, I use my head to motion toward the still-laughing Polly. Ashe glances over and sits up straighter. Unfortunately, whatever he does with his arm pulls my hair hard enough to make me wince. Polly laughs harder.

"I don't think I can take anymore," she cackles before pushing out of the chair. "I'm going to wake up our sweet girl." Ashe gives me a questioning glance as he shifts, inadvertently pulling my hair yet again.

"Ow!"

"Oh shit!" he exclaims. "Um, sorry. Man, your hair is really tangled up around this button." The more he tries to unravel the tangle, the more he pulls my hair. I see the grin he's struggling to hold back, and I threaten him, "Don't you dare laugh at me."

He smirks. "I would never laugh *at* you, but you know this is pretty funny. If you let yourself laugh, then I could laugh *with* you," he quips. My fists clench in defense. "Okay, okay. Don't get mad. Let me just take the shirt off so your hair will be easier to untangle." He awkwardly unbuttons his shirt with one hand while doing his best to keep the other still since my head is at an awkward angle. Finally managing to slide it off, he hands the dark gray shirt to me and watches as I deftly complete the untangling.

He looks so casual sitting on our couch in his black undershirt sans shoes. His midnight hair is sticking up a bit on top, and dark scruff lines his face, but somehow, he still manages to look capable. Needing a distraction, I suggest coffee. Any other day I would be stopping by The Daily Grind and seeing Tessa, but today I'll make my own. I left both a voicemail and email for my boss last night, letting him know I needed to take a sick day this morning. Thankfully, I wasn't scheduled for group today, and our director is very laid back.

After heading to the kitchen, I pop a pod into the coffee maker then follow it with a second. Not much in

Aunt Polly's house is modern, but her coffee addiction comes close to needing an intervention. I splurged on the bright-red single-serve coffee maker as a gift for her on Mother's Day.

I turn with a mug in each hand only to find Ashe right behind me. Coffee splashes on my hands when I startle. Ashe curses before taking the mugs from my hands, setting them back on the counter. He turns on the cold water before gently taking my hands in his and holding them under the stream. I should probably be saying something, but all I can do is stare. All the other times I've been around Ashe, he was in a suit or at least well put together. This morning, his eyes still have that heavy-lidded sleepy look, and he's barefoot in my kitchen with mussed hair. It's like I've been seeing him as an investigator this whole time, but now he's just a man, a very attractive man.

Ashe's focus is on my hands, intently searching for burns that probably didn't even leave a mark. If they hurt, I haven't noticed. Under the cold water, my hands feel warm in his. I both like it and fear it and wonder which one will win out. Slowly, he lifts those sleepy blue eyes to mine, our hands all but forgotten as the water continues to run. His expression is intense as he leans toward me, eyeing my lips, which suddenly feel dry. I resist the urge to lick them. My heart pounds so loudly it echoes in my ears.

"Momma! Potty!" Clemmie squeals from the kitchen doorway, clapping her hands. As I shut the water off and quickly dry my hands, I think I hear a groan from Ashe. With no time to find out, I turn and leave him staring out the window and focus on my daughter, who's straining for me from Aunt Polly's arms.

"Did you go potty like a big girl?" I ask as I take her and prop her on my hip.

"Potty!" she repeats. "Stick stick," she says, pointing to the top of the refrigerator where we keep a pack of stickers as rewards. Before I can reach them, Ashe has retrieved the pack and handed them over. Clemmie points to the one she wants then reaches for Ashe as I fumble with the stickers. He looks to me, and at my hesitant nod transfers her from my hip to his. "Man," she says, squishing his cheeks between her tiny hands.

"Ashe," he corrects with a smile.

"Man," Clemmie insists with a pout. Aunt Polly laughs as she continues breakfast prep.

"Good luck," she says. "That one is stubborn like her momma."

Ashe tickles Clemmie's belly, eliciting a giggle. I direct him toward the high chair since the bread just popped up from the toaster and Aunt Polly has eggs almost ready. He has surprisingly little trouble getting her secured. "Ashe," he says again pointing at his chest.

"Ass?" she tries. Ashe panics and looks at me and Polly, but we're way too busy laughing to offer any help.

"No, no, no. Ashe," he tries, sounding desperate. "Say Ashe." Polly and I just laugh harder, knowing he's just making it worse.

"Ass! Ass! Ass!" Clemmie yells while banging on her tray. Ashe groans and turns pleading eyes my direction.

"What do I do?"

Instead of answering, I get busy. "Clemmie, are you hungry?" I ask while scooping eggs on her plate and spreading a thin layer of jelly on the whole wheat toast.

"Hungy!" The banging continues until I place the plate on her tray with a small spoon and her sippy cup of milk. The distraction works, and her attention is now fully on making a mess of eating her breakfast.

"Thank you!" Ashe whispers in my ear, stirring my hair. I don't know what to do with the tingling I feel, so I excuse myself to run to the restroom. I take care of necessities then notice my reflection as I wash my hands. My hair is doing that crazy thing natural curls do where they hold the shape of whatever position you squished them into while sleeping. My face is pale and bruised with a few freckles making themselves known across my cheeks, and I'm not wearing a thing that matches. I debate taking a minute to change but worry that will send the wrong message. Settling for finger combing the worst sections of my hair and brushing my morning breath away, I return to the kitchen. My efforts were to no avail. Ashe is gone.

CHAPTER 27

Ashe

I feel guilty for leaving, but the moment at the sink with Eva after having spent the night with her in my arms is just too much. The excuse of needing to run home for a shower gave me the space to clear my head. I don't want to make a move too soon and scare her back into hiding. Also, while she's not an LCR client, she is a witness in our case, a witness who's in danger. My focus needs to be on finding Danielle and keeping Eva safe, not on a relationship.

By the time I return to her house, I have my game face on. Our communication last night was easy, and I didn't want to ruin it by talking about my suspicions. I need to tell her Con is waiting for us at LCR to check her phone, but I don't want to scare her unnecessarily.

"Eva, I'm worried about something, and I'd like to talk to you about it."

"Okay." She turns to me with a curious expression.

"I've been thinking. How could anyone know your favorite restaurant or favorite meal or my nickname for you?"

"Well, I ah... I guess I was so caught up in worrying about whether or not Clemmie was okay that I haven't thought about it." She turns her head to glance at her playing child.

"I don't want to worry you, but I think Demon may have gotten to your phone." I hazard a quick look and see her eyes fill with fear as she releases her phone to the floor. "Rabbit, take a deep breath. I don't intend to allow him near you again. I suspect he may have tampered with your phone when he was in your room at the hospital." Her arms wrap around herself as if in protection. "Con is waiting for us at LCR. If anyone can detect tampering, it's him. Will you go with me?" Her only answer is a nod before she moves to gather Clemmie and all the supplies she'll need for the short trip.

The parking lot is full when we arrive, but thankfully Con, Rosey, and I have reserved spots. Eva doesn't move to get out, so I walk around to the passenger side and offer her my hand after opening the door. She takes it as if still lost in her own thoughts, but her mom instincts kick in when she hears a noise from the backseat. Once standing, she opens the back door and frees Clemmie from the restraints. Little hands rub at sleepy eyes as her mother holds her tight.

Con is in his office when we make it to our floor. He greets Eva and tries to get a smile out of Clemmie, but she clings to her mother and hides her face. Once we're all seated, I hand him the phone and watch as he attaches it to a computer.

"This will take a few minutes. I'm running a scan for malware and spyware." He focuses directly on Eva. "Have you noticed anything like the battery draining fast or the phone getting hot?"

"Oh my gosh! Yes, both of those. I just didn't think anything about it because I've had it for a while." Con shoots me a significant look. "Why? What does that mean?"

She looks back and forth between us. Before we can answer, Clemmie wiggles to get down and accidently knocks a business card holder off the end table. "Oh no. I'm so sorry."

Clemmie manages to escape and wanders behind Con's desk, trying to crawl under while her mom tries to clean up the scattered cards. He chuckles and moves his feet so she can hide more easily. Girlish giggles echo from underneath.

"Poor battery life and running hot are signs that an app could be running in the background that you're not aware of. Sometimes, it actually is just an old phone, but it may mean we're on the right track."

"If something is wrong with the phone, can you fix it?" Eva asks.

"Of course."

"Though if you just want a new phone, we can help with that too," I interject. At the sound of my voice, Clemmie emerges from her hiding space and runs to where I'm seated. She raises her arms wanting me to pick her up.

"Up, Ass," she says happily as I lift her into my lap. Eva is smirking, and Con is practically bent double laughing.

"Man, she sure has you pegged, Linc," he says.

"She can't say Ashe, asshole."

"Ahem." Eva clears her throat.

"I mean jerk," I correct while flipping Con off behind Clemmie's back. How in the hell am I going to fix this? It may be funny now, but it won't be for long.

"Come on, Linc. You know you love me."

"Wink?" Clemmie asks as she plays with my watch, attempting to pry it from my arm. I recognize the lifeline for what it is.

"Yes, sweetie. My name is Linc." She leans her curly head against my chest and throws her little arms around my neck, almost choking me.

"Wuv, Wink," she says before leaning back and plopping a smacking wet kiss right on my mouth. I can't say I ever thought I'd get a kiss on the lips from Clemmie before I got one from her momma, but I also can't say it didn't melt my heart. Con's expression is as flummoxed as I feel, and Eva has flushed a pretty shade of pink. An alarm sounds from Con's computer, making the term "saved by the bell" a very real thing for me.

"Caught ya!" Con exclaims. Eva startles since her attention was still riveted on me and her daughter.

"What've you got?" I ask.

"It's an app called Spy Games. Anyone can download it from the app store. It can copy messages and even turn your phone into a microphone, so another party can hear everything that's said. That's not all it does, but it's what applies to how a killer knew Eva's favorite meal and how to get in your head with the cookies."

"That's what he meant by the note. He really was listening and wanted me to know," Eva concludes as all color drains from her skin.

"He likely knew it wouldn't take long for the app to be detected and decided to up the scare value by taunting you with it." The thought makes me furious.

Con turns back to the computer, and with a few clicks of the mouse he announces the app is deleted. "Eva, I know it will be a big hassle, but you'll need to change the passwords for all the apps currently on this phone, especially your banking apps. I'll also need to check your aunt's phone, and any other devices you have at home like computers or tablets just in case."

"But I've never even heard of that app. How did it get on my phone? I don't understand."

"It's actually pretty easy," I explain. "I told you we think the phone was accessed while you were in the hospital. Most people have passcodes that are easily guessed, which allows someone to simply unlock the phone and install the app from the app store as if they're the owner." Her hand flies to her mouth to cover her gasp. "Eva, what's wrong?"

"My passcode is Clemmie's birthday."

CHAPTER 28

Ashe

The call from Rosey comes just as I've arrived at Eva's. I excuse myself to answer the phone while Eva detaches Clemmie from the car seat and heads in the house with her bag of toddler paraphernalia. "Hey, Rosey. What's up?"

"Danielle's purse has been found."

"Where?" I ask urgently, starting to pace the front yard.

"Forty-five minutes away in Trussville. Someone found it in the bathroom of a gas station and turned it in to the owner. When no one claimed it after a week, he decided to open it up and look for a driver's license. Apparently, he found her phone instead. He used the emergency feature to get in touch with her and ended up reaching her dad. John called me frantic right after he called the Trussville police. I couldn't talk him out of heading that way. I'm leaving now. You in?"

"Definitely. Wait for me. I can be at the office in ten."

"Got it." The call drops, and I hurry to disconnect the car seat and take it in the house since Polly's sedan is absent.

"Eva?" I call out. She pops her head out of the kitchen. "I'm sorry, but I have to run. That was Rosey,

118

and we have a strong lead on Danielle."

"Okay. Will you let me know what happens?"

"I'll do my best to update you as soon as I get a chance," I say as I'm walking out the door.

Rosey is waiting impatiently in a company SUV when I pull into the lot. We're on the road five minutes later.

"So, Danielle's purse was actually found a week ago, and we're just finding out now?" I clarify.

"Correct."

"Damn."

"Yeah. It doesn't make sense. None of Julie's, Celia's, or Amy's belongings were ever recovered, so why is this purse turning up, and why now? I might have understood it if it was just after the abduction, but it's been almost three weeks. If Demon holds true to form based on what we know, Danielle wouldn't have been anywhere near here last week."

Rosey shakes his head. "So much of this case just isn't adding up. If Demon took Danielle, then history shows he should have taken her directly to some small town away from Magnolia Ridge and immediately hidden her away."

"Okay, talk it out," I encourage. "What's nagging you?"

"If he took Danielle somewhere several hours away as is his habit, then how is he also in Magnolia Ridge harassing Eva? Is he driving back and forth just riding the roads between the two? If he's still in town, then does he have a partner who's watching over Danielle? Also, why are we finding the purse? Did Danielle escape somehow and have it? Did Demon plant it there to throw us off and make it seem like he didn't have her? There are just so many variables to consider."

"The way he's toying with Eva also makes no sense. I mean, he buys her food, leaves her the Cliff Bar at the hospital, and leaves cookies for Clemmie. It's just all so innocuous until you figure in the wreck, but we both know that even the wreck could have been much worse. Maybe it was more aimed at scaring than harming. When you also figure in tampering with her cell phone, it feels more like a stalker than a killer," I conclude. "What if Demon isn't the one harassing Eva? I know the Cliff Bar has her convinced, but could it be coincidence? It would explain how Demon is in two places—he's not."

"I don't know. Something's off, and I feel like the answer is right in front of me, but I'm missing it," Rosey grumbles. The rest of the drive is made in silence, both of us lost in thought.

We arrive to find several patrol cars and John Hurst's beat-up old pickup in the gas station lot. Our interviews with law enforcement and the station owner yield no new information. Security cameras are focused toward the freestanding restroom facility in the parking lot, but apparently, they're just for show and aren't even hooked up.

Damn, what would it take for us to catch a break? A killer has had Danielle in his grasp for almost three weeks, and who knows what torture he's inflicting with every day we fail to find her? The weight of responsibility feels heavy on my shoulders as I watch her father, one of the strongest men I know, openly weep against the bed of his truck, exhausted from railing at the officers on the scene for excluding him even though he knows they have no choice.

"Come on," Rosey says, clapping me on the shoulder. "There's nothing else we can do here. I think we need to stop by the station and talk to the homicide detectives to see if they have any recent Jane Does before we head back."

We make sure John is okay to drive home then pile back into the SUV and make the fifteen-minute drive to the station. After showing our credentials at the front desk, we're directed to a conference room to await one of the detectives. A cupful of bad coffee later, a burly man who appears to be in his fifties strolls in.

"Evening gentlemen, I'm Detective Lawrence," the man says while shaking our hands. "The Magnolia Ridge department confirmed your identity and consultant status, so what can I do for you?"

"We're investigating the disappearance of a young woman from Magnolia Ridge. We discovered today that her purse was found in Trussville, so we're covering our bases and checking in to see if you guys have had any Jane Does in the last two to three weeks," Rosey explains.

Detective Lawrence fixes a cup of the horrible coffee before sitting across from us. "Well, as you know, we are pretty close to Birmingham, so we do share some of the big city problems. Homicides are not unheard of here, but rarely are they unidentified. In fact, right now as far as Jane Does, we only have one."

CHAPTER 29

Eva

I haven't heard from Ashe since he brought us home. Aunt Polly spent most of the day grocery shopping, which left Clemmie and me alone in the house, an unusual occurrence. My nerves were on end, but my daughter has always been my priority. I wanted to put everything aside and enjoy the one-on-one time with her. We'd put on our swimsuits and spent the rest of the day splashing together in her tiny plastic pool and chasing butterflies—and sometimes bees in Clemmie's case—with her little net.

Now Aunt Polly is back home catching up on her favorite show in the living room, Clemmie is down for the night, and I'm cleaning up the dishes from the simple stir-fry I made for dinner. Without the distraction of other people, my mind keeps gravitating back to my phone.

Demon was in my hospital room while I was unconscious and couldn't defend myself. I knew that already, but I'd been trying to push the information to the back of my mind and lock it away because it was more than I was ready to deal with. As a counselor I know it's unhealthy, but I learned three years ago that the locked room in my mind is essential to survival.

He basically bugged my house with my own

phone. I want to vomit, thinking he could have listened to me shower or listened to me scream after dreaming of him. That he knew my daughter's birthday makes me want to run. I have nowhere to go and no means to get there, but the desperation I feel, the skin crawling on the back of my neck, tells me to grab my daughter and my aunt and just drive away without ever looking back.

In books, the characters always buy some fake ID and hide out in some small town by getting a job waitressing or something. I happen to know that's not reality. After I was returned home to my parents, emaciated and yet somehow beyond-all-logic pregnant, I spent days and weeks being told everything was my own fault. I shouldn't have been so rebellious, shouldn't have been such a slut, shouldn't have been…well, just shouldn't have been, period.

I developed a plan to escape just like those characters in the books. I asked around in the sketchiest locations I could find, thinking I'd purchase one of those fake IDs with the small amount of money I'd still had left in my savings. Turns out, a blonde, white chick asking about illegal IDs just makes everyone suspicious. While I'm no longer blonde, I'm pretty sure the outcome would be the same.

I feel trapped, and though I know that's exactly how Demon wants me to feel, I'm too used to being the victim to feel anything else. Ashe somehow makes me feel safer, like I could be stronger, but I know I'm a means to an end *for* him and don't mean anything *to* him.

The dishes are done, and I realize I've just been standing at the sink with the water running for who knows how long. I shut it off and dry my hands. The television is dark as I pass through the living room, signaling Aunt Polly has gone to bed. I double-check the locks even though I know Aunt Polly will have done the same, and the outside of the house is still being monitored by either Villain or Moss. The cookies got into our house somehow. I can't even think about Demon in here, in the only safe space I've known since he took me.

Before I head into my own room, I pause at Clemmie's. I crack the door quietly and squeeze in. She's sleeping soundly, snuggled up on her tummy with her tushy up in the air. Her innocent little face is angelic looking in repose. It's a miracle my body allowed her to survive. *She* is a miracle, my miracle. A tear slips down my cheek and drops down to my shirt. I cover my mouth with my hand as a sob tries to erupt. Stumbling to the antique rocker in the corner, I collapse as the fear overtakes me, and I succumb to the storm that has been brewing behind my eyes all day.

What feels like hours later, I finally calm. My emotions are drained, my eyes feel almost swollen shut, and my shirt is soaked. I use the hem to wipe my face. Clemmie still rests in that deep and unburdened sleep only the young can find. Leaving the rocker, I hover over my daughter, running my fingers lightly through the curls so like mine. I have to find a way to keep her safe because I know something no one else does. She wasn't an accident.

CHAPTER 30

Eva

The marks on my thighs are even again, five on each leg. Rain hits the tin roof of my prison, and the sound is comforting since it's a break from the silence. Silence allows too many thoughts to crowd my head, too much blame to smother my lungs. Give in, the rain seems to say. Let go. Go to sleep. It's like a lullaby, a friend, allowing my thoughts to be drowned out by the pelting of water on the roof. It is the absence of anything, the only moments of peace I have. Demon never comes when it's raining. Its protection is like magic, allowing me to relax and just rest. My dreams are of nothing, and time ceases to exist as I float.

Wetness suddenly sprays my body, pulling me from my sleep. I can smell the freshness of the rain in the air ruffling my hair. It shouldn't be, but it is. I force my eyes open to see the door is ajar. The storm—it must have broken the lock! Oh my God! I'm free! I force myself to my hands and knees and use the wall for support, inching my way to standing. I stumble on unsteady legs toward the portal to my salvation.

The door swings wildly back and forth in the wind and slams into my shoulder as I pass, catapulting me outside. I land heavily on all fours in the mud, but I don't care. I'm outside! Trees are bowing under the force of the wind, and I can see the outlines of their shadowed forms, not just hear them. I see angry gray clouds racing across the sky as a streak of lightning burns my underused retinas. I breathe in the air, revel in the cleansing rain, and finally, finally take a deep breath.

"Oh, my sweet Julie." His voice comes to me from behind, and I whip around, falling to my rear in the muck. He is leaning up against the wall underneath the rotting eaves. "You failed the test, my love," he says calmly. "How can we be together if you can't be loyal?"

The haze of dark rain obscures his features as he slowly stalks toward me. I scramble backward, but my hands and feet can find no traction. He picks me up and carries me like a child cradled in his arms before gently laying me on the mattress. My muscles bunch and clench, urging me to move, to fight, but my heart has no fight left. Freedom comes and goes with the flapping of the still-open door, but it's beyond my reach now.

Demon lays beside me on the thin mattress, the wet material of his suit abrasive against my skin. "I had hoped you were ready," he says, his hands already beginning to wander my muddy body. "Soon, Julie, soon you'll be ready, and we'll have everything we ever wanted."

He forces his mouth to mine and crawls between my thighs. For long moments, I don't even exist, much less resist him. When he finally leaves and freedom's door clangs shut, my marks are not even anymore.

I come awake slowly, raindrops trailing down my cheeks, my body heavy with hopelessness. My hands go to the marks on my thighs, ever counting. Thirteen, not eleven. I jerk upright and take in the muted early morning sunlight glowing from behind my curtains. The dreams are coming more frequently than ever.

Covering my face with my hands, I feel the tears I thought were rain. My breaths heave. What do I see? I use my centering technique to ground myself in the present. What do I hear? My baby snores softly through the monitor. What do I smell? The scent of pancakes wafts from the kitchen, finally bringing me fully into the here and now. A noise sounds from the monitor, signaling Clemmie is awake. I throw off the covers and pad to the door, hoping Tessa has enough coffee to help me survive the workday.

CHAPTER 31

Ashe

Yesterday accomplished very little except to rack up miles on the road and add to our already-numerous questions, plus John has already called this morning looking for nonexistent updates on his daughter. LCR has always been at the top. We are used to getting results. The way this case is dragging on is demoralizing, especially because a life is hanging in the balance. Thankfully, last night's Jane Doe was too old to have been Danielle, but it feels like we're back to square one.

Con is reviewing the security footage from the cameras of businesses near the gas station where the purse was found. Rosey has taken over the conference room, working on the whiteboard to add new information and try to connect the dots. As for me, I've been on the phone all day talking to various detectives from all over Alabama, trying to get them to acknowledge a serial killer has been stalking our state for years, so they can add their resources to ours.

Unfortunately, the wheels of justice truly do turn slowly, and every answer seems more like a redirection, each person putting me off on another person. Those who will listen are hung up on the fact that Celia Wayne's body was too decomposed to make a connection beyond appearances and preference for dance clubs. She is the required third link in the case for a serial killer. With her case being discounted, no one wants to throw their support behind our theory.

We took this case *pro bono* as a favor to John, but we still have to keep the doors open and income coming in, so most of our investigators and specialists are assigned to other jobs while Rosey, Con, and I take the majority of the work on Danielle's case. With Villain and Moss on Eva around the clock, this case is costing us a fortune, so despite how much we want to, we can't pull any more of our assets to help. Just as I'm about to go refill my coffee for the tenth time, the desk phone buzzes.

"Yes?" I answer.

"You have a call on line three," Jillian announces.

"Thanks." I answer the appropriate line and wait for the caller to speak.

"Hello, is this Mr. Lincoln?" a female voice asks.

"Yes, it is. How can I help you?"

"Um, my name is JoBeth Williams. I was, well, I still am a friend of Danielle Hurst." My attention snags, and I sit taller in my chair.

"Thank you for calling, Ms. Williams. How did you get my number?"

"Her dad stopped by one of our shows and gave me your card. He wanted me to call, said he was trying to get word out to all Danielle's friends and acquaintances in case we knew anything that could be helpful."

"We'd definitely like to talk to you. Can you come into the office, so we can talk more easily?" I ask, knowing I would need this conversation recorded, and that Rosey would want to look her in the eyes to monitor for any evidence of untruth.

"Sure, but I'm only in town for the rest of the day."

"That's not a problem. I'll clear our schedule."

"Fine. I'll see you in about an hour," she says before ending the call. I notify Rosey and Con and ask Jillian to reserve the conference room and make sure it's ready. Before long, my phone buzzes, and Jillian lets me know Ms. Williams has arrived, and she'll be escorting her to the conference room momentarily. I grab what I need and hurry that direction. Con and Rosey are already waiting, and I take my seat with seconds to spare as a knock at the door announces Jillian.

"Ms. JoBeth Williams to see you." Jillian steps aside, and nothing could have prepared me for the woman who walks in. She is tall and curvy in an old-school pin up girl way. Tattoos in brilliant colors cover her arms, and her hair is a mix of vibrant purple and black. She sports a nose ring, multiple earrings, and some kind of retro dress covered with cherries over chunky heels.

I'm speechless for a moment but recover quickly to stand and greet her as does Con. Rosey, on the other hand, reminds me of one of those cartoon characters who sees a pretty girl and hearts start popping out of their eyes. I'm pretty sure drool is about to make an appearance. I nudge Rosey none too gently as Con is shaking hands. Rosey startles, and his usual untouchable persona slips back into place. He stands, and I make the introductions. When he takes her hand, I notice a barely perceptible twitch, not just from Rosey, but also from Ms. Williams. While I definitely find that interesting, we're on a short timeline and need to get back to business.

"Please have a seat, Ms. Williams. Can we get you some water or coffee before we get started?" I ask.

"No thank you, and please call me Joey. Everyone does," she says. I take my seat and get things started.

"Okay, Joey. Thanks for coming in. Do you mind if we record this conversation in case we need to review it again when you're out of town?"

"Sure, I guess."

"So, you're a friend of Danielle's," I state after starting the recording. "I assume you may know something you think could be useful in helping us find her?"

"Well, I'm not really sure." She fidgets as she continues, "I travel a lot with my band. We've been out of town for the last several weeks, and I didn't even know Danielle was missing until I got back into town yesterday. I don't even know if anything I'm going to tell you will actually be helpful or not, but I'd hate myself if anything happened to her and I hadn't at least tried to help."

"Everything is helpful. Sometimes it just takes one small detail to change everything, so please tell us even the small things," I request.

She takes a deep breath and begins, "Danielle and I have been friends since high school, though we haven't been as close recently with me touring and her new boyfriend."

"Boyfriend?" Rosey interrupts. This is the first we've heard about the possibility of a boyfriend.

"Yeah, she's been dating him a couple months, I guess. His name is Dustin. I don't remember the last name."

"That's okay, what can you tell us about him?" Hmm. I guess Rosey is taking over this interview. I sit back and let him handle it. I glance at Con, and I can see the anticipation of the hunt on his face. As soon as we have the details, he'll be out to get an ID on this guy.

"He's tall, like six feet or so, and maybe around late thirties. His hair is really light blond but I'm not sure what color his eyes are." The mention of blond hair has us all on edge.

"Do you remember anything about his job or what he drives?" Rosey asks as he takes notes.

"I have no idea what kind of car he drives, but he usually has on a suit, and I think he works in something like finance or real estate. The two of them were inseparable and all over each other from the start. Honestly, I liked him at first. He treated her respectfully and was always gentle and soft-spoken without a temper."

"You said you liked him 'at first.' What changed?" Rosey apparently caught the same questionable phrasing as I did.

"Look, I don't want to get Danielle in trouble," she says while fidgeting with one of the hoops in her ear.

"We're not the police. We are not concerned with anything she may have done. Our only concern is finding her," Con assures her.

"Okay, well, the night before we left on tour, Danielle and Dustin were at SubZero, the club where we were performing. We were all hanging out between sets, and I saw Dustin hand Danielle some pills. It's not like he roofied her or anything, she took them willingly, but it's not like her to use drugs."

"Could you tell what kind of pills they were?" Rosey inquires.

"What, because I have tattoos and purple hair I should obviously know all about drugs?" Joey forces out angrily.

"Hang on," Rosey backtracks. "That's not at all what I said. I would have asked the same question of anyone. These days, most people who frequent clubs know what different drugs are, whether they use them or not."

Joey relaxes marginally. "Fine. I'm not one hundred percent certain what they were. They were round and colorful, so I assumed they were Molly." Ecstasy. Danielle may have been taking ecstasy. That certainly changes our investigation.

"Did you witness her swallow the pills, or could she have been selling them?" I question.

"She definitely took them. She was high when I left, but she wouldn't leave with me. She and Dustin were dancing, and he said he was taking her home. I didn't know what to do. Dustin seemed sober, and she wasn't forced to take the pills, so I finally just left. Now I'm terrified I'm responsible for her disappearance." Tears well in her eyes, but she tips her head toward the ceiling to keep them from falling.

"You're not responsible. Whoever took her is responsible, and the information you've given us will help us find her," Rosey reassures her. "I know this has been hard, but we're almost done. I just have one more question. What day was this?" Joey snags her phone from the table and opens her calendar app before naming the date. My heart races. It was forty-eight hours before Danielle disappeared.

CHAPTER 32

Eva

Work has gone surprisingly well today. Group attendance was up, and one of my clients, a young mother, finally admitted her husband's abusive behavior. I was able to get her and the kids an emergency placement at a shelter that also provides substance abuse treatment. After months of watching her come in week after week with bruises and other injuries and sending her home with information for domestic violence support groups, I was relieved she'd finally taken my advice and left.

On top of everything else, my boss decided to treat us all to lunch, so I'm sitting in the group room, since it's bigger than the break room, laughing and joking with my coworkers over Italian. Jake complies with a request for an update on his mom while Mal tries to act like he's not staring at Jolie. For her part, Jolie is oblivious and just keeps pumping me for information about Ashe. The easy atmosphere allows me to relax enough to finish off my salad and grilled chicken. Just as we're cleaning up, my cell rings. I quickly dispose of my trash and head to my office to take the call.

"Hello?"

"Girl! I can't believe you are hello-ing me like my name didn't pop up on your phone," Tessa jokes.

"Hello?" I repeat before bursting out laughing.

"That's not funny," she says, despite the fact that she's laughing. "Listen, I know you're at work, and I am too, but I need a girls' night."

"Okay?" I say, still laughing.

"What are you doing tonight?"

"Nothing."

"Can I come over?"

"Sure."

"Awesome! I'll bring pizza, and I'll make sure there's enough for Clemmie and Polly too," she enthuses. "Okay, Gotta go."

"Wait! You know I don't eat—" The call drops before I can finish. She set me up. Pizza might as well be glued to my behind as soon as I eat it. Ugghhh! I try to call her back, but she sends me straight to voicemail. She also ignores my text. My desk phone buzzes in the middle of my fretting.

"You have a client," Jolie announces. Well, no more time to worry about pizza.

The rest of my day passes in a blur of individual sessions, and by the time I'm ready to go home, I'm exhausted. I spot Moss falling in behind me as I pull out of the parking lot. Thankfully, nothing has happened since the takeout and cookies, but I still feel safer knowing he and Villain have my back. I haven't heard from Ashe today, but it's not like he's obligated to call me. I'm really curious about why he had to leave so quickly yesterday, but I don't want to be annoying or needy.

Tessa is already in the kitchen talking to Aunt Polly when I arrive. Pepperoni pizza has been cut into small manageable pieces for Clemmie, and she's in her highchair taking a bath in tomato sauce. On the table is an open box. It's a thin crust feta-and-spinach pizza. Apparently Tessa decided to go for the gold tonight since feta and spinach is probably the only pizza I truly can't resist.

"Seriously, Tessa? You know this stuff goes straight to my hips."

"I'm pretty sure it actually goes to your ass, and these days, that's a good thing," Tessa says, eliciting a chuckle from Aunt Polly. She then eyes me up and down. "Besides, you look like you are in desperate need of pizza." She narrows her eyes. "You haven't been dieting again, have you?"

"No. I haven't been dieting. I've just been under a lot of stress."

Aunt Polly backs me up. "She really hasn't been dieting." Then she throws me under the bus. "She also hasn't been eating near enough."

Tessa claps her hands on my shoulders. "Well this is the night we fix that problem with some pizza and gossip." She releases me and snags a plate from the table and a couple slices from the box. "Girls' night calls for wine," she says, looking at me expectantly.

I grab a bottle of Pinot from my pantry. No fancy wine rack here. I pour three glasses and deliver them to the table where Aunt Polly and Tessa are now seated. Tessa wipes her hands and mouth before taking a sip. "Dang! I forgot you always buy the crappy stuff."

"It's not crappy! It's a nice bottle I've been saving. You just think wine has to be syrupy sweet."

"There is nothing wrong with a nice Moscato. You just pick dry wines because you worry too much about the calories to consider the taste," she accuses.

"You don't have to drink it."

"I swear you two fight like sisters," Polly comments in amusement as she contentedly sips her wine. We continue to joke and tease until most of the pizza is gone and Clemmie is a mess. Polly volunteers to manage bath time for me and get Clemmie to bed. Normally, bath and bedtime are my favorite times of the day because after working all day, I need time with my sweet girl, but both Polly and I can see that Tessa is practically bursting at the seams with some kind of news.

"Night, Momma," Clemmie says as I hug her tightly and kiss her on the nose.

"Be good for Aunt Polly and don't splash too much in the bath," I tell her.

"Splash!" she repeats with a grin and a splashing motion with her arms.

"Night, babycakes," Tessa chimes in with a smacking kiss to my daughter's cheek. Clemmie waves bye-bye from Aunt Polly's arms all the way down the hall to the bathroom.

"How did you get so lucky? That baby is a dream," Tessa says before noting my expression. "Oh no, I didn't mean it like that, Eva. Nothing about that situation was lucky. I'm so sorry. I just mean Clemmie is amazing." She hugs me. "That's all because of you."

I blink back the emotion in my eyes, ready to change the subject. "Thanks." I grab the rest of the bottle of wine and my glass then head for the living room to give myself a moment to pull my thoughts back out of the darkness. Tessa follows, glass in hand. Once we're seated on opposite ends of the couch sharing a quilt as is our girls' night habit, curiosity has won out over anything else. "I know you've been dying to tell me something. Now that it's just us, it's time. Spill."

"Well…" Tessa gets a dreamy look in her eyes that has me worried. "I've met someone!" While I know I try to push people away, Tessa is the opposite. She is very open and trusting and believes in the fairytale of happily ever after, the one I know doesn't actually exist. She falls in love easily, but also gets hurt and sometimes taken advantage of, making me a bit cautious and overprotective when she talks about a new man.

"Really?" I ask, trying to sound excited. "Tell me about him." She sets her wine down and bounces excitedly on the couch like a kid. I can't help but laugh. "That good, huh?"

"Oh, Eva, he's amazing!"

"I'm glad he's amazing, but I need real details."

"Okay, okay. He's tall and gorgeous. He has this sort of almost too long really pale-blond hair that kind of makes him look like the hot elf from *Lord of the Rings*. You know the one I mean?"

"Every female with a pulse knows the one you mean," I tease. "Get on with it."

"Right, so he's a hot elf."

I punch her lightly on the arm as we both laugh. "Be serious."

"Okay, he's a *seriously* hot elf." Tessa dodges my second punch with a grin. "All kidding aside, I really like him. I've only known him a couple of weeks, but it feels different, special."

"Where did you meet him?"

"SubZero. I was out with two of my baristas from the shop for drinks after work, and out of all the women there, he asked me to dance."

"Tessa, you're gorgeous, of course he asked you."

"Aww. You're the best friend ever," she says before blowing me an exaggerated air kiss. "Anyway, I had the best time with him. He has these really intense green eyes and dresses in gorgeous suits, but you know what the best thing is?"

"What?"

"He has manners. I've been seeing him ever since, and even though he's started coming into The Daily Grind most mornings, he never demands my attention while I'm working. He just waits his turn and always kisses my hand after I make his coffee. I mean, who kisses hands anymore? It's so romantic! He also pulls out my chair and opens doors for me. To be so strong, he is so gentle." She finally takes a breath and looks at me with stars in her eyes as though for confirmation that this guy is the man of her dreams.

"He sounds amazing, but you haven't even told me his name yet."

"Oh yeah, I almost forgot. His name is Dustin."

CHAPTER 33

Eva

It's been days since I've heard from Ashe. I shouldn't be surprised he could just drop me off and disappear without a word. If my life has taught me anything, it's not to rely on anyone, to handle things myself. I'm so angry, more at myself than anything. I let my guard down with him, let him in my home and around my daughter. I know he's busy and finding Danielle takes priority right now, but he hasn't even tried to send a text.

When I've asked Villain or Moss about him, they just grumble and say he's busy. I thought they were becoming my friends, but they're just covering for Ashe. He pushed himself into my life pretending he cared with his stupid little nicknames, and I fell for it. I'm so stupid. He got the information he wanted, and all I've been left with are nightmares. Concentration is impossible. I just accused my last client of failing a drug screen only to realize the results belonged to someone else. She was scared to death before I realized my mistake.

I need some air and some time by myself without other people hovering. At home, at work, everywhere I go, someone is either with me or following me. I feel like I can't breathe. The nightmares are coming every night, and my appetite is practically nonexistent. I just need to forget about this and get my life back on an even keel.

Before I can reconsider, I head toward the front of the treatment center. There's no good vantage point to watch both the front and rear entrances, so Moss has me under strict instructions to only enter and exit through the back since he stays to the rear of the parking lot. Today, I'm taking the front. My favorite bistro is about three blocks away, and pasta sounds like just the way to drown my stress. Heck, maybe I'll even have the gelato. I head out the security door and stop by the front window to let Jolie know I'll be out to lunch for the next hour.

With my purse secured across my body, I head out on foot, enjoying the walk and the sun on my face. Before Ashe crashed into my life, I used to walk to lunch every day. I miss the fresh air and the time to clear my mind.

Taking a right toward the restaurant, I pull out my phone to check the time and set an alarm, so I won't be late, but the phone flies from my hand and skitters across the dirty pavement as I'm tackled from behind. My cheek scrapes as my body makes impact with the asphalt. A massive weight settles on my back. This can't be happening. It's daylight. People are nearby. Someone will come. I try to scream, but a gloved hand wraps around to cover my mouth.

No way will I be taken again. I buck my body with all my strength and squirm to try to free my mouth. A punch to the kidney stills my movements and steals my breath. My attacker yanks me to my back, and I try to kick.

"Be still, you stupid bitch," he growls through the black ski mask. Not a chance. I jerk my knee up and connect with his groin. His grip loosens incrementally as his body caves in on itself. I fling myself in the same direction he is curled and manage to slip free. "You're dead now," he growls.

I don't stop to respond. I scramble to my feet but manage only two steps before his hand wraps around my ankle, bringing me down again. My chin meets the pavement first, and I bite my lip. Blood fills my mouth and spills down to drop on the ground. I cough, and more blood splatters. My hands scramble across the asphalt, searching for anything I can use as a weapon. A vicious kick connects with my side, and I realize in my disorientation my attacker has gained his footing. I roll into a ball and try to cover my head knowing running will be impossible.

"You thought you were better than me, you stuck-up bitch." Kick after booted kick lands on my arms, my legs, my stomach. I try to scream, but the only sounds that escape are groans and gasps.

"You destroyed my life!" he yells before sitting on my hips and raining down punches. One catches my eye as I try to block another aimed at my chest.

The whoop of a distant siren sounds from the end of the alley, and he scrambles off me. "You'll never be done with me," he taunts as he takes off in the other direction. I stay still for a moment, making sure he's gone before I try to move.

I can't tell if anything is broken, but everything hurts. My phone should still be somewhere in this alley. I spot it up against a dumpster a few feet away. Inching on my side a little at a time, I scrape my palms but don't care. Finally, it's within reach. I snatch it and reach up to grab the handles on the side of the dumpster to drag myself up to a sitting position. My first thought is to call Ashe, but I call Moss instead.

Lost in a haze of pain, I have no idea how long it takes him to find me. "Eva, oh my God!" I drag my non-swollen eye open and look at him. "I'm calling the paramedics and Ashe."

"No," I force out.

"No? What the hell? You need the paramedics. I'm afraid to move you."

"No Ashe."

"Ah, honey, I know he's a jerk, but he needs to know."

"No!" I yell as water fills my eyes. I grip the handle near my head and try to pull up, determined to help myself. Moss's hands are on me immediately, stilling my movements.

"Okay. I won't call him. Just stay still and wait for the ambulance."

I rest my head back against the dumpster and close my eyes. Before long, the paramedics arrive. They try to place me on a stretcher, but the last place I want to be is another hospital. I have Moss help me stand and sit on the gurney while the paramedics check me over. The police arrive right after the ambulance and interview me as I'm being examined. My statement is basically no, I can't identify my attacker. No, I can't describe him other than big. No, I don't want to go to have them swab for DNA because he wore gloves and a mask.

After a few butterfly bandages and some antiseptic, the paramedics recommend a ride to the hospital for x-rays even though the consensus is that nothing is broken. After signing the necessary forms to refuse further treatment, I attempt to make it to Moss's vehicle on my own. My pace is apparently not fast enough because he finally just scoops me up and carries me. I'm in far too much pain to protest.

We arrive home to a surprisingly empty house. "I called ahead while you were with the paramedics and asked Villain to come in early. He escorted Polly and Clemmie to the park. I thought you'd want a chance to clean up before they saw you."

"Thank you," I murmur.

"Let me carry you to your room," he offers, but I decline. No better time than now to stop relying on others. I use the wall to steady myself and make my way to the hall bathroom I share with Clemmie. I purposely avoid the mirror, making time only to take care of business and use a damp cloth to clean off the residual blood and gravel. Once I make it to my room, I gingerly strip off my torn and bloodied clothes and leave them where they drop. Pulling on a soft black T-shirt and a pair of sleep shorts, I fall across my bed on top of the quilt. I hug one of the pillows to my chest and curl around it before I let the sobs come.

CHAPTER 34

Ashe

Thank God tomorrow is Friday. This week has once again been a never-ending series of dead ends. The discovery of Danielle's purse coupled with the new information about a boyfriend should have given us something actionable, but Danielle has been missing for almost four weeks now. We know Eva was missing for almost eight, Amy for nine, and Celia (if we include her) for approximately two months. If Demon has Danielle, she's likely still alive, but not everyone has Eva's strength to survive that type of experience intact. No one should have to. Every day we fail to find her is another day she's at the mercy of a monster, and the thought of being accountable for that is slowly suffocating me.

I haven't spoken to Eva since I dropped her at her house days ago. I get daily updates from Moss and nightly ones from Villain, because even though I need some distance, I would never leave her unprotected. They both seem to have developed a fondness for her and think I'm a jerk for not checking on her myself, but I can't help thinking that being distracted by Eva is causing me to miss something important in the search for Danielle. Eva is safe—Danielle isn't. Danielle has to take priority.

"Yo, Linc! Get moving. You're late," Con says from the door as he lobs a stress ball at my head. I dodge at the last minute.

"Dude, why do you always aim for my head?"

Con just laughs and walks off down the hall. The stress ball rolls under my desk, but there's no time to retrieve it. I snag my laptop and join my partners in the conference room.

"Updates," Rosey demands before I can even grab a seat.

"I'll start." Con turns on the projector he has hooked to his laptop and mirrors his screen on the wall since the whiteboard is otherwise occupied. "I reviewed all the CCTV footage surrounding the gas station in Trussville as well as cameras from other nearby businesses who allowed us access. Unfortunately, with no direct shots toward the restrooms, they won't be any help without a suspect vehicle to compare them to. Fortunately, that's not all I have."

He clicks his mouse a few times, and a list pops up on the wall. "This is a list MRPD sent over this morning. It shows all males named Dustin whose driver's license places them in the range of thirty to forty years old and blond. That's the good news. The bad news is that there are twenty-eight of them, and we'll need to interview each personally."

"Shit, seriously," I groan. "Twenty-eight? I would have guessed like three."

"At least it's something," Rosey says before turning his attention to me. "What have you got?"

I shake my head, "Not a lot of anything. I've been talking to our informants, but no one is familiar with a dealer named Dustin. Most of these guys go by street names, and even a high-priced dealer is unlikely to use his real name. I'm hearing talk of a fairly new guy on the scene working the clubs who goes by Cage. Whether or not it's the same guy, I'm not sure yet. Descriptions have been a bit sketchy."

"I forgot to mention," Con interrupts. "The owner of SubZero has been less than cooperative about releasing his surveillance footage from the night Joey reported being there with Danielle and Dustin, but the MRPD is working on getting a warrant based on the official statement Joey gave at the station after she left here."

"Let's just hope the owner doesn't delete it before the warrant comes through," Rosey grumbles. He stands and walks over to the whiteboard where he has marked several more connections. "I've been trying to find additional links between our victims that might help us catch this bastard. Since drugs were introduced to Danielle's case, I went back and interviewed key witnesses from each of the other three abductions. Both Celia and Amy's friends admitted that they had at least experimented with recreational drugs." He pauses before adding, "Eva's parents indicated the same."

"What the hell, man?" I yell, lunging over the table to get in his face. "You're digging up dirt on Eva now behind my back? She's the victim, not the criminal. She's a damn substance abuse counselor!"

Rosey holds his hands up palms toward me in defense. "Calm down, Linc. No one is accusing Eva of being a criminal. I'm just saying you have a blind spot where she's concerned, and I don't want it to get in the way of saving Danielle."

Damn. He just voiced what I had already been

thinking. I just bowed up at my best friend of ten years over a girl I've known for three weeks. I fall heavily to the nearest chair. He's right. I need distance.

"Look, I know you don't want to hear it," Rosey continues, "but Eva's parents paint a very different picture of her and of the events than what we've been given. I'm not saying they're telling the truth, but I am saying we can't afford to overlook the fact that they might be."

His comments deflate the rest of my residual anger. "I get it. I need some separation to get a clearer perspective. Drugs, damn. How did I miss that?"

Con lays his hand on my shoulder. "For what it's worth, man, I think she's just a good person who made some understandable mistakes in her past. She seems like a great mom, and her coworkers seem to think very highly of her. That said though, Rosey is right. We have to look at all angles, not just the ones we like."

My throat is too tight to speak, so I just nod. As we're leaving the conference room, my phone rings. It's Moss. "Yeah, what's up?"

"We've got a problem. You need to get to Eva's now." When I don't answer, he continues. "Man, she didn't even want me to fucking call you, but you need to get your ass here."

"I'm, uh, busy," I stammer. "Con will be there in a few." I end the call and shoot Con a look. He seems disappointed.

"I heard," he says. "I'm on my way."

CHAPTER 35

Liam

Fucking Linc. I barely even know this girl, and he's tossing her off on me over some stupid comment about her past. I mean, sure, it's a big deal, but it was three years ago, and a lot has changed since then. Admittedly, I don't know her well, but in the time I've been around her, she seemed more shy and sweet than drug addict. Hell, I don't even know what I'm walking into. I should probably call Moss, but I'm practically there already.

When I arrive, Moss is pacing the front porch. If flames could shoot out of his ears, I swear they would be. "Where the fuck is Linc?" he growls as I exit the vehicle and approach. "What the hell is so important that he can't get his ass here?"

I don't think I've ever seen Moss so livid. "Take a breath, man, and tell me what's going on." I stand back a bit until I'm sure he's calm. He runs a hand down his face and shakes his head.

"You know what? Linc doesn't deserve her, and he better not even attempt to come around her again, or he'll deal with me." Whatever happened today must be big. I belatedly notice blood on his clothes.

"Moss, tell me what happened. Tell me now."

"How 'bout I show you?"

He turns and heads into the house. I follow behind, afraid whatever I'm going to see will change everything. Once inside I flip the locks on the door before following Moss down the hallway. "Don't say a word," he whispers harshly. "I've listened to her sob as though her life was ending for the last hour. She's finally asleep. I don't want to violate her privacy, but you're not going to understand unless you see it for yourself. I don't want to see it again, so I'll stay right here."

I gently turn the knob on the door he indicates, careful not to make a sound as I slip inside the room. It's a rather plain bedroom with not much more than the bed, dresser, and a couple of nightstands. The afternoon sunlight ripples through the almost sheer curtains. Nothing in the room is remarkable, nothing except the woman lying diagonally across the bed on top of a quilt.

She's dead to the world in exhausted sleep. Tear tracks line her swollen, bruised, and bloody face. Her lip is split, her eye is black, and a pale bloody trail runs from her nose to the pillow she's hugging. The short sleeve of her black T-shirt reveals a mottled arm covered in bruises and scrapes. Her other arm is hidden underneath the pillow, but I can only assume it looks the same. I fear what may be hidden under that shirt.

My gaze travels down to her legs. They match her arms with scrapes on her knees and bruises covering almost every exposed area, but that's not what catches my attention. The way she's positioned, half on her side and half on her stomach with her top knee bent, exposes the inner thigh of her bottom leg, and I have to turn away. My hand covers my mouth as I gag. I read the file. I know what those marks represent, and the thought turns my stomach. My God, how this woman has suffered. I can't look anymore. It's too much.

Exiting the room, I keep walking until I hit the front porch. "Fuck!" I yell before hurling my keys into the yard. I need to hit something. Fiery anger flows through my veins like lava. Moss steps out behind me, and I whirl around, itching for a fight. His hands are raised in surrender.

"Whoa. I get it, but save it for Linc." He grasps the railing with white knuckles and bows his head.

"I've seen, now tell me," I demand. "How did this even happen?"

"Come back inside. We should probably sit down for this."

We lock up again and have a seat in the living room. The toys discarded on the floor remind me that I haven't seen the little girl. "Where's her daughter? Is she safe?"

"Villain took her aunt and daughter to the park. He's planning to take them out to dinner too," Moss explains. "He'll also be staying inside tonight."

"Good. Now that we've covered everything else, spill." Moss covers the logistics of his protection while Eva is at work and her explanation of why she purposely slipped his guard. I shake my head in frustration. It was stupid. I understand why she did it, but it was still stupid. He goes on to explain how she called him and the condition in which he found her. After he covers the details of her statement and her attacker's threats, I'm furious. I can tell Moss is too.

"Do you want to know what makes me livid about this situation? There she is bleeding all over the place and beat to hell and back and the first thing she says to me is not to call Linc."

"What?" I don't understand.

"She was about to pull herself up off the ground and try to walk off if I called him. Bastard's been ghosting her for days, best I can tell. I've been on her all day, every day, since the beginning. Linc's been coming over, calling, messaging, and all out chasing her then suddenly, a few days ago, gets a lead and pulls a disappearing act. It doesn't take a genius to see he was using her."

"Hey, hold up," I argue. "Linc's not like that. He may have been a bit of a playboy in the past, but he's never been a liar or a user." I'm mad as hell at my partner, but I won't see him falsely accused.

"Well, I went behind her back to call him. He claimed he was busy and sent you, so you know, walks like a duck and all that…" he trails off. "As far as I can tell, she's a good person who's had a shit hand in life. She deserves better than to be all alone and in pain crying herself to sleep." I don't disagree, and I'll be damned if I betray her by breathing a word about this to Linc.

CHAPTER 36

Eva

I lean against my door listening to Liam and Moss talk about me. Tears, more of the stupid tears that never seem to stop lately, run down my face and sting the cut on my lip and the scrapes on my cheeks. I swipe them away, angry that I let Ashe close enough to hurt me, angry that I'm once again the stupid victim who brings everything on herself.

It's my own fault. I chose to leave Moss behind, so I deserve what I got. No matter, I've been closer to death than this. Clemmie needs me this time just like she did last time, and I have to buck up. Emotions will only make me weak right now, so I'm not going to feel them. The physical pain is more than enough to ensure I'm aware of my inadequacy.

Wiping my face on my sleeve, I stand as straight as pain will allow before inching along the wall toward the living room. A floorboard creaks, alerting the men to my presence. Both jerk as though I caught them stealing and stare at me. Ignoring them, I keep making my way slowly toward the kitchen, very slowly.

"Damn it, Eva! What do you need? I'll get it."

I sense Moss but don't acknowledge him. I have the oddly unrelated thought that I don't know if Moss is his first name or last. The urge to ask is overwhelming.

"What's your real name?" I ask without turning his direction or slowing my progress. A sharp pain shoots from my back straight through to my navel. I double over with a gasp, but my possibly bruised ribs protest with the agonizing result of dropping me to my knees. Moss just growls and scoops me off the floor. I hate being carried. It makes me feel fat and heavy on top of feeling weak. I need to be in control. "Put me down, Moss."

He keeps stalking toward the kitchen. Carefully, he sets me in one of the chairs before taking a step back. He stares me down, daring me to move.

"What do you want?" Moss asks in a tone that brooks no argument.

"Orange juice," I reply petulantly. He grabs an individual sized bottle from the fridge and twists to break the seal on the cap before handing it over.

"Well, hello there, Rocky," Liam says, joining us in the kitchen. "I hear you spent the day beating up bad guys." He winks at me before grabbing his own seat at the table. I can tell his levity is forced, but I appreciate the effort. I take a sip of my juice and feel the acidic citrus burn its way down my throat. "Eva, seriously, I'm so sorry this happened to you. I promise you, we will find this guy."

I just nod, knowing it's a lie. Demon has avoided the police for years. "I don't want your protection anymore," I blurt. "Can you just ask me whatever questions you have about Demon and leave? I'll answer everything you ask, but then I want to be done with LCR."

I know I'm being rude, but I'm about to shatter. I need to give them everything they want so they can have no basis for using me anymore. Moss shoots a death glare at Liam, so I stare out the kitchen window to avoid making eye contact.

Liam gentles his tone. "Eva, this guy threatened to kill you. We can keep you safe."

"I can take care of myself. I always have. I'll figure out a way."

"Can you keep your aunt and daughter safe? Can you work and keep eyes on them at the same time?" Liam's tone is deceptively soft before it takes on a sharper edge. "Will you protect them like you protected yourself today?"

My head drops to the table in defeat. I don't really care what happens to me, but I can't risk Clemmie and Aunt Polly. I won't.

"We can keep them safe. We can keep you all safe if you listen and do as you're asked." Ouch. Score one for Liam. "Can you do that, Eva?"

Clenching my fists under the table, I lift my head to look at Liam. "I think you've made it pretty clear that I'm worthless at following directions and keeping people safe, so sure, I'll be certain to shut off my brain and wait for the big men to tell me what to do, but you better keep Ashe away from me."

Honestly, those words sounded more like Julie than Eva, but I'm not sure I mind. They felt good. Standing, I stalk off, well, that's what I saw myself doing in my head. In reality, I use scratched and bruised hands to painfully maneuver myself to standing before retracing the slow steps toward my room. Before I get more than a few feet, I'm once again being carried. "Put me down, Moss!" He earns an elbow to his midsection, but the grunt he releases doesn't slow him down. He sets me gently on the edge of my bed.

"My name is Josh," he says before leaving the room. A few minutes later, he returns with my phone and juice, setting them on the nightstand. "Con is gone, but I'll be inside until Villain returns with Clemmie and your aunt. He'll be staying inside tonight too." As if he senses the protest building, he says, "Please don't argue. We can talk about how things need to change going forward, but let's get through tonight first, okay?"

I nod, and he disappears again. Though my body is on the verge of collapse, I suddenly need a shower. I need to hold my daughter, and I don't want the filth of today, of my attacker, rubbing off on her. Grabbing yet another set of fresh sleep clothes, I head to the hall bathroom. Moss/Josh doesn't try to help me this time, and I appreciate managing by myself. The hot water burns as it meets all the cuts and scrapes, but the pain reminds me that I survived yet again. I wash my hair as best I can since my arms hurt reaching that high, then I just stand under the spray until the water starts to run cold. If a few angry tears joined the water, I'm not telling.

Aunt Polly and Clemmie return within the hour, and though I dread having them see the shape I'm in, I need to lay my eyes on them in the worst way. I hear them laughing in the kitchen as I shuffle to the living room and take a seat on the couch. Villain eyes me from his perch in a chair outside the main grouping. His eyes harden, and his jaw tightens, but he doesn't say a word before returning his focus to his phone.

I feel Clemmie's sunshine before I see her. She runs in from the kitchen but stops short when she sees me. My throat closes with emotion. "Momma, owie?"

Aunt Polly answers for me after taking Clemmie's hand and drawing her to me. "Yes, baby. Momma has an owie. Momma fell. Can you kiss it and make it better?"

Clemmie nods and clambers on the couch and into my lap. Though the tight hug she gives me is physically painful, emotionally it's the most healing thing on earth. I hold her as though I'll never let her go, and my normally rambunctious toddler just snuggles her curls under my chin and lets me. Aunt Polly sits beside me on the couch and places one comforting hand on Clemmie's back while the other runs through my hair over and over. I lay my head on her shoulder and finally, I rest.

CHAPTER 37

Ashe

Distance. I keep telling myself I need distance as I try and fail to concentrate on work. It's been hours, and I'm not sure I've accomplished anything. Eva has been on my mind constantly. I keep wondering what the emergency was, why Con hasn't contacted me, why Eva didn't want Moss to call, and the list goes on. Apparently, the physical distance hasn't translated to my mind yet. Maybe I should make sure Con doesn't need me. I pick up my phone but stop myself before I start to dial.

I can't. I just can't, not after what Rosey revealed today. Drugs are a complete no-go for me. I told Eva my dad and I used to watch late night reruns together. What I didn't tell her was why. Most of the time, we were waiting up for my mom. Sometimes she came home, sometimes she didn't.

When she was clean, she was the best mom ever. She would cook pancakes for breakfast and dance around the kitchen. She loved art, so we'd visit museums and play around making our own creations. Most of them were collages we made from random magazines lying around the house, but I loved them. She was fun, and she gave the best hugs. She showed up for school events and baseball games. She and Dad would even get along. I would see him smiling at her. The problem was that she couldn't stay clean.

My mom was a binge user, which meant she'd have long periods of staying clean (like my whole fifth-grade year), but when she went off the wagon, she went way off. She'd disappear for days or even weeks at a time. When she came home, she'd be dirty and smelly and thinner, always thinner, like she didn't eat while she was gone. Dad always told me she was sick. When she was "sick", she would yell and throw things. When Dad wasn't around, she would hit. I both loved her and hated her.

When I was sixteen, she disappeared again. My father and I stayed up late every night with our reruns, hoping she'd come home. We went to the store and bought the electrolyte drinks and anti-nausea medicine, the soft drinks and saltines, everything we would need to take care of her when she showed up sick. We were ready and waiting, but she never came home that time. She never came home again. The police said it was an overdose. They found her alone, lying on a picnic table in a local park.

The day we buried her was warm and sunny and bright. It was a day for happiness, but none could be found, at least not for us. Neighborhood children made use of the small playground on the opposite side of the church from the cemetery. The sounds of their laughter filtered through the trees and left me wishing for days that would never be again.

I stood with my father beside a gaping hole, awaiting the lowering of my mother's casket. People who thought they knew her surrounded us. They had tears in their eyes, but mine were dry. My dad was sad enough for us both. He needed me to be strong. As I stood there staring down into that hole, I vowed I would never tie myself to someone who used.

It's too much of a risk. Maybe they'll stay clean, maybe they won't. Odds are they won't. Damn, I need to get out of my head. I need a distraction. I grab my keys and head for the door. When I hit the hallway, I run into Moss, literally. I reach to steady him, but he stumbles back before my hands make contact. "Whoa, sorry. I was in a hurry and not paying attention."

"It's fine," he says and heads down the hall toward Con's office without another word.

"Moss," I call after him, needing to know what happened.

"Yeah?" he says without turning around.

"Um, never mind." I walk away and head toward the elevator. I'm not getting involved. I can't.

By the time I make it through the parking lot, both my brain and body are overheated. The inside of my vehicle is even worse. I turn the air on high and debate where to go. I take a right on the highway, turn the music up loud, and decide for now, I'll just drive.

CHAPTER 38

Eva

You'll never be done with me. I woke this morning with those words in my head. A new nightmare joining the old.

Every inch of my body aches, and I dread moving from my bed. I don't have a choice though—I need to go to work. Most of my vacation days were burned when Clemmie was sick a few months ago. The last of them were used when we had the wreck. Aunt Polly is on a fixed income from my late uncle's retirement, and I have paid my way starting shortly after she took me in. I was pregnant and unable to work for the first few months due to extreme morning sickness. Polly dipped into her savings to cover my doctor visits and more until I could care for myself. I won't be the reason she has to do so again.

I roll slowly to my side and push up to a seated position. My bruised arms scream in protest. By the time I'm standing, the pain is excruciating. Coffee and ibuprofen, that's what I need. I move haltingly toward the kitchen. Passing through the living room, I see Villain sitting in the same chair as last night as though he never moved.

"Good morning, sunshine. Can I help?" he asks quickly, coming to offer me his arm.

The kindness of the gesture is unexpected but so appreciated because he actually gives me the chance to choose whether or not I want help instead of taking charge. For that reason alone, I accept. I lean heavily, but he's more than strong enough to support my weight. Thankfully, the more I walk, the less stiff I become. My job is primarily performed while seated, so maybe this day will be more manageable than I think.

"What are you doing up so early? I expected you to sleep in," he says.

"I expected to wake up on the couch," I reply.

"Oh, well, Polly asked me to carry you to your room because you were sleeping so soundly. I hope you don't mind."

"No. I think I would have been even more stiff if I'd slept on the couch." Villain seats me in the kitchen and is kind enough to quickly place a cup of coffee right in front of me before joining me at the table with his own.

"How are you feeling?" he asks, giving me a studious once-over.

"Like I need to buy stock in ibuprofen," I attempt to joke, but the serious expression doesn't leave his face.

"Moss said the paramedics recommended a trip to the hospital for x-rays and scans, but you refused."

"I don't like hospitals. I'm fine." At his pointed look, I rephrase, "I'm not broken. Is that better?"

"I don't know. Is it? You can barely move. Seems to me a hospital trip could have at least provided you with some meds to help with that."

"Yeah, painkillers and muscle relaxers. I'm a drug counselor. Don't you think I know how addictive that stuff is? If I have a legitimate need, fine, but if I can manage with over-the-counter meds, then I plan to."

Villain holds up his hands in surrender. "Fair enough," he concedes. "Where's the ibuprofen?"

I point to the cabinet above the fridge, and Villain snags the bottle before placing it in front of me. After I nod my thanks, we finish the rest of our coffee in comfortable silence. When I push myself up to standing, Villain takes my mug and places it in the sink. He offers his arm again and asks, "Couch or bedroom?"

"Bedroom. I have to get ready for work."

He brings us to a full stop and turns to face me. "No way. No how. Not happening."

"Not your call. I have a daughter to provide for and no vacation time, so yeah, I'm going to work."

"Eva…"

"No. It's non-negotiable, so you can either help me or go sit back in your chair and I'll figure it out myself."

"Fine." He resumes walking. "Moss will be here in a few minutes. At least let him drive you back and forth." I nod. "Good. I'll update him on your plans while you get ready."

Heading into my room, I hear the sound of Clemmie still lightly snoring through the monitor. I'm hoping she'll sleep later than usual after the night we had. Getting out the door will be difficult if she sees my injuries again. I find a soft navy-blue cotton dress that has a little bit of shape to it but won't put pressure on my bruises and pair it with comfortable flats. As I head down the hall to brush my teeth and tame my hair, I hear Villain on the phone. He's trying to be quiet, but I think he also underestimates how much time it takes me to get to the bathroom. He sounds angry.

"What the hell is his problem?" He pauses for a moment. "Whatever, just keep him away from her." He listens for a minute longer. "Yeah, Con, I get it. I'm on board." I lose the rest of the conversation as I arrive at the bathroom, knowing I'll need every possible minute to minimize the worst of the bruises with makeup. Twenty minutes later, I emerge to the smell of eggs and find Moss/Josh has replaced Villain, Aunt Polly is cooking breakfast, and Clemmie is still asleep.

"This is a bad idea. You get that, right?" Moss says in his signature growl.

"Maybe, but so is sitting in this house all day replaying yesterday in my head. Besides, I have responsibilities." By the time I'm seated at the table, Aunt Polly has the eggs done. She hands me a plate with a side of whole wheat toast then a bottle of orange juice. "I don't deserve you," I say to her sincerely.

"Honey, you've brought nothing but joy to my life. I'd be miserable without you." Aunt Polly sets another plate on the table. "Josh, get in here and eat before it gets cold," she yells to Moss in the living room.

His large frame fills the doorway before he takes his seat and plows into the giant pile of eggs and four pieces of toast as though he hasn't eaten in weeks. We finish at about the same time despite his amplified serving size. Moss thanks Polly before rinsing both our plates and placing them in the sink.

While he's occupied, I whisper to Polly, "You knew his name was Josh?"

"Honey," she replies with a smile while buttering her toast, "I know everything." She winks at me just before Moss turns back our direction. "Now hurry up and get going before Clemmie wakes up, or you'll never get to leave."

As we're headed through the living room, Moss asks for my phone. "It's plugged in on my nightstand. Why do you need it?" He follows me to my bedroom and waits for me to hand him the phone before he speaks.

"Con is taking charge of your security and all parts of the investigation related to you. He wants to make sure his number is in your phone for emergencies. Also, he says he may have some video footage later today he wants you to look over to see if anyone on it sparks a memory."

I know I asked them to keep Ashe away from me, but I didn't expect it would be handled so quickly. I nod my assent, lost in thought. I guess subconsciously I'd still held some hope that Ashe cared and would protest being blocked. With the confirmation that I was just a job to him, I shut my emotions down and turn my focus toward surviving the day at work.

CHAPTER 39

Ashe

The long drive yesterday helped clear my head and center my focus. Danielle remains the priority. I've avoided relationships my whole life, and this is not the time to complicate things, no matter what kind of connection I feel with Eva. I won't follow in my dad's footsteps and spend my life pining after someone who allows drugs to take precedence over family, which is exactly how her parents described her when I called them myself last night. I'll make sure Eva is protected, but that's as far as it can go.

While I'm thinking about Eva's protection, I need to check in with Moss. Neither he nor Villain have checked in. According to their usual schedule, Moss should be on the job right now. I dial his number and wait.

"Moss," he answers.

"Hey, you never checked in after your shift last night, and Villain hasn't checked in this morning. I need a status update."

"Sorry, boss. You'll need to check with Con. He said you sent him to take over Eva's protection, said you were too busy." He says the last with a little bit of an edge, but I don't have time to address it now. "Con wanted all future updates delivered directly to him."

"Is that right?"

"Yep. Con said if you had a problem with it, to take it up with him."

"Yeah, I'll do that," I snarl before ending the call and tossing the phone on my desk. I start to use the desk phone to buzz him in his office but decide this is a conversation best had in person. Stalking down the hall, I barge in his office. He's on the phone but holds a finger up letting me know to hang on. He puts the call on hold and gives me his attention. He's calm and relaxed as if nothing is going on. "What the hell did you do?"

He smiles and cocks back in his chair, propping his feet on the desk. "I don't know what you mean."

"Eva," I growl.

"Eva's protected, so what's your problem?"

"What's my problem? You—"

"You wanted me to handle it, right?

"Yeah, but—"

"So, I handled it," he interrupts, righting himself in the chair. "I'm in the middle of an important call, and I don't have time for this shit right now. You want to talk to me, Rosey and I will be in the gym downstairs sparring at 4:00, you can talk to me then. Bring your gear."

He leaves me standing with my mouth gaping and turns his back on me to continue his call. What the hell is going on? I slam the door on my way out. Four o'clock can't come fast enough. Sparring...yeah, I'm going to kill that bastard.

Thirty minutes later, I'm still fuming when Rosey shows up in my doorway. "Hey, can I come in?"

"Yeah, might as well."

"Damn, man, what's got you all pissy?" he asks as he makes himself comfortable in front of my desk. I don't get it, everything's going to shit, and these jerks act like it's just some regular day. "Seriously?" he says when I flip him off. "What is up with you?"

"I don't know, why don't you tell me what's up," I challenge.

"Dude, I don't even know what you're talking about!"

"I'm talking about changes being made behind my back at my own damn company."

"Our company," he corrects. "We're all equal, and we can all make decisions. Which one exactly is bothering you?"

"Con decided to swap everything related to Eva over to him and completely cut me out."

"Okay? And?"

"What do you mean?"

"I mean, why is that a problem for you? Look, we've known each other for a long time. Don't think I've forgotten how strongly you feel about drugs. You made it clear yesterday that you didn't want to be involved with Eva anymore knowing what you do about her using. You should be thanking Con for doing you a favor."

"That's what we're calling it, a favor?"

"Sure, why not?"

"Whatever. What did you need anyway?" I ask, ready to find a new topic.

"You know what, I'll come back later," he says before disappearing down the hall.

I swear, it's like bizarro world in this place today. My partners are losing their minds. That's okay though.

I have no problem straightening them out, and I'm starting at 4:00.

CHAPTER 40

Jackson

I'm not sure why Con decided we needed a sparring session today, but with the way he and Linc have been acting the last couple days, I can't say I mind. We work hard to stay in shape, and sparring is a part of that, but it's been a while.

The gym we share with the other occupants of the building is on the ground floor. Since we were the first tenants, we were able to request a few special additions to accommodate our employees' training needs. One of those was a small boxing ring. Linc is already warming up inside the ropes, so I hit the locker room to change. Con walks in as I'm headed out.

"Don't even think about getting into that ring before I do," he says, shoving past me in a rush. Hmm, this is going to be fun. I smile as I drop my gear bag in front of the ringside bench and take a seat. Linc looks like he's built up a good head of steam. Gloves are the only gear he has on, so I guess we're forgoing the rest. Shoving the headgear and foot pads aside in my bag to dig out the gloves, I push the rest under the bench.

Of our trio, Linc has always been the Romeo. He's a flirt, and he loves the ladies, because he knows the ladies love him. He treats them well and leaves them gently, but he does always leave. Con is our resident comedian. He rarely sits still unless he's in front of a computer monitor. Even then, he's usually bouncing a stress ball or something. Me, well, I'm the people watcher. I'm not the one others usually notice as I blend and observe.

The last couple of days have been very interesting from my perspective. Linc says he needs some distance from Eva, but as soon as he has it, he does nothing but bite people's heads off all day. Now he's ready to pound one of his best friends into the mat.

Con, on the other hand, is keeping something from me, and I have a feeling I'm about to find out what. He rarely gets involved in physical protection even though he's more than qualified. His computer skills are where he shines. Suddenly, he's never in the office and has taken over Eva's protection without consulting either me or Linc. Something's up. If this girl is playing some game pitting my partners against each other, I'll make her wish she was never born, victim or not.

Con drops his bag heavily, narrowly missing my bare toes. "Dude! Watch it!" He doesn't respond, just sits beside me long enough to snatch his gloves from the bag and pull them on, tightening the last one with his teeth. He jumps up and climbs through the ropes without even warming up, facing off with Linc. The two of them look like bulls about to lock horns. I was wrong, this isn't going to be fun, it's going to be bloody.

My phone rings from my bag while Con and Linc slowly circle each other. I dig around, intending to silence the device, but the caller ID shows MRPD. I don't want to miss the show my friends are about to put on, and quite frankly, I may have to keep them from killing each other, but Danielle comes first, and I can't risk missing something that may be time sensitive.

"This is Jackson," I answer.

"Hey, Jackson. It's Carmen from MRPD. I was trying to reach Liam, but his phone keeps going to voicemail. Is he nearby?" she asks.

"He's nearby, but I'm afraid he's a bit occupied at the moment." Occupied works since I can't exactly say Linc just caught him with a gut punch.

"Okay, well I just wanted to let him know we got lucky on that alley footage he wanted from yesterday. China King has cameras in that alley to cover their rear entrance and dumpster. The owner was more than willing to give us access to his security cameras after he heard how badly that girl was beaten. I also wanted him to know that I retrieved the victim's previous report from Detective Ayers and will be investigating both incidences."

What the hell? I'm guessing this is what Con's been hiding. "That's great. Can you send the video to my email? I'll make sure he gets it."

"Sure thing. Give me about five minutes."

She hangs up, and I turn my attention back to the ring. Linc's nose is bloody, and Con's eye is already turning purple. Currently, Con has Linc pushed up against the ropes and is leveraging some fierce body blows around Linc's attempts to block. I'm not sure I've ever seen Con this intense. I stand and move closer to the ring in case I have to intervene. Copper and sweat tinge the air. Linc breaks free from the hold and catches Con off guard with a massive uppercut just as my phone chimes with an email notification.

I open my secure account and click on the video

attached to Carmen's email. Grainy black and white video of a wide alley scattered with dumpsters appears on my screen. I'm familiar with China King, so I know this is not a bad part of town and is frequently used as a shortcut when sidewalks are crowded. A woman with a large shopping bag comes into frame, but she passes by without incident. A few minutes later, another lone woman enters from the opposite direction. She makes it halfway before I notice a large man trailing her. I'm already suspicious because he has on jeans and long sleeves in this heat. His head is down when he comes into view, and he pulls on some type of facemask. His hands are already gloved. It's easy to see what's about to happen, but what does it have to do with LCR?

The man tackles the woman from behind. She tries to fight but is easily overwhelmed by a punch to the back. He flips her over, but his body blocks her face from the camera. The man suddenly curls in on himself, and I can only assume she got in a good blow to the balls. She manages to get free and starts back down the alley but ends up on the ground again when he grabs her ankle. Just before she curls into a ball, I catch a flash of her face.

Holy shit! It's Eva. The fucker hovering over her starts landing kick after kick then sits on her and begins punching. My blood boils, and my hand tightens around the phone. I lose all concept of the fight happening in the ring and begin pacing. I thought nothing could be worse than watching that beating, but seeing Eva dragging herself across the pavement to the dumpster is more than I can take. Fuck me. I practically accused the girl of being a drug addict, ensuring Linc deserted her on the same day she was attacked. Fuck!

This is why they're fighting, only Linc doesn't know it. Oh, shit. Linc doesn't know. One glance shows Linc and Con breathing heavily on opposite sides of the ring, debating their next moves. They're tiring, so I anticipate what's about to happen before it does.

"Are you sleeping with her?" Linc snarls.

"Fuck you!" Con replies wiping blood from the corner of his lip with the back of his glove. "You ditched her, so what do you care?"

Linc charges and plows into Con's stomach, lifting him slightly off the ground before slamming him to the mat. Con lands with a grunt but recovers quickly. Going to the mat was a fatal mistake, and Linc would have known it if he hadn't been blinded by rage. Con uses his superior grappling skills to get Linc locked into a hold. Linc resists but finally realizes he's not getting free. He taps the mat, but Con doesn't let go.

"Stay away from Eva," he orders.

"I'm gonna fucking kill you, Con. Get off me!"

Con releases the hold and rolls away quickly before popping to his feet. I can tell Linc is ready to charge and start this thing all over again, so I drop my phone and dive through the ropes to get between them.

"Stop!" I hold a palm out toward each of them. "That's enough. Linc, go get cleaned up." He starts to argue, but the look on my face must change his mind. He strips off his gloves and drops them over the side of the ropes before climbing through and storming to the locker room. I turn to my other partner.

"Con, is there something you need to tell me?"

CHAPTER 41

Ashe

I'm pretty sure I'm going to throw up. I know I don't deserve to be here, and if she tells me to leave, I will. I barely remember the drive over. In my mind, I kept seeing punch after punch, kick after kick. Just imagining how Eva must have felt shames me. If she'd been in the right state of mind, she never would have left work without Moss. I knew trust was hard for her, and I pursued her anyway then ghosted under pressure. I have no doubt this is my fault. While I wasn't the one hurting her in that alley, I'm the one who made her vulnerable.

When I walked out of the locker room to Con and Rosey both waiting with serious expressions, I knew it was going to be bad, though nothing could have prepared me for that video. Con may have been right to keep it from me at first and to honor Eva's wishes, but even though I'm so grateful he took care of her when I didn't, I can't help but feel angry too.

Regardless of what Eva may have done in the past, I shouldn't have let my own issues color how I viewed her and how I treated her. Hopefully, she'll give me an opportunity to explain. Regardless, she won't be left unprotected, and the coward from the alley will be found and dealt with. I owe her that much. In my mind,

I assigned her the role of distraction even though she only tried to help. I punished her for my own lack of focus. I sat in my office while she suffered.

A knock at my window pulls me from my thoughts. Moss stands with his hands on his hips and murder in his expression. I step out half expecting a punch. "What are you doing here?" he demands.

"I just want to check on her."

"She's fine, so you can go now. She doesn't want to see you."

"Josh," Polly calls from the front porch, "let him in."

Moss doesn't move, but he also doesn't stop me as I edge past him. He shadows me to the porch and tells Polly he'll wait there in case they need him. The damn man works for me. I pay his bills, but he's willing to stand up to me to protect Eva. Obviously, he's the best man for the job. He takes a seat on the small swing while I follow Polly inside. She turns and holds a finger to her lips, motioning me to be quiet. Following her through the living room into the kitchen, I catch a small glimpse of dark and light curls woven together in sleep on the couch.

Polly indicates for me to take a seat at the table, but she remains standing. "You went from sleepover on the couch to drop off and disappear awful quick," she says in a tone more suspicious than angry. "What brings you back now?"

"I don't know," I answer honestly. "This will sound bad, but I don't know another way to explain it. Danielle Hurst is my job, not Eva. I guess I convinced myself that I had to choose between the two."

"Why would you think you had to choose?" Polly

asks before taking a seat across from me at the small table.

"Because every happy moment I spent getting to know Eva, I should have been spending searching for Danielle," I say angrily. "I was distracted."

"Are you sure about that?"

"Huh?" I don't really know what she's asking.

"Let me ask you a few questions," Polly says. At my nod, she continues, "Are you the only one looking for this girl?"

"No."

"About how many people would you say are helping?"

"I'm not sure, the police department, the sheriff's department, my partners, and others. What does that have to do with anything?"

"It seems to me like that's a kind of team, and on a team, some players rest while others work. Let me put it like this, if a paramedic does her job to the best of her ability then later is at home spending time with her husband and kids, is she responsible for someone who doesn't survive a trip to the hospital while she's off shift?"

"Well, no, that doesn't even make sense."

"Should she be on shift twenty-four hours every day?"

I think I'm starting to see where she's going with this discussion. "No. She would burn out, and more people would suffer."

"Exactly. You're part of a team. If you were the only person out there searching for this girl, then I'd back you up and say you need to be searching every minute you're not sleeping, but there are a lot of people looking for her, and while you're taking time to recharge, others are still looking."

"I hear what you're saying, but it just feels wrong to smile or laugh or start a relationship while Danielle's still missing."

Polly places her hand over mine where it rests on the table. "Asher, in your line of work, someone will always be missing or in trouble. You can trust the team you built to have your back while you have a life, or you can forfeit life for the job." She stands, signaling the end of the conversation. "Now, I'm pretty sure there's more to your story than what you said, but I'll let you talk about that with my niece." Her gaze shifts, and my attention is drawn to the doorway where Eva waits.

CHAPTER 42

Eva

There is nothing I want less right at this moment than to see Asher Lincoln, or rather for him to see me. Though I fought in that alley, I didn't win, and the evidence is written all over my body. I knew I probably couldn't avoid him forever, but I wanted to feel strong, not vulnerable, when I did. Here, after a workday from hell, with my pajama-clad body in agony, is the worst-case scenario. The look on his face assures me I look every bit as bad as I feel. Perfect.

I overheard bits and pieces of his conversation with Aunt Polly after being awakened from my nap with Clemmie by the sound of his angry voice. From what I gather, I'm a distraction who keeps him from finding Danielle. Well, I have no intention of distracting him today. I have a daughter who actually wants to spend time with me. "Aunt Polly, can you hand me Clemmie's sippy cup from the fridge?"

Polly retrieves the cup but rather than hand it to me, she waltzes right past me, sippy in hand. "I've got Clemmie. You have company," she says, leaving me alone in the kitchen with Ashe. No way am I staying in this room with him. I turn to follow Polly, not caring if he's left alone in our kitchen.

"Wait." It's not the demand I expect but more of a

plea. It stops me in my tracks. "I promise I'll leave if that's what you really want, but please, Eva, just give me five minutes."

I turn slowly to face him, noticing some slight bruising on his face. "Why should I? You didn't have five minutes to just send a text or anything else after you dropped me off and disappeared without an explanation."

"I deserve that," he admits. "I know I hurt you, and I'm sorry."

"Hurt? No, I'm angry." I don't need him thinking he's important enough to hurt me.

"Eva, Rabbit, please sit down. I can tell you're hurting."

"Don't call me that. I'm fine. I'll sit when you leave." I tighten my aching muscles and school my face to keep him from seeing how much it hurts.

Ashe stands from the table and walks around to face me in the doorway. "I was wrong, Eva. I thought I couldn't have both time with you and time to find Danielle. This is my first missing-person case, and Danielle's father is a friend. It's personal." He shoves his hand through his hair in frustration. "I was trying to do the right thing."

"And I was a distraction, the story of my life. My parents treated me like an unwanted distraction my whole life, and I let them. When I was given a second chance at life, I decided I was done being the scapegoat for everyone else's failures. I won't be your excuse, Ashe. You don't get to put that on me. All I did was try to help you." Angry tears want to escape, but I refuse to let them. "My life was finally normal before you decided to barge in," I yell, causing a spasm of pain to clench the muscles in my back, nearly buckling my knees.

Before I can catch my breath, Ashe catches under my arms and has me pulled up tight to his chest. His hold is gentle. My gaze locks on his, and a heat that should be anger but I'm afraid isn't floods my body. Either way, I don't want it.

"Let me go."

"Rabbit…"

"Ashe, let me go." He slowly loosens his hold, maintaining contact slightly longer than necessary. As soon as his hands leave my body, he pulls out a chair.

"Sit," he commands. I'd like to protest, but the spasms in my back are strengthening, and everything else just aches. I glare at him but carefully settle myself on the chair and shift until I find a position that's comfortable. "Eva, I'm sorry. I don't know what else to say or how to begin to fix this. I misjudged." Ashe rubs his hand down his face in frustration. "I let my experiences influence how I treated you."

My heart softens a little, but trust is earned, and he lost mine. I won't give it back after just a few pretty words. I start to tell him that, but his phone rings, interrupting the moment. He glances quickly at the screen.

"Damn it. I'm sorry, Eva, but I have to take this." He strides out of the room and toward the front door without another word. I halfway expect it will be a repeat performance of his disappearing act. No matter, I'm fine either way.

Standing slowly, I open the fridge for a bottle of orange juice. I should probably buy in larger containers, but I like being able to keep a lid on it in case Clemmie knocks it over or in case I don't finish it and want to keep it for later. Though I don't like to admit it, the feel of the bottle in my hands is grounding for me, always familiar, the taste of the bright citrus calming for some reason. I take a sip and let the coolness flow through my body, washing away the heat.

The sound of the front door alerts me to Ashe's return just before he reappears. "I have to go, but I'll be back." He takes my hand and squeezes it before heading out again. I swap my juice to that hand, allowing the cold to overtake the tingles.

Clemmie seems to be having a conversation with Jo-Bee on the floor and pretending to give him sips of her juice when I re-enter the living room. Aunt Polly looks up from where she sits in her favorite chair reading. "You okay, honey?"

Melancholy washes over me, and I hesitate before I reply, taking a moment to settle on the couch. "What is it about me that says I'm not worth the effort, that I'm a good target? When do I get to be the lucky one, the happy one, the one someone wants?" A tear slides down my cheek just before a small throw pillow whacks the couch right beside my face. I jerk in shock.

"You're lucky you're injured, or it would've been your face," Aunt Polly says, standing angrily with her hands on her hips. "Girl, I'm not about to let you sit here and wallow in some pity party and lie to yourself. There's not a thing wrong with you except piss-poor parents. I love my brother, but he spends all his time chasing after every whim of that creature who gave birth to you instead of being a father. That's his fault, not yours. Your mother is a whole different story, but it would take years to tell that tale. Just know that the problems lie with them, not you."

Polly picks her way around the toys scattered on the floor and sits beside me on the couch, taking my hands in hers. "You have been the sweetest girl ever since you were born. I couldn't have children, but I just know you were put on this earth for me." She squeezes my hands and smiles. "Honey, I've watched you going through the motions of life ever since you moved in. Tessa is the only one you allow close, and you do nothing but work and come home."

"I have to take care of Clemmie," I argue.

"Of course you do, but being a single momma doesn't mean you can't also have some aspects of your life that are just for you. In fact, you'll be a better parent and example for Clemmie if you do."

"Clemmie?" my daughter asks as though wondering what we're saying about her. Dragging Jo-Bee behind her, she reaches the couch and scrambles up between me and Aunt Polly. Jo-Bee falls to the floor, forgotten. She grabs our joined hands, prying them apart and taking hold of one of each. "Mine," she says with a huge smile, looking back and forth between me and Aunt Polly.

"You are most definitely the lucky one, honey," Polly says, looking at Clemmie with meaning. "As for being wanted, I know what want looks like. I was married long enough to tell, and that man who just left had it written all over his face."

CHAPTER 43

Ashe

The sight of Eva bruised and hurting will never leave my mind. Even after seeing the horrific video, I was not prepared for the level of harm that was done to her. Keeping my tone calm and my hands to myself (mostly) was a lesson in self-control. I wanted more time to talk to her, to assure myself that she was truly okay, but the call couldn't be ignored.

The tip we passed on to MRPD from Joey Williams finally resulted in a warrant, and Con called, asking me to meet him at the police station to review the footage. We could finally have an image of Danielle's Dustin to match to our list of locals. Sure, the timing isn't ideal, but police work happens around the clock. They contract LCR, so we work on their timetable.

I pull into the lot just as Con is climbing out of his sports car. "We're meeting Carmen in the second-floor conference room," he says in a clipped tone before walking off, leaving me to follow him. I guess we haven't quite buried the hatchet yet. Fine with me.

Carmen is waiting when we arrive on the second floor. She has the footage queued up on the large wall-mounted monitor. "Ashe, Liam," she greets us before suddenly laughing. "It looks like you two ran into the same door," she quips.

"Yeah, yeah, you're hilarious. Let's get to it. I'm hungry, and it's getting late," Con grumbles.

"Well, come in and have a seat." We join Carmen on the right side of the table facing the screen. SubZero has several cameras, and unfortunately Ms. Williams was unable to pinpoint an exact time since she was performing all night.

Finally, a couple hours and a couple boxes of pizza later, we spot Danielle at the bar. She's alone at first but is then joined by Ms. Williams, whose unique look is easily recognizable. They appear to be talking and getting drinks before they move toward the tables and out of the range of the current footage. We note the time and after about another hour and a half we have a pretty clear picture of Danielle's movements that night. That's the good news. The bad news is that the man we believe is Dustin seems to know all the camera angles, and we barely catch glimpses of his profile. Carmen prints a still image of the most detailed frame. She keeps one and gives a copy to Con, tasking us with trying to get confirmation from Ms. Williams and also seeing if Eva finds the image familiar.

It's close to ten before we exit the police station to the dark parking lot. Con perked up a bit after the pizza, but his banter was with Carmen. Just before we reach our vehicles, Con turns and puts a hand on my shoulder, stopping me. "I know you went to Eva's after the gym. If she let you in, fine, that's her choice, but you don't deserve her."

His lingering anger is evident in his tone. I choose not to argue with him. "I know."

"I really don't think you do. We've been friends

for a long time, man. I can tell when you want someone, and I don't doubt that you want Eva. She's taking longer to get than your conquests usually do, but will the end result be the same once you have her?"

"What exactly do you mean?" I feel my temper starting to flare again.

"You never stick. I get that everyone knows the score, and it's all up front, but Eva isn't built for that."

"What the hell makes you think I don't know that?"

"Oh, I don't know, maybe the fact that you wanted nothing to do with her once you heard she might have some mistakes in her past, but now that she's injured and vulnerable, you're swooping back in like you've got a hero complex or some shit," Con rants.

"Fuck you!" I walk away a few steps and shove my hands in my hair, gripping tight to keep from throwing a punch in the police station parking lot.

"No, fuck you for thinking you can just pop in and out on someone who's been through what Eva has."

"What the hell do you know about what she's been through?" Con just turns and starts walking toward his car. No way am I letting this drop. I chase him down and grab his shoulder to whip him around.

"Answer me! What the hell do you know?" I growl in his face.

"I saw!" he yells, shoving me away.

"Saw what?" I can tell by his expression I'm not going to like the answer to the question, but I have to know. His shoulders drop, and he runs a hand down his face. He stares down at the pavement for a moment, hands on his hips as if he's trying to figure out what to say. My anger begins to transform into fear.

"The marks. I saw the tally marks on her legs," he says quietly. That quick, the anger returns, and I shove him back against his car, my hands wrapped tight in his shirt. He doesn't resist and lifts his hands in surrender.

"It's not like that, man. *You* sent me. *You* didn't want to go. I handled things. When I went in to check on her, she'd crashed out across the bed. She was wearing shorts, and I couldn't miss them." He shakes his head. "I've never seen anything so disturbing. Reading the file and seeing the pictures is nothing like seeing in person the physical evidence of the torment one human being can inflict on another."

I drop my hold, but he remains leaning heavily against the car. "I don't really even know her, Linc, but I know what those marks represent. I can't un-see them, and I can't let her be hurt again on my watch, even if it means I have to protect her from you."

Before I can recover from the shock, Con gets in his car and drives away, leaving me standing alone in the nearly deserted parking lot.

CHAPTER 44

Eva

After a weekend of rest, my body is feeling less stiff, though my bruises are much more colorful. Clemmie has stopped constantly asking me about my boo-boos, and most surprisingly, Ashe has messaged me several times. I really believed I might never hear from him again despite Aunt Polly's words to the contrary.

The first text he sent Saturday morning was just business to ask if I could stop by LCR after work one day to look at some pictures. The next was a quick check to see how I was feeling. A conversation was sparked that continued off and on throughout the rest of the weekend. Texting seemed to make talking easier, and I even found myself smiling a couple of times. I'm not ready to trust him or depend on him, but I guess I'm okay with talking.

For a Monday, work has been surprisingly calm. Mal has grumbled most of the day, complaining that I should be at home resting. Tessa has called at least twice, and Jolie has been a bit of a mother hen, clucking over me while Jake hovers, but the rest have treated me just as they would any other day. My files finally locked away, I'm ready to head to LCR. Well, ready may not be the right word. I don't believe I will ever be ready to look at pictures that could be Demon, but I'm resigned nonetheless.

Jolie pops her head in my door just as I place my purse over my head and across my body. "These are for you," she says and places a beautiful vase full of sweet-smelling wildflowers on my desk. A cheerful "Get Well Soon" balloon is secured around the glass with a purple ribbon. "They're so pretty. I have to know who sent them," she gushes as she places a small elegantly wrapped box beside the vase. As is her habit, Jolie perches her hip on the side of my desk and waits.

Before the lunch delivery incident, I might have just opened the box, but now I know better. Not wanting to be embarrassed by having to ask Ashe if he sent me something, I text Moss. "After everything that's happened, I would just feel better if I have it all checked out before I open it since I don't see a card," I tell Jolie.

"No worries. That's understandable. If it turns out to be something good though, I want to be the first to know," she replies with a wink.

"Absolutely," I agree.

Jolie heads back up front to finish shutting down for the day while I head to the rear staff entrance to let Moss in. He's already waiting and heads straight to my office without a word. I lock up and follow, finding him checking through the flowers with gloves then carefully inspecting the package, which is tied shut with a bow.

"We need to call Ashe and MRPD. There's no card and no store label on this box, and that tells me that whatever's in it is probably not good." Moss confirms what I was already fearing.

"Can't you guys handle it though? Why do we

need the police?"

"LCR isn't equipped to deal with unknown packages. While I doubt a bomb is likely, we can't discount the possibility, so we're going to leave it alone and get everyone out of the building until it can be checked."

After Moss ushers me outside and secures me in his car, he makes the calls. The building is practically empty since we were already closed to the public, so evacuation is quick. Moss convinces my coworkers to go home and stays with me while the bomb squad x-rays the package and clears it for opening.

I'm allowed back in the building, but only to observe. Ashe arrives shortly after and joins Moss and me on the outskirts of the action. Protective gear ensconces the tech opening the box. The ribbon is carefully cut and the lid slowly raised. When nothing happens, my breath whooshes out in a rush, and I relax. Moss and Ashe remain tense and on guard.

The tech uses tweezers to remove a note from the package before placing it in a clear plastic evidence bag he hands to another officer. I realize I'm holding my breath again as he uses gloved hands to open what looks like the top of a zip type freezer bag. The smell is instantly overpowering, and I gag. Moss and Ashe exchange a knowing look over my head and barely react to the smell. The officer in plain clothes waves Ashe over.

"You're going to need to see this to believe it," she says. Ashe asks me to stay with Moss then moves to join her. He reads the note first and balks before holding his shirt over his nose and looking into the box. His eyes widen in shock.

"Is that—" he starts.

"Yep, that's exactly what it is," she confirms. "Ms. Jones, I need you to look at this note and tell me if you have any idea who could have sent it."

Ashe quickly moves back to my side and takes my hand. His actions and demeanor are scaring me. The woman approaches with the evidence bag in hand. Moss takes his cue from Ashe and moves in closer to my other side. She turns the note where I can read the typed message. *Get well soon, Sweet Julie. You're safe now. No one touches what's mine.* As soon as I read that name, my body starts to shake.

"I don't understand." My voice shakes too.

"I'm told you were attacked on Friday," the woman says. I nod my confirmation. "It appears someone is making sure that doesn't happen again."

"How?" Ashe's fingers squeeze mine painfully when I ask the question.

"The box contains ten severed fingers. My guess is they belong to your attacker." Bile rises up in my throat at her words, and my body flushes hot then cold. I retch, barely resisting the urge to vomit.

"Damn it, Carmen! That wasn't necessary," I hear Ashe say from far away as black spots begin floating in front of my eyes.

"She needed to know. She can't protect herself..." The woman's voice trails off as I find myself floating away.

CHAPTER 45

Eva

"Sweet Julie, such a good girl."

Demon's hand tangles in my dirty hair as he lies beside me yet again. I've long since left off caring about personal hygiene, or anything else for that matter. He uses my hair to slowly turn my head to face him.

"Look at me, Julie."

I lay limp in the aftermath and keep my eyes tightly shut as though unconscious, hoping he will leave. His other hand wanders down to where he just carved the thirteenth mark into my skin. A single finger lightly traces the line, smearing the still-wet blood. Though the touch is not harsh, I flinch.

"Ah, so you are awake. Don't you know you can't hide from me, Julie? You're mine now. You belong to me." A tear slips from my closed eyes. "You've done so well, better than all the others. I knew you were going to be the one." At the mention of others, my eyes open of their own accord, seeing only his shadowed profile.

"No," I whisper.

"So many failures. So much time. Finally, you're everything I've hoped for, Sweet Julie." His finger continues to move, tracing each line, each scar, over and over. "Thirteen is said to be an unlucky number,

but I believe it's the opposite for me. The thirteenth mark on my thirteenth wife. It's time, Julie."

Anticipation and fear flood my bones, anticipation that maybe he finally means to kill me, and fear of the possibility that he doesn't. Will he cut deep enough to allow me to bleed out? Will he slit my throat, or will he just leave and never return? I pray for the speed of the first. I wish I could see into his eyes, discern his intentions.

I gasp as his roving hand moves from my legs to another location and the pleasure I love and loathe sparks. Not again. He's supposed to leave now. He doesn't stay. He never stays. I cry softly, lacking the energy to fight anymore. My body betrays me before his begins to move. When he's finished, he lays his head on my stomach and cradles my body.

"You are so beautiful, so obedient. I've waited so long. Our child will be perfect."

"Eva, wake up." The voice is insistent, but I don't want to open my eyes and see the darkness again. I force myself to sink deeper, falling back into the comfort of nothing, my memories morphing into something strange and different, more terrifying.

"I've brought you a present, Sweet Julie. Wake up and meet him." Him? Demon never brings presents. This isn't right. Something's wrong. I don't remember this. *"Julie, wake up."*

My eyes open against my will to find my prison isn't dark. A dim light radiates from one corner drawing my gaze. Somehow the light is more frightening than the dark. "Do you like your gift?" I hear Demon but don't see him. My eyes dart around searching but not finding.

Something glints in the corner. I stand on surprisingly strong legs and take one step then another. No! It's him, the man in the mask. I turn to run, but my feet are stuck to the floor. The man strains toward me, but something is stopping him. Shackles, he's shackled to the wall.

"I promised you'd be safe, Julie, and I always keep my promises. He will never touch you again."

A dark shadow topped with light moves toward the masked man. My heart beats hard enough to push through my skin. My mouth is open, but the scream is stuck. The shadow raises an axe and swings.

"Eva!" A strong shake jerks me from the nightmare. I suck in a breath before turning and gagging. Dry heaves wrack my body, and my still-bruised torso aches. My eyes water as I retch, images of severed fingers flashing in my mind. When I'm finally able to take a full breath, I lay back, my arm bent over my face keeping my eyes covered. I'm so tired of always being the one who's weak when others are strong, and I just want to keep hiding from that reality for a few more minutes.

"Eva, look at me, Rabbit."

"I told you don't call me that." I meet Ashe's blue eyes with a glare. He has the nerve to chuckle.

"There you are. I knew there was fire in there somewhere."

He holds out a hand to help me sit up, but I ignore it and manage by myself. I look around, taking in the unfamiliar surroundings. "Where are we?"

"This is my office. Yours was overtaken with police, and I needed somewhere quiet for you to sleep off the shock."

The fear triggered by the thought of being brought here unaware must show on my face, because Ashe hurriedly reassures me. "Don't worry, I called Polly before we ever left your work. Moss was with us the whole way in the car, and Jillian has been with you since you arrived." He gestures behind us to the woman I hadn't noticed quietly working at a makeshift desk in the back of the room.

"What happens now?" I ask.

"Now we talk about what just happened, dream or memories?" he questions.

"Both." Ashe stands and walks to a mini fridge built into the cabinets at the back of his office. He pulls out a bottle of orange juice and brings it to me. "You like orange juice?"

"No, but you do."

He leaves me speechless and moves to the back of the room to talk to his assistant. I'm floored that he would keep the juice just for me, not knowing if I would ever be here. I break the seal, and the bright scent begins to calm me before I even take a sip. In my peripheral vision, I see Jillian slip out before Ashe rejoins me on the sofa.

"Rosey has the images we needed you to look at in the conference room, but if you're not up to it, I'll take you home."

"I'm up to it." I'm tired of taking blow after blow. I need to deliver one of my own. It's time for offense. After a brief trip to the facilities to splash some water on my face and take care of necessities, I follow Ashe toward the conference room. On the way, we pass a gorgeous woman with bright purple hair mumbling under her breath.

"Misogynist jerk!" I hear as we pass. I don't have to wonder who she was talking about for long since Jackson is the only person in the conference room when we arrive. He looks just as mad as she did and is doing his own share of mumbling.

Ashe clears his throat to get Jackson's attention. While he approaches to talk to his partner, I notice several photographs on the table. Dread clogs my throat, but I won't let anyone else get hurt. Moving purposely, I stare down at the pictures. Each one features a blond man in a club-type setting. The men are all different, and I search for any recognizable traits even though I have no memories of Demon's appearance other than his light hair.

One of the men looks familiar, but not in a dangerous way, more like he might be a client at the treatment center but on someone else's caseload. I sense Ashe move in beside me and Jackson across from me, but I keep my focus on the images. I honestly had expected to be triggered, but nothing stands out. I don't know if I'm relieved or disappointed. Just to be certain, I want to isolate the pictures and take them one at a time.

"Is anything standing out to you?" Jackson asks.

"I'm sorry. I'm not seeing anything yet. Can I move them so I can look at them one at a time?"

"Sure." Jackson picks up a random picture and turns it around. "Each picture is numbered for reference." A black number thirteen is written on the back in permanent marker. He starts to lay the photo back in the array on the table, but I stop him.

"Wait! Thirteen."

"Eva, what are you talking about?" The question

comes from Ashe.

"My dream, memories, whatever."

"Explain," Jackson says.

"He said I was number thirteen. His thirteen…"

"Thirteenth what?" Ashe asks.

"Wife."

CHAPTER 46

Ashe

Wife? What the hell? "Eva, I don't understand." I look at Rosey who looks just as confused as I feel.

"Why don't we all sit for a minute, and you can explain what you mean. I have a feeling this is important," Rosey says before gathering the pictures and removing the distraction from the table.

Eva looks a little afraid but sits and twists her hands in her lap. I let Rosey take the lead since interviewing is his specialty. "You mentioned both dreams and memories. Which one are we talking about?"

"Both. Ever since I was...well, since three years ago, I've had very vivid nightmares. The nightmares are always exact memories of things that happened. My psychiatrist initially described them as flashbacks. Some people have flashbacks while awake. Mine occur while I'm asleep. She said there were too many experiences for me to process all at once, and my subconscious would release things to me as I was capable of coping with them."

Rosey looks thoughtful. "What made you mention this particular dream or memory now?"

"I do my best to keep my memories pushed to the back of my mind. It's the only way I can function normally. If I had to relive those things every day, I'd never survive."

"You were having a nightmare earlier in my office. Was that when this memory came?" I ask.

"Yes. Demon told me he had tried and failed many times, but I was going to be his perfect thirteenth wife." Eva gets agitated. "Don't you see? Thirteen! I wasn't number three. I was thirteen!" She stands and paces. "That means there are more women out there who no one came for. No one ever comes." The last was said so softly, I almost didn't hear it.

"Eva." Rosey regains her attention. "Was there anything else about this dream or any other that stands out or that could help us?"

"I'm not sure. At the end, the dream became more of a nightmare than anything remembered." She's hiding something, I realize. Her eyes dart to the side, and her pacing increases.

"Okay, that's fine, Eva. Can you come back and sit for just a minute? I'd like to go over what we think we know and make sure you can confirm it."

Rosey opens a folder that had been lying beside the pictures on the table. Eva doesn't answer but returns. She sits on the edge of her chair as if poised to run.

"Thanks. I know remembering these things is upsetting, to say the least, so I'll be quick. I'll go through what we have, and if at any time you disagree or think we have something wrong, you stop me. Okay?"

"Yes, okay."

"Demon is a white male believed to be between the ages of thirty and forty years old. He has light-blond hair, but eye color is undetermined. No distinguishing marks like tattoos or birthmarks were observed though they can't be ruled out since lighting was limited. Your impression is that he is tall, and you remember a scent that smelled like sandalwood. His voice was whispered but 'cultured,' and he was well-spoken, which gave you an impression of being highly educated." Rosey pauses and looks up at Eva. "That's all I have physically. Is that all correct?" She nods. "And you didn't recognize any of the men in the photos we showed you earlier?" She shakes her head.

"Okay, let's move on to personality." Eva tenses and looks as though she might bolt but straightens her back and holds herself stiff. Rosey observes her behavior but doesn't comment. "You said other than the cuts he inflicted, he was gentle."

"Yes." Her answer is a whisper, and she seems embarrassed or ashamed for some reason. On pure instinct, I place my hand on top of hers in reassurance, but she flinches away. I give her space but watch intently for any sign we need to halt as Rosey continues.

"He likes to think he is offering his victims a choice by providing essentials to survive and implying they're choosing him if they make use of those things. Loyalty is important to him, and he arranges tests to ensure his victims do not intend to leave him."

Eva suddenly pops up from her chair. "I don't want to talk about this anymore. I know where this is headed, and I won't talk about that. I won't!"

Rosey and I stay seated so as not to spook her. I make eye contact with him and see that we both understand…the rapes. He nods slightly for me to talk.

"Eva, it's okay. You can leave any time you want,

and you don't have to talk about anything else. Okay?" She turns fearful hazel eyes my direction, and the pain in them is palpable. I have her attention, so I keep talking. "Rosey and I would never ask you about that, okay?" She looks skeptical. "Please, Rabbit, we just want to help Danielle and to protect you and your family. Can we talk for just a minute about things that happened before you were taken so we can help Danielle?" Rosey slides the file slowly across the table as a signal for me to continue talking.

"I'll talk, and you can just listen." She slowly sinks back into her chair. "You met him at a dance club like the other women we know of." She gives me another nod. "You remember talking to a man at the bar who was blond and attractive, though you don't remember exactly what he looked like. Things began to blur, and you believe you were drugged, right?"

"Yes."

"Did you take the drugs willingly?"

"What?" Some of the fire returns to her eyes.

"Did you take the drugs willingly?" I repeat.

Her look is incredulous. "You think I don't remember because I was already high? Seriously?"

Rosey tries to elaborate. "New evidence has come to light that Danielle may have been willingly using drugs in the days before her disappearance, and friends also mention some recreational use by the other two alleged victims." He pauses a minute as if debating what to say. "Eva, your parents claim you were using too."

"My parents? Your source of information is my parents?" she rages.

I try to calm her with our usual disclaimer. "We're

not the police even though we work with them. No one is trying to get you in trouble, we just need to know. When the information came in last week—"

"Last week?" she interrupts. "That's why you ghosted, isn't it? My parents said I was a drug addict, so of course I must be. Parents never lie, right?"

"Eva..." I try.

"I'm right, aren't I? I can see it on your face. You didn't want to be dirtied by being around someone like me. Well, you know what, I did try amphetamines once in college, trying to stay up and study for a test. I got sick, had to go to the hospital, and never used them again, but hey, drug addicts lie, so you'd probably better call my parents and verify." She stands. "By the way, those are the same parents who think I made up the whole abduction, so I guess that means you don't need my help after all." She stalks to the door before realizing she doesn't have her keys. "Where is my car?"

"It's down in the parking lot. Jillian has your purse and phone."

She leaves without another word, and I don't attempt to stop her. I'm glued to my seat with regret. I acted on hearsay and didn't bother to look into the background or dig further. I allowed my past to color my view, and I seriously misjudged her. Now I've hurt her again.

CHAPTER 47

Eva

I feel like I'm crawling out of my skin. I'm drowning in anger, and I need to hit something or throw something to get it all out, but I'm stuck in a quiet house with a sleeping toddler. At least the anger keeps me from getting lost in all the fear just below the surface. If I let my brain think about that box, nope, not going there. I've been pacing from the living room to the kitchen and back since Aunt Polly retired to her room after practically squeezing the life out of me and assuring herself I was okay. Now, it's just me, my anger, and the two pints of melting ice cream sitting on the table. I'm pretending I didn't also buy a pack of cookies on my way home just in case I failed to eat all my feelings with mint chocolate chip and black walnut. With so many emotions flowing through my veins, it might take a truck load of ice cream.

Eating my feelings is a habit I fell into once I moved in with Aunt Polly. After so many weeks of truly starving, I found myself pregnant and with access to any food I wanted. Aunt Polly shows her love through cooking. She made me anything I mentioned I craved. I found if I was depressed, cookies made it better, if I was angry, ice cream could cool me down, if I was lonely, mac and cheese felt like comfort. Soon, I didn't recognize myself. I had Clemmie, and I looked and felt like a stranger. Tessa came to my rescue. She helped me find balance and build some control over my eating patterns. I couldn't ask for a better friend. Suddenly, I know what to do. I pick up the phone and call.

"Girl, it's nine o'clock on a work night. You never call late on work nights. What's wrong?" Tessa answers.

"I have two pints of ice cream and a pack of cookies."

"Don't worry," she replies, "I'm on my way. Don't even think of touching a spoon." She hangs up, and I realize I'm smiling. Everything is going to be okay.

Soon, Tessa and I are standing in my kitchen staring at my stash of sugar. "I was angry," I explain.

"I can see that," she laughs. "So, which ice cream goes better with the cookies?"

"Mint chocolate chip," I reply without hesitation. Tessa takes the black walnut and shoves it to the back of the freezer then grabs a couple bowls and spoons.

"Check the cookies and see how many equals a serving," she orders.

"Three."

"Nice, then let's both have three."

Soon, we're snuggled into opposite ends of the couch, facing each other with our treats. "I thought you were coming to rescue me from the ice cream and cookies," I say before taking a small bite.

"Nope. I came to remind you that cookies and ice cream are not bad. Sitting alone and hiding the fact that you're eating two pints and half a pack of cookies is. Moderation, girl. You already know this, or you wouldn't have called me."

I'm still too mad and embarrassed to tell her about Ashe, so I decide to ask about how things are going between her and Dustin while I give the ice cream time to cool me down. Her face lights up.

"He's great! I'm having so much fun with him. He's so old fashioned and does all those things like open car doors and such, plus, he's just flat-out hot. I mean, it's nothing serious yet, but I really like him." Suddenly she frowns.

"What's that look for?" I ask.

"Nothing. One of my baristas is just jealous and keeps making up negative things to say about him, claiming they're rumors she heard."

"Are you sure that's all it is, just rumors?"

"Yeah, definitely." She turns her laser focus on me. "Enough about Dustin. I came here for you, so quit stalling and spill."

No way do I want to relive the events at my office, so I focus on Ashe. "Do you remember that time when I was in college and I tried the diet pills my roommate used to help her stay awake and study?"

"Of course, you were so sick!"

"Yeah, well, my parents have decided that one incident is an indication that I was a drug addict and have made their opinion known."

"That sounds like something your parents would do. Why are you surprised?"

"I'm not. What surprised me was Ashe accusing me of taking drugs willingly the night I was taken."

"Wait. What? No!" Tessa's spoon clinks into her bowl.

"Yeah. I was meeting with him and Jackson to see

if I could identify some pictures, but when I couldn't, they started telling me that they found a history of drug use connecting me to the other victims." The anger washes back over me in a wave, and I realize I've been jabbing my spoon into my ice cream and have crunched up all the cookies.

"First of all, you are not a victim, you are a survivor. Secondly, who cares what they think?"

"I do! I've worked so hard to be someone different, to put my past behind me and be a better person for Clemmie, be the kind of person who deserves to be happy. I'm nothing like I used to be, but it seems like my past just won't go away. I'm never going to outrun it." I swipe my hands angrily across my cheeks, mad that the stupid tears I haven't cried in years suddenly won't stop.

Tessa sets her now-empty bowl on the coffee table and scoots closer on the couch to pull me into a hug. "You know what? That's exactly the problem." She pulls back and looks me in the eyes. "You've divided yourself into two people, Julie and Eva, but both are just you."

"No. They're not. I left Julie behind."

"Right, you left everything behind, but did you ever consider that maybe you left some good things behind too?"

I shake my head. "I don't understand." My ice cream has turned into a melted mess, so I move back from her hug and set it aside.

"Eva, you never used to be worried about what other people thought. Sure, you took that to extremes sometimes trying to piss off your parents, but you were feisty and fearless, and so much fun."

"I'm a mom now, Tessa."

"And? Moms can't be fun and fearless?"

"Umm, I don't know…"

"Eva, you had your faults when you were younger, but at least you lived life. Yes, you've worked hard and made a lot of positive changes. You're an amazing mom, and you have a fantastic career that helps people, but you don't really live. I've watched you turn yourself into the image of what you think everyone wants you to be, but you've lost your spark, your own original personality."

I hit her with one of the nearby throw pillows. "I have personality."

"You work and come home. You wear boring clothes and eat boring foods and avoid any appearance of fun."

"Wow, tell me how you really feel," I snark. Sarcasm is the only shield I have against the pain inflicted by her words. Sure, I avoid conflict, and I don't like to call attention to myself, but I'm just trying to keep us safe.

"You need to accept that not everything about your past was bad. You didn't cause what happened, and obviously all the changes you made didn't keep this sick freak away. I just want you to find a way to bring back the good things like your determination and spontaneity. You, more than anyone I know, deserve to have a life filled with fun and laughter and someone special to share it with, but you have to give yourself permission to be happy."

"It's not that easy," I say, though I wish it was.

"I know, but one day Clemmie will take her cues from you, so live how you want her to."

"Even if that means I make mistakes like getting close to a guy who thinks I'm a drug addict?"

"Yes. Even then. Mistakes are part of life. Asher Lincoln made a big one today, and my bet is that it won't take long for him to realize it. Just be sure to make him grovel."

CHAPTER 48

Ashe

"Ashe, Detective Castillo is on line two," Jillian's voice announces from the speaker.

"Thanks," I reply before picking up the line. "Carmen, good morning."

"Yes, it is," she says, sounding surprisingly chipper.

"That sounds promising, what've you got?"

"First things first, we lucked out and got a quick hit on the fingerprints from that little gift on Monday. Turns out the victim was already in our system with a warrant for domestic abuse and child endangerment. We still don't have any leads on who killed him, but his name is Gerald Manchester."

"That name doesn't sound familiar."

"I already sent a copy of his driver's license."

I pull up the secure email account and open the image. Manchester is a large forty-three-year-old man with receding dark hair. "I don't recognize him. Any idea how he connects to Eva?" I ask.

"Yep. That's where things get interesting. Mr. Manchester was reported missing Sunday evening by his wife. She and the kids had been gone for several days but returned home to find furniture overturned and a small amount of blood splattered on the floor."

Carmen pauses for effect.

"Okay, I'll bite. What exactly makes that interesting?"

"The wife had apparently been convinced by her counselor to leave Manchester and take the kids with her to a domestic abuse shelter. While there, she filed the charges that helped us make the ID. I'll give you three guesses who her counselor was, but I'm guessing you'll only need one."

Damn. "Eva."

"Ding! Ding! Ding! Give the man a cookie."

"You're such a smart ass, Carmen," I reply without ire. "So, what was the wife doing back at the house?"

"Can't you guess? He called Sunday morning and said he was sorry. They were going to get back together," Carmen scoffs. "I know. I know. I sound jaded, but I've seen it one too many times."

"I thought they weren't allowed to keep their phones at the shelter."

"You thought right, but somehow, Mrs. Manchester managed to sneak hers in, just in case."

"Nice. So, I guess the working theory is that Manchester attacked Eva because he somehow knew she helped his wife and kids escape?"

"Exactly," Carmen confirms.

"Was there any other evidence in the package that might help us identify who attacked Manchester?"

"None. That package was completely clean. Who knows though…maybe we'll find Manchester still alive and be able to ask him."

"You really believe that?" I ask, already knowing the answer.

"Not at all," Carmen says before ending the call.

I immediately message Rosey and Con to head to my office for an update. Rosey replies that he's out finishing up a few more interviews related to our Dustin lead, but Con shows up without a reply and falls to a seat, propping his feet on my desk as usual. "Yo. What's up?"

"We know whose fingers were in Eva's gift."

"Damn! Already?" His feet drop, and he sits up straighter. "It's only Thursday. How do we have results after only three days?" Explaining the details of my conversation with Carmen, I watch as surprise slowly washes over Con's face. "Okay, so what now?"

"Now we hope MRPD finds Manchester. I think we have to assume Demon is the one who severed the victim's fingers, so even if Manchester is dead, there may be evidence with the body that can help identify Demon and find Danielle. As for us, we keep hard and heavy on the Dustin angle and start reaching out to some of the smaller rural law enforcement offices. Maybe they have similar cases that were never entered into the state or national databases." I run a frustrated hand through my hair. "I just can't get Eva saying there were thirteen victims out of my mind."

"What if she was just dreaming? She never mentioned that before from what I've read in her file." Con plays devil's advocate.

"It won't hurt to put a couple of interns on the phone calls. If they don't find any leads, then we're out nothing."

"Okay, I'm game." Con stands and turns to leave.

"Wait."

"Yeah?" he says, turning around.

"How is she?" I know better than to ask, but I have

to know. I've messaged her every day, just checking on her, but she never replies.

"Who? Are you asking about my drug addict friend?" He answers my question with his own, the side of sarcasm not unexpected.

"No. I'm asking about Eva, and you fucking know it." I trust my friend, but my anger at his ability to talk to her and see her when I can't infuriates me.

"Oh, I'm sorry, I thought they were one and the same in your mind." Apparently, his temper is flaring too. Maybe another round in the ring is in order. I bolt to my feet and move to go around the desk, but my progress is interrupted by Rosey's entrance.

"I guess I can't leave y'all unattended anymore." He puts a hand to Con's chest and pushes him back into the chair. He motions for me to sit as well. I start to balk, but the serious expression on his face makes me reconsider. "Shut it down," he says before finding his own seat. "We have more important things to talk about." Both Con and I sit silently and wait. "I think I've found our Dustin."

"Finally!" Con bursts out. "Who is he?"

"I can't prove it yet, but I believe his name is Dustin Grimes. I just sent Karo to start surveillance and get some photos we can show Joey Williams." Karoline Costner is one of our newest investigators, but she's sharp and motivated. She'll get the job done.

"Why him out of all the Dustins on the list?" I ask curiously.

"I had Con pull the surveillance from the parking lot of SubZero for the night Williams reported Dustin was there. I knew it was a long shot since he could have parked somewhere else or driven someone else's vehicle or possibly not driven at all, but hoping for only one Dustin, I ran the plates. Unfortunately, I came up with no owners with the first name Dustin. I did, however, find James Dustin Grimes."

"Okay, that's a pretty good indication," Con says. "How do you want to handle it?"

"I already notified MRPD, and like I said, Karo is watching him. I plan to alternate surveillance between her and Spock. Hopefully, he'll screw up and lead us to Danielle. I don't want to tip our hand too early and end up catching him but losing her because he refuses to give up the location."

"Let me know when you have the pictures from Karo. I'll meet with Joey and let her review them." Con smirks, deliberately trying to rile up Rosey.

"Like hell you will!" Mission accomplished. Rosey is pissed.

Con just laughs. "That was too easy." Rosey flips him off, and Con laughs harder.

Not one to miss out on the rare chance to see Rosey truly riled, I start in too. "I'm pretty sure Joey called you a misogynistic jerk the last time she was here. She probably would prefer Con follow up with her."

"Well, if I'm a misogynistic jerk, then she's a—" Rosey reconsiders. "Never mind. I'm not interested in being manipulated by you idiots. I have things to do."

"I'm sure you do." Con's tone is ripe with innuendo and trash talk.

Rosey flips him off again on his way out the door and chooses not to respond. Chuckling, I send Con out of my office too, the tension between us lessened. I need to try to contact Eva again. Not knowing how she's coping with Monday's events is frustrating and worrying.

"Hey." I jump at Con's unexpected re-appearance in my doorway. "Eva, Clemmie, and Polly are all fine. I stopped by to check on them yesterday after work. Just be aware, she is not your biggest fan right now."

A sense of relief flows over me, followed by a renewed determination. It looks like I have my work cut out for me.

CHAPTER 49

Eva

Once again Clemmie and I are spending our Saturday at the splash pad since the only way to tolerate the daytime Alabama heat is to add water. As is becoming his habit, Moss has joined me rather than staying in his vehicle. We sit on one of the many wooden benches circling the tangle of dripping kids. Clemmie's neon-green swimsuit combines with her bright hair to make her easily identifiable among the many toddlers. Her happy laughter has me smiling as she stomps hard enough to splash water higher than her head.

"You should do that more often," Moss comments.

"Do what?" I ask, shifting to better face him.

"Smile."

"I do smile," I argue.

"Not enough, and only with Clemmie," Moss counters.

"You sound like my best friend. She was on my case this week too."

"Is that the cute blonde at the coffee shop?" He looks more than a little interested.

"She'd prefer fierce, spunky, or hot to cute, but yeah, she's the blonde who owns the coffee shop. Her name is Tessa."

"Hmm. So she would agree with me?"

"I don't know. Maybe…Probably."

"Well, at least that was clear," he teases. Since the incident in the alley, Moss and I have become friends. Maybe it's because he couldn't look more different from Demon with his smooth dark skin and bald head, or maybe it's just his personality, but I feel relaxed and safe with him.

"Sorry. Yeah, she'd agree. She says I'm boring." Moss lets out a surprised chuckle. "It's not funny."

"Yeah, it kind of is," he replies just as a blast of water hits him right in the face. I can't help but laugh at the shocked look on his face and the happy one on my daughter's.

"MoMo wet!" she squeals before dropping her bucket and clapping.

"MoMo is coming to get you, little one." Moss jumps up and pretends to chase my giggly little girl. When he returns, Clemmie is laughing and squirming in his arms, trying to get away from his tickles. He plops back down on the bench, but Clemmie doesn't stay. She wiggles her lime-green-clad body off Moss's lap and runs back to the never-ending splashing.

"Well, at least it's a million degrees out here. I should be dry in about two minutes," he says while lifting his soaked shirt away from his skin and smoothing a hand over his head to catch the drops trying to fall into his eyes. "Back to our conversation though," he resumes while helping me keep eyes on Clemmie. "Why are you boring?"

"I didn't say I *am* boring, just that Tessa thinks I am. She thinks I left my personality behind when I moved on from my past. I, uh, I just needed, well…"

"Eva, you don't have to talk about this."

"No, I need to." I take a deep breath and just launch in. "I needed to reinvent myself so I could make sure I never did anything to attract attention again, so Clemmie and I could be safe."

"So you made yourself boring?" Moss jokes to lessen the tension and ease my anxiety. I smack him on the arm.

"Not boring, safe. I thought I made myself safe." I focus on my daughter, watching her smile and play, envying her freedom from worry. "I was wrong though, or you wouldn't be sitting beside me right now."

"Safe can be a lot of different things. Sometimes safe is hiding and blending in, but sometimes safe is being fierce and fighting. Eva, evil people will always be out there, and you are *not* responsible for that evil. Some things are just random. You didn't cause what happened to you, and by spending your future trying to mold yourself into the opposite of what you think he, or others like him, would want, you're letting him continue to control you."

A feeling of rightness settles over me at his words, and I sense this is what Tessa was trying to express. I didn't cause my abduction, and changing myself into someone completely different didn't keep Demon from coming back. I lean over and squeeze Moss in a spontaneous hug that surprises us both. "Thank you."

"Anytime, Eva."

"Something I need to know about?" The angry voice comes from directly behind us, and I have no doubt who it belongs to.

"Wink!" Clemmie launches herself at Ashe just as he steps even with the bench. She latches herself around his left leg, turning his light gray dress slacks dark with water and dripping on his leather dress shoe. Ignoring all of that, he lifts my daughter against his chest and bumps his nose against hers.

"Hello, sweetie." She giggles as they rub noses, and my angry heart melts just a little.

"Lo, Wink," Clemmie says and waves her hand as though they aren't just inches apart. A familiar squirming gives me a clue to her next words. "Wink, potty."

Knowing time is typically limited once she makes her announcement, I jump from the bench and pry her clinging body from Ashe's arms. He has a bit of a deer-in-headlights look as Clemmie whines and cries for him to take her. "Shhhh, Clemmie. Come with Momma, then you can go back to Ashe." I realize my mistake just as the word exits my mouth.

"Ass, Ass, Ass," Clemmie chants, drawing stares from indignant moms and quiet laughter from Moss and the few dads present. I cover her mouth with my hand and hurry her into the restroom.

By the time we exit, everyone is back to playing, and Moss is nowhere to be seen. Ashe is leaning against the back of a bench waiting for us, his half-wet clothes and sad expression giving him a surprisingly vulnerable look. Clemmie breaks my grip and flings herself into him, eliciting a grunt before he lifts her once again. She immediately lays her tangled curls against his chest and sticks the third and fourth fingers of her right hand in her mouth, something she grew out of but still does when she is very tired.

"Where's Moss? I think it's time for us to head home." Ashe follows me toward the bench where our bags still sit.

"I let him go for the day. I'll follow you home, then we need to talk," he says authoritatively, sparking my anger.

"And if I don't want to talk?" I ask.

"You do," he states decisively while following me toward my finally repaired SUV with my exhausted daughter. I unlock the doors, and he deftly fastens Clemmie into her car seat. "Go straight home," he orders before heading to his pale-gray truck.

Why I obey is a mystery to me, but I take the short route home with Ashe's truck on my bumper the whole way. He follows me inside but stays in the living room as I detour toward Clemmie's room. Quickly stripping her of the wet swimsuit, I help her into a soft pair of pajamas. She continues sucking her fingers and closes her eyes as I lay her down. I check to ensure the monitor is on and grab the receiver from my room before rejoining Ashe in the living room. Aunt Polly is out with a friend, so I'm alone in the house with a man. The thought should scare me, but it doesn't.

"What do you want, Ashe?" I ask, setting the receiver down on the coffee table.

He takes a step closer and counters with a different question. "So, you and Moss?"

"Yes. I'm sleeping with Moss and dealing drugs on the side. Anything else you want to accuse me of?"

CHAPTER 50

Ashe

The sarcasm in Eva's voice is surprising, and judging by her wide eyes, it caught her off guard too. I can't help the smile that tips my lips. That hint of fire is like a spark reigniting my need to chase her. Her lips tilt up in response to mine, and suddenly we both collapse into laughter. Eva instinctively grabs my bicep for balance, consumed with amusement, and without thought I pull her against me. I see heat in her eyes at the contact, but unfortunately, there's also a touch of fear lingering behind that gaze, and it has me locking my jaw to keep from devouring her mouth.

Gripping her upper arms, I carefully move her away from me and pace toward the door, willing my body under control. With a deep inhale and a slow exhale, I turn back around only to register rejection in Eva's hurt expression. "Don't even think it, Rabbit. I want you, but we both know you're not ready."

Blue-and-green sparks light her unusual hazel eyes, signaling the return of anger. "Why are you here, Ashe?"

"We have some new developments in the case that we need to discuss."

"If that's all, Liam was here yesterday and updated me. He already showed me new pictures, but I still couldn't identify anyone. He also told me about Manchester, but I can't talk about that due to confidentiality issues, and frankly, I don't want to even think about it."

"That's not all, Eva. Can we sit?" She reluctantly nods, and I settle on the couch while she chooses the chair farthest away. "The last time you were at LCR, you mentioned the number thirteen in relation to Demon. We made some calls to smaller, more rural law enforcement agencies and found two cases we believe match."

Eva sucks in a gasp, and her face pales. "Who are they? Where are they?"

"Hold up, Rabbit, let me finish." She nods, and I continue, "Both victims are unidentified. One woman was in Woodstock, about two hours from here, and the other was in Waterloo, a small town up north near the Mississippi state line."

"Were they recent?" Her voice holds a slight shake, and her hands are tight on the arms of the chair.

"The Woodstock case was reported a little over four years ago, but Waterloo was only six months ago." I can tell from the way her body jerks that she caught what I didn't have to say. Demon may not have stopped after her, and thirteen may only be the tip of the iceberg.

"I told the police everything I could remember. I swear I did."

"Eva, you were drugged and starved and tortured. You did all you could. This isn't on you." She nods but doesn't look convinced.

"How do you know they're connected?" I know she'll be upset by the answer, but I won't hide it from her.

"The bodies had cuts and showed signs of captivity, plus the circumstances of the disappearances fit the profile." An anguished cry escapes as she buries her face in her hands. I move to kneel in front of her and place my hands over hers. "There was nothing you could do."

"Why, Ashe? Why does no one ever come?" She lifts her head just enough to uncover her grieving eyes. "How does he know no one will come?"

"I don't understand, Rabbit. What do you mean? Help me understand."

"When he had me, I kept hoping someone would come, someone would care that I was missing and come to find me, but my friends were all new and barely acquaintances, my parents and I had never been close, and Tessa was away at college. No one cared."

"I'm so sorry—"

"No!" she interrupts. "You don't understand. No one came for these women either. No one even knows their names. How does he know?"

My jaw drops. *Damn.* Eva just made a connection we haven't considered. The victims may have all been disenfranchised in some way, alone. Maybe the victims weren't random at all.

I stand and pace while calling Con to explain the theory and have him start working through it. All the while, Eva watches me, the colors in her eyes seeming to shift with my direction.

"I need to know, Ashe. People keep telling me it was random, and I wasn't to blame, but what if it wasn't? What if it wasn't random? What does that say about me?"

"Random or not, Rabbit, it says nothing about you except that you're a fighter and a survivor."

"Ashe, there's something else you need to know. Something important that may influence his choices. You know he said I was his 'wife', but…" Eva takes a deep breath and seems to be reconsidering what she wants to say. Whatever it is, I can tell it's going to be a game changer. "He, Demon. He wanted me to…" She brushes her hands down her thighs and stands. Disappearing into the kitchen, she returns shaking a bottle of orange juice that she never opens. "What I'm trying to say is that Clemmie wasn't an accident. Demon's sole purpose was to create a family. He was trying to make the perfect child, and he did."

Sitting stunned in her brightly colored living room, I stare at all the toys scattered haphazardly over the floor and think about sweet Clemmie, about the courage Eva must have had to go through with the pregnancy. My heart nearly breaks thinking about what might have been if she hadn't, since that little girl already owns a piece of it.

The more I dwell on the revelation though, my emotions shift. Most of all, I'm angry that Eva was targeted and forced to become a mother before she was ready, but also because she withheld information that could possibly have changed the way we approached our search for Danielle. My thoughts are completely conflicted. It's not like I hadn't guessed Eva's pregnancy might have been a result of her captivity, but I assumed it was accidental rather than planned. Our profile will now need to change knowing Demon's key purpose is to create a family.

"Why would you keep something like that a

secret?" Anger seeps into my voice. "You know how important every detail is to finding Danielle."

"Yes, I do know. That's why I'm telling you now," she responds defensively.

"Well, let's just hope it's not too late."

"Don't put your failure to find Danielle on me. I didn't have to help, but I ripped myself to shreds trying to do so."

"You told us a redacted version despite knowing a young woman's life was on the line."

"You forget that I have another life in my hands," Eva says quietly.

As the minutes roll on, we sit awkwardly ignoring each other. I vacillate between wanting her to explain further and not wanting to let go of the anger. The anger serves a necessary purpose by keeping me from feeling too much for her or acting on those feelings. I'd almost kissed her, and just that much almost scared her to death.

She's too damaged, and I'm not cut out to be a dad. We just aren't meant to be. I decide it's time to let my rabbit go.

My phone rings, a welcome interruption to the silence. The news I receive leaves me in shock with no choice but to go. I start to explain, but instead walk out without a word. I convince myself it's what's best for us both.

CHAPTER 51

Jackson

Locating JoBeth Williams was not a simple task. The woman apparently lives like a nomad, roaming wherever the wind takes her. I had Con do a little research, and it turns out she earned a master's degree in music from University of Alabama but prefers performing to teaching. Her band, Bygones, tours mostly the tri-state area of Georgia, Alabama, and Tennessee.

According to their website, the band isn't scheduled to be back near Magnolia Ridge for a while, so I made the three-hour drive to catch this Saturday night show just outside of Nashville. Armed with Karo's pictures of Dustin Grimes and those of a few similar-looking men, I'm ready to get a positive ID and close in on Grimes. Sure, I could have emailed the pictures, but the woman got the best of me at our last encounter, and I aim to even the score.

The venue is a small, renovated warehouse that probably hosts around a thousand people. Once I endure the search, pass through the metal detectors, and have my ID scanned for the bracelet proclaiming me old enough to drink, I find it's standing room only. I make my way to the horseshoe-shaped bar and procure a bottle of locally brewed beer before wandering lazily

Elisabeth Scott

through the crowd, listening and trying to get a feel for the room. Bygones is opening for a popular country band who started out local, but judging by the conversations around me, Bygones has a pretty heavy following too.

Finding a spot to the right of the stage, I check my phone while I wait, only to find several missed texts and voice messages. It's been oddly dormant, but with the hectic pace of my day, I haven't had time to notice. I started out in court a county over, testifying on an older LCR case. Court was followed by a visit to Carrie Manchester for an interview that stretched on into eternity but yielded no new information that might help us locate her fingerless husband. Finally, I hit the road to Nashville with my favorite podcast keeping me company for the drive. I must have forgotten to take the phone off silent after court.

I've missed calls from both Con and Linc. The venue is playing background music, and the chatter from the crowd adds to the noise level, but I try calling Linc anyway. When the call goes straight to voicemail, I hang up and try Con, but he doesn't answer either. I make sure my phone is on vibrate rather than silent and shove it in my pocket.

Within minutes, the canned music cuts out as soft, cool lighting floods the stage. The crowd cheers as a guitar player and drummer enter followed by a keyboardist and surprisingly, a girl with a trumpet. The crowd never ceases its adoration as the band strikes up a slow swinging jazz tune. I grew up listening to jazz with my grandmother and find myself mesmerized by the rhythm. The volume surrounding me reaches earsplitting levels as Joey takes the stage.

Tonight's outfit is another retro-styled dress, this one with huge red flowers on a black background paired with some kind of red chunky heeled shoes. Her purple-and-black hair is curled in a manner reminding me of WWII pictures, and her sexy ink marches up and down toned arms. She takes the mic, and I nearly swallow my tongue at the sultry, smokey voice that proceeds from her cherry red lips.

I stand mesmerized throughout a performance that is over way too quickly. The local band that follows is pretty good, but I'm only hanging around to catch Joey once the show's over. I make my way to the merchandise tables in the lobby, and shortly after the last performance, she appears. Close up, her appeal is only more captivating, but this is business, at least that's what I'm telling myself.

Propped up against the wall, I watch as both men and women fawn all over her, gushing about everything from her singing to her sense of style. It's a little nauseating. Once the crowd thins to the stragglers and those a little too intoxicated to drive, I make my approach. Her eyes narrow when she sees me, and I can't help the smirk that forms as I see the irritation on her face.

"Hello, *Joey*." I'll never understand why a girl who looks like her wants to go by a stupid guy name.

"Hello, *Rosey*." Ouch. Apparently, two can play at this game. "Such a sweet name for such a sour jerk," she quips, turning her back and shifting to the other end of the merch table. Weaving through the few people still purchasing T-shirts, I place myself directly in front of her again.

"We need to talk," I state.

"I find that highly doubtful. You said enough the last time." Yeah, we didn't leave that meeting on the best of terms, but she's not leaving without looking at the pictures I brought.

"We may have found Dustin." That got her attention. She moves to a door behind the table and motions for me to follow, assuring the security personnel monitoring the entrance that I'm benign. I track her swaying, flower-covered hips through a crowded hallway before we end up in what I'm guessing is the band's green room or waiting area.

"Explain," she demands. I shift the bottles of warm beer and flat soft drinks to one end of the table in the middle of the room. Pulling the envelope of pictures from my back pocket, I arrange the numbered images in an array before asking Joey whether she recognizes anyone. She barely glances at the pictures before she snags the fifth image and shoves it toward my face. "This one. This is Dustin."

Just as I suspected, she identified James Dustin Grimes. "Are you certain?"

"Do I look like I'm not?" she snarls.

Man, this woman is touchy. "Just answer the question."

"Yes, Rosemary, I'm sure."

I growl, and she just grins. "Take a minute to really look at all the images—"

"I just told you," she interrupts, "I'm sure. I saw him last week at our concert in Atlanta. I'm not likely to forget what he looks like in a week."

The other members of the band begin trickling in, staring at us curiously. I grab the pictures, including the one still in Joey's hand, and place them safely back in the envelope before returning them to my pocket.

"Who is he?" she demands. "I can tell you know."

"No one you need to worry about. If you see him again, steer clear and call me."

"Why? Did being born with boobs render me incapable of protecting myself? Do I need big, strong Rosemary to swoop in and rescue me?" she sneers.

Damn! This woman is infuriating. "I'm pretty sure you're safe. He likes his women blonde and feminine." I've had enough, and I have the ID I need, so I turn and head for the door. A shoe smacks into the doorframe right beside my ear, and I jerk around to see a furious Joey with its mate in her hand. I almost think I see a tear in her eyes, but this girl's not capable of that kind of softness. She hurls the other shoe, missing by a mile, before stalking off.

By the time I exit into the steamy night, I've calmed down. I consider going back in to at least apologize for letting my professionalism drop, but my phone starts buzzing with notifications. When I check, I have several missed calls from both Linc and Con plus one from Carmen. This can't be good. Something about the building must interfere with phone signals. I call Linc first while walking toward my vehicle. He answers on the second ring.

"Where the hell have you been?" he yells. "We've been trying to reach you for hours."

"I'm in Nashville. I—"

"I don't fucking care. Get to Atlanta. I'll send you an address."

"What's in Atlanta?"

"We found Danielle."

I break into a run.

CHAPTER 52

Ashe

Too late. The words threw kindling on the fire of my temper. Two hours ago, Con's devastating call resulted in a mad dash east. The area where we've ended up isn't the worst in Atlanta, but it certainly isn't the best either. Underground Atlanta was once a thriving attraction, but now it hosts only a few entertainment venues. Just blocks away, police officers have to guard fast food restaurants to keep tourists safe from the many people begging for money or looking for something to steal.

We cross under the arched sign and make our way down the many steps following the sound of police radios and the shine of flashlights. People litter the walkway, and bass booms from the small concert venue at the far end. Officers are busy stringing up caution tape and keeping away the half-drunk gawkers filing out of the waning event.

Apparently, Saturday nights are a busy time for murders in Atlanta since the coroner is otherwise occupied, and Danielle's body remains covered with a tarp, not yet removed from the scene. Con and I pull the requisite protective booties over our shoes and step under the tape. A couple officers are familiar, and as a professional courtesy, we're granted a "look but don't touch" pass.

The tarp is pulled back to reveal a version of Danielle who appears to have aged years in the weeks she's been gone. She's propped up by a brick wall, her legs sprawled haphazardly. Her outfit is skimpy and her makeup heavy, typical of a night spent partying or clubbing. What grabs my attention though isn't her clothing but what appears to be track marks littering her left arm.

Her body's positioning leaves little to the imagination, and I notice even before Con points it out that her thighs are free of marks. The hand closest to me bears the ink of a stamp I'd bet money belongs to the venue we can still hear booming in the background. The death isn't ours to investigate, so we back away and move out of the area when the young officer approaches to replace the tarp.

Karo joins us as we find a place to observe without hampering the crime scene technicians. Her eyes are flat and cold and her expression grim. "Sorry it turned out this way," she says glancing toward the body. "I did what I could, but it was no use."

"We know you did your best," Con says with a conciliatory hand on her shoulder. "This is not on you."

"Can you talk us through exactly what happened?" I know Karo's had a shock, but she's a professional, and we need to get all the details while they are still fresh on her mind.

"Sure."

Just as Karo's about to recount the events, the coroner arrives, causing a commotion among the crowd of professionals and onlookers. The distraction is momentary but enough to delay the conversation. We watch the proceedings closely, hoping to pick up any clues or overhear any helpful conversations.

In the meantime, the loud bass of the concert fades, and crowds of people flow out to flood the common area and gape unashamed at the real-time crime drama playing out before their eyes. Their brash words and ever-filming phones scream their insensitivity to the reality that someone died, someone who was loved and will be grieved. We scan the people, hoping to catch a glimpse of Grimes returning to the scene of the crime, though we all know it's unlikely. Officers try to maintain a perimeter, but drunken feet stumble where they shouldn't.

Tired of the circus before me, I turn back to Karo and motion her and Con farther away from the chaos. "Start at the beginning. What happened?"

"I tailed Grimes here. He parked in the deck above then went straight down into the concert."

"Was Danielle with him?" Con asks.

"No. He was alone. Once I was able to buy a ticket and make my way to the upstairs balconies, I spotted her though."

My temper flares. "Why didn't you call us as soon as you saw her?"

Karo gives as good as she got. "Maybe because I didn't realize it was her at the time," she snarks with a glare.

"Ignore Linc. He has PMS. Please continue." Con plays referee and gets the story moving again.

"Like I said"—Karo shoots me another angry look—"I didn't recognize Danielle until I saw her face as they were leaving. It was dark and crowded. She was dancing with Grimes and hanging all over him. From my vantage point, I couldn't see what she was taking, but Grimes kept her supplied with pills and shots she was tossing back with abandon. She seemed very willing. They were practically having sex in the front row before she started swaying and stumbling around."

"What happened next?" I ask, already knowing but needing to hear Karo's version.

"Grimes held her around the waist and wove through the crowd to the exit. I saw where he was headed and made my way down. They exited slightly ahead of me and seemed to be moving toward the stairs when Danielle started convulsing. Grimes spotted me behind them and just dropped her and ran. I didn't have a choice but to try to help."

"You did the right thing," Con assures her.

"So Danielle seemed to be acting of her own free will?" None of this is making sense to me.

"Definitely," Karo affirms. "She—"

A grief-stricken moan cuts off any further words Karo might have been about to say. John, Danielle's father, pushes through the last of the crowd and tries to cross the crime scene perimeter. I rush to hold him back, not wanting him to see his daughter that way. Con and I reach for his arms but miss as he falls to his knees in the middle of the sea of people and weeps. It's a sight I'll never forget.

The anger I expect him to direct toward LCR is absent. If anything, John seems grateful for our presence. While some professional courtesy is directed his way because of his retired status, he knows no one is going to include him in the investigation, especially now that it's morphed from missing person to possible homicide. We can get information he can't, at least we can if there is any information to be had.

Con and I do our best to bolster John while detectives rehash with him all details of Danielle's disappearance and Karo works to keep the press out of hearing range. When there is nothing else to be done, we escort John to his hotel where he parts ways pleading privacy.

Rosey meets us at the hotel, and we're lucky enough to find vacancies. The night is spent tossing and turning as well as updating our people regarding the new course of our investigation. Sure, initially we were tasked with finding Danielle, and that job is done, but nothing about this is making sense, and I'm never one to leave a puzzle half finished. Additionally, despite my lingering anger, I still feel a need to ensure Eva and her family are safe.

CHAPTER 53

Eva

I need my best friend. Tessa thought Ashe was going to grovel, but she couldn't have been more wrong. My time with him yesterday started off angry and ended angry. Ashe was supposed to stay last night until Villain came on shift, but after my revelation, he barely spoke and ended up rushing out without an explanation. I'm thankful he arranged someone else to cover for him and didn't leave us unprotected, but why couldn't he have taken the time to have a rational discussion?

Clemmie is everything to me, and I have to keep her safe. Making her parentage public can only hurt her. Sure, people probably assume, but assuming someone is the child of a killer and knowing for sure are two very different things. Once I realized I was pregnant, the awareness that Demon wanted my baby kept me from telling the police. Tessa and Aunt Polly are the protectors of my secret, and right now, I need Tessa. I need reassurance that I did the right thing.

I tried to call her last night, but she didn't answer. That's not unusual since she's an early bird, but she's still not answering calls or texts this morning. I put Clemmie down for her nap and ask Aunt Polly to watch her. Tessa knows if she ignores me, I'll just show up.

Like many businesses in the South, the coffee shop is closed on Sundays. Tessa usually goes to an early Mass and spends the rest of the day at home.

Seeing her car in the driveway fills me with relief. My chest is so tight from holding everything in that I can barely breathe. I'm not sure I would have survived having to hunt her down. Snagging my phone from the passenger seat, I climb out and head toward the door. Before I reach the porch, I notice her door is open a crack. She is forever forgetting to close the door after letting her puppy outside.

Knocking on the open door, I call out a few times with no answer. I head inside leaving the door cracked in case Taco, her puppy, is still outside. Calling them both, I hear tiny feet clambering across the wood floors before Taco runs toward me full tilt, barking and jumping at my shins. He's typically pretty calm, but he starts darting back and forth toward the kitchen like he wants me to follow.

No one is in the sunny yellow space, and Taco's food and water bowls are empty. I refill the food, and Taco dives in as though he's starved, increasing my worry. Taco is Tessa's baby, and he is never without anything.

Crossing the living room, I look outside the French doors to the backyard. Next, I check the bathroom and the guest bedrooms before finally getting to the master suite. They too are empty, but what sends my heart into overdrive is Tessa's purse and phone lying haphazardly on her dresser. Without stopping to think, I run straight out the door toward Moss's vehicle, which is never far behind mine. He is out and sprinting my direction, gun at the ready, before I ever make it off the porch.

"What happened? Are you hurt?" His questions are succinct, and his eyes somehow rove our surroundings while also visually checking me for injuries.

"I'm fine. It's not me. It's Tessa." Moss moves us quickly into the house and secures the door behind us.

"What's wrong? Where is she?" He moves through the house as he speaks, checking as I did, only much more efficiently.

"That's just it. I don't know." Anxiety pushes my voice into a higher pitch at the end.

"Calm." Moss shoves his weapon into the back of his waistband and places himself directly in front of me. "Explain."

"She didn't answer my calls last night or this morning, so I thought maybe she was having boyfriend troubles or something was wrong. I came over to talk to her and found her door open. I didn't worry initially because she sometimes leaves it open, but…" My thoughts are tumbling one over the other just like my words. I slow for a quick breath, but once again Moss stops me.

"Breathe, then tell me about the door."

I take a deep breath, feeling my thoughts begin to center. "She leaves it open for her dog sometimes, so I wasn't worried, but I can't find her. Everything is here, her purse, phone, car, but she's not. Taco was starving, like he hadn't eaten in a while, and that's not like Tessa."

"Taco?"

"Her dog." Moss grunts and rolls his eyes at the name.

"Stay right here, and don't touch anything. I need to make some calls."

Wrapping my arms around myself, I shiver despite the heat outside. Taco whines at my feet while Moss heads into Tessa's bedroom. I hear his voice rumbling, but I can't make out who he's talking to or what he's saying. On shaky legs I walk toward the couch but reconsider sitting when I remember Moss said not to touch anything. Taco whines to be picked up, so I snuggle him to my chest, instinctively knowing he needs comforting as much as I do.

"Let's go," Moss orders. I didn't even see him return to the living room, but I follow him to the door. Noticing Taco in my arms, he pauses at the entrance long enough to grab the leash hanging on a hook then ushers us out and into my vehicle. I sit sideways with the door open and hold the leash, allowing Taco to roam somewhat free while Moss paces and talks on the phone.

Within a few minutes, I hear sirens. I had honestly expected to see just Ashe or Liam pulling in, so the noise ramps up my fear to astronomical proportions. Magnolia Ridge Police Department vehicles screech to a halt from two different directions, and suddenly Tessa's yard is looking like a crime scene.

Moss talks to the officers but stays outside with me as they enter the house. A nondescript third vehicle parks in the road behind one of the police cruisers, and a petite woman with wildly curling brown hair barely constrained by a ponytail stalks toward us. I recognize Detective Castillo from the scene in my office.

"Carmen," Moss greets.

"Stone," she replies. Stone? I make a mental note to ask Moss later. "Where're your bosses? I figured Linc would at least be here."

"Atlanta," he says shortly.

"Oh. Yeah, I guess that makes sense. Have they—"

"I'm sure you remember Ms. Jones," Moss interrupts and directs her attention to me. Obviously there's something he doesn't want me to know, but right now, I don't care. I just want to find Tessa.

"Sure. It's not every day I get to open a box of severed fingers." I wince at her nonchalance. Apparently, she wasn't nearly as bothered by that as I was. "Now, why don't y'all tell me what's going on."

I explain once again, pausing only to answer the many questions Detective Castillo fires at me. She jots down details in a small notebook while Moss stands sentry beside me, and Taco strains at his leash, yipping at passing cars.

"You mentioned a boyfriend. Do you have a name?" Pen poised, Detective Castillo waits for my answer.

"I don't think she ever mentioned a last name, but his first name is Dustin." Moss and Castillo exchange an urgent look over my head. "What? What was that look about?"

"Would you recognize Dustin if you saw a picture?" Moss asks, his expression intense.

"She showed me a picture on her phone once, so probably. Why? What's going on?" Stress is making my heart race, and someone needs to clue me in.

"I'm taking her to LCR."

Moss all but drags me away from Detective Castillo and puts me in his car, Taco in my lap. Stalking away, he returns moments later to load the puppy carrier in the back and secure Taco inside. He doesn't speak, but I feel his urgency as we race toward LCR.

The elevator ride when we arrive is eventful since Taco is terrified and barks at everyone we see. Thankfully he calms once we're in the quiet offices. Moss leads the way through a door displaying Liam's name and turns on a computer. He places Taco's carrier on the floor and motions me into a chair. He makes a call while the computer boots up, and I hear Liam's voice giving Moss instructions as his fingers fly over the keyboard before finally stilling.

"Eva, I need you to look at something." I move around to the back of the desk. Moss has a driver's license blown up large on the monitor. The name says James Dustin Grimes.

"Why do you have that?" I ask sharply, knowing the answer can't be good.

"Eva, I'll explain everything, but I need to know, is this Tessa's boyfriend?"

"Moss, I don't understand what's going on, but yes. That's him."

CHAPTER 54

Ashe

My sleepless night in no way prepared me for this morning's traffic. Atlanta can be a mess on a good day. Today is not a good day. Presently Con, Rosey, and I are at a standstill gridlocked on I-20. Con rides shotgun while Rosey follows behind in his own vehicle. The sky is gray and dreary, and the rain hitting the windshield is enough to make wipers necessary but not enough to keep them from making that annoying squeaky sound. Combined with a lack of sleep, the crawling pace has tempers flaring.

"Could we go any slower?" I rant from behind the wheel.

"In Atlanta? Probably." Con grumbles. "Don't jinx us." As soon as the words leave his mouth, the drizzle outside turns into a downpour, and I find myself trying to navigate without the benefit of being able to see more than two feet in front of me.

"Seriously?" I gripe.

"I told you not to jinx us."

I flip Con off and try to stay focused on the road. The monotony of the stop-and-go movement has me needing a distraction in order to keep my sanity. I turn down the music Con likes to blare and wait for his attention to divert from the window to me. He gives me the evil eye and reaches for the control to turn the music back up. I knock his hand away and start talking.

"All this time we've been operating on the premise that Demon chose his victims at random. The information Eva withheld changes that perspective. Our profile has been all wrong. Nothing was random. Demon targeted disenfranchised young women specifically for the purpose of finding one he could turn into some freaky captive bride and force to carry his child. I can't help wondering if the police having that information years ago could have prevented what happened to Danielle." There, I said it out loud, the thought that had been bothering me since last night.

"We don't really even know what happened to Danielle at this point, so speculating helps nothing," Con reasons.

"But how could she make a choice like that, ignoring the damn consequences?"

"How could she not?" Con fires back. "Acknowledging Clemmie's parentage and the circumstances surrounding it would have just put a permanent bullseye on Clemmie's back. Eva was protecting her daughter the best way she knew how. You and I both know that as soon as law enforcement found out Clemmie was the daughter a killer wanted but never knew he had, someone would have leaked that shit to the media. She would've forever been known as the daughter of a murderer."

Though I hate to, I have to admit he's right, and I might have overreacted. I don't have time to dwell on it though since we're almost at the coroner's office. Today looks to be a day full of meetings. Rosey will be accompanying John to the morgue to officially identify

Danielle. Con and I will try to learn anything we can about what happened to her, even though the official cause of death and most other details are likely days away. The buzz of Con's phone interrupts my thoughts. He snatches it from the cupholder and answers after looking at the display. The one-sided conversation sounds serious, but I can't determine the subject matter from Con's non-committal grunts and curses. He stares at me for a long moment after ending the call, and my nerves ramp into overdrive.

"What's going on, Con?"

"We need to get back to Alabama. Tessa's missing."

CHAPTER 55

Eva

As soon as Moss ends his phone call, I insist he take me home. Fear is suffocating me, and my mind keeps drifting into areas best left forgotten. I need Aunt Polly and the comfort of the familiar. I also need my eyes on my daughter, ensuring she's safe.

Moss is unusually quiet on the way back to his vehicle. I can tell there are things he isn't telling me. Taco's barking is the only interruption to the silence. When we reach the parking lot, I take a quick minute to let Taco do his business before loading up. Moss gives me the option of going straight home or stopping to get my 4Runner first. I like to have my own transportation in case of emergencies, so I choose option two.

With no evidence of foul play other than Tessa's purse, phone, and vehicle left behind, her house is not considered a crime scene. Evidence was taken earlier, but there's no tape across the door or any other sign that something so monumental as Tessa's disappearance occurred. It's like she was here and then she wasn't. The world just moved on. Is that what happened when Demon took me? Was it like I'd never existed at all? I won't let Tessa be forgotten. No one came for me, but I will always come for her.

Moss sticks close behind me as I use Tessa's spare

key to enter and grab Taco's food and soft bed. As I load Taco and his paraphernalia in the SUV, I realize tears are falling. I lock up, casting one more sorrowful look at my best friend's house and silently promise her I won't stop until she's found.

Aunt Polly is waiting on the porch when I get home, her eyes filled with tears. Falling out of my 4Runner, I run toward her outstretched arms, forgetting about everything but my need for comfort. Our embrace is interrupted by Taco's barking, and I realize Moss has liberated him and his accoutrements from the 4Runner and also shut the door I didn't bother to close.

"This must be Taco," Aunt Polly says, pulling back from the embrace. "He's a lot smaller than I expected from Tessa's larger-than-life stories of his escapades."

"His mouth isn't smaller," Moss gripes. "My ears are bleeding." Though his words complain, his face registers affection. He's obviously a dog person. He pauses to herd us through the open doorway. Setting Taco's carrier down in the living room, he heads to the kitchen to put the dog food in the pantry.

Clemmie is strapped in her highchair, devouring a cup of pink yogurt that appears to be more on her than in her. "MoMo!" she squeals, clapping and reaching for Moss.

"No way, little one. You're too messy for me today." He smiles and taps her lightly on the nose as he passes, eliciting a bout of giggles.

"Let's get you cleaned up," I say, grabbing a paper towel and wetting it at the sink. Before long, her face and hands are clean, and she's headed to hunt down Moss. The sight of Taco, who's now out of his carrier and investigating the living room, stops her short.

"Doggie!" Clemmie exclaims.

Moss sneaks back outside while she's distracted chasing Taco from chair to chair and finally under the coffee table. The two of them roll around and play like the old friends they are. Taco has always been Clemmie's favorite part of visiting Tessa's house. That thought has my eyes welling up again, but I stare at the ceiling willing the tears not to fall. I can't fall apart. Aunt Polly squeezes my shoulder as she walks by to take a seat on the couch.

I need to do something, so I grab a notepad and pen from the junk drawer in the kitchen and curl up in the large purple chair to make a list. Before I can even start, my phone rings from my purse on the entry table. I don't remember bringing it in, so I'm guessing Moss must have.

I rush to answer hoping it's Tessa. My heart sinks when the caller ID reads Mobile. It's probably Tessa's brother. Her parents were killed in a car accident when Tessa was sixteen, and Luke, who was twenty-one and in the Army at the time, gave up his career to come home to Mobile and take custody of her. Signaling Aunt Polly to let her know I'm heading to my room, I fall on the bed, taking a deep breath before I answer.

"Julie, what happened? The police just called, asking if Tessa was with me," Luke starts. "They said you reported her missing. What's going on?"

"I don't know, Luke. I wish I did, but I went by her house this morning since she wasn't answering my calls, and she wasn't there." I can hear myself talking faster and faster and pause to take a breath, trying to push some of the anxiety down.

"Why didn't you call me?" Luke asks, his anger

evident in his voice.

"I'm so sorry. It's been years since we've talked, and I just wasn't thinking about calling anyone other than the police."

"All right, slow down and then tell me everything you know," Luke orders. I do exactly as he instructs and explain everything from this morning until now. "I'm heading that way. It will take me about five hours, but I'll get there as fast as I can," he promises.

We disconnect, and I let out a relieved breath, glad Luke will be here to help. Though I don't remember exactly what his job entails, I know he works remotely and travels a lot, allowing him to pick up and head here immediately. Tessa and I spent most of our time at my house growing up, so I don't know Luke very well. According to Tessa, he was always fiercely protective of her, so I'm sure he will help me put pressure on the police to find her.

Knowing Tessa's finances won't be able to withstand the loss of income, I take a minute to call her manager at The Daily Grind. After Allie assures me she'll keep the business running, I hang up and make my way back to the living room. As soon as I sit, Clemmie climbs into my lap for a big hug and a slightly sloppy kiss on my cheek.

"Love, Momma."

"I love you too, baby." Tugging her in for another hug, I inhale the baby scent of her curls. I would hold her forever, but she scrambles down much too soon so she can rejoin Taco on the floor. Seeing Taco reminds me that he probably needs to go outside.

I let Clemmie follow me and the leashed puppy out into the backyard. She toddles around on bare feet picking blow-out flowers, her name for dandelions, and blowing the seeds all over the yard. She tries to blow a few on Taco, but he's having nothing to do with it and just barks at the floaty seeds. Clemmie laughs and tries harder. When Taco is finally ready to go back in, I let him off the leash at the back door and scoop my now-dirty daughter into my arms to head to the bath. As we pass through the living room, I literally run into the last person I expect.

CHAPTER 56

Ashe

"Whoa." I catch Eva by the upper arms as she plows into me with Clemmie on her hip. For a second, I think I see relief on her face, but it's quickly replaced with a blank stare.

"Let me go," she says quietly at the same time as Clemmie reaches for me. I release her immediately and catch the toddler diving from her mother's arms.

"Wink!" she squeals, bouncing on my hip.

"Hey there, sweetie." The smell of dirt and little girl makes me smile.

"Doggie," she says, pointing to what looks like a long-haired chihuahua.

She immediately squirms to get down and runs after the dog. Eva starts to go after her but stops at my words. "We need to talk."

"What I need is to give Clemmie a bath. I don't have anything else to say to you right now."

"Eva, it's important." I sense her resolve weakening. "Can we just go out on the porch for a few minutes?" I throw in a please for good measure. She looks over at Polly.

"It's fine, honey. I'll get the bath started and see if I can get our little munchkin clean." Polly snags Clemmie faster than I would have thought possible and whisks her protesting captive off toward the bathroom.

Eva follows me out to the porch and takes a seat in the middle of the swing, ensuring I can't sit beside her. The belligerence of the move causes me to smile before I move to lean on the porch rail facing her. "I'm sorry about Tessa," I begin. "I would have been here sooner, but I was in Atlanta when Moss called."

"Why?" Eva questions.

"Why, what?"

"Oh, I don't know. Why are you sorry? Why would you come sooner or even at all? Why were you in Atlanta in the first place?" Eva doesn't try to mask her anger. She's practically yelling by the end of her tirade.

"Shit, okay. Um, I'm sorry because I know Tessa is your best friend and she's very important to you. I came because I'm going to help you find her. LCR is going to help you find her. As for why I was in Atlanta, we'll get to that in a minute."

"Fine. How can you help me find Tessa?"

"We may have a lead, but I need to ask you some questions."

Eva stops the swing she's been angrily pushing back and forth. "Anything. Ask me anything if it will help Tessa."

"You told Moss that Tessa has a boyfriend named Dustin. Is that right?

"Yes."

"You identified him as James Dustin Grimes based on his driver's license, right?"

"Yes. You know all of this, so why are you asking me again?" Her impatience shows.

"Hang on, I'm getting there. Can you start from the first time Tessa mentioned Dustin and tell me everything you know?"

She starts the swing moving again before telling me how and where they met, how long they've been dating, and a few other details I doubt will help. Eventually, she mentions something about rumors.

"What were the rumors?"

"Tessa didn't say. I just know it was one of the female baristas at The Daily Grind who was sharing them." She stills for a minute then asks, "Why is all of this important?"

"Dustin Grimes was dating Danielle before she disappeared. We also believe he may be a drug dealer known on the streets as Cage."

Eva bolts up from the swing. "No! Tessa would never date a drug dealer. Never!"

"Please sit back down. That's not all." Stepping forward, I take her hand and pull her to sit beside me on the swing. I'm surprised she allows me to do so, but I can tell her thoughts are racing. I rake my free hand through my hair before taking a deep breath, trying to figure out how to say the words I know will hurt and terrify her. News stations are already covering last night's events, and I want her to hear it from me first, so I finally just blurt out what Eva needs to hear. "Danielle was found last night. She was dead."

Her hand pulls from mine to cover her face as she folds double. I rub my hand gently up and down her back. She raises up just enough to turn her face to look at me.

"So, you're telling me that Tessa's new boyfriend killed Danielle and now has taken Tessa?"

She narrows her eyes before asking angrily, "How long?" At my quizzical look, she clarifies. "How long have you known about Dustin?"

"We just identified him as a suspect a few days ago. I had no idea he was dating Tessa."

"But you suspected he was Demon then did nothing while he murdered one woman and abducted another?" Eva near shouts.

I stand and pace. "That is not at all what happened." Stopping, I look her in the eyes for a moment. "You should know me better than that." I resume walking the length of the small porch. "From the moment we knew he was a possibility, we had surveillance on him. One of our investigators trailed him all the way to Atlanta last night. She watched him just like she was supposed to, but when he came out of the concert with a stumbling blonde who fell and started seizing, she had a choice to try to save the girl she recognized as our missing person or chase down Dustin, who fled as soon as Danielle fell. Danielle came first. Karo had no way of knowing where he would go or what he would do from there. She was just trying to save a life."

Eva's expression morphs from anger to chagrin. "I'm sorry," she whispers. "I shouldn't have accused you." Her hazel eyes water before she hangs her head. "I just don't know what to do. I can't let Tessa think she's alone, but I don't even know where to start. She's the strong one. I'm completely useless!"

Striding to the swing, I grip her upper arms, lifting her to stand only inches in front of me. Shock is painted on her features, but I maintain my grip and stoop to stare straight into her eyes. "Stop it, Rabbit. Stop it right now," I order. "You are a survivor, and you are the strongest woman I've ever known. I know you're scared and upset, but a pity party is not going to save Tessa." Eva opens her mouth as if to argue, but I don't let her get a word in. "You don't have to know what to do. You just have to know the right people, and trust me, Rabbit, LCR is the right people. We *will* find her."

Eva's shoulders shake with silent sobs, and I pull her into me, tucking her head under my chin. Some of the tension leaves her body, and I know it's time for me to make my apology. "Eva, I'm sorry I was angry with you. I should have taken the time to really listen and try to understand why you omitted details instead of reacting in anger." Her body regains some of its stiffness, but her cheek remains against my heart.

"The more I thought about it, the more I realized you were only protecting Clemmie. That doesn't make you a bad person. It makes you a good mom." Eva looks up at me, and the relief in her eyes is palpable. I can't resist kissing her forehead. The sound of a car door slamming has me jerking around and pushing Eva behind me. A tall man with preppy blond hair and a furious glare stands with his hands on his hips.

"What the hell, Julie? Tessa's missing and you're making out on the front porch?"

CHAPTER 57

Eva

"Luke," I say, maneuvering my way out from behind Ashe. I haven't seen Tessa's brother in almost eight years, but his use of my first name makes his identity obvious. "It's not what you think." Dang! Did I really just use the most clichéd line in the world? "Um, I mean…"

"Who the hell are you, and what makes you think you can talk to Eva like that?" Ashe demands while trying to force me back behind him. A pinch on his arm gets the result I need. He lets go with a curse.

I dart down the steps, only to have Luke pull the same move, shoving me back and stepping in front of me. "Fuck you, asshole. Get away from her!" Tired of all the male posturing, I kick the back of Luke's knee. It buckles, almost sending him to the ground. "Damn, Julie, what was that for?" he asks, rubbing his leg.

"I'm not some toy for you two idiots to fight over. We're all on the same side, and when you both figure that out, you'll be allowed inside." I leave them both gaping and head inside, slamming and locking the front door.

"I heard yelling, honey. Is something wrong?" Aunt Polly exits the bathroom with Clemmie close behind. Her hair hangs in damp ringlets that drip onto the shoulders of her green, unicorn-covered nightgown. She runs toward me on bare feet and tackles my legs, almost knocking me over. I bend down and tickle her, knowing her innocent laughter will help calm my irritation.

"It's nothing, Aunt Polly, just an overload of testosterone."

"If you say so." She shakes her head and moves toward the kitchen to start preparing dinner. A knock sounds on the front door as she walks by. She diverts to answer it but continues on her way when I hold up a hand.

I pick up Clemmie and perch her on my left hip. She lays her wet head against my shoulder, and I squeeze her tight before waving Aunt Polly on and opening the door a crack. Ashe stands on the porch with Luke right behind him. The adversarial posturing is no longer present.

"Can we come in?" Ashe is the first one to speak. I open the door and step aside, letting them enter.

"Wink!" Clemmie perks up and gives him her best smile.

"You're all wet," he says fingering a damp ringlet. "Did you get a bath?" She gives an exaggerated nod, looking somewhat like a demented bobblehead and causing us to laugh as she intended.

"Who do we have here?" Luke asks, stepping to the forefront.

"Oh, Luke, I forgot you've never met my daughter, Clementine, or Clemmie as we call her."

"Tessa never mentioned you had a daughter, Julie. For that matter, she never told me you lived in the same town. For all I knew, you disappeared off the face of the earth three years ago." Luke reaches out to gently caress Clemmie's cheek.

I feel bad for keeping him in the dark, but I swore Tessa to secrecy, fearful of anyone knowing the details of my new life, even Luke, although Tessa was convinced it would be safe. Clemmie squirms out of my arms, bored with the adult conversation, and runs to Aunt Polly. Ashe's curious eyes never leave my face. "I just, well...I just needed a new start. It felt safer, I guess."

"Hey. It's okay." Luke squeezes my upper arm affectionately, like he used to when I was young. "I shouldn't have pushed. Right now, I just want to know what happened to my sister."

Guilt overwhelms me for taking even a moment to focus on anything other than Tessa. "Let's sit down, and Ashe can update you on what he knows."

Luke follows me into the living room, looking around in awe like most first-time visitors, taking in Aunt Polly's colorful style before sitting uncomfortably in one of the chairs. I take the other one, leaving Ashe with the couch. Taco darts excitedly back and forth between us. Ashe immediately launches into all that led up to this moment while I contribute the details of finding the empty house and the dog. Luke asks multiple questions, his fear for his sister evident.

Excusing myself when Aunt Polly calls from the kitchen, I find Clemmie sitting in her highchair pretending to stir her small bowl of mashed potatoes. "Tayduhs. Yum!" she says taking a messy bite.

"Honey, can you grab the biscuits from the oven? I'm afraid the chicken will burn if I don't get it out of the oil." Aunt Polly pulls a piece of golden fried chicken from the skillet and places it on a plate lined with paper towels. My mouth waters, and I groan as I reach for the oven mitts, noticing an old favorite, macaroni and cheese, is also on the menu.

"Aunt Polly, you know I can't eat like this," I protest, placing the hot pan of biscuits on the counter before grabbing the butter from the fridge.

"Why not?" Ashe asks, having suddenly appeared in the doorway.

"I…uh…" I stammer.

"Girl thinks it's a sin to eat anything other than rabbit food," Aunt Polly scoffs.

"Really? *Rabbit* food?" Ashe asks with a sly wink for me. I stick my tongue out at him behind Polly's back and immediately regret it as Clemmie starts imitating me, causing Ashe to full-out laugh and then respond to her in kind. I can't help but smile at his interaction with my daughter and notice Aunt Polly glancing at the pair with a soft affectionate look as well.

The sweet moment is interrupted when Luke enters with a scowl, reminding me that my focus needs to be on Tessa. I immediately sober.

"Luke, I thought the voice I heard in the living room must be yours. I haven't seen you since before you joined the Army years ago. You don't even look like the same person," Polly says, greeting him with a hug as though he's still the young boy she remembers. Indicating the table, she directs, "Y'all have a seat. Supper is almost ready."

"Thanks, but I'm really not hungry right now," Luke replies.

"Nonsense. You're gonna need some energy to

find our sweet Tessa, so sit down and help yourself." She places the heaping containers of food on the small table, and we all crowd around. Polly says a quick blessing and a prayer for Tessa's safe return, setting a somber mood as we all plate our food.

I take a small portion of my favorites and try to set aside the perfectly crispy crust to eat my chicken plain. Ashe eyes me suspiciously but keeps any comments to himself. Halfway through the awkwardly silent meal, Ashe's phone rings.

"Excuse me, I need to take this," he says as he wipes his hands and steps out the back door. Clemmie continues to make the only noise in the room other than the occasional clanking and scraping of forks on plates. I finish and rinse my plate in the sink then wish the bath had waited until after eating as I attempt to liberate my little mess maker from the "tayduhs" covering her hands.

"Thank you for dinner," Luke says with a halfhearted smile for Aunt Polly. "I know it's after business hours, but the detective I spoke to said she'd be at the station late. I'm going to head over there and see if she has any new information. I also need to see if I'll be allowed to stay at Tessa's. I'd like to be there, just in case."

Not wanting him to have to face that alone, I ask if he wants me to go with him, but he declines. Once he leaves, Aunt Polly and I busy ourselves putting away the leftover food while Clemmie pounces on Taco, waking him from a nap. Apparently, playing copycat is entertaining her tonight because she crawls around barking. Taco seems more scared than amused and runs to hide under a chair.

Ashe flings open the back door a bit harder than he means to and barely catches it before it impacts the wall. "Sorry." He shuts the door carefully before turning and pinning me with an intense look. "I have to go. That was one of my informants. Cage is rumored to have a big drug deal going down tonight. This could be our chance to prove Cage is Dustin and force him to lead us to Tessa." He grabs and holds my hand for just a moment as he passes then strides out the front door. Hours later, when my phone rings, the news is devastating.

CHAPTER 58

Ashe

After making all the necessary calls to get personnel in place, I change into more unobtrusive clothing, grab the weapon I prefer from my gun safe, and meet Con downtown. He fastens his seat belt then double checks his weapon. All LCR employees, including our office staff, are required to be firearms proficient and maintain their concealed carry permits. Though Con typically prefers staying behind his computers, he's the second-best marksman in the company. He used to be first until Karo joined us and knocked him out of the spot. She's on standby tonight in a separate vehicle, ready to take down the man who slipped past her.

We pull into the dark loading area behind an abandoned retail store, dousing our lights as soon as we hit the parking lot. Mouse, a skinny teen around nineteen, is already waiting in the shadows of a rusted-out dumpster. Ensuring my shirt covers my weapon, I exit the truck slowly, keeping my hands in plain sight. Mouse straightens as I approach. He's even thinner than the last time I saw him, and his unwashed smell is strong. The eyes underneath his hoodie are a little too bright, and I suspect his meth addiction has overtaken his brief stint of attempting to stay clean.

"Mouse, what've you got for me?"

"The better question is what've you got for me? I'm in a bad way, man. I need some cash."

"You know I'm not giving you money to shoot into your veins. It's the same deal as always, a room at Smokey's Motel is waiting for you. You can get a shower and sleep and order all the pizza you want. The value of the information determines how many nights."

"No way, man. That won't work this time. This dude is psycho. He'll kill me." I turn to leave, knowing Mouse will give in. "Wait," he calls out. I rotate to face him. "Look, I need to get away, leave town."

"I can help with that. You know the offer of a rehab placement always stands."

"Fuck!" he swears. "Fine, I'll take it, but I need to go tonight."

"The earliest I could get that arranged would be tomorrow, but I can make sure you're protected tonight."

"Fine, all right. Whatever."

"Done. What've you got?" My patience is running thin. We already lost Danielle. I can't lose Tessa too.

"An hour from now under Carver Bridge, Cage has a big deal going down. I heard he's moving a large shipment of some kind of new drug using the Devil Kings." Mouse licks his dry lips and scratches his arm as his eyes dart around in drug-induced paranoia. "Look, that's all I know. You gotta help me now."

"I will. I have a guy on the way. Name's Spock. He'll be guarding you tonight and be your escort to rehab tomorrow." Mouse nods. I describe Spock and the vehicle he's driving. Spock was already slotted to follow Mouse from here, so this will make his job easier. Mouse pulls his hoodie tighter around his face and fades back into the shadows while I rush back to the truck.

Con slides his weapon back into its holster as I make it back safely. "Carver Bridge. One hour," I bark. Con needs no further instructions. He's on the phone to Karo before I pull out of the parking lot. We pass Spock on our way out, and I'm relieved Mouse is finally taking me up on rehab, even if he's just looking for a place to hide.

The bridge is about thirty minutes away on the other side of town, the side where people know it's safer to keep their mouths shut. Con calls our county drug task force contact to update him on the location. Our role tonight is observation and support since the drug task force will be making the necessary arrests. It's pitch-black and nearing midnight as we approach Carver Bridge. The old wooden railroad bridge spanning the Coosa River is still in use, but not this late at night. The age-darkened support beams offer untold places to hide, and the nearby dock provides the means for a quick water exit.

Parking in an adjacent shopping center, Con and I exit and keep to the darkest shadows. We find a concealed spot behind a small maintenance shed and settle in to wait. Karo has already touched base and is positioned near the water to try to cut off that route of escape. The drug task force crew might as well be nonexistent for all the luck we have trying to spot them. That's a very good thing. We hold our position for what seems like an eternity but in reality is about an hour past the indicated meet time.

"Fuck, Linc. I think Mouse screwed us over."

Con's patience is at an end.

"Yeah, looks like," I reply, calling off Karo and sending her home. Not long after, the drug task force also decides to pack it in for the night.

Captain Jamison stops by and claps me on the shoulder. "Better luck next time, I guess. Damn informants are as bad as the ones we lock up sometimes."

"Yeah," I agree, but Mouse has always been reliable before. We'll be having a serious talk in the morning. "Sorry to have called you guys out for nothing."

"Honestly, that's a possibility with every call we get. Hell, at least it was a little excitement on a slow Sunday." We shake hands, and the captain and his team head out, leaving just me and Con.

We're both sweaty, tired, and ready to crash. Calling Spock as we make our way to the truck, I update him and warn him Mouse is a flight risk. A few steps later, I stumble in a pothole concealed by the early morning blackness. Con yanks me up just as a searing pain streaks across my arm, followed quickly by a sound we both recognize.

"Gun!" Con grits out while yanking me behind one of the many boats left on trailers in the lot each night. It's poor cover, but better than being exposed. "Fuck! You're hit."

I look down and spot the crimson covering my left bicep and dripping off my elbow. "I think it's just a graze." Lifting the gun, I'm thankful the injury is not on my dominant side. Additional blood flows when my left hand steadies my grip, but I ignore it. "I'll cover you. Get ready to move."

Con points to his next position of cover and motions a countdown before taking off in a crouch. My gun is propped on the top of the boat as I peer over just enough to scan our surroundings. Nothing moves, and no shots are fired. Once Con is safe, I drop back down and repeat the process as he covers me.

A ping sounds as a shot ricochets off a minivan just as I dart behind. The shooter is too far away for Con to safely return fire. "Sniper," he says, indicating a rifle with a long-range scope.

"Fuck." There's no way we can defend against that kind of firepower with the weapons we have. Our best bet is to try to evade and make it to the truck. We continue our game of tag from one cover to the next, but no further shots sound. When we finally make it to the truck, Con hops behind the wheel, and we tear out of the parking lot. As the adrenaline wanes, the sharpness of the pain increases. I push it out of my mind and call in the ambush to MRPD.

"Shit, man. That's a lot of blood. I'm taking you to the ER."

"Just head to the office, you can patch it up there."

"Sorry, bro. Not happening." Con ignores my preference and heads toward Magnolia Regional. By the time he wheels into the parking lot, blood is now soaking most of my clothing and has even dripped to the seat and floor. Okay, maybe it was deeper than I thought. Nausea churns in my gut as the ER attendants race out to the truck.

CHAPTER 59

Eva

My stomach cramps as I wallow in misery on the wretched mattress that smells of sweat and dirt and blood. I drift in and out of consciousness as the wind batters the walls of my prison, causing them to shake. Water seeps under the seam of the door, but I don't care. Between the humidity stealing my breath and the pressure in my abdomen, all I can focus on is my suffering.

I run dry, cracked hands down my body as has become my habit every time clarity returns. The scars still number thirteen. Demon hasn't been back since he revealed his real purpose, some kind of sick family with me as the obedient adoring wife and our child. Oh, God, our child...I can't. I can't give him a child. My already labored breathing wheezes in and out of lungs overwhelmed with the heaviness in the air.

My mind blanks momentarily, but another cramp bends me double, and the fingers that were exploring my scars encounter fresh fluid. I can't see it, but my touch has grown used to the sticky viscous feel of my own blood. My hand shakes as I retrace the healed and healing scars. The blood isn't from the cuts. That must mean...but I haven't had a period since I've been here, malnourishment having at least kept me from that humiliation.

A moan transitions into a scream as unbelievable agony radiates from my lower stomach around to my back. The very walls seem to shake and vibrate with my pain as the volume of the storm increases to the point that my ears pop. My addled brain struggles to make the connection between the blood and the pain. Realization strikes along with a flash of lightning visible under the door. Could I be pregnant? Demon took me repeatedly after claiming he was consummating our hellish union. I blacked out before he finished but woke up smelling of him and hurting. Being pregnant shouldn't feel like this, should it? Please, God, don't let a child be born into this. Please help me!

A crash sounds just outside. No! Please! Don't let him be back! The door creaks and groans before breaking open. Splinters from the frame embed in my legs. My breath is sucked away as the walls begin to move and the mattress lifts and flips and floats. Finally, finally it's the end. I smile as my body flips and floats too.

I wake with a gasp to the shrill sound of my phone. My mind struggles to make the transition from memories of the tornado that saved my life to the present, causing me to almost miss Liam's call. "'Lo?" I manage.

"Hey, Eva. It's Liam. I'm sorry to wake you, but I thought you might want to know. The drug bust was a setup. Dustin wasn't there."

"So we still have no idea where Tessa is?" My voice cracks with emotion.

"No. I'm sorry, Eva. That's not the main reason I

called though. Ashe was shot."

"What?" I exclaim, already climbing out of bed and searching blindly for clothes.

"He's okay. It was just a deep graze. I guess I should have said that first. Sorry."

"You've said that quite a few times already," I point out.

"Shit, sor—" He cuts himself off. "I mean, well, never mind."

"Liam, where are you? I'm on my way."

"We're at Regional, but just stay put. I need a favor."

"Sure. What?" I ask.

"Ashe is dosed up on pain meds from the stitches, and I need to head straight to the police station to give a statement and follow up on what happened. Rosey, uh Jackson, is still in Atlanta, and I don't want to drop Ashe at home alone. Can I drop him at your house for the rest of the night, so Villain can keep watch for him too while he's incapacitated?" His tone is hesitant as though he expects a refusal.

"Sure. I'll be waiting," I agree before ending the call. I'm not sure about starting a relationship with Ashe, but I'm not afraid to be alone with him. I know he won't hurt me. I'm also not sure why Liam thinks Ashe needs Villain's watchfulness, though maybe it's just because of the meds like Liam said.

I grab the receiver for the baby monitor but can't resist the compulsion to look in and make sure Clemmie is okay after the horrors of my dream. I hope she never knows of my thoughts during captivity. She is so very much wanted and loved. Cracking her door open, I peek in to find she has wriggled out from under her covers. She insisted Taco be allowed to sleep in her room, and he has somehow migrated from his dog bed to Clemmie's, no doubt at her direction. The two are cuddled up, and one of them is snoring, but I'm not sure which.

Blowing Clemmie a kiss, I move toward the living room so Ashe's arrival won't wake the rest of the house. I turn on the porch light and grab a pillow and blanket from the hallway closet, positioning them on the couch. By the time I finish, I hear a soft knock at the front door and pull it open to find a smiling Ashe leaning heavily on Liam.

"Hewwo there, little wabbit," Ashe says in a horrible imitation of Elmer Fudd. I snicker and push the door open wider so the two can enter.

"Sorry, Eva. He really doesn't tolerate pain meds very well, never takes them. We had to practically force him tonight. He was hurting so bad that he kept tensing up and making things worse. The doctor refused to sew him up without the meds. I can take him to the office and get an employee to watch over him if you think he'll be too much trouble," Liam offers.

"I'm coming for you, little wabbit," Ashe singsongs. I giggle at this usually serious man pretending to be a cartoon character and hurriedly shush him before he wakes Clemmie.

"Just put him on the couch," I direct as Liam maneuvers Ashe around the furniture. Eyeing the bandage wrapped around his left arm, I ask, "How many stitches?"

"Ten." The number causes me to wince. Ashe trips over a toy but thankfully crashes directly on the couch. Liam eyes the way Ashe is awkwardly sprawled and moves to reposition him.

"I've got him. Just go ahead. I know you said you had to get back to the police." He shoots me a grateful look.

"Villain is up to speed, and he can help if you need him." Liam impetuously squeezes me in a quick side hug. "Thanks, Eva." He's out the door before I can even respond.

Switching off all the lights except a small lamp in the far corner of the room, I turn back to Ashe, who's snoring with his mouth wide open. The coffee table makes a convenient seat so I can remove his shoes. He doesn't move a muscle as I lift his heavy feet, setting his shoes under my perch. I settle the pillow on the left-hand end of the couch so he can lie on his right side if he wants and then slowly raise his feet to the couch. He's not a short man, so his feet sort of dangle over the sofa arm. Surprisingly, his socks don't match, and that has me silently laughing again.

The new position of his feet has his body falling over toward the pillow. Moving around that end of the couch, I place my hands under his arms from behind and position him flat on his back, mindful of his injury. The blanket is still draped over the back of the sofa, and not wanting Ashe to get cold since Aunt Polly keeps the air conditioner running constantly, I start to place it over his body.

One swift move changes everything. Ashe's right arm whips out quick as a flash and snags mine, pulling me down on top of him. The blanket falls to the floor forgotten as I find myself face to face with Ashe's blue eyes. His arm holds me tight to his body, and his features fully relax. He kisses me on the forehead as his eyes close again.

"Don't run. Stay with me, Rabbit. Let me catch you this time," he mumbles, causing my heart to beat faster against his. Though his eyes are closed, his uninjured arm is locked tight, and his fingers move lightly up and down my side. His heat seeps through my thin shirt and warms all the places left chilled by my earlier dream. No one has held me or comforted me other than Aunt Polly since I was taken. Even though Ashe may not remember this when he wakes, I allow myself just a moment to rest in the security of his embrace. Closing my eyes, I fall into a dreamless sleep.

CHAPTER 60

Ashe

I wake slowly, a warm weight on my chest and a subtle vanilla citrus scent floating on the air. It would be like a dream except my head is pounding, my arm is burning, and my mouth feels like I gargled sand. I try to shift, but the weight has me pinned. A groan escapes, and I crack my eyes open to find I'm staring into warm hazel pools that appear more gold today.

"Oh my gosh, Ashe, I'm so sorry." Eva starts to move off my chest, but I still her movements, tightening my grip and pressing her cheek down to my chest. I'm not sure why she allows it, but she relaxes and lets me tangle my fingers in her unruly hair.

"Good morning, sweet rabbit." I feel Eva's laughter before the sound reaches my ears. Placing her hands to either side of my chest, she pushes herself up to her knees with a smile, not realizing she's straddling a part of me I'm struggling to ignore. The pained groan escapes before I can swallow it.

"I'm so sorry! I didn't mean to hurt your arm," Eva exclaims as she scrambles off and plops down on the coffee table. I miss her immediately, and damn if I understand that. Using my good arm, I push to a seated position and lean over, cradling my head.

"Headache?" she inquires. At my nod, she rushes

off to the kitchen and soon returns with a glass of water and a couple pills. "Just ibuprofen," she assures me.

"Thanks, Rabbit." Again, she giggles, actually giggles. "I don't get it. What's so funny?" She begins to outright laugh but quiets herself, probably trying not to wake the rest of the house.

"I was just remembering your Elmer Fudd impersonation," she says with a grin.

Huh? "My what?" I ask, knowing I must have misheard.

Her smile grows. "Your impersonation."

Shit. Is she serious? "Explain," I demand.

Not only does she explain, but this lighthearted Eva I've never seen before reenacts the whole scene and has me laughing too when Polly makes an appearance wrapped in a fuzzy robe over her pajamas.

"Asher Lincoln, I thought that was you I heard." She starts to pass by like my presence on her couch is nothing out of the ordinary but does a double take when she spots my bandage. "What on earth happened to your arm?" she asks, coming around to take a closer look.

"He was shot," Eva blurts before realizing a little pair of ears has joined us.

"Wink gots a shot?" Clemmie questions while climbing up beside me. She pats my arm, thankfully just above the bandage. "Owie." she says, giving me sad eyes then turning to her mother. "Sucker?" she asks hopefully.

"Okay," Eva answers. Clemmie cheers and bounces down to tear into the kitchen with Eva and Taco following. In a few minutes, she returns, holding a purple lollipop that she presents to me by shoving it toward my mouth. I look to Eva for clarification as she and Polly laugh. "She thinks you got a shot at the doctor, so you need a sucker like she gets when she has a shot."

Oh. Now I get it. I take the purple treat and remove the wrapper, so I can pop it in my mouth. Clemmie claps as if I've just won a prize and dances around in circles.

"All right, girlie girl. It's time to make breakfast," Aunt Polly says while ushering Clemmie to the kitchen. I track their progress before looking back to find a surprisingly serious Eva.

"I was worried about you," she admits softly.

"Thanks for letting me stay," I reply. "I'm so sorry I couldn't find Tessa for you last night. I promise Con and I will be doing nothing but focusing on her again today."

"Thank you." A knock at the door startles us both out of our melancholy moment. Eva rises to answer it, letting in Villain.

"Morning," he greets us both. "Moss will be here shortly to take Eva to work, so Con asked me to be your chauffeur to wherever you need to go," he directs to me.

"Oh no! Work. I forgot it was Monday." Eva disappears down the hall at warp speed, leaving a shocked Villain in her wake.

"Okay," he drawls, heading to the door. "I'll just wait outside."

After his exit, I pry myself off the couch and visit the facilities before heading into the kitchen to find Clemmie happily eating yogurt and Polly plating bacon, eggs, and toast. Taco's face is buried in a bowl of food near the back door.

"Grab a seat, Asher. The bacon's turkey, the eggs are white, and the toast is sprouted whole grain, but Eva might revolt if I tried to pass off two fat-filled meals in a row." She places a plate in front of me as I sit at the table then places one on the highchair as well as one at Eva's empty seat before taking her place. "Go ahead, eat up. I promise it's good."

A cup of black coffee already waits at my place as well as a milky-looking one at Eva's. I take a sip and enjoy my first gulp of heaven and caffeine before digging into my food as instructed. It's not what I'm used to, but it is actually good. I'm almost done by the time Eva sweeps in clad in a monochrome gray outfit with her curls springing out of a slightly off-center ponytail. She gives Clemmie a squeeze and a loud smacking kiss before practically inhaling her food.

"Thank you, Aunt Polly. You truly spoil me." Eva places her empty plate in the sink and rushes toward the foyer table where her keys and purse rest. I follow, hoping to get a word before she takes off again.

"Eva?" A light blush moves up her cheeks as she stops to look at me.

"Um, yeah?"

"Thanks," I say with all sincerity. The blush darkens.

"I, uh, I have to go," she stammers. "I won't have time to stop and get my latte from Tessa if…" Her eyes widen in shock at her mistake before her face crumples into misery. "What am I going to do? We have to find her Ashe," she pleads.

"We will. I promise." I lift her chin to look in her eyes. "I won't give up."

"I need to stay, to help."

"There's truly nothing you can do, and we both know you don't have any days off left. Don't risk your job. Just trust me to do mine." She nods and heads out the door, almost running into a shocked Luke, fist raised to knock. He eyes my sleep-disheveled hair and sock-covered feet then glances back and forth between me and Eva with a glare. Taco races to the open door and barks at Luke. Eva ushers the dog back inside, pulling the door shut behind her.

"Where are you going, Julie?" Luke asks, frustration in his voice. "I need your help."

Eva glances toward the open car door Moss holds and then back again. The pressure to stay sits heavy on her shoulders despite knowing there is nothing she can do right now. Even though I'm guessing she'll get angry, I answer for her while placing a gentle hand at her back to usher her off the porch.

"*Eva*," I start, stressing her name, "doesn't have the option to miss work today, but she asked me to help." Eva rushes on toward Moss. "Why don't you follow me to my office? We can talk there. My associate and I have some new developments."

Luke looks like he wants to argue but gives in and moves toward his car. I duck back in to grab my shoes and let Polly know I'm leaving. My phone rings as I walk to Villain's vehicle. Pulling it out of my pocket, I hope this call won't cause as much trouble as the last one I received. The screen shows it's Con.

"Hey, man. I'm on my way," I answer.

"Linc, we have a problem." Well, so much for hoping, I guess.

"Okay. What's going on?"

Con hesitates for just a moment before blurting, "Mouse is dead, and Spock is in critical condition."

CHAPTER 61

Tessa

Pain is not something I'm a stranger to, but this pain feels different, sharper, not like the pain of my childhood. That was the pain of breaking or bruising. This is a pain of burning. My whole body feels slightly over warm, and weight presses down all around me.

Slowly opening my eyes, I blink to relieve the dryness and see only white walls and the sturdy rails on my bed. Rails. I look to my right and see machines with flashing lights and a clear tube leading under the blanket. Hospital, I'm in the hospital. My breathing speeds up, and something nearby beeps. A whiteboard near the door cheerfully tells me my nurse is Terri with a heart over the I.

Tears leak from my previously dry eyes, and when I reach up to swipe them, I feel the cannula that must be sending oxygen to my lungs. I also feel the pull of the IV in the top of my hand and see the layers of tape holding it down. Covering my skin are bandages, plural. Heavy blankets weigh me down, but even though their heat feels stifling, I can't find the energy to push them off.

Without warning, the door swings open. A perky redhead in kitten-covered scrubs blows in with a smile. This must be Terri with a heart. "Good afternoon, sweetie." She introduces herself and starts checking my vitals. "How are you feeling?"

My voice croaks when I try to answer, and she pours water into a small plastic cup from the pitcher on the tray table beside the bed. She adds a bendy straw and presses it to my lips. The first drink tastes like heaven, but the second leaves me feeling a bit nauseous, so shake my head for her to take it away. "I'm hot."

"That's probably a good thing as long as you don't have a temp." She runs a device over my forehead and pronounces me ready to remove some of my coverings. "You were going into shock when you arrived, so the warming blankets were necessary as were the fluids," she says pointing to the IV stand. "You lost a lot of blood, but luckily not enough to need a transfusion."

Blood. My mind flashes to the knife, cutting, cutting, cutting…crimson everywhere, splashes and puddles. My breath wedges in my throat, and my hands clutch the sheets anchoring me to the bed.

"Whoa, hey sweetie, look at me." She gently uses my chin to turn my face toward hers. "Look at my face. Tell me five things you see," she commands in a voice that brooks no argument.

Surprisingly, I almost smile at the technique I always have to use for my best friend. Wait, where is Eva? Where is anyone? Why am I alone? "Where is everyone?"

Terri with a heart laughs. "Well that's not what I expected you to say. I was expecting something more along the lines of eyelashes or nose, but you're breathing normally again, so all's well."

"Is my friend here?" Eva would never leave me in

the hospital alone.

"There are a couple of detectives waiting outside to talk to you, but we didn't have any information to be able to call anyone else." When I look at her quizzically, she explains, "You didn't have a phone or ID when you collapsed in the parking lot. We don't even know your name, sweetie."

Shock races through me. "Tessa. My name's Tessa Taliaferro."

"Nice to meet you, Tessa. Your doctor will be in soon to discuss your injuries and treatment plan, and administration will have some paperwork for you to fill out, but in the meanwhile, is there anyone you want me to call to be with you before we let the detectives in?"

"My friend, Eva Jones." I recite the number, and Terri promises to call and hold the detectives off until Eva arrives. She then blows back out as quickly as she blew in, leaving a heavy silence in her wake. Suddenly, I wish she would come back so I wouldn't have to think, so I could pretend I don't feel. I stare at the door as if by thinking about her, I can summon her with my mind. Of course, nothing happens, leaving me with only silence and time, time to think about everything I should have done differently, time to remember all that was done to me. Time is the last thing I want, and the only thing I have.

I know I need to take an account of my body before Eva arrives, so I won't flinch or give away my feelings. Eva's not like me. I'm the strong one, and I'm not about to trigger her anxiety if I can help it. Just like when I was young, I'll smile and play it off. I learned early how to lie and how to shut off my feelings. Lifting the sheet, I prepare myself to do so again.

My hospital gown is loose at the back, and it's the only clothing I have, which causes me to feel really vulnerable. Maybe I can get Eva to bring me some underwear, so I'll be better protected, although I guess it's too late now. I don't think I'll ever be the same, and neither will my body. Bandages cover most of my thighs, and one is perilously close to where I hurt the most. Shame overwhelms me. I trusted him, slept with him willingly, well not this time, but I did before. If there were signs, I didn't see them.

Raising the bottom hem of my gown, I view my stomach, which also sports a large bandage. That cut was the first. I lost track of them all after that. Blood from one had seeped into blood from another and another, forming a maze over my body and leaving me too weak to put up more than minor resistance when he… No. I can't go there yet. No one has to know about that.

I survived. I got away. He left me bleeding on that bed, thinking I wouldn't have the strength to move while he went in the bathroom and cleaned up, but I crawled to his button-down shirt and wrapped it around me before pushing to my feet and stumbling out the door. The bright light on the roof of the hospital in the distance was the only thing I recognized, so I pushed myself beyond my limits to get there. I couldn't even begin to explain how and don't remember anything past my relief at feeling my bruised and torn feet touch the pavement of the parking lot.

Now, here I lie, bandages covering so many burning slices, covering the soles of my feet. Eventually, they'll heal, but I'm not sure I ever will. My feelings are all over the place. One minute I want to tell everything so he's caught and punished, the next minute I don't want to tell anything at all, to just say I don't remember so I can bear my shame alone. I want to kill him myself for what he did to me, but at the same time, I never want to look at him again. I want to fight and recover and prove he didn't win, but I also want to sleep and sleep and never wake up.

CHAPTER 62

Eva

Minutes move at the pace of hours today. The clock haunts me, staring down at me with a reminder that every passing moment is one where Tessa is in danger and I'm doing nothing to help her. My stomach rolls with nausea, this morning's breakfast the last food I could tolerate.

The group room is still empty as the second hand ticks slowly by. Jake and I are working together to teach a class on setting healthy boundaries. Clients are required to attend two group counseling sessions per month but can choose their times without registering ahead, so we don't know whether to expect one or twenty-five.

"Have you got the handouts ready?" Jake asks in his typical quiet tone as he draws a diagram on the whiteboard.

"They're sitting on the sign-in table by the door," I reply, unable to resist another peek at the clock.

Raking his sandy hair back, Jake stares at me for a moment then blurts, "You keep staring at the clock. Is there something going on?"

"Uh, no. It's just been a really slow day. How's your mom?" I ask in an effort to divert attention.

"What?" Confusion briefly crosses his features

then clears. "Oh, yeah, my mom. She's about the same, just needs a lot of care." We sit down across from each other at the front of the table to wait for clients to arrive. Jake looks at me and leans forward to prop his elbows on the table.

"When was she diagnosed?"

"Um, a couple years ago, but I don't really like to talk about it." Of all my coworkers, Jake is the quietest. We've spent a good bit of time together because we started working here just weeks apart. Much of our training was done together. He talks to me more than he does the others, but his abrupt nature sometimes makes conversations uncomfortable.

"No worries. I'm sure we'll be too busy to talk in a few minutes anyway."

"Maybe. Are you sure you're okay? You just looked at the clock again." He glances that direction himself. "It's only been two minutes. You're not waiting for another delivery, are you? The police questioned us all like suspects because the deliveries arrived here at work."

"I'm sorry, Jake. I can't imagine how that felt."

He stares at me intently. "It might not have been so bad, but the interview room was dark and stuffy and closed in. I don't know about you," he leans in and lowers his voice to a whisper, "but tight spaces make me feel trapped."

My throat feels clogged, and my chest feels as though a weight has settled on it, squeezing out the meager breaths I can suck in. The scent of blood mixed with dirt fills my nose, and nightmare images fill my mind. My hand moves of its own accord to grasp my throat.

"Miss Jones, are you okay?" I jerk around almost expecting to see Demon but finding a client staring at me while entering the door with a few others behind her.

"I...uh..." I glance at Jake, who's staring at me with concern. "I just had something stuck in my throat," I lie. "Excuse me." I grab my keys from the table and quickly edge past the people entering for group then push into the bathroom across the hall. Locking the door, I turn around and lean against it, gulping in oxygen. Leaning my head back to touch the door, the fear of seeing a repeat of the images has me afraid to close my eyes. Finally, I dampen a few paper towels and gently dab them over my face so as not to erase my makeup and look even more out of sorts than I already do.

Knowing I have to get back, I toss the paper towels in the can and open the door. Jolie is hurrying down the hall, waving at me, so I change direction to meet her near my office. "You have a phone call on line one. He said it was urgent."

"Okay. Thanks," I say, unlocking my office and closing the door behind me before grabbing the phone receiver. My finger hovers indecisively over the flashing button that will connect my call because I can't take any more bad news. I just can't. The phone beeps, startling me into action. "Magnolia Treatment Center, this is Eva."

"Eva Jones?" an official sounding voice inquires.

"Yes."

"Excellent. This is Grant Henson at Ridgeview Hospital. We were asked to contact you by a patient, Miss Tessa Taliaferro." The receiver falls from my hand, and I sit heavily in my chair.

"Ma'am? Ma'am?" I hear the tinny-sounding voice from the dangling receiver and snatch it back up.

"Sorry. I'm here! I'm here. Which hospital did you say you were with?"

"Ridgeview. Can I assume you know Miss Taliaferro?"

"Yes. I do. I'll head that way right now." I start to hang up, but Mr. Henson stops me to explain where to go. Once off the phone, I buzz Jolie to let her know I have an emergency then gather my belongings and run out the back door. Moss meets me before I even get down the steps.

"What's wrong?" he asks anxiously, his hands meeting my biceps to stop my progress.

"We have to go. Now!" I insist, trying to push past him.

"We will, just as soon as you tell me what's happening."

I start to explain, but as soon as he hears me say, "I found Tessa," we're moving. The drive to Ridgeview only takes about fifteen minutes, but like everything else today, it feels so much longer. Moss has been on the phone the whole time, but I couldn't quote a word he said. My mind has been offering up scenario after possible scenario for what happened to Tessa and what shape I will find her in.

The slam of Moss's door gets me back on track. I jump out of the vehicle and follow his long strides to the elevators then to room 454. Moss stands to the side to allow me to knock. At what sounds like a muffled response, I crack the door and push it open.

CHAPTER 63

Ashe

Villain gets us to the hospital in record time, and surprisingly Luke follows. I guess he's figured out by now that we detoured from our plan to go to the office.

"What are we doing here?" he asks with a tinge of anger as we exit the vehicles.

"Sorry, man. I had an emergency call regarding the serious injury of one of my employees and forgot you were following me. Villain can show you the way back to the office and make sure you're up-to-date on all we know and all we're doing." Before the angry reply can leave his mouth, I'm already headed toward Ridgeview's main entrance. My phone rings just as I reach the covered portico, and though I'd love to ignore it, I can't with so many important things going on. It's Rosey.

"Hey, man. What's up?" I delay entering the building and lean against one of the stone-covered support columns.

"I have news, and it's not pretty."

"Likewise. Par for the course at this point. Let's hear it."

"I just left the Fulton County medical examiner's office. John made the official identification then headed home to be with his wife and start planning the funeral.

Damn, that was rough." Rosey pauses. "In any case, I've got the report on Danielle, and I've gotta say, man, it doesn't exactly add up."

"What do you mean? Something's wrong with the report, or something doesn't match our theories?"

"The report's fine, but I just don't think this was Demon. She had barely healing cuts on her thighs, but she also had them on her stomach and elsewhere. The cuts don't look methodical or planned, but rather like a random angry attack or some kind of sadistic sexual kink. She also had a system full of drugs and possible evidence of sexual trauma but no evidence of malnourishment or captivity."

"Damn. Demon uses drugs initially to subdue, but no evidence points to him continuing their use. Do we know where she might have been held?"

"That's just it. I don't think she was. Once news of her death hit the media, a number of people contacted the police to report sightings of her over the past weeks. They go back almost to the day she disappeared." Rosey sounds frustrated. "I don't think Dustin Grimes is Demon. I think he's just a sadistic fucking lowlife rapist drug pusher."

"Fuck."

"Exactly."

"Are you on your way back yet?"

"Yeah. I'm stuck in traffic, but I'll get there eventually. What's your news?"

"You already know about the ambush, so I won't rehash that. Other than zero leads on Tessa, even though we have several of our investigators working on the search with the police, Mouse is dead, and Spock is in critical condition. I'm not yet current on what exactly happened. I'd just arrived at Ridgeview when your call came in."

"Damn it! What the hell is going on? Nothing is adding up," Rosey rants.

"I don't know. Hopefully I'll have more after I talk to the PD and check on Spock. You know this all has to fit together somehow. We're just missing a few pieces of the puzzle. I mean, how likely is it that we have multiple killers operating in the same area with similar MOs?"

"Not very."

"Just get here and get all the information regarding Danielle to Con."

"Will do." He ends the call, and my brain is racing, suggesting and then quickly rejecting theory after theory. Accepting that I don't have time to keep leaning against a column, I head in and locate the intensive care unit. A sign on the door announces that visitors won't be allowed for another hour. I find Spock's wife sitting in the ICU waiting area with a couple of familiar MRPD officers. I hug Sandy and shake hands with the officers before taking a seat.

"Mr. Lincoln, what can you tell us about this morning's happenings?" Officer Clark asks.

"I was about to ask you the same thing. Spock, I mean Kane, was protecting an informant overnight. I didn't hear of any problems until I got the call to come here."

"Did this informant have anything to do with last night's shoot-out at Carver Bridge?" asks Officer Stuart, narrowing her eyes suspiciously.

"Shoot-out? You sent Kane into a shoot-out?" Sandy interrupts, looking at me accusingly, her eyes catching on the bandage on my arm.

"No, Sandy," I assure her. "He should have been as safe as he ever is in this job." After she calms and nods her acceptance of my answer, I turn back to the officers. "The informant Kane was guarding gave us the tip that led to the bridge ambush. I understand he didn't make it."

"Correct." Stuart glances meaningfully at Sandy before asking, "Can we speak for a moment in the hall?"

"Of course." I follow her out while Clark stays with Sandy.

"You want to cut the shit and tell me what's really going on here? I know LCR was helping with the Hurst investigation. Is this connected?"

"Yes," I say without hesitation. "I believe it is. It can't be a coincidence that Danielle is found one night, then we're led into an ambush the next, all proof dying with the informant by morning. Couple that with the incidents surrounding Eva Jones and the disappearance of Tessa Taliaferro, and we have one big shit show. We just have to figure out who's pulling all the strings."

"Wait. I thought the guy who attacked Jones in the alley was identified, and her case was closed."

"Her alleged attacker's severed fingers were identified, but the rest of him hasn't been located, nor has whoever separated him from his fingers."

"Shit. That's obviously not my case, so you have fun with that. Seems our guy is fond of knife work though. Your informant's tongue was cut out, and your man in there was practically gutted. It's a wonder he survived." She motions to her partner before continuing. "At least Taliaferro was found. That's some good news."

"Wait, what?" Shock hits me in the gut.

"You didn't know?" One look at my expression confirms her answer. "Well damn. Yeah, she was found in the parking lot as a Jane Doe around three this morning. She woke up about an hour ago and was able to give the nurse her name. Castillo is waiting downstairs to talk to her now. That's all I know."

Clark rejoins Stuart, and they head out. I call Jillian and ask her to send someone to sit with Sandy and watch out for Spock before stepping quickly back into the waiting room and letting Sandy know who's coming. By the time I reach Tessa's floor, I've tried to call Eva twice with no answer, and I'm seriously about to lose my shit because Moss isn't answering either.

Carmen is easy to spot when I near the room but difficult to bypass. "I know you don't think you're about to barge into that room I've been impatiently waiting to get into," she says with plenty of attitude.

I definitely was, but I guess I'm not now. "Of course not."

"Right. She's not seeing anyone anyway. Apparently, the doctor advises against interviews right now, at least that's what the nurses claim. It seems more like they're waiting for something. My guess is they're waiting for your girl to get here."

My girl? Eva's not my girl. She's just...hell, I don't know what she is. "I don't have a girl."

"Yeah," she affirms, but disbelief colors her tone. "So, I hear you had an encounter with a bullet last night."

"Just a graze." Changing the subject, I ask, "Any idea who hit our safe house?"

"Not my case, so I got nothing for you. Sorry about Spock though."

"Yeah." I guess it's my turn to use the one-word answer. We stare at each other in silence until a curly-headed blur zips past us to knock on Tessa's door before barging right in. Moss follows close behind.

"Finally. Let's hope that means we can get this show on the road. I've got a pile of paperwork waiting on my desk." Carmen is knocking on the door, and pushing in without waiting for an answer, less than three minutes after Eva enters. Her no-nonsense stride announces she's all business. I follow but stop just inside the door, frozen by the pain I see on Eva's face.

CHAPTER 64

Eva

This can't be happening. I was so happy to know Tessa had been found, but even though various scenarios had played through my mind as we drove, nothing could have truly prepared me to see my fierce and strong friend huddled in on herself. Her eyes fill with tears as they meet mine, and I rush to sit on the edge of the bed and hold her as sobs wrack her body. Moss looks stricken and moves to leave us alone but instead takes up a defensive position in a seat near the bed when Detective Castillo barges in with Ashe on her heels.

Tessa hides her face and wipes the tears with the sheet while my eyes meet Ashe's over Castillo's head. To her credit, Castillo looks uncomfortable, but that doesn't erase the intrusion. "Miss Taliaferro, I'm Detective Castillo. I need to ask you a few questions about what happened. Would you like everyone else to step out of the room?"

"No," Tessa says firmly, squeezing my hand in a silent command not to move. She stops and looks down, fidgeting with the covers. "I don't remember anything." She doesn't meet my eyes but rather continues to stare at the blanket.

"I understand, Miss Taliaferro, but perhaps if we

start slowly, the details will come back to you," Castillo coaxes. Both Ashe and Moss stay completely silent, watching the exchange.

"No!" Tessa explodes, her shame-filled gaze finally locking with mine and silently begging me to help her.

"I think Tessa's had enough. She's obviously not ready for your questions and can't help you right now." I stand and slowly remove my hand from Tessa's grip then step toward the detective.

"I really don't think it's your place to determine that," Castillo counters.

"Carmen, maybe it'd be better if you came back tomorrow," Ashe intercedes.

"Really, so now you want to tell me how to do my job too?" she snarks.

"Out!" This time the order comes from Moss, who's on his feet ushering both Ashe and a protesting Castillo into the waiting area, leaving me alone with Tessa.

"Tessa?" She doesn't reply, just continues to occupy herself with the sheet. I use my finger to lift her chin, but she still refuses to lift her gaze. "Everyone's gone, and it's just us. You don't have to be strong." A slow trail of tears flows from her lowered lashes before she finally lifts watery eyes to mine with an expression I recognize from my own mirror. "Oh honey, whatever happened, it wasn't your fault," I promise her.

The dam breaks, and a flood of tears drops to the sheets before she lies back down and curls in on herself away from me. I adjust my position behind her so I can stroke her hair and comfort her. Just when I think she's found sleep, she reaches behind to grab my hand.

"Don't leave me. Promise you won't leave me," she whispers.

"Never."

Within about fifteen minutes, she is really and truly out. Her grip on my hand relaxes and slips away. I move to a chair on the other side of the bed. A perky-looking nurse in outlandish scrubs pops in and sets the blood pressure cuff on Tessa's arm to take a reading, but my friend never stirs. With a few more checks and adjustments to machines, she lowers the lighting then leaves, but the door swings back open right on her heels. It's Luke. In the rush to get here and the emotions of the last hour, I completely forgot to call him.

He takes in the low lighting and slows his approach. His pain and fury are evident as he looks down at his sleeping sister. "I'm going to kill whoever did this to her." His voice is a low growl, and conviction backs up his words. He gently touches her hair and tugs the sheet up higher.

"I'm so sorry I forgot to call, Luke. She just needed me, and I didn't think."

"It's fine, Julie. You did the right thing taking care of my sister." He takes my hand, and I can't read the expression in his eyes. "You always do the right thing." With a light squeeze, he lets go and returns his focus to Tessa. "What happened to her?"

"I don't know. She says she doesn't remember."

"Has the doctor been in?"

"Not since I've been here." He nods and pulls a second chair up beside the bed. Covered by the sheets and blankets, only Tessa's face is visible, giving the impression nothing is wrong. I'm afraid to find out what the layers of fabric hide. I'm afraid she was targeted because I was too protected. The blame is on me.

"What are you thinking, Julie? Whatever it is, stop." I glance up in surprise to find Luke's eyes on me, his stare intense.

I cringe a little at his repeated use of my old name. "I go by Eva now, Luke."

"I know, but you've been Julie to me since you were little, and you probably always will be."

"I'm not little anymore."

"Believe me, I know." Luke says nothing more, and the silence starts to bother me. The air feels heavy and stuffy inside the room, and the darkness is messing with my sense of time.

"I'm going to step outside the room for a minute. Tessa asked me not to leave, so I'll stay close. Do you want anything from the vending machines while I'm out?" I ask.

"No, Julie. I have everything I need."

"Um, okay." I exit the room, closing the door gently behind me then barely suppress a scream as I run straight into Ashe.

"Shhhh." His grip is gentle as he steadies me then leads me to a seat nearby.

"What are you doing here? I thought you left."

"No. I sent Moss home and took his place. I wanted to be here in case you needed anything." A smile takes over my lips even though I try to force it back. I shouldn't be smiling while my friend is hurting.

"You are so beautiful," Ashe says quietly, tucking wayward strands of curls behind my ear and gently caressing the side of my face in the process. That heat he inspires returns, and I shift slightly away, not because it doesn't feel good, but rather because it does.

"I'm sorry, Eva. I know this isn't the time." As he frequently does, Ashe drags his hand through his hair causing it to stick up a bit on top. "How is Tessa? Has she said anything?"

"No. She's just been sleeping. Luke's with her now."

"Yeah," he huffs.

"What's that for?"

"I just don't like the guy. He keeps calling you Julie, and he has a bad temper."

"He doesn't mean anything by it. He's just always known me by that name." I repeat Luke's excuse, finding it more believable as I say it. "He used to have a temper when we were young, but he never directed it toward me or Tessa. Their father was abusive, and Luke came back from the Army determined to be his dad's opposite. According to Tessa, he never even raised his voice."

"Let's talk about something else," Ashe suggests, looking irritated.

"Sure. Have you found Dustin?"

"No. MRPD plus several LCR investigators are tracking—" He cuts off abruptly as a bloodcurdling scream echoes from Tessa's room.

CHAPTER 65

Ashe

Eva and I rush into Tessa's room to find Luke comforting his sister after what must have been a nightmare. As much as I dislike the guy, Tessa seems to feel safe with him. Her arms are secured around his waist, and her face is hidden in his shirt. Eva steps to the other side of the bed and adds her comfort to Luke's. Not wanting to make Tessa uncomfortable, I head back out to the waiting area and decide to call Rosey back while I wait.

"Hey, man. Anything new?"

"You mean other than still being stuck in traffic?" Rosey asks facetiously.

"Yeah, other than that."

"Not much. Any developments on the ambush?"

"Unfortunately, not much. The sniper appears to have been a professional. According to trajectory calculations, he or she set up on a maintenance platform under the bridge, but nothing was found up there. Based on a round recovered from a boat in the lot, it looks like our shooter was using a TAC-50. The combination of gun type and the lack of significant evidence tells me it was not likely an amateur. My guess is military experience, but I have no proof to support it, just a gut feeling."

"Yeah, Con said as much right after. He mentioned that the shooter's reactions reminded him of his own training."

"Exactly."

"Con also said the shooter seemed to be targeting only you. That true?"

Damn. It was definitely true, but I was hoping I was the only one who'd noticed. The last thing I need is both my partners on my ass about it. "It's possible, but who knows?" I hedge. "That's not what I called you about anyway."

"Then why did you interrupt all the traffic fun?"

"Tessa Taliaferro's been found."

"What? By whom? When?" Rosey questions.

"She showed up at the hospital as a Jane Doe. Officially, she reports she doesn't remember anything, but unofficially, I think she's afraid. Carmen was here when I arrived. The interview didn't yield anything actionable, and Carmen and I were ushered out pretty quickly. We sat in the waiting area for a while, and here's the interesting part, according to our MRPD contacts, the injuries sustained by Tessa are consistent with Danielle's. Traces of drugs were also found in her system, though in her case they were not likely taken voluntarily."

"Well, shit. That shakes things up a bit."

"Yeah."

"So, are we—" Rosey starts before I hear the blare of horns and cursing from his end of the call.

"Rosey? You all good, man?"

"Yeah, damn idiot in a Corvette just flew off the on-ramp and decided to cut across all lanes of traffic and go straight for the carpool lane. I had to slam the brakes and nearly got rear-ended by a not-too-happy trucker."

"Sounds about right for I-20."

"Well, back to what I was asking," Rosey continues. "Are we thinking Dustin Grimes killed Danielle then headed back to Magnolia Ridge and straight to Taliaferro? She was dating him, right?"

"According to Eva."

"Okay, so we like Grimes for both Danielle and Taliaferro, but do we like him for Demon?"

That was the same question I'd been asking myself since our last call. "I just don't know."

"Our assumption was that Dustin was both our drug dealer, Cage, and Demon…one and the same, but is this guy really smart enough to stage a kidnapping and an ambush on the same day?"

"Seems doubtful since he almost let himself get caught with Danielle," I reason. Grimes doesn't have a military background or any known firearms proficiency either, according to the information we've gathered.

"So, like I said earlier, maybe we're actually working two interconnected cases instead of one, and our killer is actually killers, plural."

"Fuck." I hang my head and rub my tired eyes. This is getting so tangled and complicated that I don't know how we'll ever unravel it. How can I keep Eva protected if attacks are coming from two fronts? I glance toward the door to Tessa's room, relieved she's safe right now.

"Linc, you still there?"

I must have missed something. "Sorry. I'm here."

"Look, we're both tired. Let's meet with Con tomorrow and hash things out," he suggests.

"Sounds good." I end the call and stash the phone in my pocket, my thoughts racing, trying to build connections. Thirty minutes and two trips to the vending machines later, Eva drags herself out of Tessa's room. Her eyes are red and puffy, and she looks exhausted. She drops down into the seat beside me, and her head falls to my shoulder as if it's the most natural thing in the world, as though the action didn't completely shift the ground under my feet. She trusts me.

I wrap my uninjured arm around her and run my hand over the curls now springing in every direction. With every stroke of my hand her body relaxes more and more into mine. "You okay, Rabbit?" I ask quietly, resting my cheek against the top of her head.

"Yeah. I just needed a minute." I can't see her face, but I hear the heaviness in her voice. I resist the urge to speak and just wait her out, continuing the calming strokes. "I, um…" She pauses and blows out a steadying breath. "I remember what that feels like, what Tessa feels like. I convinced myself Demon died in the same storm that saved me and let myself try to move on. Instead of fighting to remember and fighting to keep him from hurting anyone else, I made myself forget. Now my best friend is lying in there hurt the same way I was because I did nothing. I hid and hoped someone else would worry about whether or not Demon was found or stopped. I focused only on my own needs." Eva's voice has gotten quieter with every word she speaks until she's barely audible by the end.

"Eva, Rabbit, this is not your fault. You did what you needed to do in order to be a healthy mom for Clemmie." I take her chin with my free hand and try to turn her eyes up to mine. She resists. "Rabbit, look at me. It's important." Eyes swimming with unshed tears hesitantly meet mine. "We don't think this was Demon." She jerks back in shock.

"What do you mean? It has to be!" Realizing her voice was raised, she glances around to make sure no one is listening before continuing. "Who else could it be? It's exactly the same."

"That's just it, it's not exactly the same." I briefly share some of the differences and our reasoning that Dustin and Demon are likely two different people. Eva's eyes reflect her confusion and fear.

"So we're back to having no idea who Demon is, and Dustin is nowhere to be found. *Two* men are out there hurting women, including my best friend, and no one can stop them?" She bolts from her seat and starts pacing. "I don't know what to do. Maybe I should try hypnosis or regression therapy or something. Maybe I could remember something new."

"Okay, but how certain will you be that what comes to mind are accurate memories?"

"I don't know," she practically growls. Frustration is evident in her voice as her pacing increases and fists clench. "I can't just keep doing nothing. I need to help." Her voice breaks. "What if he…" She shoves her fist to her mouth and leaves the thought unfinished. I stand to intercept her and pull her gently into me.

The moment is interrupted when the elevator dings. The doors open to expel a very determined-looking Carmen Castillo. "Linc. Somehow I knew I'd find you still here." She turns to Eva. "Having you both together will save me some time. Let's have a seat." She gestures to the same uncomfortable chairs I've occupied for hours. I settle in, knowing whatever she's about to say can't possibly be good.

"Did you find Dustin?" Eva asks hopefully. I can tell by Carmen's expression the news is not that positive.

"No, but we did find someone else." Eva stares in confusion, but the puzzle pieces are clicking together in my brain, and I know whose name is about to come out of her mouth even before she says it.

CHAPTER 66

Eva

Gerald Manchester is dead. Thankfully, Detective Castillo spared me the specifics yesterday, but my attacker was found deceased, actually not just deceased, but murdered. Judging from the expression on Ashe's face when she'd briefed him, it must have been bad. I didn't want to know.

Since Luke wanted to stay the night with Tessa, I'd had Ashe drive me home in time to eat dinner with my family and spend the rest of the evening playing with Clemmie before bath time and stories concluded in bedtime. My sleep had been surprisingly calm and restful, but my workday was turning out to be the exact opposite.

Despite my lack of details regarding Gerald Manchester's death, my mind had no problem using every spare moment between seeing clients to conjure up various scenarios, each one more gruesome than the next. Seeing Gerald's wife in the treatment center today had just made things worse. She'd been transferred from my caseload to Jake's due to conflict of interest, so I only saw her in passing, but her eyes were red from crying and her stare had been vacant. While I'd certainly held no goodwill toward the man, I'd never wished him dead.

A knock at my door has Jake poking his head through the barely cracked opening. "You have a minute?"

"Sure. Come on in." I close the file I was working on and spin my chair to face him where he takes up residence on the love seat.

"Carrie Manchester. Today was my first session with her. She used to be yours, so is there anything you can tell me that might help me work with her? She was pretty closed off today. I just got a lot of one-word answers."

Our treatment consents cover our ability to staff cases, and Jake is already in possession of her file, so I have no issue with reviewing her situation. Jake listens intently as I describe Carrie's previous home situation and shelter placement. He seems angry when I briefly gloss over my related attack and subsequent "gift" but calms when I reveal that Mr. Manchester is now deceased.

"So, he won't be hurting you again. You must be relieved," Jake comments, staring at me intently.

I shift in my chair, uncomfortable with both the attention and the idea that I could be relieved by someone's murder. "I, um…I don't know. I mean I'm relieved to be out of danger, but—"

Jake interrupts me. "Are you? Are you really out of danger?"

Slightly creeped out by the unusual turn of this conversation, I stand and turn to place the file from my desk into my locking cabinet. I shove a few unruly tendrils behind my ear as I face Jake again, intending to usher him out. His eyes are focused on the action of my hand.

"Is your hair naturally blonde?" His question stops me in my tracks before I find myself taking a step back. Thankfully, my cell phone chimes from the desk, breaking the awkward silence between us. "Well, I need to get back to work," Jake says as though he never asked the previous question. "Thanks for the update on my client." In less than a minute, he's gone.

I sit heavily and take a minute to check my text, finding an update from Luke to let me know Tessa is being released in a few hours. The momentary relief distracts me from the discomfort of Jake's visit. Pretty soon, I'm too busy to think about it as client after client requests a portion of my time.

Finally, we close to the public, and I have a moment to catch up on my clinical notes and treatment plans before time to lock up my files and head out. Mal is locking his office as I start down the hall, so we walk out together. Waving at Moss, I unlock my 4Runner and climb in. I toss my belongings into the passenger seat and hurriedly crank the steaming-hot vehicle, turning the vents right toward my face to fully blast air conditioning as I fasten my seat belt.

I reach for my purse so I can plug my phone into the charger while I drive, but the handle catches on something between the seat and the door. My hard yank causes the purse to fly free, flinging its contents all over the floorboard. Groaning and griping under my breath, I try to reach everything, only to be pulled up short by the seat belt.

My patience is running thin as I unfasten the belt and lean over the center console to drag all my belongings toward me. The one thing I actually needed from my purse, my phone, is conspicuously absent. I shove my hand up under the passenger seat, feeling around for the wayward device but finding something unfamiliar and round instead.

I snag the object and pull it out. It's an orange. Holding the small fruit, I straighten up and stare. Clemmie doesn't like oranges, and I typically stick to juice, so I don't understand how this got in my car. Could it have been in my purse? A small sticker on the side rolls back and catches on my finger. I fling the fruit and spring from the car when I read the small print, "California Clementine".

My breath is coming in pants by the time Moss reaches my side because I recognize the clementine for what it is, a threat. Demon is claiming his daughter.

"Call Polly. I need to know where Clemmie is." Moss looks at me questioningly. "I don't have time to explain," I yell. "Just do it!" Jake and Jolie exit the back door as Moss is dialing. They're headed for their cars but change direction when they see us.

"Car trouble?" Jake asks. "Do I need to grab my jumper cables?"

I shake my head but don't otherwise respond, too busy listening intently for Polly to answer the call Moss has on speaker phone. At the sound of her happy voice, my knees turn liquid, and I find myself sitting on the pavement.

"Well, hello there, Josh. Is everything okay?"

"Yes, ma'am. Everything is fine. Eva just needed to talk to you." Moss leans down and hands me the phone.

"Aunt Polly, is Clemmie okay?" I hear the slight tremor in my voice and clear my throat.

"Of course she is. Is there some reason she

wouldn't be?" I hear my baby babbling in the background, and it's the sweetest sound I've ever heard. "She's just pretending to feed that purple bear she drags everywhere."

"Jo-Bee."

"Yeah, that's the one."

"Aunt Polly, can you and Clemmie stay inside until I get home?"

"Sure. It's like a million degrees outside anyway. Something I need to know about?"

"I'll explain when I get there."

I end the call and accept the outstretched hand Moss offers. He pulls me to my feet, and I realize Jolie and Jake are still beside us.

"What was that about?" Jolie questions with hands on her hips. "Please tell me you didn't receive another delivery."

"No. No delivery, just a false alarm," I evade.

"Okay, well if you're sure, I need to get going." Jolie gives me a one-armed hug and heads toward her car. Jake nods at me and Moss then leaves as well. I grab my keys from the ignition and quickly lock my car. Moss is already ushering me toward his vehicle without needing an explanation.

"Drive fast," I beg.

CHAPTER 67

Ashe

Eva's call came in as I was wrapping up a debrief with Rosey and Con. We'd spent most of the day huddled in the conference room going over everything we had so far. Based on our theory of two killers, we grouped similar crimes together and subtracted everything that could be attributed to Gerald Manchester, such as the physical attack on Eva and also her wreck, since forensics matched the paint transfer on Eva's 4Runner to his large work truck.

We'd received more information today from MRPD as well as Atlanta. Toxicology showed traces of the same sedative in both Danielle and Tessa's systems. No DNA was found related to the sexual assaults, but initial opinions pointed to the same weapon being used in both cases, though nothing was determined conclusive yet. Because a knife was also used in the attack that killed Mouse and injured Spock, we've tentatively attributed those to Dustin Grimes also since Mouse was informing on the drug dealer Cage, who we believe to be one and the same with Grimes. This would also make him responsible for the ambush and the graze on my arm, which is barely more bothersome than a scratch today.

If it weren't for the delivery of Manchester's

fingers in a box, we could almost attribute the other deliveries, excluding the Cliff Bar at the hospital which never yielded any clues, to him and call it case closed once Dustin Grimes is found. Unfortunately, since it would be impossible for Manchester to cut off and deliver his own fingers and then eviscerate himself, we now believe we have a third person to find. We can't completely rule out the possibility that Dustin Grimes is Demon or even that our gift giver is someone other than Demon, but both possibilities seem so unlikely that we've pushed them to the backburner.

We need to determine Demon's ultimate motive. Why send deliveries at all? Why mainly send them to Eva's work? Why protect her from Manchester? Nothing is adding up, and we have way more questions than answers where Demon is concerned. We had taken everything as far as we could without new information, so when my phone rang, Con and Rosey gathered their things and left the room to me.

"Hey, Rabbit. How was work?"

"Ashe, please get to my house now."

The desperation in Eva's voice has me rushing toward my office for my keys. "Eva, what's happened?"

"He's coming for Clemmie. He knows!"

"Where are you? Is Moss with you?"

"Yes. He's driving. Just get there, please," she begs.

"I'm on my way." The call ends before I can say more or try to figure out what happened, but by that time I'm already in my truck and driving. I use the hands-free feature to call Rosey and let him know what's happening so he and Con will be prepared should I need them.

I pull in right behind Moss and jump out to intercept Eva as she runs full tilt toward the house. My legs are longer, and Eva's speed is hampered by the dress shoes she wore to work. I catch her easily and place myself in front of the door.

"You're going to scare Polly and Clemmie. Slow down a second and breathe before you go in there." I glance over her head to Moss, who's come up behind her, but he just shrugs. I guess he's as in the dark as me. "Tell me what happened so I can help."

"He left it in my car, or in my purse, or...I don't even know, but it was there, and I know what he meant, and I have to protect her." Eva barely takes a breath, and her thoughts are so disjointed, it's hard for me to follow.

"Okay. Slow down. We'll make sure Polly and Clemmie are protected. I promise, but I need to know what happened. What was in your purse?"

"An orange, well, not an orange, but you know what that means, right?"

I take Eva's hands and lead her to the swing. Kneeling in front of her, I try to walk her back through events. "Did anything unusual happen at work today?"

"No, well, not really. I had a weird conversation with Jake, but whatever." I look at Moss, and he nods, assuring me he'll check out Jake. "After work, I got in my car and when I tossed my purse in the seat, it spilled. While I was trying to find my phone under the seat, I found the orange, except it wasn't an orange. It was a clementine. Do you get it? It was a *clementine*. He knows about my baby." Eva's voice pitches higher and higher as she speaks, and her breathing increases to near hyperventilation. With my hands on either side of her face, I bring her focus to my eyes.

"Slow down. Breathe with me." In and out, I breathe with her until she's back to normal. "I'm going to stay with you, and Moss is going to go check out your car. Where are your keys?"

"In Moss's car." Moss disappears without a word, but I know he'll contact Rosey and Con and update me when he has news.

"All right. Let's go in so you can assure yourself everything is fine." We stand, and I step aside to let her open the door. Happy laughter and excited barking greet us as Clemmie clambers up from the floor to run to her mom.

"Momma home!" she squeals as Eva scoops her up and hugs her tightly. "Owie, Momma." Clemmie wiggles and squirms to get out of Eva's unbreakable hold. With a kiss to her head, Eva eventually lowers Clemmie back to the floor.

"Clemmie, let's go show Momma the cookies we made." Polly rises from the chair and places her book facedown on the seat to hold her place.

"Cookies!" Clemmie grabs her mother's hand and mine and drags us toward the kitchen, following Polly. Taco runs wildly and tangles around everyone's legs as we walk. A platter on the table holds a stack of chocolate chip cookies, and Clemmie drops our hands to climb a chair and grab two. She holds one out to me. "Cookie, Wink."

Half the cookie falls in crumbs to the floor, but her happy grin is contagious. I take the mangled cookie and make a big deal of enjoying the gooey chocolate. "Cookie, Momma." Eva gets the same offer and responds in kind. Her face is smiling, but her eyes still reflect worry.

The rest of the evening is spent eating a healthy stir-fry dinner, returning Taco to Tessa, who is at home in her brother's care, and watching Clemmie play. Once bedtime arrives, Polly retires to her room to read while Eva takes care of the bath and story time ritual. While she's occupied, I call Karo and arrange for her to start a daytime detail protecting Polly and Clemmie. I also check in with Moss who reports finding a single clementine in Eva's car but no prints or other evidence. A quick look out the window assures me Villain has the house covered for the night, so I grab the go bag I always keep in my truck and wait for Eva.

I'd already assured her I wasn't leaving tonight, so it's no surprise when she returns with a pillow and a couple blankets. "Are you sure you don't mind staying?"

"I'm sure. Get some sleep, and don't worry. Villain is outside, and I'll be right here. You've got your monitor in Clemmie's room, and everything will be fine."

Eva smiles slightly and deposits her load on the opposite end of the couch from where I'm sitting. "Thanks, Ashe. Maybe I'm overreacting. It's just a piece of fruit, but it seems like so much more."

"Either way, it doesn't hurt to be overly cautious." I snag the pillow and lean back, wedging it behind my head. "Get some rest. Everyone's fine right now. We'll talk more tomorrow." She nods and heads toward her room, leaving me alone with the TV.

CHAPTER 68

Eva

"You are so beautiful, so obedient. I've waited so long. Our child will be perfect." Demon croons in my ear. My body is weak and sticky with blood and fluids. What child? I don't understand. My mind is like quicksand, sucking up my thoughts and refusing to return them.

"You are the one, sweet Julie. My other wives weren't strong. They gave up before they were fully pure." His hand strokes the raw wound he just created. The pain barely registers anymore as one ache blends into another, making individual issues indecipherable.

"This is it, the thirteenth visit to my thirteenth wife. It's perfect. Our child was created today. I just know it." His whispered voice sounds almost giddy with excitement. "Do you think it will be a boy or a girl?" He strokes my concave belly as though conjuring a child within.

"I hope it's a girl who looks just like you. Soon I'll be able to take you home. I just have to know you're pure and you won't hurt our baby. You're safe here. I made sure there was nothing dangerous." His words barely have any meaning to me at all. I roll to face the wall and curl up around myself, seeking the escape of unconsciousness.

He prevents the oblivion by curling his body around mine. One arm slips under my head, and the other reaches around to pull my body tightly to his before finding and squeezing my breast. "Nothing is more important to me, Julie. Our child is the most important thing in the world, and I will never give her up." His hand moves back down to my belly. "Don't fail me, Julie. I can't keep you if you fail."

As always when I dream, I wake gasping for breath and checking my scars to make sure they are no longer fresh but long healed. Just as I sit up and swing my legs over the side of the bed, I hear a quiet knock at my door that can only be Ashe. I debate taking the coward's way out and pretending I went back to sleep or doing what I really want and inviting him in. The first option should be my gut instinct, but it isn't. For years, I've faced these dreams on my own, but tonight I want comfort. I don't want to be alone.

Decision made, I walk to the door and open it. Ashe is dressed in athletic shorts and a thin T-shirt. His eyes meet mine, searching as though trying to discern what I need in this moment before the distraction of my state of undress draws his eyes downward to the hem of my oversize shirt and farther to my bare legs and red-painted toes. No words are spoken, but then again, none are needed.

When I take a small step forward, Ashe closes the distance. I find myself crushed against his chest, his mouth on mine. He doesn't so much kiss as devour. It's not gentle, but it's exactly what I need. I pull him farther into the room and quietly close the door behind us. The light of the hallway fades, leaving us lit only by the glow of the nightlights I keep on each side of the room. Ashe's grip at my waist loosens as he breaks the kiss and looks into my eyes. I hope all he sees is desire, that the darkness hides the vestiges of fear I shove to the background. I lift to my toes and this time I kiss him, pouring my certainty into the action. Again, he breaks first.

"Little Rabbit, you're playing a dangerous game, and I'm not sure you're ready for the consequences." One of his hands at the back of my waist drifts lower, pulling me close enough to feel his meaning. I should be terrified, but surprisingly, I feel nothing but safe. I push myself even closer. "Eva, are you sure? You know I want you, but the last thing I want is to hurt or scare you."

"You don't scare me, Ashe. I want new memories to replace the old. I want them with you. Can we just try?"

"We can do whatever you want, rabbit. I'm yours. Take what you need." With that statement he spins us around, putting his back to the bed. He sits on the edge and releases me completely, giving me the freedom of the next move. I place my hands on his shoulders and climb up to sit astride his lap. I can feel his desire, and no doubt he can feel mine, but still he makes no move to touch me.

Confidence spiking, I laugh and shove him backward before following him down for another kiss. "Touch me." As though he was waiting for my command, his hands find my hair and tangle within the messy curls. He kisses me hard, almost bruising my mouth, but I return his fervor full force. My body begins to move of its own accord in rhythm with his. He gives me full control, never trapping or leading me.

It's like nothing I've ever experienced and everything I've ever needed.

His hands move to my bare legs, and I tense for a moment, knowing he'll discover my scars. "Don't run now, little rabbit. We're just about to get to the good part." I can feel his smile as his hands caress the tops of my thighs, never once veering toward the scars he knows are there. "Do you trust me?" I nod. "Then let me show you what I think about your scars."

Still astride his body, I sit up and focus my full attention on his hands and his words. I can feel his body straining with need beneath me, but he takes his time and stares directly into my soul. "Scars are just your body's way of reminding you that you won. If you forget the battle, then you also forget the victory. That's what these scars say to me. They say here is a courageous woman who fought over and over and over. She never gave up, and in the end, it was she who was victorious, not her demons."

As he speaks, he traces each mark with the softest of touches until every mark has felt his reverence. A tear flows down my cheek, followed by a trail of them. He sits up and kisses them away. My heart overflows with gratitude for this man who has taken marks I always felt were shameful and to be hidden and turned them into a badge of honor. In that moment, impulse wins out over common sense and I blurt, "I love you, Asher Lincoln."

He laughs. "I'm pretty sure I've loved you since you tripped over my feet and made me chase you, Rabbit. It's about time you realized you loved me too." A huge smile stretches across my face. I tackle the man

I love and proceed to make him mine in every way possible.

CHAPTER 69

Ashe

I wake to the sound of soft snoring and masses of curls attacking my face. My body is pleasantly warm, and my hand is full of the softness and curves that are Eva. Her body is the little spoon to my big spoon, and my first thought is that I never want to leave this bed, or this woman for that matter. My second thought is to wonder why I hear two sets of almost identical snores. I cautiously peek through the curls with one eye and spy Clemmie snuggled up on top of the covers in front of Eva. She's clad in a pair of dinosaur footie pajamas, and her curls are just as crazy as her mom's. The two of them lying beside me paint a picture of the future I want more than I want my next breath.

Since my clothes are on the floor, and I'd rather not have Clemmie wake up before I'm dressed, I cautiously detangle myself from Eva, immediately missing her warmth. I slip slowly out of the bed and throw on my boxer briefs and shorts before locating my shirt on the other side of the room. Wishing Eva's room had an en suite, I slowly open the door to the hallway and take a cautious step toward the bathroom.

"Good morning, Asher." Aunt Polly's voice sounds from behind me. Damn. I turn slowly, glad my untucked shirt hides my morning, um, discomfort.

"Uh, good morning. I was just um—"

"I know what you were just doing. I'm not that old."

"Um, I—"

"Well, quit hem hawing around and get to it. Breakfast will be ready soon." With that, she heads off toward the kitchen and leaves me grinning in her wake.

By the time I take care of business and return to Eva's room, Clemmie is jumping on the bed and Eva is fighting to keep the covers pulled up and her daughter from taking a tumble. The grin I was already sporting grows even bigger. Eva looks my way as I laugh, and her eyes reflect her feelings about our night together. Unable to help myself, I jump on the bed and plop a kiss right on her mouth. Clemmie laughs and dives on top of us, planting her own sloppy kisses on our cheeks. If she wonders why I'm in her mother's room, it's not evident.

"Alright, little dinosaur. It's time for us to go get breakfast." I swoop Clemmie up and toss her over my shoulder amid peals of those sweet little girl giggles that have stolen my heart and head toward the kitchen to give Eva an opportunity to get dressed.

"Wink! Wink! Wink!"

I reorient my captive to the upright position and prop her on my hip before responding. "What's up, buttercup?"

"Potty, Wink." Okay. Um, how do I take a little girl to potty? I'm way out of my league here. Clemmie wiggles to get down, and as soon as I set her on her feet, she takes off for the bathroom. In no time, she has her pajamas unzipped and discarded on the hallway floor before she runs into the bathroom clad only in some kind of pull-up diaper.

She leaves the door slightly ajar, and a few minutes later I hear a flush and a baby voice calling me. I look around, hoping to spot Eva or Polly for a save, but no such luck. Peering around the door, fearful of what I might find, I spot Clemmie simply standing in front of the sink with her hands raised as though waiting for a lift to wash her hands. I oblige before helping her dry her hands and zipping her pajamas back on. Apparently zipping up is a bit more complicated than unzipping.

Polly has eggs and bacon, the real kind this time, ready by the time we reach the kitchen. I fasten Clemmie in her chair and hand her the small plate of eggs Polly has set aside along with a toddler spoon. Eva enters just as the bacon is being plated, and I don't miss the wink Polly gives her or Eva's resulting blush.

"Ashe, can you drive me to work since I don't have my car?"

"Of course. I just need to introduce Karo to Polly and Clemmie first."

"Karo? Who's Karo?" Eva asks.

"She's the new security detail for Clemmie and Polly so they have protection during the day when Moss is with you."

"Oh. That sounds great. Thank you." I kiss the top of her head as I walk by then head outside.

"Morning, boss," Karo greets as she climbs out.

"None of that. Ashe or Linc. I'll answer to either."

"Sure thing."

"You ready for this?"

"Of course. I love kids. That's why I volunteered to take this assignment. Villain says Polly is a sweetheart who likes to feed people, so I'm sure everything will be fine."

"Come on in. I'll cover the introductions."

Karo pulls an overnight bag from her car. I've asked for close protection since Eva and I both will feel better knowing eyes are on Clemmie and Polly all day rather than a detail that stays outside.

As soon as we get inside, I realize Karo was perfect for this job. She and Polly are quickly chatting like old friends. Clemmie shortens her name to "Car" and adds a few vroom vroom sound effects, and Eva visibly relaxes. After placing our breakfast dishes in the sink, Eva and I leave the others still finishing up and head toward her room. On the way, I grab my bag from where I'd dropped it beside the couch last night.

As soon as the door closes, I have Eva in my arms, wishing we had time for a repeat of last night. She's already dressed in another of her bland work outfits, so I don't mess her up even though I want to. I do land a kiss on her gorgeous mouth though. She tastes like orange juice. I can't say I'm surprised. She responds with a beautiful smile and lifts eyes that shine golden green in the morning light to meet mine. "What was that for?" she asks.

"Just because I finally can. That's the only reason I need."

"Ashe, I'm so happy." She loops her arms around my neck and lays her cheek on my chest. "I wish we could just stay here and never have to think about what's outside these doors."

"I wish that too, Rabbit. Facing what's out there is hard, and I know you're worried about Clemmie. I am too, but we've stepped up protection in all areas, and we're doing everything possible to keep you all safe, including Tessa."

"Oh my gosh! I forgot. I have to go see Tessa." Eva breaks loose from my arms and starts rushing around hunting shoes. "Ashe, hurry up and get ready. Luke said Tessa refused to stay home from work today, and I need to stop by to check on her. I understand why she needs to get back out and do things on her own, but I'm worried because physically she's nowhere near ready."

"I'm on it," I reply, quickly snagging and throwing on clean clothes from my bag. We head to the bathroom to brush our teeth at the same time, and the experience is a little surreal. I could see myself making this a morning routine with Eva by my side. Soon we're out the door and on our way with Moss following behind.

Halfway to the coffee shop, my phone rings. The Bluetooth connects automatically when I crank the truck, so the screen on the dash reads Carmen Castillo. I let the call go to voicemail, not wanting to have a confidential conversation in front of Eva. She pays very little attention since she's engrossed in a text conversation with Luke about his sister.

Once we pull into The Daily Grind, I have Eva wait for Moss and let her know I'll be inside after I check my messages. I pull up the voicemail from Carmen and tap play. "Call me ASAP. We found Grimes."

CHAPTER 70

Eva

Moss is right on my heels as I enter the coffee shop. Tessa is behind the bar delivering orders and smiling as usual, though it's impossible to miss the strain in her eyes and the slump of her shoulders. Her manager, Allie, has taken over greeting the customers, allowing Tessa to focus on making drinks, which keeps her back to the crowd for the most part. Though most people wouldn't notice, the slowness of her movements is obvious to me. I can't believe just forty-eight hours after she was found, she's already back at work. No way her doctor could possibly approve, though obviously I understand needing to get back to a regular routine rather than dwelling on the darkness.

Luke is sitting at the end of the bar, and if his face is any indication, he also doesn't approve. He watches Tessa like a hawk, on a mission to spot any sign of weakness. When it's finally our turn at the counter, Moss orders his typical triple-shot espresso while I request a skinny latte with two extra shots and cinnamon. Tessa stays busy, and though I know she could make the drinks with her eyes closed, she acts as though they take her total and complete focus.

When she turns to hand us our coffee, I manage to catch a quick glance between her and Moss though she quickly covers it by turning to me. Moss's stare never leaves her face as I lean over the narrow counter to give her a quick hug. "Shouldn't you be at home?" I ask in concern as she winces.

"Yeah, she should," Luke pipes in from his stool. "The doctor told her to take the rest of the week off, but here we are."

"We already had this discussion, Luke. What am I supposed to do, continue to sit around holed up in my house, waiting and wondering if something else is going to happen or get out and get back to my life?" Luke rolls his eyes but says no more.

"Listen, why don't you come over tonight, and we can have a girls' night. I'll even make sure we have plenty of ice cream and other junk food." Before she can respond, I add, "Clemmie has been asking for you." I know playing the Clemmie card is probably a bit low, but I see the refusal brewing and know Tessa can never resist my daughter.

"Fine. Give me time to go home and change after work, and I'll be there." She doesn't sound happy about it, but at least she's coming. Allie calls for her to make another drink, so Tessa returns her attention to work. Moss heads toward the exit. I follow him, accepting a hug from Luke as I pass by.

Back outside, Moss stops beside a nondescript car and starts speaking to the man inside. Curious, I step up beside him and wait for an introduction. The man behind the wheel has latte skin and close-cut, dark facial hair. The rest of his hair is cut in a fade with lots of dark spiky twists all over the top. He wears sunglasses that he removes when he spots me.

"Hello, gorgeous. Who might you be?" he asks

with a friendly smile.

"Nope. Not happening. Don't even think about it. This one belongs to Linc," Moss cuts in.

"Belongs? I don't belong to anyone except myself."

"Whoa, hold up, feisty. I didn't mean anything by it. I was just making sure Bond here knew you were off-limits before he gets his fool self killed by the boss, who's staring daggers from his truck."

Sure enough, when I turn around, Ashe's stare is directed straight at us though his mouth is moving, letting me know he's still on his call. I turn back to the new guy. "Your name is Bond?"

"Actually, it's James Carver." He sticks his hand out the window for me to shake.

"Moss just called you Bond."

"Yep. Haven't you figured out yet that no one at LCR goes by their actual name?" He laughs. "I guess they figured Bond went with James, like 007."

"Oh. I see. You're Tessa's new guard?"

"Yep. I've been assigned to Ms. Taliaferro. Not a bad gig if you ask me. She's very easy on the eyes," James says, eyeing Moss with a grin. The comment earns him a smack on the back of the head. "Ouch! Shit, man, that hurt."

"Just keep your eyes in your head and your mind on the job," Moss gripes before taking my elbow, leading us toward Ashe's truck. My guess is that James isn't just called Bond because it matches his first name. I'm sensing he must have a reputation with the ladies. The idea amuses me.

"Nice to meet you," I call over my shoulder.

"Likewise," I hear as Moss opens my door.

Too late, I realize as I climb in that I should have grabbed a coffee for Ashe. I wait for him to end his call and start backing out before I apologize.

"No big deal. I'll grab some when I get to the office," he replies.

"What did the detective want?" I know I shouldn't ask, but my curiosity gets the best of me.

"There's been a new development." Ashe briefly shifts his focus from the road to me and back. "Dustin Grimes was found this morning."

"That's wonderful! Did he admit to being the one who took Tessa? She says she doesn't remember, but I think she's just scared."

"Eva," Ashe tries to interrupt, but I'm on a roll.

"If it was him, she'll be safe now, and Danielle's family will have justice. Wait, if he's Demon, then Clemmie and I will be safe too! I feel so relieved!"

"Eva, there's more." My excitement deflates at the serious nature of his tone. Whatever he's about to tell me isn't going to be good. "He's dead."

"Dead like just died, or dead like murdered?" I ask, hoping for the former so we can lay all the recent events at his feet and move on.

"Dead like murdered."

"Oh." I don't know what else to say to that. Murdered means there's still a killer out there somewhere.

"From initial reports, it appears he was killed in the exact same manner as Gerald Manchester. The fingers weren't with the body." I gasp, and Ashe clears his throat before continuing. "He was also missing another body part."

"What?" I'm not following.

"Think eunuch." Oh. Oh! I gag on the sip of coffee that now feels lodged in my throat. "Eva? Are you okay? Do you need me to pull over?"

I shake my head and manage to swallow. "You, uh, you think this is the same killer?" I stammer. "Is it Demon?" The last question comes out as a whisper.

"It's too early to say conclusively, but yeah, that'd be my guess."

"But why? Why kill Gerald and Dustin?"

"That's exactly what we have to find out."

CHAPTER 71

Ashe

After dropping Eva at work, I arrange to meet Carmen at our offices and make Rosey and Con aware. I'm the first to arrive other than Jillian. I ask her to send Carmen to the conference room when she shows up and head to my office to gather my thoughts before we get started.

Eva's question about why the killer targeted Manchester and Grimes weighs on my mind. The note sent with Manchester's fingers implied a sense of possession over Eva and possibly an urge to protect, but Grimes never hurt Eva, only her friend. How can I keep my family safe if I can't figure out what exactly is going on? Wait. My family? I love Eva, but...but nothing. I love her, and she trusts me to protect her and Clemmie and Polly. That makes them mine. I'll worry about the logistics of that once I've ensured their safety.

Jillian's voice startles me as she announces Carmen's arrival and lets me know Con is here and Rosey is five minutes out. I grab my laptop and a pen and notebook before heading to the conference room. Carmen is alone when I enter, perusing the various boards displaying our work.

"Impressive," she comments. "Looks like you guys have made much the same conclusions as we have, but your setup definitely makes things easier to see."

"That's because we have all the fancy toys. You could always come over to the dark side and go private. We promise to play nice," Con comments as he strolls in and takes a seat at the table.

"I know better, Connery. Playing nice is not in your personality."

"Sometimes it can be more fun to not play nice," he replies with a wink.

"Sometimes when you don't play nice, you lose body parts," Carmen says with a smirk as she tosses a file open in front of Con.

"Oh, shit!" he exclaims as he jerks away from the table, splashing the coffee he was drinking over his hand. "Fuck, Carmen. Was that really necessary?" he asks, shaking the coffee off.

"Completely." She wears a satisfied smirk as she retrieves the images of Dustin Grimes sans vital appendage. I can't help but laugh. Gallows humor is better than no humor at all.

Rosey chooses that moment to join us. "What did I miss?" He scans the room, noting Carmen's smirk and Con's scowl.

"I'll be happy to show you," Carmen begins as she settles into a seat near Con.

"Nah, man. Don't fall for it. Trust me, you do not want to see that," Con states, carefully moving to place himself farther away from the offending file.

Rosey just shrugs and takes a chair, leaving me the last man, uh person, standing. I guess that means I'll start. "As Con just learned, we've had a new development. Dustin Grimes was found dead this morning. His body was missing fingers and—"

"Don't say it, man." Con cringes and places a protective hand over his lap. "We get it, just don't say it." Carmen laughs, and Rosey just shakes his head.

"Yeah, well. In any case, Grimes and Manchester initially appear to have been taken out by the same killer. We just need to determine motive," I begin.

"Motive is easy. Our guy fancies himself a protector. Manchester used his hands to beat Eva Jones. Our killer then cuts off his fingers, rendering his hands useless before killing him. Grimes then cuts up and rapes Tessa Taliaferro and loses his fingers and his dick—"

"Damn it, Carmen. You just had to say it, didn't you?" Con grouses.

"I can say it again if you want to keep interrupting." She looks pointedly at Con who shakes his head and runs a pretend zipper over his lips. "Anyway, now Grimes is dead too. Seems like a punishment fits the crime kind of thing. I almost think we should be looking for a woman." She turns to me. "How well do you know Ms. Jones? I'd say she has the best motive."

I feel my blood boiling and open my mouth to lay into Carmen, but Rosey, ever the voice of reason, speaks up before I can. "That's a valid theory, but what about the deliveries she received at work, the food delivery, the fingers, and yesterday the clementine?"

"We only have her word that she didn't call in the restaurant delivery herself. Nothing was wrong with the food, and by all accounts, she enjoyed the meal. She also could have grabbed the orange from the break room at work," Carmen counters.

"Okay, what about the cookies that showed up at

her house?" Rosey replies.

"Same thing. She could have easily sent them herself. The restaurant says the order was paid for with a Visa gift card, and the person who took the order couldn't remember if the person ordering was male or female due to the sheer volume of orders. The cookies were from a local bakery, but again, they're a popular item, and no one remembers who purchased them. Jones is one of the few people who had access to the house, and even her aunt thought she'd left them. Also, let's not forget all the drama she created over a Cliff Bar that probably came from the hospital cafeteria."

"That's all speculation, not proof. What about the gift box? You saw her black out in her office at the sight of the fingers. Are you saying she sent those to herself too?" I ask, incredulous at the turn of this conversation.

"It's not impossible. Passing out can be faked. She's intelligent and has a degree in psychology. It wouldn't be hard for her to figure out how to play us." Carmen taps her pen on the table as though considering her next words. "Look, I'm not saying she did it, but you all know as well as I do that violence changes people. Maybe everything that happened to Ms. Jones altered something inside her. I'm just saying we can't ignore the possibility."

"Noted," I say, hoping to close the topic. "What else do we have?"

Con pipes in with his first useful comment of the day. "We still have to consider the fact that this may be Demon, that we may have a notorious and dangerous serial killer in town. Just because we now know he didn't take Danielle and are relatively certain he didn't take Tessa, doesn't mean that he can't be responsible for these murders and Eva's deliveries."

"True," Rosey adds. "He could be trying to prove something to Eva. She mentioned his comments about wanting a child and how he referred to her as his wife. That could imply a sense of possession, that he can hurt her, but no one else can. I just don't understand why he retaliated for the attack on Tessa unless he felt Grimes was some sort of copycat."

"What's the MRPD's official stance?" I ask Carmen.

"At present, Ms. Jones is considered a suspect, but we are not ruling out the possibility that she could be a victim or a target. Either way, we plan to keep her under surveillance and bring her in for another interview."

"It's not her," I state definitively.

Carmen stands and gathers her things before tossing out on her way to the door, "Yeah, well, sleep with one eye open. You wouldn't be the first man to be led around by the wrong head."

CHAPTER 72

Eva

My day was relatively uneventful if you disregard two clients testing positive for methamphetamines on their random drug screens. Such is normal in the realm of substance abuse treatment. Their court referral officers weren't too happy, but outpatient treatment just can't provide the same insulation from the real world as inpatient. We do the best we can, but ultimately, it's the client's choice whether they choose to stay clean or not.

As I walk out, I make a mental list of all the snacks I need to pick up for my night with Tessa. I lock the treatment center door and turn to find Moss leaning against my driver's side door. While he's always in the parking lot, he doesn't typically wait for me like this. His serious stance sets off alarm bells in my head and has me picking up my pace.

"What's wrong?" I can't keep the note of fear from my voice.

"Ashe called and said we needed to go down to the police station for an interview."

"An interview? Has something happened? Is Clemmie okay?" I forget to breathe as my apprehension increases.

"Everyone is fine. Nothing new has happened. I think they just want to ask you a few questions," Moss says calmly. "Hop in, and I'll follow you over."

The trip to the police station is shorter than I would like, but I take the opportunity to call Aunt Polly and make sure she and Clemmie are okay. She tells me they're at the park under Karo's watchful eye. I inform her we're having company later and then call Tessa to let her know I'll be late. She sounds exhausted, but hopefully I can pamper her tonight and make sure she rests.

Too soon, I'm pulling into the parking lot, and I'm not the least bit prepared. Moss comes up beside me, and we enter the station side by side. He seems to have his protective face on, but I can't imagine why that would be necessary here. If I'm safe anywhere, it should be the police station. At the front desk, Moss gives our names, and we take a seat in the waiting area.

Detective Castillo appears and summons us down a dimly lit hallway. "Josh, you can wait out here," she says, indicating a cracked red vinyl chair. I catch a glimpse of Moss's angry face as I enter a small room with Detective Castillo on my heels.

"Take a seat, Ms. Jones." Her tone is very formal, bordering on hostile as she indicates the lone chair on the right side of the dated metal table. She takes the seat on the left, and once we're both settled, she pushes a button on a device in the center of the table and informs me that she's recording. I halfway expect to be read my rights, but that's not what occurs.

What follows is a series of questions that seem completely random. She asks about everything from my job to my parents. She asks about my stance on capital punishment and my whereabouts for the past forty-eight hours and whether or not anyone can verify I actually was where I claimed. Not wanting to throw Ashe to the wolves, I just list Villain and Moss as my verification along with Aunt Polly.

As thirty minutes ticks over into an hour, my patience is wearing thin, and Detective Castillo shows no signs of nearing a stopping point. "Look, I'm not sure what is really going on here, but could you just tell me or let me go?"

She studies me for a few minutes then opens a file that has been on the table since we entered. "Okay, if that's how you want it, let's cut to the chase." She starts laying out pictures along the center of the table. I have a suspicion what I'm going to see when I look, so I delay as long as possible, keeping my focus on the mirrored glass behind the detective.

"Take a look, Ms. Jones. An abuser and a rapist both dead. Not bad. It's about time someone stood up to those kinds of men, right? I mean, they deserved everything they got. It's not like anyone's going to be sorry to see them go. You did the world a favor in my opinion."

"I did what? Wait, no! No, no, no! I don't know what you're talking about. I wouldn't. I couldn't!"

"Sure you could." She takes a picture of a hand without fingers and shoves it at me. I gag and turn away. "He'll never hit his wife or kids ever again. He'll never hit you again. That's justice, right?"

"No, please." My breathing speeds up, and I feel like a weight is compressing my chest. Another picture is shoved in my face. It's a close up of a man's naked torso, a pool of blood where his missing penis used to be. It's too much. I stand and stumble to the garbage can in the corner before falling to my knees and losing everything I'd consumed all day. Tears streak down my face and mingle with the mucus and saliva as dry heaves wrack my body.

When I'm finally spent, I drop to the floor and lean back against the wall. A bottle of water and a handful of tissues appear in front of my face, and I look up to see sympathy on Detective Castillo's normally hard face. "Sorry. I had to know. I'm still not ruling you out, but I'm leaning toward believing you."

"I'm watched twenty-four hours a day. There's no way I could've done this." I take the water and wash my mouth out, spitting into the can before wetting the tissues and doing my best to clean my face. "Am I free to go?"

"You've always been free to go. This was just a voluntary interview."

Now she tells me. I'd be furious if I had any energy. As it is, I just want to find a bathroom and clean up before anyone can see me. Reluctantly, I accept her outstretched hand and her assistance to stand. She directs me to the restroom down the hall before opening the door. Moss catches one look at me and loses it.

"What the hell did you do to her? This was just supposed to be an interview, not a full-fledged interrogation," he rants.

"I did my job," Detective Castillo replies unapologetically.

"Well fuck you and your job." Moss wraps his arm around my waist and supports my stumbling gait as I try to push the gruesome images out of my mind. He stays outside as I practically fall into the dingy bathroom.

The mirror over the stainless-steel sink isn't a

mirror at all, but rather a piece of some sort of reflective shatterproof plastic. It distorts my image, making me appear even more frightening than I thought I'd look. My makeup is a lost cause, so I use the hand soap to quickly wash my face. The cool water does wonders to restore my senses even though my body still feels weak. I take a few small sips from the bottle I'd settled on the edge of the sink and prepare myself to leave the solitude of this room.

A knock at the door ends my procrastination. "Eva? You okay in there? Do I need to come in?"

Rather than answer, I push the door open and meet Moss's worried gaze. I don't have to say anything. He tucks me under his arm and shuffles me out of the station and into the humid evening air before I even have time to realize we've moved.

"Ashe is going to be pissed," he grumbles under his breath. I don't even think about trying to drive as Moss fastens me into the passenger seat of his vehicle and heads toward home. I try not to think about anything at all.

CHAPTER 73

Eva

Moss must have called Aunt Polly while I was with Detective Castillo, because she has completely readied the house for girls' night. Snacks are arranged on the kitchen table, and I suspect if I open the freezer I'll also find ice cream. Tessa lounges on the couch while Luke sits on the floor pretending to make stuffed animals dance for Clemmie. I wave but head straight to my room and then to the shower. My experience at the police station needs to be washed from my body before I can feel human again.

Changing into yoga pants and an oversize T-shirt, I leave my damp hair to air dry so the curls will hopefully still look okay in the morning. As soon as I step outside my door, Clemmie yells for me and runs to jump into my arms. I bury my nose in her ginger ringlets and breathe in today's dose of her sweet baby sunshine scent. She gifts me a sloppy kiss on the cheek before heading back to coerce Luke into more play. Thankfully, he's a good sport and seems enamored with my daughter. Aunt Polly sits in her favorite chair, seemingly engrossed in a novel, and Tessa hasn't moved from her position on the couch.

I plop down beside her and ask, "Which one first, salty or sweet?"

She smiles. "Salty."

"Hot or not?"

"Not."

"Okay, chips for the win." I push myself off the couch with what little energy I have left and snag the bag of cheese curls off the table. Bless her, Aunt Polly always knows just what we need. I drop back down with our snack and a couple bottles of water from the fridge.

Tessa opens the bag and grabs a handful of fake-cheesy goodness before asking, "Where were you?"

"Later," I whisper after a meaningful glance at Clemmie. Since I was already late, bedtime comes quickly. Luke takes his leave when my sleepy girl hits the whiny stage of the night. Polly has already given her a bath, but she requires a story from both me and Tessa before she's ready to close her eyes.

As is her habit, Aunt Polly retires to read in her room after making sure we know that there is, in fact, ice cream in the freezer. I have no idea what I did to deserve her, but I'll be forever grateful. She is the mom I always wished I had.

Ashe has messaged to check on me a few times, and I'm surprised at how much I miss him. He supports my need to take time out for Tessa but reminds me he is just a phone call away if I need him. I assure him that Villain is on duty outside, and all is calm inside before wishing him goodnight.

Finally, it's just me and Tessa. Ice cream is scooped, and sitcom reruns are playing quietly in the background. "I know," she says.

Not understanding what she means, I clarify, "About my interview at the police station?"

"What? No! You had to go to the police station and didn't tell me? What the heck is wrong with you?" Tessa smacks me hard with a throw pillow, nearly toppling my ice cream.

"Hey! Easy on the ice cream. It's not like I eat this often."

"Whatever. Spill. Why were you at the police station?"

"Nope. Not happening. You first. What did you mean when you said, 'I know'?"

Tessa focuses her attention on her ice cream as though it holds the secrets of the universe. I wait her out, knowing she'll cave eventually. Finally, she blows out a beleaguered breath and blurts, "I know Dustin is dead."

"Oh." The image of his mutilated body pops into my mind and almost has my ice cream making a reappearance. I set the rest of my bowl aside, no longer hungry. "Who told you?"

"No one. I saw it on the news."

"How do you feel about that?" I don't want to discount the possibility that she may be sad since she doesn't remember her attack.

"Honestly, I feel relieved."

My head pops up at that answer. "You want to talk about it?"

"I don't know. I guess I can now that he's gone. I was just afraid, you know?" A rogue tear drips down her cheek. "I was afraid if I told what happened to me, he would come back and take me again." She finally looks me in the eyes. "I'm not strong like you. I thought I was the strong one, but I'm not. You are."

"That's not true. We're both strong in our own

way. It's not weak to protect yourself. It's smart. He's gone now though, and it's okay to talk about what happened if you're ready, though I'll understand if you're not."

"I just don't know if I'll ever be okay again," she sobs. "I thought he was handsome and nice. He was always buying me things and taking me out. I didn't know he was selling drugs. I really didn't." Her eyes plead with me to believe her.

"I know. I know you would never be okay with that."

She shakes her head and continues through the tears. "I was just sitting at home watching a late-night movie when he pulled up. I wasn't worried. I just let him in, but then he started pacing and talking crazy about not meaning to kill someone and how we needed to pack and run away. His eyes were dilated and bloodshot like he was high. I was terrified, so I tried to call 911, but he caught me. He…"

She stops and hides her face in her hands. I scoot over and pull her into my arms, offering comfort in the only way I know how. She cries until her tears turn to hiccups then takes a sip of water before pulling away and starting to pace.

"He punched me in the stomach, and while I was down he pushed pills into my throat and held my mouth and nose until I swallowed. When I woke up, I didn't know where I was. He had taken my clothes and shoes and was on top of me. I fought hard. I promise I did, but he cut me, and he just kept on cutting me, screaming that I knew too much, and he could never let me go. I stole his shirt and ran while he cleaned up." She pauses her pacing to look at me. "I willingly slept with a rapist,

Eva, and I never even knew it until it happened to me. What kind of person does that make me? How many women was he hurting during all the weeks I allowed him in my bed?"

"That's not on you. You are completely innocent in all of this. As soon as you knew, you tried to get help. Sometimes the bad guys are just bigger and stronger, and they win. It's fucked-up, but it's the truth. We can't take the blame for that. We just learn how to fight better so we can win the next time."

Tessa gives me a watery smile. "You said fuck."

I stand and grab my friend into a hug filled with laughter and tears. Looking her in the eyes, I state, "Next time, we win."

CHAPTER 74

Ashe

Staying away last night after receiving the call from Moss regarding Eva's interview-turned-interrogation was nearly impossible. I'd spoken with her several times to assure myself she was okay, but there was no way I'd be able to wait until tonight to actually see her and judge for myself that she was fine. Thankfully, her work schedule was light for today, and she invited me to join her for lunch. I stopped by a local deli and ordered a large grilled chicken salad for her and a sub for me.

Takeout bag and drinks in hand, I wait my turn for the receptionist and am surprised when she buzzes me straight back and sends me directly to Eva's office. The door is open, but I knock lightly on the frame to alert Eva to my arrival. She's on the phone but waves me in toward the love seat. I set my cargo on the desk and make myself comfortable while I wait.

When she ends the call, I stand and cross to stand in front of her. Placing my hands on the arms of her chair, I lean down and place a quick kiss on her startled lips. "Hello, Rabbit."

"Hmm, well, if that's how you always plan to say hello, maybe you need to leave and come back in," she says with a smile.

I laugh at her unexpected humor. "So, you have all the jokes now, huh?"

"I don't know about *all* the jokes, but I can hold my own."

"Good to know. I'll keep that in mind." I point to the bags on the desk. "You hungry? I stopped by the deli like you asked."

"Definitely. Do you mind if we eat in the break room with the others?"

I'd been hoping for some time alone to talk about yesterday, but I am here for her, so I agree. She grabs the bag while I manage the drinks. Within a few minutes we are seated at a table in the small break area with Jackass, Jolie, and a quiet guy with sandy blond hair. Conversation is practically non-existent, and the tension is thick in the air. For Eva's sake, I take the initiative by addressing the group.

"I know we started off on the wrong foot, and then my last time here was more than a little traumatic. I just want to assure y'all I didn't bring any drama with me today, just lunch." I smile, but only the redhead smiles back. Okay, awkward silence it is. Great.

Eva manages to engage her coworkers in a few work-related topics, but I mostly just eat my sandwich and observe. It hasn't escaped my notice that most of the incidents involving Eva have occurred here at her work. If Demon really is who we're looking for, then Jackass has the wrong color hair. It looks natural, but I won't rule out dye. He seems to be way more interested in the receptionist, Jolie, than in Eva though. Despite Carmen's insistence that the killer could be female, I'm not buying it, so Jolie pretty much flies under my radar.

The third member of our party, Jake, is quiet, unusually so. He speaks when spoken to, but his answers are short and abrupt. I don't notice him showing a particular interest in Eva, but truly, he's only showing interest in his reheated leftovers. I make a mental note to check back in with Moss to see if he had a chance to run the check we'd planned after Eva mentioned having a strange conversation with this guy. I'd like to get him talking, but I doubt starting off with "So, I hear your mom has Alzheimer's" would get me very far, and beyond that, I don't remember Eva saying anything else helpful.

"Jake, is your mom doing better today?" Jolie asks, unknowingly giving me the opening I need.

"Um, yeah. She's good today."

"Your mom's sick?" I ask.

Chatty Kathy, otherwise known as Jolie, answers for Jake. "She has Alzheimer's, and Jake is just the best son, always taking care of her."

"Sorry, man. That must be hard." I give a concerned look.

"Yeah."

"I almost forgot," Jackass pops in. "I have some notes you need to pick up from your group I covered yesterday."

"Okay." Obviously, this is more conversation than Jake is used to, because he quickly gathers his trash and tosses it in the garbage before making an abrupt exit. No one else at the table acts as though this is unusual, so I guess it must be par for the course. Red flags are popping up everywhere related to this guy, and knowing he wasn't at work yesterday just makes me even more suspicious.

I debate whether or not to warn Eva but decide tipping her off might cause her to act differently and place her in more danger instead of less. She's surrounded by people day in and day out, so she should be safe, deliveries notwithstanding. None of the deliveries have been designed to harm her, so her physical safety should be secured within these walls. I'd prefer to have Moss posted inside rather than outside, but confidentiality laws make that impossible. I will make sure he knows to be hypervigilant and to keep an eye on Jake.

Finally, what has to have been the most boring lunch ever comes to a close when Jolie and Jackass head back to their posts. I guess I should start calling the guy Mal before Jackass accidentally pops out of my mouth. He actually doesn't seem that bad, but I'm reserving judgement for now. Eva tosses her empty salad container into a recycle bin, then leads the way back to her office.

I follow her in and pull the door closed behind us, needing a brief moment of privacy to ask if she is really okay after her encounter with Carmen. She beats me to the punch and speaks first. "I need to tell you something."

"Okay. You can tell me anything."

"Tessa is going to the police today. She remembers what happened to her but was afraid to speak up. It was Dustin. She knows he's dead, and she's willing to talk. I just thought you should know in case it helps."

"Thanks, Rabbit. That will help me tie up a few loose ends."

"Also, I need to ask a question, and I need your honesty."

"Of course, anything."

"Did you know what Detective Castillo was going to do to me yesterday? Did you know what she was going to ask?"

"I knew what she suspected, but I didn't think she would take the interview as far as she did. She told me it would just be a few questions to verify an alibi." I take her in my arms and look her in the eyes. "I'm so sorry that happened. I never would have let you go in there alone if I'd known it would go that way."

"Do you suspect me too?" she asks quietly.

"Never. You value your daughter too highly to do anything that would separate you from her."

She tucks her head under my chin and squeezes me in relief. We talk for a few more minutes before her intercom buzzes to notify her a client is waiting. I drop a quick kiss on the top of her head and take the rear exit. Stopping by Moss's car, I update him on the changes I want in the security procedures and inquire about the background check on Jake. Unfortunately, nothing is back yet, so I climb in my truck and head back to the office. I'm barely parked when my phone alarm goes off. Unfamiliar with the tone, I check the screen, shocked to see it's the companywide emergency alert. All employees have it on their phones, but no one has ever had to use it before. Fuck! Immediately, I pull out and head back toward Eva, somehow knowing it's related to her.

CHAPTER 75

Karoline

Though the guys are teasing me that I'm on babysitting duty, I really enjoy spending time with Polly and Clemmie. It's an easy detail, and so far, nothing has even come close to being a problem, well nothing except Sebastian Villani, Villain to everyone at work. He was getting off shift when I arrived this morning, and I could tell from his derisive look that he wasn't over being angry with me.

I'd give anything to go back in time and do things differently, but that's impossible. It feels like a lifetime ago anyway. Having grown up in foster care, I was in awe of Sebastian's huge family with all their love and hugs. When we started hanging out as teens, his family welcomed me and made me feel special. They felt like my family. Sebastian felt like my family.

I'd loved him with every beat of my young heart, and he'd returned that love. We were inseparable, until we weren't. It was my fault, and I accepted it, but I'd missed him, missed being a part of that family. I'd hoped six years would have taken some of the heat out of his hatred, but apparently not. No matter. I needed the job, and I didn't need his help to do it.

"Karoline," Polly says as she walks back into the living room. "I just put Clemmie down for her nap. I'm going to head out back and work in my herb garden for a bit. I find myself in need of some fresh air. I've got the monitor, so I'll hear if Clemmie wakes."

"Okay. No problem. I'll pull the curtains back, so I can keep watch outside while staying close to Clemmie in here."

"There's some tea in the fridge and homemade cookies in the jar on the counter."

"Yes, ma'am. Thank you." Polly reminds me a lot of Sebastian's mom, only she would never be caught dead in such a colorful house or in bright hippie clothes. I've thought about visiting her since I moved back to Magnolia Ridge, but it would kill me if she hated me too. I'm better off not knowing and preserving all my happy memories.

Wandering into the kitchen, I search for the cookies Polly mentioned while keeping an eye on her through the small window over the sink. In any other house, the rainbow-colored unicorn cookie jar would have been completely out of place. In this one, it seems right at home. Three giant chocolate chip cookies end up on a small plate, and I grab a bottle of water from the fridge to accompany them.

I peer out again as I enter the living room. Polly should be visible in the small herb garden at the back corner of the yard, but she's not. A few small trees hinder the view, but my senses say something is wrong. I rest my plate and water on a small end table and pull the weapon hidden by the long pants I wear over my ankle holster. As I edge for the back door, I hear a muffled cry from Clemmie's room.

Shit! I quickly turn my phone to silent and text an SOS to Rosey. I can't be in two places at once, and though I don't want to prioritize human lives, Polly has a much better chance of defending herself than a two-year-old. Decision made, I plant my back against the hallway wall and creep toward Clemmie's door.

Sounds still leak from her room, but this time it's more like whispers than cries. Knowing I can't afford to wait for back up, I decide it's now or never. Standing to the side of the door, I slowly test the doorknob but find it locked. Those room breaching skills from my time with SWAT are about to get a refresher course. I take a deep breath and blow it out before spinning and planting a kick just at the right place to fling the door open.

Staying low, weapon in front, I enter the room. Clemmie is sitting on her toddler bed sucking her fingers and holding a purple bear. She appears to be the only occupant of the room, but the hair on the back of my neck alerts me to the intruder just as a knife imbeds itself in my upper back. My left shoulder burns hot as the blade is ripped out. I manage to turn and clip the man's knee with a kick before he catches me just below my right eye with his fist and the bulky hilt of the knife.

Clemmie wails from the bed, and my gun is useless because I can't guarantee she will stay in place, and I won't risk hitting her. My vision is blurry from the blow anyway. My only chance is to delay him until backup gets here. Steeling myself against the pain I know is coming, I lower my right shoulder and charge for his midsection. I don't feel the knife going in, but I certainly feel it as he yanks it out, preparing to plunge again.

Still practically doubled over, I go for the target in

my field of vision and use the butt of the gun to ram this guy's balls into his throat. His pained grunt is satisfying, and as he grabs his crotch, I have a moment to move. I snatch a screaming Clemmie from the bed and shove her in the closet, turning the lock as I do, so I know she's out of harm's way.

The intruder recovers faster than I would have thought and slams me face first into the wall. I feel my nose snap, then blood drips into my mouth and down the front of my shirt, adding to the liquid warmth I can feel flowing down my back. Time, I just need to keep taking up time. I'm so tired. I can feel everything in my body slowing down, but I can't give up yet.

Clemmie's terrified screeches from the closet spur me on. I gather what strength I can and shove backward with all my might. The momentum takes us both to the floor, I land on top of him, stealing his breath before he regains his strength and flips our positions. I buck and flail, but he outweighs me by at least fifty pounds.

His gloved hands wrap around my throat, and even as my breath starts to slow, I realize if his hands are around my throat, he's not holding the knife. A glint registers to my left, so I reach blindly, feeling for the blade. Agony rips through my injured shoulder, and I only manage to grip air. The hands at my throat loosen momentarily, allowing a few gasping breaths before the steel of the blade I could never reach impales my lower abdomen again and again.

My movements still as the floor beneath me flows with a river of red. It's strange to watch my life as it drains from my body. The suffocating weight lifts, but I lack the strength to move. Through dimming vision, I watch as the man uses his knife to pry open the closet door. Clemmie flails and screams, but the man tightens his grip and steps over my body on his way out the door. My last thought as black invades my vision is that I failed.

CHAPTER 76

Sebastian

Damn. I've just barely gotten to sleep when my phone rings. Working nights and trying to sleep during the day sucks. All my phone does is ring off the hook. I turn over and yank the covers over my head, intent on ignoring it, but as soon as it stops, it starts again. I groan and reach out from under the blankets yanking the phone off the charger.

"What?"

"Villain, get up. It's an emergency." The urgency in my boss's voice spurs me to action.

"I'm up. Sitrep." Requesting a situational report comes as easy to me as breathing after my years in the Marines. I'm dressed in last night's clothes and checking my weapon before Rosey even finishes speaking.

"Karo sent out an SOS from Eva's. I can't get her on the phone. Backup is on the way, but you're much closer. Consider the situation life-threatening and go in accordingly."

"Fuck! On it." I don't bother to end the call knowing Rosey will have already hung up. I grab my backup piece from my nightstand and shove it in the waistband of my jeans. Snagging the keys on the hook by the door, I hit the driveway at a run and back the company vehicle out with a screech. I'm only a few miles away, but it feels like forever, knowing that Karoline is in danger. I may hate her, but I don't want her hurt. I told Linc not to hire her, but the jerk never listens. Fuck.

I pull in a couple houses down and cut the engine before opening the door. Safety off, my weapon leads the way as I move quickly from cover to cover, staying in the shadows. The house is quiet, and the front door is slightly ajar. Staying to the side, I use my gun to nudge the door open. The creak of the hinges sounds deafening in the heavy silence but doesn't spur any type of reaction. I enter at a low fast run, noting nothing out of place in the living room. The kitchen is also clear, but the hallway shows signs of action. One of the bedroom doors is barely hanging on its hinges. As I was taught, I open the first bedroom door and clear it before moving to the second and then the bathroom before finally reaching the open door to the left.

I keep my back to the wall and yell, "I'm armed, and I will fire. Come out with your hands up." No response. I repeat the words once more with the same result. Fuck it. Time to go in.

The smell of coppery blood hits me as soon as I enter the room. A body is on the floor, but I need to clear the room before I allow myself to look closer. I'll be no help if I'm dead too. The small toddler bed is unoccupied, and the closet looks like it was jimmied open, but it's currently empty. Satisfied I'm not about to be ambushed, I drop to my knees beside the body, keeping one eye on the door.

Blood is everywhere, seeping into the fabric of my jeans. My body moves by rote as I feel for a pulse that's slow and thready. I don't let myself look until I know she's alive. Karoline. Her face is bruised and bloody, and her abdomen is littered with what appear to be stab wounds. "Fuuuuck!" I yell, tears of rage falling unbidden down my face.

I pull my phone from my pocket and activate the LCR emergency beacon. It's the signal that will have all of LCR plus first responders converging on my location in record time. I rip off my shirt and use it to press hard on Karoline's abdomen. She grunts, and her indigo eyes peer up at me through a haze of pain. "Seb?"

"Yeah, baby. It's me. Don't talk, okay? I've got you, and everything's going to be fine." Her eyes start to close, but I know if I let her sleep, she'll slip away from me. "Wake up. You have to stay awake." Her eyes pierce me, more alert this time.

"He has Clemmie. I tried..." She coughs, and blood splatters my chest.

"Stop, Karoline. The paramedics are almost here. Just focus on me and stay awake."

"Failed," she wheezes. "Failed her, failed you." Her final words are barely a whisper. "Always fail."

"No, baby, no." I speak knowing she can no longer hear me. Sirens sound outside, but it feels too late as her eyes roll back in her head and her body begins to seize.

Paramedics are shoving me out of the way before I even realize they've entered the room. Karoline is loaded up and gone in a heartbeat, and I realize I've wasted too many years pretending to hate this woman. Now I may never get the chance to tell her I still love her.

CHAPTER 77

Ashe

The emergency beacon led me to Eva's. I just left her at work, so I know she's okay, but I see Polly's sedan and spot Villain's company car a few houses down. Paramedics are on scene. One ambulance rushes off in the opposite direction, and another remains parked in the driveway. MRPD has three cruisers blocking the street, but after showing my credentials, I'm able to get through. Officers Stuart and Clark are on the porch when I approach.

"What happened?" I know my tone comes out short, but I don't have time for niceties.

Clark speaks up. "Your man inside may know more, but from what we can gather, a toddler age two was taken from the residence by an unknown male. A young female was found inside with multiple stab wounds, and an older female was found in the backyard with a knife wound to the throat. Both victims are on their way to Ridgeview. Crime scene techs obviously haven't been here yet, so grab gloves and booties before you enter."

Oh, God. No. Not Clemmie. Eva warned me. She said Demon would come for his child. Fuck. I jerk on the protective gear and enter as quickly as I can without disturbing evidence. I have to get to Eva and get to the hospital, but I need all the information I can get first. Villain is on the floor in Clemmie's bedroom. His back is against the bed, and his head is on his knees. The carpet is soaked with blood, and his posture screams devastation. "Tell me. Now."

"Karoline," he chokes out. Shit. Villain is going to be no help to me right now.

"Sebastian, let's go now." I reach a hand down for him to grab and lever himself off the floor. His grip is slippery, and my hand comes away bloody. Fucking hell. He follows me out as though in a daze, stepping where I step until we're outside.

LCR has descended en masse. After turning Villain over to Rosey, I grab Con and pull him into my truck without an explanation. I have to get to Eva before she hears about this. Con is briefed on the way as we break every traffic law to reach the treatment center in record time. I swing into the parking lot and just breathe for a minute after I shove the truck in park. Con's eyes are on me, but for the life of me, I don't know what I'm going to say to Eva. I promised her I would keep her family safe, now Polly is in the hospital and Clemmie is missing.

"Man, don't think. Just go," Con urges. I force myself to exit the truck and find Moss waiting for me. Even though he got the emergency alert, Eva couldn't be left alone.

"I'm in the dark. What's going on?" he asks as we hurry toward the front door. I give him the quick rundown. "Wait. You can't tell her in there. Let me go in and get her. She's not going to want to be vulnerable in front of her clients like that." Moss is the voice of reason. "She'll freak if she sees your face right now."

"Yeah, okay. Just hurry." I return to the truck and pace. Con gets out and joins me.

"I'm gonna ride with Moss. We'll follow you guys to the hospital." He doesn't wait for my response because he knows me well enough to know I'm still struggling with what to say. Minutes later, Moss and Eva exit through the back. She looks anxious but strong, and I'm about to destroy her. Shit. I climb in the truck knowing Moss will deposit her in the passenger seat so we can get to the hospital while we talk.

He gives me a significant look as Eva fastens herself in as if to say, don't fuck this up. I nod and pull out into traffic.

"Ashe? What's happening? Where are we going?" Eva's voice reflects her fear.

"We're going to Ridgeview." I take a deep breath and just tell her in one fell swoop. "There was an intruder at your house. Karo was gravely injured. Polly was too."

"No! This isn't happening. No, no, no!" she wails, tears streaming down her cheeks as she keeps repeating that one word over and over. "Oh my God. Who's with Clemmie? Who has my baby?" One look at my agonized face has her shaking her head. "Ashe, don't say it. Don't tell me she's gone. Please, Ashe, please!" she begs.

I've never felt so helpless in all my life. There is nothing I can do or say in this moment that won't hurt. "I'm so sorry, Eva."

She folds over with her hands clenched tightly in her hair and rocks back and forth. "This can't be happening. I can't do this. I won't survive it. I won't. I know I won't." She mutters under her breath as the rocking continues.

She doesn't even notice when the truck stops in the hospital parking lot. I get out and walk around to open her door and unfasten her seat belt then lift her out to stand before wrapping her in my arms. "What am I going to do, Ashe?" She sobs brokenly while I hold her up. When her knees eventually buckle, I lift her up and carry her inside, Moss and Con flanking us.

Con has apparently called ahead and seems to know exactly where to go. He leads us to a surgical waiting area on the fifth floor. Much of our team is already there, and several law enforcement officers are also crowded to one corner. Carmen is among them, and I glare to make sure she knows to back the fuck off. She's the last person Eva needs to see right now.

I place Eva in a chair near Villain but away from everyone else. He looks almost as shell-shocked as she does. Rosey walks over just as every phone in the waiting area peals with a sharp tone. It's the Amber Alert for Clemmie. Eva just looks at her phone and starts sobbing again. Villain scoots closer and throws his arm around her to pull her tight while I look to Rosey for an update.

"Both Karo and Polly are still in surgery. It's touch and go at this point, just a waiting game." He sighs. "I know you don't want to hear this, but we need to talk to Carmen."

"Why?" I spew angrily. "She's a homicide detective, and we are dealing with a missing child."

"We also have two attempted homicides." His comment is sobering.

"Fine." I motion to Villain and Moss who are on either side of Eva, letting them know where I'm going, then follow Rosey and Con over to the law enforcement corner.

Rosey is the first to talk. "What can you tell us?" he demands.

"Shouldn't we be asking you that?" Carmen starts, but one look at the anger on my face shuts her down.

Stuart steps forward. "Clark already gave you the basics back at the house. Once the injured were dealt with, we found the apparent entry point, an open window in the child's room. Based on the evidence, the initial theory is that the intruder first attacked the older woman outside, believing her to be dead. He then entered the house through the child's window, which was either accidentally left unlocked or was somehow unlocked by the intruder at an earlier time. Before he could leave with the child, he was surprised by your employee. From the looks of the room, she put up one hell of a fight, but was ultimately too injured to continue. The lock on the closet was jimmied, so it's possible the toddler was hidden in the closet at some point."

Clark adds, "The Amber Alert has already gone out, but we don't have a lot for people to go on since we don't know anything about the kidnapper's vehicle or appearance."

"Has the FBI been contacted?" Con asks.

"Yes." A tall dark-skinned guy in the back speaks up. At our questioning looks, he introduces himself. "I'm Jaquay Larken, Missing Persons. We've spoken on the phone several times regarding the Hurst case." I nod my recognition. "I contacted the Birmingham FBI field office personally. An agent will be here within the hour. It would help if I could have more information to share when he gets here." He looks over at Eva. "Your guard dogs have her pretty well surrounded, but it's in her best interest to talk to me. I'm very good at what I do, but without information, my hands are tied."

Before anyone can answer, a grim-faced doctor wearing a surgeon's cap steps through the double doors and into the waiting area.

CHAPTER 78

Eva

My heart stops as the doctor looks around the overly full waiting room before asking, "Jones family?"

I stand on shaky legs. The doctor winds through the seating area to where I am. Ashe arrives by my side as well. The doctor speaks in a quiet voice with a slightly musical accent. "I'm Doctor Anand. Can I ask your relation to Ms. Jones?"

"I'm her niece, Eva Jones."

"Very well, Ms. Jones. Your aunt survived surgery but will be in the ICU for the near future." He goes on to explain the details of the knife wound to her neck, but my brain stopped comprehending at the word survived. I'll deal with the rest later. For now it's enough to just know Aunt Polly is alive.

"Do you understand, Ms. Jones?" I jerk my attention back to the doctor and nod without even knowing what I'm agreeing to. "Are there any other questions I can answer?" I shake my head. "The ICU waiting area is on the fourth floor, and visiting hours are posted." He shakes my hand and disappears back behind those double doors.

"I need to call my dad. He can come stay with Aunt Polly while I find Clemmie. I have to go find

Clemmie." I head toward the elevators intent on starting my hunt. Ashe moves to block me. "What are you doing? I have to find Clemmie!" My voice raises until I'm yelling at the end.

People turn and stare, and the hospital security guard down the hall looks like he's getting ready to approach. Ashe motions to Moss and whispers something before Moss moves to speak with someone at the main desk for this floor. "The police need to talk to you, Eva. They can help find Clemmie, but they need information only you can give. Moss is arranging for us all to move to a conference room or meeting area so we don't have to leave the hospital but can have more privacy."

I nod, realizing his plan makes more sense than my gut reaction to just drive around until I find my baby. My fingers twist my hair over and over while I wait for Ashe to round up a few police personnel and give directions to what must be more LCR employees. Within a few minutes that feel more like hours, I find myself in a room with a long table and fancy burgundy rolling chairs.

All the pent-up anxiety has me wanting to pace, but Ashe leads me to a seat. Liam and Jackson join us as well as Detective Castillo, two uniformed officers, and another man who has the look of a plainclothes detective. The last man speaks first. "Ms. Jones, I'm Jaquay Larken. I work with missing persons. I'd like to ask you a few questions, if I may."

At my nod, Larken proceeds to take notes on everything from what Clemmie was wearing to vital statistics and identifying characteristics. I answer, but with each question, I grow angrier, feeling like my daughter is being reduced from a living, breathing ball of sunshine to a still image with a generic description. I don't sob, but I can't contain the silent tears that flow in a never-ending stream down my face. Trying to dry them would be futile, so I don't even bother.

"Ms. Jones?" I refocus my attention on Larken. "Most kidnappers want something. The best-case scenario is that the abductor will contact you in some way within the next twenty-four hours. The Birmingham FBI office is sending agents to aid in the search and help with the response should a ransom demand be received."

Talking and debate ensues between the rest of the people present in the room about the best way to handle things, but I just tune them out and pray. I picture my sweet girl with her bouncing copper curls. I try to picture her in the light, but the darkness keeps encroaching. Fears that the father she was never supposed to know may be hurting her or scaring her swamp my emotions and overtake my thoughts. My breathing stalls. I need air.

I dash from the room and dart down hallways full of offices. Stumbling around corners and down flights of stairs, I finally see a door leading outside. I fling myself through and double over, sucking in deep breaths of hot air tinged with the essence of the honeysuckle growing along the nearby fence. Not having heard anyone follow me, I'm surprised when arms circle me from behind and Ashe's clean scent overtakes all others. He folds his body over mine and just holds me until my breathing slows. He doesn't speak as I straighten and turn into his chest. Ashe just strokes my hair and lets me anchor myself to his strength.

When I finally pull back, he looks straight into my eyes, anguish evident in his blue gaze. "We will find her, Eva. I promise." I have no words, so I just nod. "Will you come back inside with me? The FBI will be here soon, and we need to get a tap set up on your phone so we can trace any calls that come in." Again, I nod, too drained to resist.

Ashe leads the way back to the conference room, taking the elevators this time. When we enter, I grab my purse from the table where I'd abandoned it and excuse myself to freshen up in the bathroom. I dig through my bag as I walk, searching for ibuprofen and tissues but finding neither. My phone falls out and hits the tile of the hallway with a cracking sound. Not caring, I snatch it up and push through the swinging door to the women's restroom.

I set my purse and phone on the metal shelf below the mirror that runs the length of the sinks and snatch a handful of paper towels. I don't bother waiting for the water to warm. The frigid liquid I splash on my face helps bring my brain back online and return my focus. As I'm using the paper towels to blot the last vestiges of moisture, my phone dings. Desperate for any news on Clemmie, I grab for the device but end up fumbling it into the sink. It slips through my grasp and hits the porcelain again before I use more paper towels to retrieve it.

The screen has spiderwebbed, but I can see enough to know I don't recognize the number. Desperate, I open the text anyway.

Unknown: —Soon our family will be reunited—
A current picture of Clemmie follows.

CHAPTER 79

Ashe

Eva is asleep sitting up in the LCR conference room. Afternoon transitioned to evening and now night, and other than the text Eva received at the hospital, we have nothing to go on. That text prompted the shift from the hospital to LCR so we could utilize our technical resources in tracing the message. Unfortunately, the phone was an unregistered burner commonly sold all over town.

The FBI agent and Larken have set up shop at one end of our conference room table, and both Con and Rosey are still here trying to drum up leads by revisiting all our evidence on Demon. Our resources are spread thin with both Karo and Spock in the hospital and Villain and Bond on protection detail there. Karo made it through surgery, but she's still listed as critical. Thankfully Spock was able to transition from ICU to a regular room, but both Karo and Polly remain in need of intensive care. Con contacted Eva's father to come stay with Polly so Eva could devote her time to the search for Clemmie.

So far, I haven't been able to get her to eat and have had to force her to sip from the bottle of water beside her. She has made impassioned pleas to all the local news outlets and radio stations and tried to have

Moss carry her to put up flyers everywhere, but after that text, I didn't want her out of my sight.

She used our copy room to make the flyers and sent Moss to do the posting. Once they started going up, the phone rang continuously with tips. Agent Brandt and Larken have been fielding the calls, but Eva insisted she be allowed to listen in. Her eyes started slipping shut about thirty minutes ago, and I decided any sleep she could get would be better than none. She was running on emotions, adrenaline, and fumes, and her body had hit a wall.

Moss walks back into the chaos that is now our conference room and drops a bottle of orange juice on the end table near Eva before touching base with Con and Rosey. Larken and Brandt are still on their phones, so I gather the LCR crew, hoping a recap will help us find something we've missed. "Can you tell me anything new?" I focus on Con since he's our tech expert.

"I've been checking out Eva's coworker, Jake Martin. Moss said you wanted him run through the system. Interesting fact, he doesn't have a mother with Alzheimer's. His mom is dead. She died in a car accident when he was a teen." My suspect radar adds to the red flags I had already raised in my mind.

"Was he at work on the days Eva received packages?" Rosey asks.

"He was," Con confirms.

"What about his financials?" I need to know if we can match any of the purchases to him.

"Technically—" Con starts, but I interrupt.

"Don't even give me the whole 'technically' speech. I know you probably don't have permission from MRPD to access the financials yet, but I also know you well enough to know that in this situation you would have gone in anyway and covered your tracks, so what did you find?" My patience is at an all-time low, and I'm not concerned about whether or not information can be used in court, because I'm not concerned with bringing this killer in alive.

Con doesn't try to deny his actions. "Your guy doesn't have any purchases I can track back to the bakery or the restaurant that delivered Eva's takeout, but he does have some massive gambling debts. I suspect the stories about his mom are simply to cover up gambling excursions."

"Okay, so we don't have a financial link. Where was he three years ago when Eva was taken?" I'm desperate for anything since our only other suspect is dead.

Con taps away on his laptop. "Looks like he finished an undergrad degree in counseling at the University of South Alabama in Mobile four years ago before moving to Biloxi, Mississippi for a while. He eventually finished up his graduate degree at University of Alabama in Tuscaloosa."

"Biloxi is well known for gambling, and it's only an hour from Mobile. Can we find any links between him and Eva in Mobile?" Moss asks.

Rosey shuffles through a stack of papers in front of him, preferring old-school paper notes to Con's need for electronics. "When I first interviewed Eva, she said she graduated from USA like Martin. Perhaps they crossed paths in some classes." He shuffles some more and comes up with a different list. "This is the original list of people she dated, but no one has the last name

Martin."

"Okay, any other places their lives could have intersected? Where did Eva work?" Moss brainstorms.

"She worked at Grand Bay Addiction Recovery Center, but I don't recall seeing that on Martin's work history." Con busily taps keys for several minutes. "Wait. I may have something." He keeps typing and clicking.

"Damn it, man, spill. We don't have all night," I growl.

"I just need to make sure I'm right." My pen taps impatiently on the table until he finally yells, "Yes! I'm right."

"Then let the rest of us in on it," Rosey grouses. We're all exhausted and worried sick for Clemmie, so I predict tempers are about to flare.

"Martin has a ton of old unpaid medical bills screwing up his credit. One of them is listed as Gulf Coast Medical Group. Anyone want to take a guess as to who owns Grand Bay Addiction Recovery Center?" Con looks very pleased with himself.

"Fuck, so he was a client there?" I can't believe we could have missed such a huge connection.

"Look," Con cautions, "the company owns a few other facilities, but Grand Bay is by far the largest. We'd need the police to get a warrant for the records to know for sure, but it seems like too much to be coincidence that they went to the same school, that he lived within an hour of where Eva was taken, and then ended up living in the city where she was found, and now is working in the same treatment center. When you add the possibility that he could have been a client where she worked, I vote we pass all this along to

MRPD so they can bring him in for questioning."

"Agreed. Rosey, can you handle that?" He nods and heads out of the room with his papers.

"Con, keep digging and check into property records in his name or his parents or grandparents. We need to look for something rural and likely isolated. Also, check for any military or firearms experience. Moss, can you grab some takeout and keep the OJ coming? I know Eva is going to need it even if she doesn't think so." I glance at the other end of the room to check on her, only to find she's disappeared.

CHAPTER 80

Eva

My head is filled with fog as I slowly come awake. The back of my neck feels stiff from accidentally falling asleep sitting up on the couch. Everyone is busy, and I think they've forgotten I'm here. Honestly, I'm glad. I want them focusing on finding Clemmie rather than constantly asking me if I'm okay while keeping me trapped inside this room instead of out searching for my daughter.

Impotent rage overwhelms me and makes it hard to focus, to think, to sit still. How will we ever find her if we don't even know who has her? I know in my heart it's Demon, but that doesn't help at all since we still don't know his identity. My impatience says I should just get in the car and drive. I have no idea where to even start, but at least I'd be doing something other than just sleeping while a murderer has my daughter.

Everyone else is doing something. Liam is typing away, his eyes glued to his computer screen. Jackson is on the phone, and Moss is conferring around the whiteboard with Ashe. The end of the conference table closest to me is occupied by Larken and Brandt. They too have eyes glued to screens and ears to phones. They don't even realize I'm awake...or maybe that I'm even in the room. They are all searching while I'm sleeping.

Needing a quieter place to gather my thoughts and come up with a plan, I grab the bottle of orange juice someone has thoughtfully left for me and slip out to the breakroom to see if I can find some food to go with the juice. I need to wake up and refocus. The break room selections are proof positive that this office is primarily staffed by men. Beef jerky, strange spicy flavors of chips, and various brick looking protein bars that make me physically cringe make up the available offerings. Juice will just have to suffice. I'm not really hungry anyway.

Sitting down at the table, I put my head in my hands, pulling my hair to try to bring my brain back online or maybe just to punish myself for falling asleep. I let my forehead tap the table and rest there for a few minutes while I run memories through my mind, trying to find some clue I may have missed, some detail to tell me who Demon is. His face was always hidden and his voice well disguised by his whispered tone, but there has to be something. Lifting my head slightly, I let it fall back to the table. I feel like banging it, but that would do no good.

Calling my father to get an update on Aunt Polly turns out to be a big mistake. I get a scathing commentary on my utter failure as a parent and orders to stay away from my aunt. I don't suppose I can be too mad though because "utter failure" seems like an accurate description at the moment.

Still paralyzed by a lack of direction and uncontrollable fear, I start to pace, orange juice all but forgotten. I'm on lap thirty-three when my phone chimes with a text. Snatching it off the table, fearing another taunt or worse, a demand, I'm relieved and chagrined to find it's Tessa. I haven't even told my friend anything that's happened. It was all so fast. I haven't been there for her like she was for me.

Tessa: —I need you. Please! I think I'm having a panic attack.—

Me: —I'm coming. Where are you?—

Tessa: —In the LCR parking lot. I tried to come to you, but I don't want anyone to see me like this. Please help me!—

Me: —I'm coming right now.—

My body is already moving even as I'm typing the last of my message. I spent too long trying to handle panic attacks on my own, and I won't leave Tessa to fend for herself or expose her to others when she's so vulnerable. I don't wait on the elevators but speed down the stairwell instead. The lobby is deserted as I sprint across. The door flings back with a loud clang as I rush outside and right into a trap.

Strong arms grab me from behind. One is banded around my arms and torso. The other presses a damp cloth over my mouth and nose. I kick and flail and try to scream, but the sweet scent of the fabric invades and brings sleep with it.

CHAPTER 81

Eva

Every part of my body aches as I try to open my eyes. My teeth clatter painfully as though I'm freezing, but I experience neither heat nor cold. The shaking is uncontrollable.

I don't understand why I feel so bad. My brain feels sluggish as though full of sticky oatmeal, and my thoughts are disconnected and fleeting. Something is important, but I can't remember. Tessa. I need to help Tessa. Where is she?

Softness and scratchiness register beneath my shaking fingers. My eyes finally open, though there is nothing to see but more darkness. It is familiar yet not. I must be dreaming. This is just a nightmare, and when I wake everything will be better. I just need to go back to sleep.

My heavy eyelids drift back down, dragging me deeper into the oatmeal-filled nothing. The shaking increases, but I can't seem to care. The fleeting brush of a hand over my hair barely registers before the voice of my nightmare croons, "Sleep, sweet Julie. Everything will be better soon."

The next time I wake, cold is the first thing I feel. My body still shakes intermittently, but my thoughts are clearer. This time my eyes open easily. The darkness is still pervasive, though a small sliver of what looks like the muted light of early morning streams through a small window near the ceiling. I turn my head attempting to get my bearings. The room shifts and spins around me as nausea churns. Having experienced vertigo before, I lie still, then keep my eyes tightly closed the next time I attempt to move.

I sit carefully and feel around, realizing I'm on a bed. The sheet feels cheap and scratchy. A heavy weight pulls my ankle to the floor, and I keep feeling around, afraid to open my eyes and set the room spinning again. My freezing body shakes. I try to find covers to wrap up in, but the sheet below me is all I feel. My heart pounds, and my breathing becomes labored as I run my hands over my body. My eyes pop open to confirm my nakedness before I lose focus and vomit all over the floor.

When the heaving ends, I fall back against the bed. The churning in my stomach has calmed though the dizziness persists. This can't be happening. I can't survive this again. The creak of a door sounds, but I refuse to open my eyes, refuse to see him again. I cower and hide inside my mind, in the place I created years ago to escape him. I go there again now. It's my happy place. Flowers and beauty fill the space just like before, but something's different, something's new. Sweet laughter invades my senses, and a sunshine scent tickles my nose. Clemmie. She has become my happy place, my world.

The laughter is getting closer. "Momma," her baby voice calls. It sounds so real.

"Open your eyes, sweet Julie. Our daughter wants to see you." The indistinguishable raspy voice is exactly as I remember it.

Oh, God. Oh, God. Oh, please no. I squeeze my eyes more tightly shut, willing the voice to go away, willing this to be a dream and my baby to be safe.

"Momma?"

"Momma's sleeping. Daddy's here now. We'll come back tomorrow when she feels better," his voice says. The fear of never seeing her again overcomes the fear of seeing him as the creaking of the door signifies his intent to take her away.

"Momma! Momma!" Clemmie cries.

"I'm awake! Don't take her. Give her to me," I beg, swaying as I sit and lay eyes on the shifting image of Clemmie settled on the hip of the only person on this earth I wish was dead—her father. In the dim light, my swirling vision only registers the height of his outline, but his whispered voice is unmistakable. "Give her to me," I repeat.

"Don't you remember how this works, Julie? You need to earn your rewards. You've proved yourself disloyal and impure. You'll have to correct your behavior before we can be a real family. You should be grateful that I prepared this nice place for you before I found out you were a cheater. Maybe you'll learn your lesson faster this time. Clean up your mess, Julie, and maybe we'll visit tomorrow. Tell Momma bye, Clementine."

"No! Please! Don't go. Let me see her. I'll do anything you want." I stand and try to give chase, but dizziness combined with some kind of tether at my ankle takes me down to the floor.

"I know you will," he says softly before closing the door and separating me from my daughter, who continues crying out for me.

Anger and hatred boil over into a scream of rage. Once I start screaming, I can't stop. I scream and scream and scream, begging for my daughter, demanding my freedom, threatening harm I have no means to inflict, and finally just incoherent sobs. He doesn't respond, but I knew he wouldn't.

The tears coating my body and the slate tile on which I'm sprawled combine with the frigid air conditioning to increase my shaking. My ankle throbs from kicking at the restraint during my fit of rage. It's a metal cuff with a chain. From my vantage point on the floor, I see it's welded to some kind of plate built into the tile. The sight terrifies me because it tells me he has been planning and preparing for this for a long time.

Not yet trusting my legs, I crawl back to the bed and pull myself up off the floor. The bed is warmer, but only minutely so. I rip the fitted sheet off the mattress and wrap it around me like a cocoon. The crying has made my eyes puffy and my nose runny, but my thoughts are finally clearer. Whatever he must have drugged me with is either wearing off or flowing out in my tears, if that's even possible.

I need to think. I survived this before, I can do it again. What did he say? I need to remember. He called me a cheater. What did he mean? What do I do? How do I get my daughter back? Does he have Tessa, or did he steal her phone? Was he just waiting in the parking lot for any chance I left?

My thoughts are racing. I need to slow down, to take things one step at a time. I take a few deep breaths and just lie still. My eyes find the sliver of light near the ceiling, now much brighter. It leads me to my first task.

I need to explore this room and figure out if there is anything I can use. Taking my sheet with me, I sit up slowly, testing to make sure the vertigo is gone. Finding myself stable, I stand.

Though muted light trickles in from the small window, the room is still extremely dim. I move toward the wall with a hand outstretched and encounter what feels like painted concrete blocks. I'm guessing the window is likely level with the ground outside and my prison is a basement room. Shuffling farther as the chain scrapes along the floor, I find the unexpected, a door with a knob that turns. It's not locked. I don't know what I expect to find, but the rudimentary bathroom isn't it.

A toilet and a stainless-steel sink are the sole inhabitants of the room. The toilet is a commercial style without a tank. There is no mirror, no soap, no towel. A single roll of toilet paper sits at the back of the sink. Otherwise, the room is empty, devoid of anything I could use as a weapon. I feel around the wall near the entrance searching for a light switch, but there is none, just another of the small windows near the ceiling.

Wanting to ensure the drugs are out of my system and knowing from experience how important hydration will be to my survival, I turn on the sink and cup my hands to hold water. First, I rinse the stale vomit taste from my mouth, then I drink as much water as I can stand. I use the restroom, conserving toilet paper, knowing he will probably want something I don't want to give up in exchange for more.

Once I return to the other room, the sour smell has me nearly losing all the water I just chugged. Retching the whole time, I use small pieces of toilet paper to clean and flush my mess from earlier before rinsing my hands in the sink and returning to the bed. It's the only piece of furniture in the room. Exhausted, I lie down and will my eyes not to close. Once I'm still, I begin to hear noises from above my head, the scrape of a chair, the muffled tones of a male voice, and the final sound before I fall into a cold sleep…my daughter's laughter.

CHAPTER 82

Ashe

It's been over forty-eight hours since Clemmie disappeared, and thirty-six since I lost Eva. I'm beyond furious. She was safe here with us. Why did she leave? What the hell was she thinking? My fist meets the wall, and not for the first time. Professional repairs will be needed, but I don't really give a shit. Finding Eva and Clemmie is all I care about.

Con was able to track Eva's movements using the building's security cameras, but they only led us as far as the parking lot outside where we found one of her shoes and a sweet-smelling cloth we suspect was soaked with sevoflurane to subdue her. Watching her try to fight off a masked attacker on the security footage was gut-wrenching, but the thought of her now being unconscious and at the mercy of her rapist burns like lava flowing through my veins.

Every second we delay in finding her is another opportunity for this monster to hurt one of my girls. Rosey believes Demon is unlikely to harm Clemmie due to some daddy fantasy in his head, but I'm not willing to rule out anything. The man is a batshit crazy rapist and murderer who sees nothing wrong with keeping women as his starved captives for months at a time. He's capable of anything.

LCR remains a command center of sorts since we have the finances for better equipment and more room than MRPD. Agent Brandt is keeping to himself for the most part, doing who knows what, but Larken is working to keep us in the loop, and even Carmen is putting all her efforts into finding Eva and Clemmie. Well, she's primarily hunting Demon, but it's all one and the same now.

Officers Stuart and Clark tried to pick up Jake Martin for questioning, but he wasn't at his residence. His vehicle was also missing. Local law enforcement has the description and tag number along with an order to be on the lookout. He's our only viable suspect at present, so we're devoting all available energy to researching anywhere he could have taken Eva and Clemmie.

Tips are still coming in. They have ranged from plausible possible sightings of Clemmie at grocery stores or playgrounds to the completely ridiculous theories of alien abduction. One caller legitimately believed Clemmie had been kidnapped by gypsies. It's the kind of crazy you just can't make up. MRPD has been chasing down the more plausible sightings, but nothing has proved valid yet.

"I've got something," Con yells from his favored position behind the computer. We all flock behind him to see what has him excited. "Martin had a great aunt who lived here in Magnolia Ridge. She died a few years ago, but her property seems to have been tied up in probate and forgotten."

"Is it in a neighborhood or rural?" Rosey asks.

"From what I can tell, it seems to be a farm of sorts, pretty far off the beaten track. Definitely rural,"

Con confirms.

"Is there any recent utility activity at that address, any power or gas bills?" Castillo joins the discussion.

"No. I already checked. The need for that could easily be circumvented by a generator though," Con reports.

"Good point. So, how do we want to play this?" I ask.

Castillo is the first to respond. "I've got a judge on standby to sign a warrant. I'll send all this her way and see if she'll sign off on it."

"In the meantime, let's send Clark and Stuart out to run surveillance," Larken suggests.

"No way. Our guy will spot them miles away. They're in a marked cruiser. Let me and Moss take it. We're authorized for surveillance work through the MRPD," I argue.

"You seriously want me to believe that you can objectively run surveillance on a man suspected of kidnapping and raping your girl? Do I look stupid?" Carmen, as usual, says exactly what she thinks without any filter.

"I'm a professional, Carmen. I just need to get out of this room and do something, anything."

"How 'bout I go with you instead of Moss? I'm not your friend and not likely to let you go off half-cocked and screw anything up," Larken states.

Carmen looks back and forth between us appraisingly before reluctantly agreeing. In no time, we're loaded up in Larken's unmarked vehicle and weaving up and down back roads to get to the Martin farm. Larken parks down a small dirt side road, and we proceed on foot once our weapons are secured.

Though it's approaching evening, the southern sunlight burns until almost eight. Without the cover of darkness, we stick to the shaded edge of the woods surrounding the property. A large but dilapidated barn looms in the distance with an unkempt farmhouse in the foreground. As we move around, I see a set of hinged doors at the side of the house leading underground to what must be a basement storm shelter or an old root cellar. Farther along, despite all odds, we spot a car matching the description of Martin's, though it's too far away to read the plate.

Larken updates the team via text and tries to rush Carmen with the warrant. The two of us settle in using overgrown bushes and trees for cover to observe. Sweat trickles down my back as adrenaline flows through my body, demanding an outlet and making stillness nearly impossible. "Rein it in, buddy," Larken says quietly.

I try, but the impotence of it all, having the training and being in the right place at the right time with the right weapons but not able to do anything, is eating at me. Typically, I'm the one trying to remind others to be patient and do things the right way, but every second we wait is another second Demon could be hurting my girls. I don't even care anymore that I'm thinking of Clemmie and Eva as my girls. Once I get them back, that's exactly what they'll be.

A sudden flash of headlights in the approaching dusk has us dropping farther into the brush. Martin is already here, and our warrant hasn't had time to arrive. Who the hell is this? We never accounted for Demon having a partner. An expensive sports car pulls up to the front of the house, and a suited man walks right in the front door. Lights flicker on in one of the windows, so apparently the generator theory was a good guess.

One by one, more-impressive vehicles arrive, bringing the total number of people other than Martin to six men and one woman. I'm itching to try to get closer, but the area is open with no real cover, making the risk of exposure high. Have we stumbled on a trafficking operation? It doesn't fit Demon's profile, but we've been wrong before. Warrant or not, if one of those fuckers tries to walk out with Eva or Clemmie, my waiting is over.

Thirty minutes or so pass with no more movement in or out. Larken receives a message that a limited warrant has been issued. He leaves me keeping watch and returns with two vests from his trunk as well as helmets. Thankful for the protection, I pull on the armor and once again wait.

Pretty soon, all hell breaks loose as the warrant is served. Police and FBI in full gear move all over the property. Larken and I join the group near the vehicles as ordered, but my eyes keep straying to that cellar entrance, knowing it's the most likely place for Eva to be.

Finally, an officer moves that direction and flings open the door. He moves carefully down the steps, weapon at the ready, until he disappears. At his shout of "Clear!", I don't hold back any longer. I take off at a dead run. Yelling a warning to the officer inside so I don't get myself shot, I descend into the musty darkness, needing to assure myself that Eva and Clemmie are okay. The officer gives me an irritated glance before heading back up and leaving me alone in a cellar devoid of anything other than rows and rows of dusty jars filled with home canned goods. Eva's not here.

Back at the top, the level of urgency in the air, and in the movements of people in the area, has dropped significantly. Carmen approaches. "It was nothing more than an illegal high stakes poker game," she says with disgust. "There's no evidence that anyone has been held here. We're taking everyone in, but they'll all be out within hours on misdemeanor charges that will likely go nowhere. We'll have an opportunity to interview Martin, but I don't think he's our guy. He doesn't seem to have the discipline to stay under the radar."

I yank off my helmet and hurl it toward the tree line as I stalk off. The vest follows. I tear at the Velcro straps until I can fling it over my head to join the helmet wherever it landed. My hands fist in my hair, and a growl of rage and frustration and fear I don't want to acknowledge escapes from my gut. I'm going to find this guy, and when I do, I swear I'm going to kill him.

"Linc!" I turn to see Rosey running at me full tilt, his phone at his ear. "We know who he is!"

CHAPTER 83

Eva

I don't know how long I've been here, but I'm past the point where my hunger bothers me. Demon hasn't returned, but I expected his mind games, for him to punish me after I demanded he return my daughter. I should be scared, but strangely, I'm just angry. No, actually, I'm furious.

The light comes and goes, but I wish it didn't. It makes the passage of time move more slowly and reminds me how long I've been separated from Clemmie. I hear her sometimes, and I don't know which is worse, hearing her laugh or hearing her cry. I could never wish for her to be scared or upset, but my skin crawls to think of her being conditioned to like her sadistic father or worse, love him. She's mine. She is nothing like him.

Wearing my sheet like a toga, I make another trip to the bathroom for water. The cold dankness keeps me from feeling thirsty, but I know I need to drink, or I'll get weaker and weaker. I've had years to analyze my nightmares and memories and consider what I would have done differently the last time Demon took me. I guess my subconscious was preparing me for this day.

This time, I won't let myself get despondent or give up. I will hold on to my anger, and I will fight. The cold may hurt, and shivers may wrack my body, but it doesn't drain my energy nearly as much as the oppressive heat had. I know his brand of torture disguised as pleasure, and I'm ready to fight. I can be deceptive too. Sometimes fighting is more effective with your brain than your fists, though I'm not ruling out either option.

He wants the perfect wife and perfect family. I can make him believe I want that too, that I want him to be Clemmie's father, that I'm ready to be his wife. I'll say whatever is necessary to get him to unlock the cuff at my ankle.

I've tried many times to break it. I've banged it on the bed frame, on the floor, and on the wall. I've pushed and pulled and tried to fit my foot through the cuff. I knew it wouldn't work, but I had to try. My ankle is so bruised and swollen now that the cuff is cutting off circulation to a degree and causing me to limp. I've contemplated using the chain to strangle my captor when he returns, but I'd still be trapped, and it would put Clemmie at risk of being left with no food and no one to keep her from getting hurt.

I've explored as far as my tether allows. Unfortunately, the windows are beyond the scope of my reach. The bathroom has nothing other than toilet paper, and my bed is bolted to the floor and welded together. The mattress has no springs, just lumpy filling, like one you might find on a bunk bed at summer camp as a kid. My search for weapons or a means of escape turned up nothing. My assets are the sum total of half a roll of toilet paper, a sheet, and the chain attached to my ankle...not exactly encouraging.

I keep telling myself that I'm stronger now, that

I've survived this before, and I will again. If I only had myself to worry about, I think I'd rock the strangulation move and risk never being found just for the satisfaction of knowing that no woman would ever have to fear Demon again and that Clemmie would always be safe. It would be worth it, my life for hers.

I lie down on the mattress as the light gives way to deep darkness once again. All the thinking and battling with the chain has worn me out. The lack of food has weakened me, but after some rest I'll be ready to try again.

Sleep comes with dreams, and dreams for me exist only as nightmares. I wake as I do most nights, with my heart pounding and a scream on my lips. I can still feel Demon's hands on my body in the blackness and hear his whispered words in my ear.

"Sweet Julie, how I've missed you. I couldn't wait any longer to spend some time with my wife now that our daughter is safely asleep."

Wait, those are not the words of my dream. Oh, God, please help me. Those words were just breathed in my ear by the creature behind me sharing the mattress. My body shakes in fear, but I hope he attributes it to shivers from the cold. He'll never release me if I act scared. He has to believe I want the same things as him. I force myself to lie as still as possible and slow my breathing. My sheet twisted while I slept, leaving me feeling more vulnerable since I'm exposed, but I don't dare try to cover up.

My skin crawls as his hands rove down to trace each scar he inflicted upon my body. I know he sees them as marks of *his* ownership, of *his* "purification," but Ashe told me they were marks of *my* victory, signs of *my* courage. As Demon strokes each stripe of puckered flesh, it's Ashe's words repeating in my head that allow me to be still and suffer Demon's caress.

"Did you miss me too, Julie? You knew I was watching you all along, didn't you? I've watched you raise our daughter. Clementine, such a beautiful name. You were such a good wife, staying home and keeping yourself for me."

The raspy whisper in which he always speaks somehow begins to sound familiar, recently so. My brain tries to make the connection, but I'm distracted by his next words.

"You stayed pure for me, Julie, until now. That's why I had to save you. You let yourself be distracted by another man, to become his whore. I won't let you destroy our family. I have to protect you from yourself until I can remove the evil temptation."

"I...I'm sorry," I stammer, trying desperately to compose a convincing response. "I...uh...I thought you cheated. They told me you took other women."

"Never, Julie. There was no one after you, but don't worry. It will all be okay." He strokes my hair as though trying to soothe, but the motion only serves to frighten. "Soon there will be no more temptation. He will be out of the picture forever. He has a lot of powerful enemies. They already tried to take him out once. All I had to do was provide a little direction and incentive."

No, please, not Ashe. I have to work to hide my reaction. Any sign that I care will just place Ashe in greater danger. I won't do that. Demon's hands slide to more intimate places, and I can no longer think at all. I can't let him force me again. I won't survive it. I won't.

My breathing becomes labored, and my heart speeds up.

"Ah, my sweet wife. Your body still responds to me. I can feel your excitement and hear your breath." He slows his touch. "Soon, but not yet. You must be purified again."

My relief is profound until I feel the burn of the first slice. His knife digs into my flesh over and over again as I fight his hold and scream until my throat is raw. "Tonight, you will bleed away all your impurities just as you did before. I know exactly how many cuts it takes now, but don't worry, tomorrow, we will be one again."

He kisses my temple and stands from the bed, leaving me covered in blood and writhing in pain from the thirteen new cuts that overlay the old.

CHAPTER 84

Ashe

Rosey and I rushed to the hospital in response to Villain's call. While Bond was still keeping watch over Spock and his wife, we'd obtained permission for Villain to guard both Polly and Karo inside the intensive care unit. The glass walls allowed him to sit just outside in the hallway and monitor both women. The possibility that one of them might be able to identify the killer was too great to leave them unprotected even inside the secure unit.

The name Villain gave was unbelievable. Con was already digging into the background, searching for properties, and relaying his findings, but I needed to confirm with the source. Apparently, Polly regained consciousness a short while ago and became very agitated when Eva wasn't there. The injury to her throat prevented speech, but a nurse had procured a white board and marker. As soon as she had the marker in hand, Polly wrote one single word, *Luke*.

Villain called us immediately and was waiting on our arrival for further questions so as not to overtire Polly before we could get the most important details. Carmen was following close behind. As the lead detective on the murder/attempted murder cases, she needed to get an official statement in case warrants were needed.

Carmen shows her badge, and Rosey and I produce ID at the desk, but only two are allowed back. Villain makes his way out, and Carmen and I leave him with Rosey in the waiting area where a man I assume is Eva's father still waits. He eyes us suspiciously, but I don't have time to address it.

Polly looks like a shell of herself when we enter the room. Her eyes are closed, and the boldly feisty woman somehow looks fragile, hooked up to machines and devoid of all her usual vibrant colors—at least until she opens her eyes. Those eyes are full of fight and fury. Machines beep faster, and a nurse pops in to warn us not to get Polly overly agitated.

Polly immediately points to the whiteboard and marker discarded in a chair beside the bed. I grab them and introduce Carmen as I hand the supplies over. "Have you found Eva?" she writes with a slightly shaky hand.

"No. We need your help. You told Villain that Luke was your attacker." She tries to nod but ends up using the whiteboard to affirm.

"Did you see his face?" Carmen asks urgently.

No appears on the board followed by *Tattoo*.

"Polly, I know it will be hard to explain everything in writing, so I'm going to try to ask questions that will enable you to write short answers. Is that okay?" I ask.

Yes, hurry up, so you can find Eva and our baby girl!

I almost grin, relieved to realize that Polly is going to be fine. After I assure her that others are already on the hunt while I'm here, Carmen and I ask a series of ~uestions that Carmen documents and has Polly sign once we're done. The information we receive is enlightening. Polly confirms Luke was in the military and had some trouble overseas years ago, for which he was treated psychiatrically once home. She answered affirmative to having noticed signs of Luke's attraction to Eva, going back to her teen years.

In regard to her attack, she affirms that the attacker wore gloves, but she reports she fought back and scratched as she was grabbed. The sleeve of the attacker also pushed up to show part of a tattoo she recognized as being Luke's. It was a distinctive image of a heart and knife. With a final edict from the older woman to get our "asses moving" and bring Eva and Clemmie home, we leave Polly to rest.

Not bothering to explain, I pull Rosey away from what appears to be a heated discussion with the older man in the waiting room and nod for Villain to get back to his post. Carmen dashes off with barely a wave, Villain moves, and Rosey reluctantly follows me.

"What the hell was that?" I ask as soon as we're alone in the elevator.

"Eva's dad. He wanted to make sure we were aware that his sister's injuries are all Eva's fault and that he plans to get a restraining order to keep her away from Polly and also plans to file for custody of Clemmie. You pulled me away mid-rant before I could finish telling him what a piece of shit he is."

"We'll definitely get back to that later. No way any judge is going to take that lunatic seriously."

"What did you get from Polly? Is it really Luke Taliaferro?" Rosey asks, ready for action.

"The information is not conclusive because her ID is based on a partial view of a tattoo on his arm as he was trying to hold her from behind. She claims the tattoo is distinctive, but we have no way of knowing that for sure. Carmen is working on warrants, and Con is still looking at properties Luke may own, but we also need him to get more in-depth access to military records or find people who served with Luke who might talk to us about an incident that happened overseas. Moss is bringing Tessa in since we couldn't reach her by phone, but she is not in the know at present."

"Okay. That's a lot more than we knew an hour ago. Finally."

Our trip back to LCR takes just minutes, and we go directly to the conference room where Con has set up additional computers and monitors. Agent Brandt is still working silently at one end of the table, though now joined by a few other FBI agents, but Larken doesn't seem to have returned, nor have any other MRPD representatives. No matter, we have what we need to work the hunt, and we won't be waiting on the police if I have a say in the matter.

"I have information," Con announces.

"Go," Rosey says as we move to take up position behind him where we can view the monitors. Con pulls up a military service record, and I know better than to ask how he got it. From what we see, Taliaferro had an expert rating as a marksman and was moving up in the ranks until he was given a medical discharge three years into his service.

"Any idea what spurred that discharge?" I ask.

"No, but I have the contact information for some of the people from his unit," Con replies, waving a printed

"On it," Rosey says, snatching the list and hurrying out of the room.

"Properties?" I ask.

"Well, that's where things get weird. Luke supposedly came up here from his residence in Mobile when Tessa was missing, but I can't find any records of home ownership or lease agreements for him in that county in the last three years."

"Three years, but that's when…"

"Yep," Con interrupts. "He's been off grid for the past three years."

"Damn it. Any properties in Tessa's name or any other family members?"

"Just the house where Tessa now lives."

"So how the hell are we supposed to find this guy?" I rant. The sound of a throat clearing has me looking toward the doorway to find Moss and a frightened looking Tessa. Fuck, how much did she hear?

"Guys? What's going on?" Tessa's timid voice and the way she shies away from Moss are evidence of her recent trauma. I know we need to be gentle since in all likelihood, she has no idea about her brother's possible actions.

"Tessa, come have a seat. Thanks for coming." She settles into a chair noticeably distant from us. "Time is short, so I'll be brief. Eva and Clemmie are missing."

Shock registers on her face. "No. That's not possible. Aunt Polly would have told me."

"Polly was attacked when Clemmie was taken. She's been in the hospital. I'm sorry, Tessa."

"I don't understand. How did I not know? How were my best friend and my goddaughter taken, and I'm only just now finding out?" she rages with tears streaming. Moss takes a step toward her, but her glare stops him.

I quickly explain everything we know so far, leaving out only the details related to her brother. "We need to talk to Luke too. Do you know where he is?"

"No. He was hovering and treating me like a broken piece of china since my attack, so I sent him home."

"To Mobile?" I ask. She nods, rattling off the address when asked. Con turns a monitor discreetly to show me that the address is listed as purchased by someone else three years ago.

"Tessa, I wish I had time to lead into this better or to protect you from it, but Eva and Clemmie's lives are on the line, and we need your help finding your brother." I take a deep breath, debating with myself on how to continue but decide expedience is essential. "We believe Luke may be Demon."

CHAPTER 85

Eva

I wake slowly. The light is here again, but the orangish tinge tells me it's waning. I try to move, but my body feels as though it's weighted down by piles of sand like when kids bury themselves at the beach. That was never my life, but I know some kids do.

My mouth feels like I may have swallowed some of the aforementioned sand, dry and gritty. I attempt to sit up but fall back immediately. I need water, but the blood loss has left me weak. Last time I might have just waited to die. That was the old me though. That was Julie. No matter how many times Demon calls me Julie, I'm Eva now, and I can't let myself forget it.

I use every bit of strength I can muster to shove myself up with my arms and roll off the bed. I hit the floor on my hands and knees with a jarring impact. The burning sensation searing my thighs along with the feeling of a sluggish flow rolling down my legs lets me know I ripped open cuts that must have dried to the mattress. It's a feeling I'm not unfamiliar with, but he's never cut me like this before. They were only ever single cuts and always only…after.

He said he was coming back today, and if the color of the evening light is any indication, I'm running out of time. I force my liquid limbs to crawl toward the sink. Every movement rubs the fresh cuts. The pain is excruciating, but I bite my lip to keep silent, needing time to prepare before he comes.

Reaching the bathroom takes forever, and a trail of blood I can't afford to lose follows me. I reach up with one arm and turn on the faucet, trying to hold enough water in that hand to drink, but it just dribbles out before it reaches my lips. Gritting my teeth, I grab the edge of the sink and pull myself to my feet. I can't fully contain the whimpers, but I try to keep them quiet. Unable to let go of the grip on the sink that holds me upright, I lean forward and tilt my head up under the faucet and drink until I can't maintain my hold and slide back to the floor.

The creak of the door comes all too soon. I haven't had time to plan. I don't know what to do. I just know I will die before I will let him inside my body ever again.

"Sweet Julie, it's time, my love."

The familiarity of his voice strikes me again, before he steps into the room, and for the first time, the light from the overhead window streaks fully across his face. *No. No! NO!* I scream incoherently in anguish, unable to withstand the grief, the betrayal. It can't be. My head shakes back and forth in denial, not Luke, not my best friend's brother. I can't accept it.

"What's wrong, Julie?" He no longer speaks in concealed whispers, and I can't fully grasp Demon's words spoken in Luke's voice. "Deep down you always knew it was me."

He steps closer, and I try to push farther into the bathroom, only to be stopped by the chain still strangling my ankle. "You couldn't have really believed that jerk flirting with you at the club cared enough to purify you like I did, love you like I did. I was so proud of how you protected me by directing the police toward him. It's how I knew I could trust you to raise our daughter. It's why I let you keep her."

"Luke, please. What are you doing? I don't understand." I belatedly realize I've trapped myself by moving into the bathroom. The chain is so taut I couldn't pull the strangulation move if I wanted to, and I don't even have the space to move away from him. I am well and truly without options.

"You ruined my first time meeting my daughter by forcing me to act like I didn't even know she existed. You left me no choice but to bring her home with me."

A cry from upstairs startles us both. Clemmie. "What's wrong with Clemmie? Luke, where is my daughter?" My hands shake with fear and rage.

Luke just smiles. "Don't worry. Our daughter is fine. She loves being with her daddy. I made sure she would stay safe so we could have some time alone now that all the impurities have drained away," he says while staring at the blood dried on the bed and the trail leading to me.

I follow the path of his eyes—the bed, the chain, my shackled ankle, the ruined sheet, and my mutilated legs. Wait! The sheet, I didn't notice the sheet. It must have stuck to some of the blood on my legs and trailed behind me.

Another shrill cry sounds from upstairs, this time angry and scared and followed by a crash. Luke runs from the room without even bothering to close the door, and I hear his feet thudding up the stairs. This is my only chance, so I forget the pain and will my body to move. I gather the sheet and crawl back to the bed. I don't even try to get on top. Instead, I slide myself underneath on my stomach. I twist the sheet to form a makeshift rope that I tie to the bed, and I wait for Demon to return. He will never be Luke to me ever again. I can't think of him by that name and do what I'm planning to do.

Movement sounds upstairs, and with the door open, I can hear him talking to my baby. I hear her say "Dadda," in her sweet baby voice, and the rage that washes over me burns like a fire under my skin, fueling my fight. The urge to kill is strong.

The heavy steps sound on the stairs again, and Demon reappears in the doorway. "Ah, Julie. What are you trying to do? There's nowhere to hide. Clemmie is ready for us to be a family. Don't you want to see her?" He inches closer.

"Where is she? Bring her to me! I want to see that she's okay."

"In due time, sweet wife. I've spent three years waiting for you, working to make this house a home for us, making sure we would be safe. Our time is finally here, and I won't let you take it away again. We will have our family."

I bide my time and wait until he's within reach, then lash out with my foot to hook it around his and sweep it out from under him. It doesn't work like I'd imagined it would in my head. He stumbles but doesn't go down. His placid expression morphs into rage, and he reaches for the chain, using it to pull me across the bloody floor and out from under the cover of the bed. His ever-present knife makes an appearance from a sheath I never suspected he wore on his leg. I turn over and try to grab the sheet but it's just out of reach.

"No! I won't let you do this, Liyana. Our daughter is alive this time. I wanted us to be a family, and I won't let you take her away again."

Liyana? I don't understand, but I don't have time to think as his knee lands on my stomach and my breath whooshes out. The knife rises above his head, and I use the only thing I remember from long ago self-defense classes. I grab his groin and squeeze with every bit of strength I can muster.

He chokes and his body collapses on mine as he claws at my hand, but I refuse to alter my grip. The knife clanks to the floor as he uses both hands to pry my clawing fingers away. My hand is bent backwards then twisted to the point of resistance and beyond. I hear the snap of my wrist before he releases me and falls to the side.

My hand is useless, but somehow, I don't even feel the pain. I can see the awkward angle, but my brain refuses to comprehend. I had planned to use my twisted sheet as a kind of noose, but with only one hand, the knife is my only option. My knees slip out from under me on the tile when I dive toward it, but I won't stop moving. I belly crawl until my fingers touch the blade.

The howl of rage is my only warning before Demon is on my back and has ripped the blade from my hand.

CHAPTER 86

Ashe

I wish I could say the conversation with Tessa went well, but it didn't. She was understandably angry that we would suspect the brother she loves, who took her in as a teen and raised her. Thankfully, clearer heads prevailed once Rosey returned and convinced her that the best way to clear her brother was to help us find him.

She was shocked he had sold his house in Mobile and had no idea where he had been living. I could see that detail cracked her confidence in his innocence to a degree. Dustin's murder also made a lot more sense when viewed as revenge taken by her brother.

Con continued to search for properties tied to the Taliaferro family but was coming up blank. Agent Brandt joined the conversation, and his missing persons experience, coupled with the fact that he was a stranger to Tessa, lent a different slant to the questions and made them feel less pointed and personal.

He was able to draw out a few possibilities within an hour or so of Magnolia Ridge, which Con promptly started checking into. It was only after a series of questions about favorite vacations that a usable lead developed. Apparently, the siblings' father had a best friend who had the honorary title of uncle. They spent a few memorable summer vacations at "Uncle" Jerry's lake house on the outskirts of Magnolia Ridge.

From the map Con pulled up, the property was secluded and almost in the next county but still inside Magnolia Ridge jurisdiction. The property was listed as being purchased three years ago by a company called LD Holdings. Tessa didn't recognize the name, but stated her brother's initials were LDT, Luke Denver Taliaferro.

Carmen was contacted to have a warrant ready once we could verify LD Holdings was in fact owned by Luke Taliaferro. Agent Brandt was able to pull some FBI strings and before long, we had a list of four different companies, which eventually traced back to Luke Taliaferro with land developments in Alabama and neighboring states. One of those companies was LD Holdings.

Fresh off the raid earlier today, we had to impatiently wait for law enforcement to restock supplies and recheck gear even after the warrant was issued. Moss was assigned to stay at LCR with Tessa, both as protection and to prevent her from warning her brother, while I met up with members of SWAT, Hostage Negotiation, Missing Persons, and the FBI. Con and Rosey had my back, and we'd all three donned our own protective gear and double-checked our weapons. We wouldn't be allowed in until all was clear, but I wouldn't be held back for long if my girls were in there. I wanted to be ready for anything.

Finally, hours later, we are ready to go. We follow the route mapped out for us so that all possible exit points are covered and park to block the narrow dirt road out of view from the main house. Exiting the car, everything feels like a repeat of the raid on Martin. I can't help but fear that somehow we are wrong yet again, that Eva and Clemmie will be lost to me forever.

"We're going to find them," Rosey says with uncanny intuition as he lays a hand on my shoulder.

The team is more prepared than they were for this morning's impromptu raid, so once everyone has radioed they are in position, the hostage negotiation team takes the lead, hoping for a peaceful resolution. No response comes from within the house or from attempts to reach Luke via cell phone. No lights are on despite the dusky hour, and no one breathes as SWAT members are sent in to try to get images and sound from inside the house. The wait seems interminable.

My heart truly feels like it explodes when I hear over the radio the confirmation that Clemmie is inside and alive, but my relief is tempered by my worry for Eva. Without warning, SWAT converges on the house from every direction, telling me the situation is dire. My body moves without conscious thought, but both Con and Rosey grab an arm to restrain me.

"You'll distract them from their job. You don't want to risk getting them hurt."

Con is right, but I need to be in that house. I need it like I need to breathe. I try to be still, but my muscles are strung tight, and my jaw hurts from being clenched so hard.

A noise from my left draws our attention, and I see a fully outfitted SWAT member run to hand off a screaming Clemmie to one of the uniformed officers before heading back in. Con and Rosey relinquish their hold, knowing I won't be kept from her. In minutes, I have her in my arms. Her screaming continues, and I realize she can't tell who I am under my helmet. I toss it off and speak softly and calmly. Within a few minutes, the screams turn to cries then taper off into sniffles. She doesn't speak but nuzzles her face to hide against my neck.

Ambulance sirens pierce the night, and I pray they're for Taliaferro and not for Eva or anyone trying to save her. SWAT pronounces the house clear, but still I see no sign of Eva. I pace while patting Clemmie's curly hair and rubbing her back. The first ambulance pulls in, and personnel tumble out to rush inside with a stretcher. Minutes pass, but they never exit.

A second ambulance arrives, and Carmen tries to take Clemmie to be checked out, but her screeching is earsplitting. Con walks with me, looking more serious than I've ever seen him. I sit on the bumper of the ambulance, feeling an odd sense of déjà vu as the paramedic checks Clemmie, takes a blood sample for toxicology, and pronounces her physically unharmed. Still, no one exits the house.

I'm contemplating who I'd need to take out in order to get inside when Agent Brandt walks out with Officer Stuart by his side. When had she gone in? They walk directly to me. Stuart looks grieved but determined.

"Don't tell me she's gone. Don't." I shake my head and feel my breathing coming too fast.

"Linc, no. It's not that," Stuart speaks up. "I just need you to let me take the baby, so you can go with Agent Brandt."

"Not happening. You tell me what the hell's going on. Tell me right now!" My vehemence upsets Clemmie, who starts to cry again. I bounce her on my hip and try to calm her. Con gently pulls her from my arms and gives me a look that tells me he'll protect her with his life. I nod and turn back to the duo in front of me. "Let's go." Brandt and Stuart follow as I stalk off, determined to get in that house.

I'm stopped at the porch and made to put on booties so as not to contaminate any evidence. While there, Brandt speaks up. "Listen, Lincoln, your girl is injured but not fatally. We're trying to help her, but she refuses to be touched. Before we have to try more extreme measures, we need you to try to get through to her."

I swear I'm ready to tear down fucking walls at those words. No one will be touching Eva but me. A hand lands on my arm and I jerk in response, bowing up at the person who dared to try to stop me. "Whoa," Stuart cautions. "Take a deep breath. You'll scare her if you go in hot like that."

She's right, so I do as she suggests then follow her along a hall and down a set of stairs to a basement that smells of must and copper…blood. A room veers off to the right. It's dark inside, but light spills in from the main area where I stand and from a small window near the ceiling. Eva is on the floor, huddled under a twin bed. I can hear her sobs and her panicked breaths. I take a step in, and she screams and shifts farther away. Realizing the light is at my back obscuring my face, I speak softly. "Eva, Rabbit, it's me. It's Ashe. Can I come in?"

She looks at me intently as though trying to study my face before nodding. My eyes adjust more to the dimness, and the true horrors of the room are revealed one by one. A chain is attached to Eva's ankle although it appears to have been cut away from its mooring on the floor. Blood is everywhere, the floor seemingly mopped with red. Another step closer reveals a mattress also soaked in crimson. One more step, and I see a body I assume is Taliaferro. He lies face down on the floor, a knife beside him. There is no risk of him waking up to grab it since most of his head is gone. I make a mental note to find and personally thank whichever SWAT member is responsible.

"Ashe?" Eva's voice is scratchy and barely audible.

I turn my attention away from the nightmare surrounding me and back to the only thing that matters, Eva. "I'm right here, Rabbit. Can you come out?" Lowering to my haunches, I hold out my hand. The shadows from the bed obscure most of her form, but I don't miss her hand reaching out slowly to grab mine. I don't want to hurt or frighten her, so I don't pull. I let her move on her own. Her pained moans and whimpers only serve to drive into my heart how badly I failed her, failed to keep her safe.

As she moves farther into the light, I realize she's naked and covered almost completely in blood. I have no idea how much is hers and how much is Taliaferro's. Letting go of her hand, I move quickly to strip off my vest and overshirt. I reach to place the shirt around Eva, but she jerks away. My movement was too fast. I slow my motions and talk softly to explain what I'm doing.

"Do you want my shirt?" She nods. "Can I help you put it on?" She gives another nod. Moving fully out from under the bed, she tries to sit up, but has one arm clutched to her chest. "Can I touch you?"

"Yes," she replies softly. Reaching around her

slowly, I use an arm behind her back to help her sit. I suck in a breath when the movement reveals her mangled legs. Curses run wild through my mind, but I can't risk scaring her. I help her slip what looks like a broken wrist through the sleeve first before fully wrapping her in the oversized garment.

"The paramedics are here. Can they come in and help you?"

Eva shakes her head wildly. "I want to get out. Please take me out. I need out." Her urgency increases with each plea. "You, just you, get me out."

"I'm going to pick you up, okay?" She nods but cries out as I lift. Trying not to jostle her too much, I do my best to make sure she's covered before carefully carrying her up the stairs and out to the stretcher waiting near the porch.

"Where is Clemmie? Is she okay?" Eva asks as I lay her down.

"She's perfect. Con has her."

"Don't let her see me like this, please."

I nod. "I'm so sorry, Eva. So very sorry." I want to continue begging for her forgiveness, but her eyes have closed, and I know she won't hear me. The paramedics load her up as I swipe at the salty droplets I didn't realize were flowing down my face. Torn between my girls, I do what Eva would want. I find Con, so I can take care of my baby.

CHAPTER 87

Eva

After two nights of fluids, food, and rest at the hospital plus several days of Ashe hovering over me at his house, I'm feeling more like myself. Aunt Polly came home from the hospital today to join me in the realm of Ashe's coddling, and by some miracle, my father left without having ever put actions to the threats I'm told he issued.

Because of her age and inability to describe what happened to her, the doctors kept Clemmie for observation and allowed her to share my room at the hospital. It was unorthodox, but somehow Ashe made it happen. He also had a sleeper chair pulled in so we were never alone.

Surgery was required to set my wrist and suture the deepest of the cuts on my legs. They would scar, and badly, but what's a few more? The cuff was cut off when we arrived, but my ankle had to be wrapped until the swelling could go down enough to treat the damage. Ashe was there through everything. He and Clemmie played and cuddled, and when she cried, he held her. When I cried, he held me too. He made sure we both had everything we needed. If he cried sometimes too, I'll never tell.

We had more than enough visitors, except one who

was noticeably absent, Tessa. One of the first questions Ashe asked at the hospital was why I left the building that awful night. I explained how fear had overwhelmed me when I'd gotten Tessa's text, and he assured me Tessa's phone had been missing since her abduction. She hadn't replaced it yet because she was avoiding everyone. Ashe said he believed Luke must have found it with Dustin Grimes before he killed him. It was recovered in the evidence from the estate where I was held. He'd also had Tessa's spare key to my house, which explained how the cookies had gotten inside.

I don't know what to do for Tessa. What happened to the brother she knew and loved who beat up bullies for me in middle school and who later raised his sister? I was never close to him after he returned from the Army, but I still can't reconcile his actions with the boy I knew. I need to know so I can help Tessa. Luke was all she had, and now she probably thinks she's alone, but I won't desert her, because she never left me. As soon as I'm mobile again, I won't let her keep me away.

Once Clemmie is down for the night and Aunt Polly is comfortable in the room Ashe set up for her, I pull him down next to me on the sofa. Now that we're all home, I think I'm finally ready to talk about why I was targeted. I listen as he fills in the blanks and helps me understand what happened.

Apparently, Rosey was able to get in touch with two of the guys from Luke's old Army unit. The story they told made me sad for the young man Luke was, even as I couldn't excuse all that he had done. He could have sought treatment for his pain, but he allowed it to consume him and destroy so many lives.

According to Rosey, Luke received a medical discharge from the Army that coincided with his parents' death and his need to come home and take custody of his sister. The deaths were listed as the official reason. Unofficially, the men Rosey spoke to both confirmed that Luke had been in a relationship with a local woman while deployed to the Middle East. Neither of the men could remember her name, though I guessed it must have been Liyana. Both distinctly remembered that she had reddish-blonde hair, since it was a very rare trait in the Middle East. The relationship was hidden from her radically traditional family, but somehow one of her older brothers had discovered her secret and threatened to kill her as a point of honor. This was two days after she told Luke she was pregnant.

Luke had apparently bragged to his buddies of his excitement to be a father. He also shared his plans to marry the mother before her family discovered the pregnancy and then bring her home to the United States. One of the guys, Wilcox, said he'd warned Taliaferro that his plans were not realistic and the situation was dangerous, but Luke was too blinded by young love to see it. Two days later, the woman was dead. She'd chosen to take her own life rather than be dishonored and murdered by her family.

Wilcox said Luke couldn't function after the loss of his love and his child. He started raving about how some curse from her family must have made her kill herself. Ancient Middle Eastern customs, rituals, and superstitions became his obsession.

Though his relationship was unsanctioned, he had the sympathy and favor of his higher ups. The matter was covered up. When the news of his parents' deaths came only days later, it provided a more legitimate reason for the discharge.

"So, Luke killed Dustin because he hurt Tessa?" I ask.

"That's what the evidence points to, and he killed Manchester for hurting you."

"Why? I don't understand? Why did he care if I was hurt? He hurt me so many times." I look down at my legs, which are covered by a blanket.

"I wish we knew, Rabbit," Ashe says as he pulls my head to his chest and strokes my hair. "My guess is that he didn't see what he was doing as harmful. Maybe he saw his actions as having some kind of purpose."

"Like purifying me to be his wife? He mentioned purification a few times."

"Exactly."

"I feel so stupid. How could I not have recognized him? How did I not know?" I drop my gaze, unable to hold eye contact.

Ashe tips my chin up in his usual way. "You were drugged then kept starved, probably dehydrated, terrified, and alone in the dark. Don't underestimate what that can do to your mind."

"I'll never understand this. Never."

"Don't try. You'll waste all your moments of happiness drowning in the unexplainable." Ashe wraps his arms around me more tightly. I snuggle into his comfort and run my uninjured hand up his arm. My fingers encounter the scar from his bullet wound, and a memory resurfaces.

I sit up quickly, almost knocking Ashe's chin with the top of my head. "I forgot. While I was in the basement, Luke said I was the last one. He said he never took anyone else, then he threatened you. He said you had a lot of enemies, and he helped them try to kill you. What did he mean, 'a lot of enemies'?"

Ashe straightens and says, "You have nothing to worry about. We are perfectly safe. Luke was an expert marksman, and a gun was found at the estate that is likely going to match the ballistics of the bullets recovered from the ambush. Luke was the shooter. He was just trying to use your fear to manipulate you."

I stand, needing to grab a bottle of orange juice. "What are you doing?" Ashe stresses as he moves to block my way. "You shouldn't be up."

I realize I look broken with my wrist in a cast, my foot in a walking boot, and wraps protecting the stitches on my thighs, but as much as I appreciate the love and care Ashe has shown me, I need to do some things for myself. Deep down, I think he needs that too, so he can relax and know that I'm okay. "I'm fine." I reach up and caress his cheek before pulling him down for a kiss.

"Hmm. Maybe you are fine." Ashe laughs.

"Not that fine yet, but soon." I wink at him, knowing I've won our little standoff but also knowing he let me. I love him for it too.

I hobble to the kitchen and grab the orange juice Ashe has taken to stocking for me. He eyes my return, looking for any sign of pain so he can swoop in and carry me. The pain is there, but I want him to see my strength.

A cry sounds from down the hall, and Ashe is gone before I move two steps. He returns moments later with a tearful, sleepy Clemmie. Her arms are around his neck, practically strangling him. As he has done for the last few nights, he simply carries her to the room I now think of as ours and waits for me. Once I lie down, Ashe places Clemmie in front of me to be my little spoon then he climbs in behind me. His long arms wrap around us both, and together we find sleep.

EPILOGUE

Eva

Summer has transitioned into fall, and I inhale the crisp scent of the cool air as I walk to my car after work. For the most part, life has returned to normal, if there is such a thing. Aunt Polly's voice is back, and she has no problem making sure we're all aware of it. Clemmie has been seeing a play therapist, and Ashe and I finally have our bed to ourselves. Aunt Polly has listed her house to sell since none of us ever want to return there. Eventually we'll have to figure out new living arrangements, but for now we're all happily crammed in at Ashe's.

I've reached out to Tessa several times to let her know I love her and that I'm here for her, but she never returns my calls or messages. I've even stopped by The Daily Grind, but each time she's been absent. Ashe tells me to keep being present and give her time. I'm trying, but I miss her. What happened to me was not her fault. She was my friend when I was sure I deserved none, and she can never be replaced.

The beep of a horn startles me out of my thoughts and brings me back to the present. Jolie waves as she pulls out of the almost-empty parking lot. I return the gesture and climb into the 4Runner, ready to start the weekend. Ashe took a rare Friday off today, and I'm excited to meet him and Clemmie at the large community park downtown.

Today was Football Friday at work, so I'm ready to play in jeans and my favorite jersey. Ashe just shook his head this morning when I walked out wearing the crimson jersey that completely clashed with his orange and blue one. I couldn't help but laugh and yell, "Roll Tide!" as I ran out the door.

I pull into the small parking lot near the pavilions where Ashe said we'd meet. The lot is unusually crowded, but the park is big. I'm sure we'll be able to find a good spot to picnic and play. Music is playing as I lock my car and head down the shaded path toward the first pavilion.

Moss is the first person I spot when I round the last corner. His dark bald head gleams in the sunlight as he smiles and leans up against a support post. Behind him is the whole LCR crew, including Spock and his wife, and even Karo, who is on paid administrative leave though she has tried to resign several times. She looks better than the last time I saw her, but her movements are still somewhat stiff. She's keeping to herself, but I see Villain's watchful gaze focused on her every move from across the pavilion. Jolie's red hair catches my eye despite being partially hidden behind Bond. Mal stands on the outskirts, hands in his pockets. The tables are loaded with food, and Aunt Polly is bustling around at the back helping fill coolers with drinks. I must have missed the memo, because I have no idea what's going on.

"Eva," Ashe calls as he appears, still wearing his orange-and-blue jersey and holding hands with a giggly Clemmie who has on her favorite elephant-covered

Alabama sundress with a brand new giant Auburn bow in her hair.

"What's going on?" I ask suspiciously. "When you said to meet you for a picnic, this is not what I thought you meant."

"Clemmie and I have a present for you, and we thought a party would be a fun way to give it to you."

I glance around to see everyone smiling, even Mal. Aunt Polly has made her way to the front and is snapping pictures with an honest-to-God disposable camera with actual film. She only breaks those out for what she calls special days, so I'm starting to feel nervous.

"Ashe?"

"Clemmie, go give Momma her present."

My daughter skips over with something floppy in her hand. "Here, Momma," she says, thrusting her gift up to me with a big smile. I take it, giving her a big hug and thanking her. I look down and realize she's given me one of those cheesy bumper stickers for football fans who take things a little too far. It's half orange and blue and half crimson and white and says, "House Divided."

I turn to ask Ashe what this means only to find him down on one knee. Clemmie runs over and sits on his other knee, and everyone laughs. I can hear the near continual clicking and winding of Aunt Polly's camera as I take a step closer.

"Rabbit, I have chased you for long enough," he starts. "Clemmie and I think it's time to make things official." I smile as he leans down to whisper in Clemmie's ear.

"Mawy Wink, Momma!" she shouts then starts

jumping up and down, clapping when Ashe produces a beautiful ring.

"Will you marry me, Rabbit?" he asks with a grin that says he's confident of my answer. Catcalls, whistles, and applause sound from our friends, but I ignore them.

"Any day, anytime, anywhere," I say, stealing my daughter's seat on his knee and stealing a kiss as well.

A word about the author…

I am a fun-loving Army and Air Force mom of four and Nonni to the sweetest baby ever. My first novel, Thirteen Scars, is the realization of a generational dream. Upon my father's passing from Alzheimer's, I found partially written stories, books, poems, and recipes hidden like a wonderful treasure trove throughout his home. As a child, he always told me one day he would write a novel in the style of Isaac Asimov, his favorite author. I eagerly adopted his dream and decided I too would one day write a novel. He died never having accomplished that dream, having even forgotten he ever had one. I am excited to be chasing that dream in his honor.

https://www.elisabethscottbooks.com/